M
KIENZLE

Kienzle, William X.

Dead wrong.

$18.95

DATE		

Dead
Wrong

Dead
Wrong

William X.
Kienzle

**Andrews
and
McMeel**

A Universal Press
Syndicate Company
Kansas City

This is a work of fiction and, as such, events described
herein are creations of the author's imagination.
Any relation to real people, living or dead, is
purely coincidental and accidental.

Library of Congress Cataloging-in-Publication Data

Kienzle, William X.
Dead wrong / William X. Kienzle.
p.   cm.
ISBN 0–8362–6129–1 : $18.95
1. Koesler, Robert (Fictitious character)—Fiction.
2. Detectives—Michigan—Detroit—Fiction. I. Title.
PS3561.I35D36   1992
813′.54–dc20   92–46287
CIP

Credits:
Editorial Director: Donna Martin
Senior Editor: Jean Lowe
Production Manager: Julie Miller
Copy Editor: Matt Lombardi
Book Design: Edward D. King
Jacket Design: George Diggs
Editorial Coordinator: Patty Donnelly
Typography: Connell-Zeko Type & Graphics
Printing and Binding: R.R. Donnelley & Sons

FOR
JAVAN

Acknowledgments

Gratitude for technical advice to:

Robert Ankeny, Staff Writer, *The Detroit News*
Ramon Betanzos, Ph.D., Professor of Humanities, Wayne State
    University
Gerald Dziedzic, Executive Assistant, Wayne County Clerk's Office
Sergeant James Grace, Detective, Kalamazoo Police Department
Sister Bernadelle Grimm, R.S.M., Pastoral Care, Mercy Hospital,
    Detroit
Marge Hershey, R.N., Pulmonary Care Unit, Detroit Receiving
    Hospital
Timothy Kenny, Assistant Wayne County Prosecuting Attorney
George Lubienski, Attorney at Law
Charles Lucas, M.D., Professor of Surgery, Detroit Receiving Hospital
Thomas J. Petinga, Jr., D.O., FACEP, Chief of Emergency Services, St.
    Joseph Mercy Hospital, Pontiac
Werner U. Spitz, M.D., Professor of Forensic Pathology, Wayne State
    University
Karen Webb, Social Worker
Inspector Barbara Weide, Criminal Investigation Bureau, Detroit
    Police Department

Any technical error is the author's.

In memory of Commander Robert Hislop

1960

CHAPTER

1

SHE NEEDED HELP. That's what most of her friends told her.

Actually, she believed herself beyond help.

But she was willing to live with that. She had for thirty-two years now. God made some women beautiful, some plain, some ugly. That's what she believed. She considered herself lucky to be among the merely plain.

Then something happened that made her think that there might be exceptions to her philosophy. She had been noticed! She, Agnes Ventimiglia, one among many in the Wayne County Clerk's Office, had been noticed! And it wasn't what you might think. It wasn't one of those cheap pickups. This was a fine young man. Peter Arnold was his name.

She remembered—God, she would never forget!—the first time he'd come in. He was so good-looking she had noticed him right off the bat. She was too shy to let him know; diffident, she kept her head turned half away. But she was watching him out of the corner of her eye.

He stood back near the windows on the north side of the rectangular room. He too was doing some studying.

Business in the clerk's office was brisk as usual. People wanting documents: birth, marriage, death. For as many reasons as there were people needing one of life's milestone records.

The young man was not weighing which was the fastest line. He was concentrating on the clerks. Agnes could tell. She was a people watcher. Usually she went undetected in this hobby, as so few paid any attention to her.

His inspection completed, he selected *her* line.

Agnes had no idea why she'd been singled out. Hers was by no means the fastest moving nor the shortest line of customers. But her heart seemed to skip a beat.

His presence in her line prompted her to move things along with more dispatch than usual. Not that she was curt or short with any of her customers. Agnes tried never to upset anyone anytime. However,

1

this day she was eager to learn if there might be some special reason this handsome stranger had chosen her.

As the line steadily progressed, Agnes moved imperceptibly back and forth from right to left to get a better view of the stranger as he gradually neared.

Then he was there.

Not tall. Not short. Not physically imposing. Yet there was something . . . His thick dark hair was brushed back and it clung tightly to his patrician head. Heavy eyebrows accentuated his riveting eyes.

His eyes. She wouldn't call them cruel; no, they stopped just this side of being cruel. But there was no nonsense in those eyes.

Peter Arnold needed a copy of his birth certificate.

After a few self-conscious fumbles, Agnes located the record. *Peter Arnold, born November 7, 1939.* Twenty-one years ago this very day.

She made a copy of the record and handed it to him with a sunny smile. "Happy birthday."

"Thanks." Then, after a moment's hesitation, "Today I am a man, as they say. Uh . . . I don't mean to be too forward, but . . . would you be willing to help me celebrate? Dinner . . . maybe?"

It did not take Agnes more than a split second to recognize a once-in-a-lifetime opportunity. "Well . . . yes . . . I guess that would be all right." What comes next, she wondered. She'd never before been asked for a date.

"Great," he said. "What time do you get off work?"

"Five-thirty."

"I'll pick you up here, then."

"Okay."

So that's how it worked. Simple.

IT HAD BEEN A LOVELY DATE. He had been a perfect gentleman. And he remained a gentleman on all their subsequent dates, which, during this singularly marvelous month of November, took place almost every night.

On November 8, their second date, for instance, they mutually confided that each had voted for John Kennedy and that each happened to be Catholic. Over the following days and weekends they continued to find similarities and happy coincidences in their backgrounds. It was as if each of Agnes's revelations found a like circumstance in Peter Arnold.

There had been but one flaw.

During their time together the previous weekend, Peter had asked a favor of her. Actually, "asked" might not be the precise word. The request had overtones just short of an ultimatum. Yet his manner had been so sweet and affectionate that the overall effect had been ambiguous. He asked her to alter a record.

Agnes's first instinct was to flatly refuse.

He had an explanation, which, while admittedly not totally convincing, nonetheless gave some weight to the argument. Further, she did not want to chance losing this man.

In the end, she had consented. And nothing more was said of it. She took his subsequent silence on the matter as testimony to his trust in her. He had asked, she'd agreed; case closed.

And, in fact, she had done as he asked.

After which, her sensitive conscience began to trouble her.

She knew of no one in whom she could confide. Not in her friends certainly. She was not on the best of terms with her parents, and she had no other close relatives. Nor could she even confide in her parish priest. Oh, he undoubtedly would have kept her secret. But, with his celibate life-style, he would never be able to understand what one person will do for another person for love. Particularly when, as in her case, there was a real danger of losing the loved one.

But at last it was over. She and Peter could get on with their life together.

And tonight promised a major development in their so-far brief relationship. To date, physical intimacy had progressed in cautious, deliberate steps. Agnes of course was a virgin, and a good Catholic girl as well. Peter? It was difficult to tell. Agnes simply assumed that any man of twenty-one years or more would be sexually experienced.

In any case, all indications were that after dinner this evening they would go to his flat and, perhaps after holding hands and kissing chastely, as they had so often in the past, they would actually make love.

Agnes had one very good friend at work, Rosemarie, a young lady whom God had seen fit to make beautiful.

As the days of November passed, Agnes could not help but radiate happiness. She confided the source of that joy to Rosemarie, who was almost as happy over it as was Agnes. The only thing she did not confide was the favor she'd done for Peter. No one, not even Rosemarie, would comprehend what she'd done for love.

Rosemarie kept the advice coming on how to carry on a romance. The cautious development of the affair was, to Agnes, a matter of morality. To Rosemarie it represented a slow but inexorable seduction.

The two women agreed that tonight very likely would be the night.

With that in mind, they had visited the nearby Hudson's during lunch hour and picked up some tantalizing lingerie—just in case.

Then, before Agnes left work to meet Peter, she and Rosemarie spent nearly an hour in the ladies' room, working on makeup and hair styling. Whether or not Agnes needed it, she had gotten help.

As Agnes left the office, with much more than her usual trepidation, Rosemarie reflected that she had never actually met Peter. She found that odd and somehow disquieting. She shrugged away her doubts with the supposition that Peter and Agnes were shy about having an affair. On further thought, Rosemarie concluded, in this day and age, such modesty was refreshing.

Agnes found Peter, punctual as always, parked and waiting for her on Woodward near the City-County Building's exit.

They drove a couple of short blocks, parked in a convenient lot, and walked a few yards to the Pontchartrain Wine Cellars, one of downtown Detroit's favorite restaurants. Everything about dinner seemed special. Peter urged Agnes to order one of the more expensive entrées. And he selected a fine wine to accompany each course.

Agnes grew increasingly certain: Tonight would be the night.

After their leisurely dinner, Peter drove them to his apartment on Detroit's near west side. Again, as he had done repeatedly all evening, he complimented her on her appearance. Agnes was delighted. She surreptitiously eased open the clasp on her large handbag and fingered the lacy black gown she'd purchased earlier that day. Would she, she wondered, be bold enough to confide the details of this night to Rosemarie tomorrow?

It was only a short distance from the parking area to Peter's apartment. Though it was a chill November evening, for Agnes it might as well have been spring.

As they entered Peter's apartment, Agnes reflected on how far she'd come in such a relatively brief period. A few short weeks ago she would have denied out of hand that she would ever go unchaperoned into a man's quarters. Actually, the first few times, she had literally trembled. But now she knew, as she knew there is a God, that she could trust Peter. Indeed, theirs was a relationship founded on trust.

As she settled into a corner of the couch, he asked, "How about a drink?"

"That would be nice."

She almost wished he had specified a nightcap. She envisioned herself tossing down a fairly stiff drink in order to cast off the last vestiges of inhibition. Then, in her fantasy, she would go into the bathroom, shed her clothing, don the negligee, and emerge, making a present of herself to her beloved. The mere thought of such a scenario told her that no matter how nervous she felt, deep down she was ready for tonight.

From behind, Peter reached over her shoulder, offering a delicate glass containing an amber liquid. "Here you go."

She smiled, accepted the glass, and inhaled. Sherry. How nice! From slight experience she knew this wine would undoubtedly make her feel as if she were floating. Just right. She sipped. It was delicious. A perfect evening.

Behind her, near the wet bar, he spoke. "By the way, Aggie, did you do that favor for me . . . in the records?"

She smiled. So much time had passed since he had first made the request, there was no possibility that there was anything more to his query now than the simple explanation he'd given her. It was only natural that he would want to close that chapter for good and all.

"Yes, I took care of it. . . . There was no problem; nobody will ever know—"

She never had a chance to complete the statement. The blow landed exactly where he had aimed.

Such a blow to the temple would, he knew, inflict the desired fatality. In the human skull the temple bone is thinnest. Her skin was not broken, so there was no external blood to elicit concern. But inside Agnes's head the bones were fractured; they had penetrated the brain, causing massive bleeding. There was nothing now but to await death.

It was, he thought, merciful as violent death goes. She couldn't have felt more than an instant of pain. The weapon was a cousin of the ancient slingshot with which David killed Goliath. Colloquially, it was known as a blackjack. A narrow leather bag with a spring in the handle to protect the user's hand. In the striking end was a heavy metallic object about the size of a dove's egg. The blackjack long had been a favored instrument of injury and death.

Agnes had been unconscious since being struck. The best emergency care would have been hard-pressed to save her. And even then, it would have been questionable that she could ever function normally. Of course, there would be no medical intervention now; he was just waiting to make sure there would be no miracles here.

Her excruciatingly labored breathing sounded ghastly. Foam oozed from her nose. A deep bruise was forming where the weapon had struck.

While this ineluctable process progressed, he moved about the room, making sure everything would be left in perfect order. He paid no attention to her until he was done.

It was now about forty-five minutes since the attack. He checked for vital signs. There were none. No pulse, no breath. Her face was a bluish purple. Her eyes, which had been open when she was struck, would remain open.

Awkwardly manipulating her dead weight, he maneuvered her body into a heavy sack, hoisted it over his shoulder, turned out the lights, and left.

PLAN A was to drop the body from the Belle Isle bridge into the Detroit River, whose strong current would carry it to the depths, thus effectively burying it for the foreseeable future. Unexpected traffic rendered that plan infeasible.

Reverting to Plan B, he drove down Atwater, at the river's edge near the foot of Woodward, until he came to a deserted stretch. He pulled over, got out, wrestled the sack from the trunk, dragged it to the water's edge, and let it tumble in.

He wasted no time at the scene, but reentered his car and drove away.

1993

CHAPTER

2

REPRESENTATIVES of what passed for civilization named the land Ville d'étroit, or City of the Strait. It became known as Fort Detroit.

Antoine de la Mothe Cadillac introduced the French to native Americans here. It was an ideal location for a settlement. One segment of the Great Lakes, from Lake St. Clair to Lake Erie, squeezed through this narrow passageway named the Strait River, or Detroit River.

To this day, the river continues to flow between Windsor and Detroit, between Canada and the United States.

Over the years, the city of Detroit grew. Unfortunately, the city's southward growth occurred largely along the river's bank, so that the majority of inhabitants had precious little unobstructed access to the water's dreams and memories.

This river—so near and yet so far—was on the mind of Father Robert Koesler as he drove east on Jefferson Avenue.

Father Koesler was pastor of St. Joseph's parish—or Old St. Joe's as some called it to distinguish it from all the other St. Joseph's; it very definitely was the eldest by far.

The river was within walking distance of his church, but he could not actually see the water until almost on top of it. It was not unlike this avenue called Jefferson: It ran along the riverfront, but the water was a rare sight.

How could this situation be remedied? By planning such as that of Minneapolis with all its city lakes. In Minneapolis, there is no private property abutting any of the lakes. There is the lake, then the shore, then the street, and only then does one find housing. It could have happened in Detroit. All these apartments, businesses, and factories might have had to locate removed from this glorious river. Then not only would it have been completely open to the public, but it would have been spared a measure of pollution.

The few parks that dotted the shoreline were insufficient for general patronage. Hart Plaza, across from the City-County Building, was an exception. Still, even that area offered no free parking, and the city's mass transit was a nightmare.

9

Another exception was beautiful Belle Isle, nestled midway between Windsor and Detroit at almost the halfway point of the strait. A bridge connected the island to Detroit. There was no such connection between the island and Windsor. And there was no charge for parking on the island.

There it was, even as he thought of it. Belle Isle. And across from it, on this side of the river, was his destination, one more highrise. However, girded as it was with greenery, this building did not completely block a view of the river.

Father Koesler parked in the visitors' lot. He studied the building, recalling a time some years earlier when this complex had been the scene of a murder. A professional football player had been killed in this very building, and Koesler had been drawn into the investigation of his death.

He shook his head. The longer he lived, the more Detroit sites held personal significance for him.

He shrugged and started toward the building, pulling up the collar of his coat as he walked.

A Michigan axiom has it that if you don't like the weather, wait a minute and it will change. Take March, for instance: One might expect spring, and one might get it. Or one might get a blizzard. This day, with a stiff wind off the river, was bone-chilling.

Koesler registered with the guard in the lobby. This building's security had been beefed up following and because of the murder.

The guard checked. Yes, a Father Koesler, identified by his driver's license, was expected by Mr. Nash. The guard gave directions to the penthouse suite. A bit redundant, since the penthouse occupied the entire top floor. One just went up until there was no more up.

He stepped off the elevator into a rather stark foyer. Behind him was the elevator, doors now closed and descending; on his left a full-length mirror, on his right a nondescript painting, and ahead of him a closed door.

A young man in a white uniform opened the door and invited Koesler in. The guard had obviously alerted the occupant.

The room he entered was large, taking up one corner of the penthouse. Floor-to-ceiling windows displayed Detroit's east side, and the Pointes, as well as a healthy slice of Windsor, including the airport, and, of course, the river. If not breathtaking, the panorama was at least dazzling.

The man, obviously a servant, took Koesler's coat and hat and said he would get Mr. Nash. He disappeared through a door at the far side of the room.

Koesler, alone with his thoughts, gazed absently at the scenery. Old Charlie Nash! It had been ages since Nash had packed it in as far as personal publicity was concerned. Although much younger than Joe Kennedy, Charlie Nash in his heyday had been Detroit's version of the late patriarch. Though not quite as wealthy as Kennedy, still Nash was well within the *Forbes* 400.

Like Kennedy, Nash was very much a Catholic, though only by his definition, not the Church's. Charlie's personal life was reportedly unbridled and his business affairs allegedly unprincipled. Unlike Kennedy, Nash had but one child, a son—though gossip suggested the boy was the only offspring Charlie knew of or admitted to.

In any case, some fifteen years ago, Nash had handed the business—real estate development—over to Teddy, who, according to knowledgeable reports, was a chip off the old block.

The far door opened, and Charles Vincent Nash entered the room in a wheelchair pushed by the young man in white.

KOESLER WAS SHOCKED. Nash could not have been more than in his midseventies, a little more than ten years older than Koesler. Yet he easily could have passed for one in his nineties.

Nash had no picture of Dorian Gray in his attic.

The two men regarded each other for a few moments. Then, without taking his eyes from Koesler's, Nash barked, "Get outta here, kid!"

Without a moment's hesitation, the servant left, closing the door behind him.

"Yer better than six feet, aren'tcha?"

"Six-three," Koesler replied, " . . . or at least I used to be."

After a second, Nash began to laugh, a near-cackle that segued into a violent coughing fit—the harsh hack common among smokers.

Koesler, thinking there must be something he could do to help, started forward. But Nash, while continuing to cough, waved him off. "Emphysema . . ." he managed to gasp. "It'll pass."

He pulled a device from a pouch at the side of his wheelchair, and inserted the instrument into his nostrils. The inhaler helped.

While Nash struggled with his breathing, Koesler took a more observant look around the room.

It was a study in white—all four walls and ceiling plus a pristine white carpet. It reminded him of . . . a hospital room, but larger of course. He noticed that one corner of the room actually seemed to be a duplication of a hospital room, complete with hospital bed. One does not normally expect to find a hospital bed in a private living room.

Koesler was reminded of a change of pastors in a suburban parish many years previous. The outgoing pastor, a modest-living and pious priest, had required but a small pickup truck and his own car to move all his earthly goods in one trip.

The incoming pastor, the notorious Ed Sklarski, arrived accompanied by two large moving vans, the combined contents of which threatened to require the building of an additional rectory. Along with a collection of furnishings that included a concert grand piano was a hospital bed, "just in case."

Quite obviously, in the case of Charles Nash, the bed served a pragmatic need.

"Used to be six-three, eh?" The inhaler had done its job. Nash's words were accompanied with the hint of what might generously be described as a smile.

"Uh-huh. It's been a while since I measured. I suppose we all settle in with age," Koesler said.

Nash raised his eyebrows and gestured to include the chair, the bed, the medical equipment that spelled out the life-style of a chronic invalid. The effects of age were no stranger to him.

Except that he lived in a penthouse and had everything money could buy, Nash might have been any abandoned old man in a nursing home. His skin seemed to shrivel into deep wrinkles—creases that threatened to bury his eyes in some sort of cosmetic implosion.

But those eyes were lively. His gaze never left Koesler's face. Nash appeared to be carefully studying the priest. Koesler wondered why; as far as he could recall, they had never met before. Of course once Nash had begun to build his empire with the creation of strip malls, he had basked in celebrity status. He went on to the construction of more pricey shopping centers. Then, seemingly, no report of any top society affair was complete without the notation that Mr. and Mrs. Charles V. Nash had been in attendance.

But as quickly as he had broken the plane of prominence, after many years of notoriety Charles Nash slipped into seclusion. Some surmised he was in the throes of a fatal illness. There was even a rumor that he had "gotten religion," and was dedicating the remainder of his life to repentance. No one really knew for certain.

His wife had joined him in seclusion until her death several years ago. And his son Teddy had, without a backward glance, taken over the business with a vengeance.

With all this in mind, Koesler was wondering why he had been invited into the inner sanctum. He now broke the lengthy silence: "Is there something I can do for you, Mr. Nash?"

Nash wheezed. "Maybe."

Another pause which Nash did not seem inclined to interrupt.

"You're not a parishioner of St. Joe's," Koesler said finally. "As a matter of fact, this building is not even in my parish."

"The value of one immortal soul," Nash said.

"What?"

"I heard you say that once in a sermon."

"When did you . . . ?" Koesler stopped himself in midquestion. Of course he would have been able to recognize Nash in that small but growing and faithful congregation at St. Joe's. But he'd been a priest for almost forty years. There'd been lots of congregations, many of them so large he would be hard put to remember some few individuals, let alone everyone. Besides, the "value of one soul" phrase he used with some frequency.

"Yes, of course, the infinite value of one immortal soul. You'll have to forgive me, Mr. Nash. We parish priests do tend to become a little provincial . . . only we call it parochial. So, back to the beginning. Is there something I can do for you?"

"Maybe." Nash's breathing was less labored. The inhaler apparently continued to help.

"Did you want to go to confession?" It was a natural question in these circumstances.

"Maybe I want a spiritual guide." Nash's eyes danced as if he were enjoying some private whimsy.

"Confession is for the past. Spiritual direction is for the future."

"Cute." Nash cleared his throat, accompanied by that mucus gurgle in his chest. "So, you think the past's gotta be cleared up before you go on to the future?"

"Seems to make sense. At least to me."

"I got a problem with that."

Koesler waited for an explanation.

"You gotta be sorry . . . don'tcha? You gotta stop sinning . . . promise never to do it again?" Nash wiped his lips with a napkin that he carried on his lap.

"Yes, you do."

"Well, I'm not sure I am."

Koesler smiled. "Our old moral prof told us a story you may find helpful. Seems an old sailor was dying in a rundown room in some remote port. A priest came to give him the last sacrament.

"In trying to remember the sins of a long life without confession, the sailor could recall lots of fights, most of which he'd lost. He was sorry about that—especially the losing part. His language had been . . . well, salty. But that was the only way he could be understood aboard ship. He'd missed Sunday Mass just about all the time. But most of that time, he'd been out to sea.

"Then there were all those women. At least one per port. When he got to that part he paused. No excuses, no explanations.

" 'Are you sorry for all those affairs?' the priest asked. The sailor thought for a moment. 'No, can't say I am.'

"The priest thought about that a while. 'Well, are you sorry you're not sorry?' 'Yes,' said the sailor, 'I guess so.'

" 'Well,' said the priest, 'I guess that's good enough.' " Koesler laughed at his own anecdote. "Of course the old salt was at the end of the line. He didn't have to worry about sin in the future." Koesler's unspoken thought was, . . . *and probably neither do you.*

Nash looked at the priest. The old man's eyes may have been laughing, but nothing else was.

After a moment's silence, Koesler said, "Well?"

"Well?" Nash responded.

"Well, can you go at least that far in repentance? That you're sorry you can't be more completely sorry?"

Nash shrugged, glanced out the window, then turned back to Koesler and said, "You really want to save me, don'tcha?"

"You sent for me," Koesler said. "What other reason could there have been? I can't help you in any other way but spiritually."

The priest was baffled. Perhaps Nash wanted to test the waters, as it were. Maybe to make sure this confessor would not be judgmental. Koesler had had many such penitents in the past—people who wanted, sometimes desperately, to get something off their chest, some shameful failure in their past perhaps. But they were afraid they would be misunderstood, that they would be embarrassed by the harsh reaction of a confessor. So they would waltz around the principal problem until they were fairly sure of an understanding and receptive ear.

Could that be Charlie Nash's problem?

"How long you been a priest?"

"Uh . . . thirty-nine years—and counting."

"Uh-huh. You always been a Detroiter?"

"Yep. Born in old St. Joseph Hospital on the Boulevard."

"Where the GM Cadillac plant is now."

"Exactly." Maybe this was Nash's way of establishing his confidence in a confessor, but Koesler felt as if he were interviewing for a job.

"So, all that time in Detroit."

"Well, in Detroit and environs. Before I was ordained, yes, I lived in the city exclusively. Since I've been a priest, I've been assigned to a bunch of different parishes, some in the city, some suburban—but always in the archdiocese of Detroit."

"Uh. Family? You got family?"

"Not much anymore. Parents are gone. No brothers or sisters."

"No cousins? No close cousins?"

"Well, yes. My mother's only sister had three daughters. We kind of grew up together. They still live here. They're about the only cousins that still live here. But where is this leading? I mean . . ."

"I'm interested in your background. The reason will get clear later on. I'm interested in your cousins. What about them?"

Koesler was beginning to feel a lurking touch of claustrophobia. It was not uncommon for him to become defensive whenever anyone impinged on his private life. Such a mechanism might have been anachronistic in the nineties—indeed, any time after the sixties and the Second Vatican Council.

By the seventies, a great deal of the mystic cultic character of the priesthood had vanished. Priests were now frequently on a first-name basis with their flock. "Father Jack" was one of the boys who happened to be ordained and had a supernatural aura only when vested and supervising worship.

Koesler, however, could not be or become "Bob" or even "Father Bob." His clerical roots were deep in the pre-conciliar Church. From his seminary days on, he saw the priesthood in an extraterrestrial dimension. Priesthood for Koesler—and for many of his contemporaries—shared in the mission of Jesus Christ and was a sublime vehicle for helping others. Emphasis was on the role and not on the individual. So he was uncomfortable when anyone attempted to burrow into his personal life. Not that there was anything in it of which he was ashamed. But the intrusion seemed to him counterproductive.

The familiar level was completely open to his family, and fellow priests and personal friends. But when he was operating professionally, as he was now with Charles Nash, he was more comfortable with recognition of his professional character.

However, in the hope that Nash's promise or relevancy would finally emerge, Koesler was now willing to humor the man and follow his lead. "What was it again you wanted to know?"

"Your cousins . . . tell me about them."

"Uh . . . okay. There are three of them—about my age, in their fifties and sixties."

"Old maids."

"Maiden ladies. They never married."

"Names?"

"Oona, Eileen, and Maureen Monahan."

"Irish."

"My mother's family was Irish."

"Children?"

"They're unmarried."

"Doesn't mean they couldn't have children."

Koesler suppressed irritation. "Not these women!"

"How about the last one? Maureen?"

Koesler tipped his head sideways, as if taking a fresh look at Nash. "This is where you've been going all the while, isn't it? You already know about Maureen—and her two girls. Maureen took them in to live with her. If you knew of their existence, you have to know they were adopted—maybe not technically, but for all intents and purposes."

"I want to know more about them. Then you'll know why I sent for you."

Koesler knew he'd reached the end of his tether. "I think we've delved into my life far enough, Mr. Nash," he said firmly. "I don't know what there is about me or my relatives that piqued your curiosity, but I see no point in continuing this conversation." He stood up. "If ever I can really help you sometime, feel free to call. Or," he added, "you might consider calling the parish that serves this area. Which, incidentally, is St. Charles—"

"Wait!" Nash said, with more animation than he'd shown previously. "Wait, don't go." He turned his head and looked out the window for a moment. Then he turned back to Koesler. "All right, all right: I know your background. I know about your cousins. And I know about the young ones—Maureen's children."

Koesler sat back down, but he still was far from satisfied with continuing this conversation. "They're not Maureen's children—not her natural children; they're adopted."

Nash hesitated. "I know about that. But they're as good as hers. She raised them."

"Not from their earliest years. They were foundlings. No actual parent can be completely responsible for every decision children make, especially as they become adults. Still less if the child is not in the care of the adopting parent during the child's early, most formative years."

Nash almost smiled. "You know where I'm heading, don't you?"

"You're going toward a rumor, nothing more." Koesler had been maneuvered into a defensive position, and he did not like it at all.

Nash spread his hands, palms up, as if he were speaking an irrefutable if unpleasant truth. "It is no rumor, Father Koesler. Your cousin Brenda is the paramour of my son Teddy. You know that's true, don't you?"

"No, I don't *know* it's true. I have heard the gossip. As far as I'm concerned, that's all it is—gossip. It isn't even reliable enough for this hearsay to appear in print. We have our share of gossip columnists locally as well as nationally. From time to time, one or another of them will climb out on a limb and publish or broadcast a thoroughly scurrilous story. But nothing—nothing!—about Ted Nash and Brenda Monahan!"

Nash sank back into his chair. "My son is a powerful man—even though he has little more power than what came from me. But above all, Teddy is cautious, I'll give him that. Anyone who published a word of his affair would be hard-pressed to prove anything. And any publisher who okayed the story would be flirting with a serious lawsuit. But it's real, Father Koesler; put your bottom dollar on it: It's true."

Nash fished through the pouch on the side of his wheelchair until he came up with a pack of cigarettes. Koesler could hardly believe his eyes. Most probably, Nash owed his emphysema—the disease that likely would kill him—to smoking. He needed an inhaler just to breathe normally . . . or what passed for normally.

Koesler had been a smoker. In his youth, he, like many smokers of his era, had lit up one or another of the unfiltered cigarette brands. There were no filter tips in those days. Nor, he noticed, was Nash's cigarette filtered. In later years before he quit, Koesler could not bring himself to smoke any but the most thoroughly filtered of brands. And now here was Charles Nash delivering an almost self-inflicted coup de grâce.

The priest leaned back in a futile attempt to get as far away as possible from secondary smoke inhalation. "Suppose . . . just suppose, I grant for a moment that my foster cousin and your son are—and I really don't admit this—having . . . an affair. So what? It may or may not be of concern to you. But . . . me? If I wanted to intrude unasked into someone else's life—which I seldom if ever do . . . but, say I did: What could I do about it?"

"We're talking adultery here!" Nash's raised voice was forceful. "Your cousin may not be married. But my son, by God, is very much married. He's got a family, for God's sake!"

Two thoughts occurred to Koesler almost simultaneously. If anyone should be an expert in adultery, surely Charles Nash would be that person. At least so spoke his universally accepted reputation. Plus, why should his son's adulterous affair bother this old master of infidelity? By Nashian standards, merely one woman on the side was hardly even getting into the game. Neither of these unspoken considerations, thought Koesler, deserved airing.

Instead, Koesler said, "Mr. Nash, Ted's wife must have at least heard the rumors. As far as I know, she hasn't done anything about it." Koesler could not imagine a woman of Mrs. Nash's standing putting up with such a situation. Divorce was not uncommon even among Catholics now. And any financial settlement in such a case would leave her with a very comfortable future.

"Also," Koesler added, "Ted is a businessman—a builder, a developer. His position in the business community could scarcely be changed, let alone damaged at all, merely by an extramarital affair.

"Don't misunderstand me: I'm certainly not condoning adultery. I'm saying I don't know this accusation to be true. How could I broach a matter like adultery to Brenda when it's no more than a rumor? And even if it were true, Brenda knows I'm available if she wants to talk."

"You don't understand! You don't understand, dammit!" Nash pounded feebly on the arm of his wheelchair. "Teddy has created the impression that he is more Catholic than the Pope—courtesy of the training his mother gave him. If the Vatican needs a new electronics system, they've got it, courtesy of Teddy. If this city gets into deficit spending over a visit from the Pope, Teddy picks up the tab. Christ, he's even got his own goddam chapel and his own goddam priest! On top of all that crap, little Brenda works in the chancery for the arch-diocese of Detroit."

Koesler had to admit privately that all Nash said was true: Ted had indeed made himself the most "official" Catholic layman in Michigan—perhaps in the country—maybe even the world.

"The thing that's gonna happen when Teddy's affair becomes public . . ."—Koesler noted that Nash eschewed the conditional "if" for the more definite "when"—"the thing that's gonna happen when Teddy's affair becomes public," Nash repeated, "is that this whole Catholic fable gets exposed and destroyed. And that means that Teddy's whole world is gonna crumble and so is Teddy. If he can't be Pope Teddy, he ain't gonna be nobody. See?"

"Yes, but—"

"What you don't see," Nash continued as if Koesler had not spoken, "is that when this masquerade is over, Teddy is gonna be left impotent in every which way.

"And then . . . and then . . ."—Nash seemed to be unwinding like a tired spring—"my whole empire, everything I worked for, everything I built, is gonna be nothin'. All my enemies, all my competitors that've been snapping at my heels all these years, they're gonna be all over Nash Enterprises. And there ain't gonna be anything left of it. It'll be gone. Everything."

Koesler thought he saw a tear trickle from Nash's eye. There was no way of being certain; if it was a tear, it vanished in one of the many wrinkles.

Ah, so that was it! Koesler now thought he understood. This had absolutely nothing to do with religion, God, the sacraments—any sort of consolation or hope that Koesler could and was prepared to deliver. Nash couldn't have cared less about the state of anybody's soul: not his, not his son's—certainly not about the soul of his son's paramour. It was simply business as usual. Or, rather, keeping the business thriving as usual.

Not for nothing had Ted Nash created this image of himself as super-Catholic. Apparently and against all odds he saw himself as God's embodiment of the One True Church—although how he was able to accomplish this, given his private life, Koesler had great difficulty imagining.

Charlie Nash could perceive, even predict, the outcome of this charade. Teddy would be unmasked—probably sooner rather than later. And when that happened, when his feet of clay were exposed, he would not have the bravura to tough it out, laugh it off.

And with Teddy frozen and vulnerable, the vultures would gather and devour about the only thing Charlie Nash valued in this life or the next: Nash Enterprises, Inc. And the news media—the news media! What a field day they would enjoy lampooning this holier-than-thou fraud! Not only would he be stripped of his every Catholic costume, but his girl-on-the-side would be revealed as an employee of the Church.

Among the avenues open to Charlie Nash to avert this catastrophe was the one he was now pursuing: Get to Father Koesler and convince him to in turn convince his cousin to break off her liaison with Ted.

So far, it did not seem to Nash that he was accomplishing his mission.

"Look . . ." If Nash had been a less formidable individual, one could almost have taken his tone as pleading. "It can't be that hard. You can talk to your cousin—all right, your *foster* cousin. She got at least some Catholic school training; Maureen saw to that. She's gotta know this is wrong. Besides, what kinda future is this for her? What's she gonna get outta it? Teddy is not gonna leave Melissa and the kids. They're his respectability. Brenda's got hold of the short end of this stick and it isn't gonna get any better. You'd be doing Brenda a favor—a very big favor."

"And if I do," Koesler said, "and if Brenda denies that there's anything going on between her and Ted . . . ?"

"But it's true, dammit! It's true!"

"I'm not some sort of private investigator, nor did I ever want to be. If . . . *if* I were to bring it up with Brenda and she denied it, that would be that as far as I was concerned."

They sat in silence regarding each other for a few moments. Nash seemed markedly drained by the intensity of his effort to convince Koesler.

Finally, in a declining effort, he shrugged. "Okay, let's do it your way for now. You go think it over. But remember . . ." He smiled faintly. "You could save her soul. Remember? 'The value of one immortal soul.'"

Koesler nodded.

Nash pushed a button on the arm of the wheelchair. Instantly, the young man in white appeared and piloted the chair and its occupant from the room.

In a few moments, the man returned to usher Koesler to the elevator. Koesler would ponder this morning's extraordinary conversation not only on the elevator but all the way on his drive home.

The nearest he could come to a resolution of the situation was to pursue the matter in as nonconfrontational a way as possible. Perhaps he could find an opportunity to speak with Maureen about it. Or maybe with one of her sisters . . .

It couldn't hurt.

And it might save one immortal soul.

CHAPTER

3

At 7:00 P.M. it was a bit late for rush hour traffic. Yet traffic on I-75 northbound was moving at a crawl.

Ordinarily, Ted Nash would have been extremely irritated. Not tonight. Too many things had broken for him today. So he was able to scrunch into the generous upholstery of his half-million-dollar custom Jaguar and enjoy the wraparound sound of Mozart coming from the CD player.

Today's major conquest had been over that ragtag group of environmentalists. He and they had been at each other with increasing frequency. So often, indeed, that he was becoming familiar with their names, their fields of expertise, even their odors.

The latest battle had been over Ford Park. The group argued that Ford's acres represented the final vestige of wetland within the corporate limits of the city of Detroit.

Ted Nash needed that land. Translated into a large strip mall it could attract the patronage of one of the last best neighborhoods in the city. He had already secured Mayor Maynard Cobb's assurance that the city would offer one sweetheart deal after another, including nonmetered parking.

Of course the parking would not actually be free. Parking costs would be reflected in higher office rents or higher retail prices. But that was not Nash's concern.

The group's arguments were the same tired complaints they always advanced. The animals, the birds, the fish, the trees—all endangered, all precious, all entitled to protection.

They did not know their Bible.

Why, in the very first chapter of Genesis, the very first book of the Bible, it said, "God created man in his image: in the divine image he created him: male and female he created them. God blessed them, saying: 'Be fertile and multiply; fill the earth and subdue it. Have dominion over the fish of the sea, the birds of the air, and all the living things that move on the earth.'"

These crazy nature lovers had it all backward.

22

According to their interpretation of Scripture, the fish of the sea, the birds of the air, and all living things that move on the earth have equality with man. Why, if that were even partly true, most of the marvelous accomplishments of Nash Enterprises would have been some sort of crime against nature, since, after all, nature had been pushed aside for the sake of all the malls, shopping centers, highrises, and residential developments that constituted Nash Enterprises.

Such considerations had never bothered his father, Charlie Nash, in the least. Progress, for the old man, was a case of damn the torpedoes, full speed ahead.

Ted's conscience, however, had always been a much more tender instrument of judgment and punishment. If he had not had his unique facility for making moral decisions armed not only with Scripture and tradition but with a healthy dose of reason, logic, and pragmatism, why, Nash Enterprises would have disintegrated in the wake of old Charlie's retirement.

Of course Ted had to admit that his rationalization was aided and supported by the spiritual direction of Father Art.

Good old Father Art.

In the beginning there was Father Charles E. Coughlin, controversial Detroit radio priest of the thirties.

Little Teddy Nash was a teenager during the years of the Second Vatican Council. Looking back at that event now, Ted realized that his dad had paid absolutely no attention to the council—which had been a considerable media happening, even for the secular media.

Charlie Nash's parish church was lucky if he darkened its door even twice a year. So Charlie had been mildly surprised one Christmas when the service was held totally in English. The priest was no longer muttering in Latin. But the mild surprise was quickly displaced in his mind by plans to acquire land in Bloomfield Hills.

It was left to Teddy's mother to plant the seeds of religious conservatism in Ted's psyche. Mother also led him to the hero worship of Father Coughlin, who never did release his hold on the preconciliar Church.

With the passing of Coughlin in 1979, the mantle of leadership fell on the willing shoulders of Father Arthur Deutsch.

Later, Father Art had been able to retire to Boca Raton in a splendid place he had prepared for himself. He would probably have joined Opus Dei, a reactionary conservative subculture of the Catholic Church, except for Teddy Nash's having made him an offer he could scarcely refuse.

As virtual court chaplain for Teddy, Father Art could stay in harness and be far more influential by the continuing formation of the young man's conscience than ever he could have been in retirement.

Ford Park was a case in point. Instinctively, Ted Nash had known that it was financially imperative that the animals inhabiting the park be ousted for the sake of progress. After all, there were plenty of other habitats to which they could migrate. Besides, relocation to a pristine environment in some other state would be good for them. Breathe cleaner air. And if those ground animals that couldn't fly away got run over by cars and trucks, that was just part of the "dominion" that God wanted man to exercise over nature.

The latter argument had been supplied by Father Art.

Of course, none of these arguments came close to influencing the crazy environmentalists. But then again, they did have their own interpretation of Scripture.

What mattered was that Nash Enterprises had won. It had cost the company under the table, but that's the way things moved along in the real world. The company had Ford Park. All was right with the world.

Thus Teddy, even mired in crawling traffic, was a happy man.

Adding to his euphoria was the anticipation of a leisurely weekend with Brenda. His wife and children were off to Palm Springs, so he was relieved of having to concoct some excuse for spending yet more time away from home.

Ted had never regretted marrying Melissa Dwyer. She had been just what the doctor ordered. Her family was yin to his family's yang. Hers was Old Money. His was nouveau riche. While his parents had been invited to most of high society's doings after Charlie had struck it rich, they had never really been accepted into anything resembling the elite . . .

Melissa's family, on the other hand, went back to the original families that had settled Detroit. In marrying Melissa, he had wed respectability. God was good.

Teddy didn't even mind the children. It was difficult to be bothered by them. He hardly ever saw them.

Ted and Melissa had three children in four years. As far as Ted was concerned, it would have been very acceptable to have ten in ten years—or twenty in twenty. However, Melissa was not amused. Eventually, one night several years ago, she had announced, "We've got to talk!"

To Ted's surprise, Melissa didn't want to have a baby every year for the rest of her fertile life. Ted said he would discuss the matter with Father Art and see what the official Church position was on a hysterectomy when the organs in question were perfectly healthy.

Melissa, when she recovered from astonishment at Ted's imperious presumption, declared she didn't really give a damn what current Church teaching was, but if he was going to check out anything, let it be the present stance on vasectomy, again when the operation involved not only healthy but robust plumbing.

Ted very definitely was having none of that, no matter what the Church taught.

They argued for quite a while until both came to realize that neither "ectomy" was going to take place.

They debated noninvasive methods of birth control . . . until they came to the conclusion that while Melissa, on the one hand, had no intention of depending on unreliable methods, Ted, on the other hand (citing the papal encyclical "Humanae Vitae" as definitively condemning any form of artificial birth control), had no intention of utilizing any such thing.

By this time, neither thought it productive to mention the rhythm method. In the end, both could have sung "Let's Call the Whole Thing Off."

All things considered, Melissa figured she could do without sex at least until such time as it would be worthwhile to divorce Ted—certainly not until the children were grown—or until she chanced on a safe affair of the heart.

Ted was not nearly as tranquil with the arrangement. It was perfectly acceptable for women to be continent; abstinence came naturally to them. And of course priests freely chose to be celibate and chaste. But he felt no call whatsoever to lead a temperate existence.

And then, like a miracle, Brenda came into his life. God was good.

THEY MET AT A Marygrove College Christmas celebration, at which he was the guest of honor. She was a graduate of what had been a Catholic college for women. It was now coed, and Ted Nash was one of its benefactors.

The timing was perfect. He'd been barred from Melissa's bed just long enough to build up a smoldering hunger. He certainly could not bring himself to seek relief either with a prostitute or by himself.

Had Ted not been the honoree, he would never have considered attending the party. It was neither his kind of party nor his sort of group.

It was held in a huge room with a vaulted ceiling. In the center of the room were tables holding trays of finger sandwiches and hors d'oeuvres. Other tables against the walls held liquor and generic wine. A student choral group was singing carols.

Bored, Ted was eager to leave, when he spotted her, as the song had it, across a crowded room.

She was tall—easily his height, slender, and dressed in what for some reason was his favorite color scheme—black and white. He caught her looking at him. But when he returned the gaze, she quickly turned her head.

He approved such modesty.

Who can say why one person is attracted to another? There can be countless reasons, many of them intangible. But something ignited between them.

He crossed to her and introduced himself. She blushed and acknowledged that she as well as everyone else in the room knew who he was. She introduced herself. Brenda Monahan.

Irish. He liked that too.

When he discovered where she worked—the chancery of the archdiocese of Detroit—their conversation would not suffer an awkward silence for the rest of that evening, nor for all the evenings to come. With his abiding interest in Catholicism—on his terms—he was fascinated with the inner workings of what was in effect headquarters.

Ted did not particularly cotton to Detroit's Catholic hierarchy. Far too liberal. He felt that was a just charge to make against Detroit's archbishop, Cardinal Mark Boyle. And of course the archbishop set the tone for the entire archdiocese.

Not that every priest marched in lockstep to the official drummer. There was Father Art for one, and many who agreed with him.

But there just wasn't much one could do to an archbishop, especially when he happened to be a Cardinal as well. Only the Pope could rein in a Prince of the Church. And even the Pope would be hesitant to meddle, particularly publicly.

Nonetheless, Ted was always curious about what made the ecclesiastical wheels grind. Even the redoubtable Father Art could not hold forth very authoritatively on that subject. Oh, sure, Father Art had his pet theories about what went on behind Chancery doors on the highest local levels. Such theories might be accurate or not; at best they were informed guesses.

Now, here was this young woman sent not only as a relief for his concupiscence, but also as an instrument of inside expertise that could satisfy his curiosity about the chancery.

God was indeed good.

And here he was, on his way home, as it were, to Brenda.

CHAPTER

4

TED NASH turned off the CD and Mozart's *Eine kleine Nachtmusik,* and began to softly whistle *Camelot.* More and more this Sterling Heights high rise reminded him of King Arthur's redoubtable fortress. And it also reminded him of God, since God had directed him, just as He had guided Arthur, to all the fortress contained. Not the least of this bounty was Guinevere—Brenda.

The structure was christened Nebo, after the mountain from which Moses had viewed the Promised Land. Ted's suite in this building was his promised land. The building was Ted's baby. In erecting it he had avoided some earlier mistakes, from which he had learned. Measured by the standards of the 1990s, it was about as perfect as a condominium building could be. There were few if any complaints from the resident-owners.

But most of all, with unwonted prescience, Ted had incorporated into Nebo his unassailable nest.

The idea had first occurred to him when, many years before, he had read of the French king who had built into his palace a double staircase leading to his chambers, the configuration of which made it impossible for his wife to encounter any of his mistresses coming or going.

Although at the time Nebo was planned and built, Ted had had no practical need for such a protective hideaway—relations with Melissa were then at least adequate—still and all there might come a time when he would require utter seclusion. So he had tucked into Nebo a mazelike retreat. Now he needed it, had it, and used it.

He pulled into the ramp adjoining Nebo, drove up two levels, pressed the automatic door opener, and entered the ramp's only garage. In effect, it was a garage within a garage.

From there, he took a private elevator to the eleventh floor, exited, and took another private elevator—which masqueraded as a janitor's closet and required a special key for entry—and arrived at the twenty-first floor, one floor below the penthouse.

Besides Brenda and himself, only two others knew of this ultra-private suite, and only one of those two had access to the apartment.

Ted's architect was the draftsman of the entire building, including the Nash retreat. The architect's financial future was linked to the Nash fortune. Thus the architect could be trusted. And he, in turn, had involved so many subcontractors in the construction of the suite that no one of them knew the entire configuration.

The only other confidante was the housekeeper, who, along with her family, was in this country illegally. Thus she was even more dependent on Ted Nash's good will than was the architect.

It was Ted's conviction that it paid to protect one's rear.

Utilizing his key, Ted entered the suite.

"THAT YOU, TED?" Brenda called from the kitchen.

Nash smiled as he put down his briefcase and hung up his hat and coat. "If it's not, it's got to be Mandrake the Magician."

"It could have been Valeria."

"She hasn't been here today?"

"Oh, she's been here. But she forgot her groceries. I thought she might have come back for them."

Nash reached the doorway to the kitchen. Brenda stood, her back to him, at the sink. She was mixing a pitcher of martinis.

She was wearing a white, frilly blouse, and a dark, knee-length skirt. Black and white, his favorite colors. She never forgot. Besides, it was a sensible ensemble, considering this is what she'd worn to work at the chancery.

Ted renewed his admiration for her figure. He reveled in her wasp waist, the curve of her full hips, the slope of her calves, her slender ankles. That was just one of many fascinating things about Brenda: One could admire every portion of her body separately. And that was one of the joys of seeing her fully clothed: It enabled one to appreciate sights that were otherwise lost in the beauty of her total nakedness.

Ted could never understand how some thought Brenda plain. They just had not had the fortune to experience the complete Brenda. He had. And he could not get enough of her.

He approached her. As soon as she felt him behind her, she leaned back against him. He smelled her straight brunette, shoulder-length hair. Vintage Brenda. He inhaled the fragrance of her shampoo. "Thank God for Palm Springs," he murmured.

She stirred the ice in the pitcher. "What's in Palm Springs?"

"Melissa and the kids." In Brenda's presence he never used the designation "wife" for Melissa. Melissa was certainly not fully a wife; and, by Ted's peculiar lights, Brenda was at least as much a wife as Melissa. Somehow, it just didn't seem suitable to use the term in either's presence.

"That means we've got the whole weekend," Brenda said.

"That's what it means, okay. Any problems?"

In no way did the query imply that a problem would be permitted to interfere with their time together. Merely that if Brenda had any prior commitment, it would be canceled or postponed. Brenda understood. She shook her head. "No, no problems."

"Great. Are you going to keep stirring until you melt that ice?"

She laughed. "Go make yourself comfy. I'll be there in a minute."

In the living room he kicked off his shoes and snuggled into the leather recliner. His chair. He looked about him. The decor was as appealing as any ad for interior design. Brenda had a talent for that—among other things. Ted felt good—very, very good.

Brenda entered, bearing a tray with two martinis straight up and some cheese and crackers. She set the tray on the end table alongside his chair. She took her martini and sat on the couch across from him. "How was your day?"

With a broad smile, he raised his glass to eye level.

"That good!" she exclaimed. "You're toasting it?"

"We got the Ford Park deal!" he exulted.

"Marvelous! None of the media thought you could pull it off."

He took a sip of his drink, then set the glass down and spread some cheese on a cracker. "Bleeding hearts! They all get upset about killing Thumper or Bambi. Well, we're not killing them; they just have to move when they get in the way of progress."

"It's a sure thing?"

"It's a done deal." He cheesed another cracker, leaned forward, and offered it to her. "By the way, with the park gone there's going to be room for much more than just the mall. We're going to put up some additional condos. Should be a significant increase in population for that area. We may even buy up some of the existing buildings and gentrify them." He gestured with a cracker. "This would be an excellent time for your boss to scoop up some of that land for a new parish. The final head count will more than justify the move. And if he waits until the development is well along, things will get tough." He leaned back in the chair. "Matter of fact, if the Department of Finance and Administration doesn't get off the dime very, very soon—like now—there just might not be any land at any price."

Brenda looked thoughtful. After a slight pause during which she took a small sip of her drink, she asked, "Now, how am I going to do this? Without, that is, blowing my cover . . . *our* cover."

"I've thought of that. The deal between Nash Enterprises and the city will be on radio and the tube tonight and in the papers tomorrow. Only the news about the mall, not the part about the condos and further developments. But the mall is the essence of the whole idea . . . and you can speculate as well as anyone else."

Her concern appeared to dissolve. "That's pretty good. But how's this: Isn't this just about the same M.O. you used in the Conner-Jefferson development?"

"Come to think . . . yeah, it is. Just about."

"So the possibility of your doing it again is strong . . . strong enough so that the archdiocese would be foolish not to move on it."

"You're right! You're absolutely right. The risk is minimal while the gain could be significant. Good thinking."

Ted felt a bit ambivalent about Brenda's mental powers. On the one hand, he was pleased that she was so much more than a mere sex object. On the other, he occasionally felt threatened in that she might just possibly be significantly smarter than he. But for the moment, that emotion was buried deep beneath the surface.

"As it turns out," he went on, "you're in a no-lose situation. If you make this suggestion, it doesn't really matter whether McGraw moves on it or not. You're going to be absolutely correct. If he buys your recommendation, he'll be a very happy man. If he doesn't, he loses . . . and so does the archdiocese. Either way, your stock climbs."

Brenda knew all that. But she let him think he had reached this conclusion on his own. "How about another one?" She didn't wait for an answer.

Watching raptly as she left the room, he marveled at her sinuous movement.

"While we're at it," he said, loudly enough to be heard in the kitchen, "how was your day?" The times he had addressed the same question to Melissa, the interest was nonexistent and the words simply pro forma. He didn't really care what the kids had done in school or what was the gossip in the beauty parlor. With Brenda, however, he was very definitely interested in what went on in the chancery. He found the inner workings of the Church fascinating.

She returned and refilled his glass, then topped off her own drink, of which she had taken only a few sips. She returned to the couch, a smile tugging at her mouth.

"Something did happen that I thought you'd find interesting. There was a letter that arrived a while back. It was addressed just to the chancery, correct street number and all. But because it wasn't addressed to anybody specific, it was delivered to the Cardinal's office. It was written in some foreign language, but none of the secretaries could figure out what the language was.

"To make a long story short, the letter traveled all over the Chancery and the Gabriel Richard Building. Some of the younger priests in the various offices saw it, and so did just about all the lay employees. Nobody could figure it out.

"Finally, they figured that since it had an Egyptian postmark it probably came from some missionary priest. So they sent it to the Propagation of the Faith office in hopes that someone in the office of the missions could at least identify the language."

"And?"

"And the Prop office solved the mystery." She paused. "It was written in Latin!"

"Latin!" Ted roared. "It was written in Latin? And it went through all the downtown bureaucracies and no one recognized it?"

Brenda nodded vigorously. "Of course, the Cardinal didn't see it. Nor did the few elderly priests who work there. Any one of *them* would have recognized it immediately.

"And," she added, "rumor has it that this isn't the first time this has happened."

"Worse yet! To think that no one in the administrative offices knew or realized it was Latin. That really tells you something. And it makes you wonder whatever happened to the Latin Rite of the Roman Catholic Church."

Ted was on the verge of getting himself all worked up. For him it was just one more indication of the damage and destruction that had been inflicted on his Church as a result of that damned Ecumenical Council in the early sixties. It was bad enough that ranking lay people working at headquarters of the Archdiocese of Detroit could not even recognize the Latin language. Worse, some young priests, who represented the Latin Rite of the Catholic Church, but couldn't and wouldn't remember anything that preceded Vatican II, couldn't even make out the tongue of their own rite!

"Anyway," Brenda said, "it's a true story. Kind of interesting and kind of funny. I thought you could call that editor at the *Free Press*— Nelson Kane, isn't it? It's just the kind of story he likes. It should give him a whole column. Then he'll owe you one."

"Good thought. Very good thought. I'll give him a call tomorrow."

"Seems we've got something going here," Brenda observed.

"Huh?"

"We're helping each other one-up people who will then owe us. You gave me the ammo to get an advantage over Muggsy McGraw with that land parcel deal. And I give you a story that can win you a favor at the *Free Press*. Not bad."

"Not bad at all. And relatively painless. Now . . ." Ted held up his empty glass. ". . . how about one more, honey, before dinner?"

Brenda, who still hadn't finished her first drink, immediately got the pitcher and refilled his glass. She glanced at his eyes. They were beginning to glaze. Would he stay awake long enough to have supper? Would he be conscious enough for sex? She didn't bother adding anything to her own glass. Instead, she went back into the kitchen. He watched her go, again appreciatively.

Another great thing about Brenda: By now, Melissa would have been all over his case for having three powerful drinks on virtually an empty stomach. With Brenda, whatever he wanted he got. No fuss, no argument, no recriminations. Bless Brenda. "What's for supper, by the way?"

"Looks like a leg of lamb," Brenda called back. "As usual, Valeria left heating instructions." She grinned. If Valeria were a man, she'd be accused of having the belt and suspenders syndrome; she never left anything to chance.

Brenda returned to the living room. "Just to let you know ahead of time: I probably won't be home till late Wednesday evening. It's Aunt Oona's birthday. I really should drop in for the party."

"Juss as well," he slurred slightly. "M'lissa is having some people over. I've already been informed I've got to be there."

Ted understood that Oona was not really Brenda's aunt; it simply was the easiest term of reference. "Anything else cooking downtown?"

"Not much," she replied. "Outside of the Latin letter, most things seem to be in remission, or dead in the water, especially in our office. McGraw had an appointment with the Cardinal this morning. But it went nowhere."

"Oh? What about?"

"The ADF."

Ted put his glass down definitively. "That thing is a mesh. That thing is a mess," he corrected himself. "Should bring in three, four times what it does."

"That's what McGraw thinks too. His idea was an old one. He keeps thinking the time is right for the Cardinal to okay it."

"Quotas," Ted pronounced.

"Yes. He thinks it's feasible to set reasonable quotas for every parish. With most of the parishes banking with the chancery—and even with those who bank independently—McGraw is confident that we can set realistic goals for everybody."

"And if they don't meet 'em?"

"That's McGraw's fail-safe clause. We know they've got the money. If they don't reach their goals during the drive, we simply take it from their reserves."

Nash smiled contentedly. "A fund-raiser's dream come true."

"Uh-huh."

"Jussa way it oughta be. *Just* the way it ought to be," he corrected. "Wassa matter with that? What's the matter with that? The Cardinal didn't buy it?"

She shook her head. "He keeps going back to the goals Cardinal Mooney set when he started the ADF."

She knew that Ted was aware of Mooney's design for the Archdiocesan Development Fund. She also knew that at just this moment, he couldn't recall the philosophy.

"You remember, Ted: The idea was to explain the needs of the diocese. Services that were too complicated to be provided by individual parishes—things like a seminary, social services and so forth. Then, simply call on Detroit Catholics to rise to the challenge. No quotas, no demands."

"And what's it got 'em? Two million tops . . . right?"

"Uh-huh. But in this presentation today, McGraw proposed not only the setting of goals but publishing the results in the *Detroit Catholic*."

Ted smiled. "Show what each parish contributed? Uh . . . gave?"

"Uh-huh. Show what each parish gave, along with the preestablished quota."

"Jus' 'xactly. And the Cardinal didn't buy it?"

"No. Said it didn't square with the intent of the ADF. We have to depend on the free will offerings of informed Catholics. He was particularly negative about publishing the results of the drive. Said it would embarrass the poorer parishes and the ones who for one reason or another didn't, or couldn't, contribute very much. He said what use was the money if it came from coercion? The Church ought to be able to rely on the growing generosity of Christians."

Ted's lip curled. "Makes you wonder why they made him a . . . a . . . Cardinal, dunn't it?"

"I'd better get dinner going." Brenda wondered whether she had waited too long. It was Ted's habit to be abstemious with hors d'oeuvres. That meant that the drinks hit him harder. She usually tried to tuck the beginning of dinner between drinks two and three.

"Whadja say it was?"

"Lamb."

"Good. Tired of roast beef."

With that, Ted listed to his right and fell asleep.

Brenda pursed her lips and shook her head. Too late. She went to the rear of his recliner and pushed the back down as far as it would go. He was nearly horizontal. Almost immediately he began to snore.

She returned to the couch, picked up the remote control and turned on the TV. There wasn't much to watch. Mostly game shows and reruns of old sitcoms.

It didn't matter. She just wanted some background noise.

This evening would be the "B" format. Ted would nap for an hour or two. When he woke he would have trouble establishing clear consciousness. But he'd come around.

They'd eat. Then probably they'd watch cable. Later they'd make love. Ted was very good at that. He was very active. And he was always careful to make sure she was completely satisfied.

Her mind turned toward the coming Wednesday evening—Aunt Oona's birthday party.

Brenda's presence at such occasions always turned out to be a mixed bag. She was very certainly expected to attend, but usually the party would end badly, with angry, hurtful words. There seemed no way out of it. Even the knowledge of how it likely would end could not excuse her absence.

She wondered whether her "uncle" the priest would be there. Probably.

They would all call him Father Bob. Even Brenda herself would be expected to follow suit. It was worse when the Koesler side of the family visited. Most of them were Lutheran. Then it became a battle of names: The Lutherans would go out of their way to call him "Bob," while the Irish would extend themselves just as far in calling him "Father."

What a family!

There were stirrings from the recliner. Apparently, Ted was not going to nap as long this evening.

Brenda busied herself in the kitchen, reheating the meat, potatoes, and vegetables, and tossing the salad.

Repeatedly, from one or another of the sisters, she'd heard how the Monahans and Koeslers had lived in adjoining flats on the corner of West Vernor and Ferdinand across from what had been the Stratford Movie Theater. They might just as well have been brother and sisters as cousins.

Yet, as close as they had been as children, now they treated a visit from their priest relative as if Moses were coming down from Mount Sinai with the Ten Commandments. And they treated him not as the kid with whom they'd grown up, but as some sort of cultic abstraction.

As far as she was concerned, she liked Bob Koesler—Father Bob. He had helped to get her the job with the archdiocese. That was more important than he realized.

The snoring had stopped. There were sounds of stretching movements. Ted was coming around.

Without turning, she knew he was standing in the kitchen doorway looking at her.

"You know something?" The slur in his pronunciation was gone. "I couldn't live without you."

"That's nice." She smiled. It was true: He couldn't live without her.

CHAPTER

5

TRAVELING SOUTH, a motorist would ordinarily take Interstate 75. However, this was weekday rush-hour traffic, so Father Koesler chose the alternate and ancient route of Jefferson Avenue. The traffic was not nearly as clogged as that on the freeway, the traffic lights were favorable, and it was the shortest distance between two points.

The two points were downtown Detroit, where Koesler lived, and Grosse Ile, where Eileen Monahan lived and where the birthday party for Oona Monahan was to be held.

Via Jefferson, he would drive through the heart of River Rouge, Ecorse, Lincoln Park, Wyandotte, Riverview, and Trenton. All old cities and all known by Detroit-area natives as "downriver." All bordered on the Detroit River as it flowed toward Lake Erie, the next in the chain of the Great Lakes.

Grosse Ile, an island just east of Trenton, was connected to the mainland by two bridges. In addition to mostly beautiful homes with plenty of lawn, the island also boasted a naval air station and a Catholic parish, Sacred Heart, coveted by many priests as a haven for virtually early retirement as well as for the access it provided to a fine golf course.

Eileen had lived on Grosse Ile almost as long as Koesler's memory stretched. Her home fronted on the river, across which lay Amherstburg, Canada. The house rested on the water's edge. Its rectangular lot ran almost forty yards back to the road. Over the years, the property had been guarded by a series of dogs, with none of whom had Koesler been able to make friends.

On his first visit to Eileen's home many years ago, Koesler had pulled up at the garage displaying the numbered address. A high metal fence delineated the property. Koesler had wondered how to announce his presence; there was no sign of a doorbell. He had rattled the fence; instantly, a small but loudmouthed spaniel mix had hurled himself at Koesler as if the fence weren't there. The dog, Koesler had reasoned correctly, was the doorbell.

Eileen had appeared shortly after the dog announced Koesler's arrival. She was distressed that the animal was making such a commotion. Assuring him that the dog did not bite, she opened the gate. Instantly, the animal dove for Koesler's ankle. But before it could strike, Eileen scooped it up, whapped it across the snout, and admonished, "That's Father Bob!"

The spaniel proved to be the first in a series of anticlerical dogs owned by Eileen. Once it was established that, for whatever reason, there would be enmity between Koesler and Eileen's sentinels, she routinely locked them away when her cousin was expected.

Trenton. Almost there.

Koesler thought again on what awaited him. He considered this type of family reunion more a duty than a pleasure. But since he was conscientious in the fulfillment of duty, he nearly always attended the gatherings.

There would be six people. There were always six. None of whom had ever married.

He, of course, had promised a celibate, or unmarried, life. There was no other way the Church would have ordained him. Willingly he had taken on this obligation. He had no other desire in life but to be a priest.

The three sisters were another matter.

Oona, the eldest, whose sixty-fifth birthday they would be celebrating, was an often mean-tempered hypochondriac who frequently actually was ill. Koesler could remember once visiting her in the intensive care unit of a hospital. She complained that she was getting insufficient care. Since she was already receiving the maximum care of which the hospital was capable, he could do little for her.

Eileen, at sixty-one years, was next. As she aged, a bit more rapidly than the others, particularly in recent years, she reminded Koesler of one of the maiden ladies—it didn't matter which—in *Arsenic and Old Lace.* Eileen walked in a rush of tiny steps. Her dresses overflowed with an abundance of lace. She managed to be occupied with "busy-work" most of the time. And she seemed dedicated to making peace. There was lots of peace to be made.

Maureen, at fifty-eight, was the baby. She was the nuts-and-bolts practical one. She had been employed most of her life at a series of diverse jobs. She'd been a waitress, a butcher, and a lifeguard. Those were the more colorful occupations in her résumé. In addition, she had been a secretary in a long list of business offices. And it was she who had adopted the two girls.

Each was now thirty-three years old. Both had been foundlings. Mary Lou had been first. And then, because Maureen sensed a loneliness in the youngster's life, Brenda had been brought into the household.

The two girls had such similar backgrounds. Each had spent her earlier years in various foster homes. Each had found her way to St. Vincent's Orphanage on Detroit's east side. The home was owned, operated, and staffed by the Sisters of Charity, those wondrous women whose bonnets brought to mind giant gulls—the precursors of TV's "Flying Nun."

Mary Lou had hated everything about St. Vincent's. Not that she was abused in any way. But she desperately wanted a home. So when Maureen took pity on her and brought her home on holidays and isolated weekends, Mary Lou tried to blend into the furniture, and wept bitterly each time she was returned—dragged back—to St. Vincent's at the conclusion of each sojourn.

Maureen began bringing Brenda home with Mary Lou, hoping the companionship of the other girl would neutralize the trauma of return for Mary Lou.

It didn't work out quite as hoped.

Brenda, for the most part, kept her feelings locked inside. She seemed so thoughtful—contemplative. She also seemed passive. On those occasions when they were returned to the orphanage and Mary Lou would go into her tantrum, Brenda would watch as if she were part of the audience at a play.

When the girls reached the fifth grade, all of their care and education to that point having been provided by St. Vincent's, Maureen was able to take both of them permanently without legally adopting either.

As to the spinsterdom of the sisterhood: It is not all that uncommon for the Irish to postpone marriage. It often happens that this delay in marrying becomes set in stone. To a degree this was the case with the Monahans.

In addition, Oona, as the eldest, took on a heavy load in caring for her younger sisters, as well as supporting the family when their father died prematurely. As sometimes happens in such circumstances, Oona's social life was all but nonexistent. She glided into her later years having experienced few interpersonal relationships, fewer thrills, and no romances.

Eileen was naturally shy. As a child she seemed foreordained to become a nun. During her formative years, she prepared for that vocation. But when, after high school graduation, it came time for her to enter the convent, a medical exam found her health to be extremely delicate. The doctor's opinion was that Eileen was destined for a brief sojourn on earth and that she was utterly incapable of enduring the physical demands of religious life. The doctor's prognosis for her life span eventually proved inaccurate. But for Eileen, the die had been cast. She had been brought up to be a nun, not a wife and mother. Her virginity appeared to her and her family to be a gift from God. And so she embraced it. This much should be said for Eileen: Her celibacy was a much more fulfilling and positive experience than Oona's.

Of all the sisters, the one most likely to break the cycle of spinsterdom was Maureen. The baby of the family, guarded and guided by two doting older sisters, Maureen enjoyed a relatively carefree childhood. For an Irish Catholic girl attending parochial school, she dated extensively and often. Unabashed, she confided in her sisters, and, through her, the sisters lived a vicarious storybook adolescence. Except that for Oona and Eileen it was fiction.

Maureen hid no dating detail from her sisters' eager ears. There was nothing much to hide. While her dates included dancing, roller skating, ice skating, swimming parties, and a good deal of necking, she never went "all the way." So her Catholic conscience did not much trouble her. But for her, unlike her sisters, her social and romantic life was an embarrassment of riches. There were so many boyfriends, some more serious than others, that Maureen never seemed able to settle down and select the one who would be a life's companion. And so it went until her prospect of marriage thickened and finally congealed. The two little girls became her life.

As time went by, Mary Lou seemed to grow closer to Maureen. She certainly was more dependent. It was likely she never lost the deep fear that she might be returned to the orphanage. That might explain why she virtually became Maureen's shadow. Occasionally, friends would observe that Mary Lou was becoming a clone of the sisters. As an adult, she flitted from one job—usually clerical—to another. The problem had nothing to do with incompetence. It was more a case of thin self-confidence.

As more time went by, Mary Lou came to alternate employment with learning experiences. The testimonials to her accomplishments piled up. On the walls of her room were certificates of graduation from schools of cosmetology, financial management, floral design, and the like. It was difficult for Mary Lou to grow close to Brenda because . . .

Brenda was the antithesis of Mary Lou. Brenda was filled with quiet self-confidence. Life was marked with goals and achievement of goals. Thus it surprised many when she took a job with the chancery of the archdiocese of Detroit. A secretarial position, even at the top, in the chancery's Department of Finance and Administration paid only a fraction of what she could have earned in a secular office. The only logical conclusion was that it had to be a stepping-stone to something else—though what that something else might be certainly was a mystery.

That made up the dramatis personae of Oona's birthday party.

Father Koesler pulled into a parking space near Eileen's property. As he approached her gate, somewhere inside a dog was barking furiously.

Three other cars were parked nearby. Given the likelihood that all were here for Oona's party, they were still one guest shy. Eileen's car would be in the single garage. That left two sisters, two "nieces," and him. Five. But there were only four cars in the lot. Since he was just two minutes early, someone was going to be late. As he had not memorized who drove what, he had no clue as to who was tardy.

With some trepidation, he eased open the gate. No dog in view. Thank God. But the barking grew more frantic. It must be Eileen's latest mastiff. As long as the beast was confined to the basement, Koesler could be unconcerned if not downright fearless.

He tried the doorknob. Locked. How like Eileen. If the gate was unlocked, the door certainly would be locked. Come to think of it, she would be happier with both locked.

He knocked several times, loudly.

Finally, the door opened. Eileen, smiling, stood on tiptoes and delivered a cousinly kiss. She gestured for him to go on in, passing him on the porch as she went to let the beast out into the yard. He renewed his vow that he and the dog would not be in the same space at the same time. He would continue the charade of fearlessness, but he would be sure the dog had been confined once more in the basement before he left.

Appetizing aromas greeted him. Maureen and Mary Lou were doing the cooking. Mary Lou checked her watch. "Good old Uncle Bob," she said, "right on time."

Because of the age difference and in spite of the lack of blood relationship, both Brenda and Mary Lou always referred to Oona and Eileen as "Aunt" and to Koesler as either "Father" or "Uncle." However, both addressed the remaining sister as Maureen. Evidently they did not feel comfortable calling her "Mother."

Mary Lou greeted Koesler with a cursory hug and a peck on the cheek. Maureen was up to her elbows mashing cooked rutabaga. She looked up and winked at him. He returned the wink.

Eileen entered the kitchen, closing the door quickly behind her. The dog's roar was restored to the yard. The tenor of its bark had changed. It knew that Koesler had breached the neutral zone—but he would never get out alive.

Koesler volunteered to assist or relieve, even to the mashing of rutabaga. But his offer was declined by all, and he was ordered into the living room; dinner would be ready in a little while.

He removed his jacket and clerical collar and hung them in the hall closet.

In the living room, seated near the picture window, was Oona, complete with a white sling supporting her right arm.

"Happy birthday," he said. "Hurt your arm?"

Oona audibly sucked in a breath of air in the Irish way of foretokening some sort of doom. "It's getting harder every year. And now . . . sixty-five! God have mercy."

"Go on now, sixty-five isn't that old." He was speaking from the vantage of sixty-four. But he was convinced it was a matter of health. With good health, great old age had a measure of youth to it. Without health, youth could have all the disability ordinarily attributed to old age. For Oona, then, sixty-five might just as well be ninety. But Koesler did not want to play to her hypochondria. He would try to keep the conversation light. "And your arm?"

She shrugged. "Arthritis kicking up again."

Was it arthritis? He knew that in her medicine chest was every conceivable medication, palliative, and supportive bandage, pad, and compress that could be found in a well-stocked pharmacy.

Koesler recalled years before when a smattering of male relatives had attended family parties. Oona had stated that if there were anything to reincarnation, she was going to come back as a man, have a huge dinner prepared by womenfolk, then settle into a comfy chair, loosen her belt, and, while the ladies cleaned up, belch.

Maybe the sling was her version of reincarnation. It clearly had gotten her out of the meal's preparation and undoubtedly would do the same for the cleanup later.

Oona began to detail the extent to which arthritis had limited the few remaining potentials of her already circumscribed life. Oona had the standard number of joints in her body. But he would offer odds that she could match and surpass anyone in afflictions to those joints.

As Oona ran on, Koesler's attention wavered. He looked past Oona out the picture window. Floes were sweeping toward Lake Erie.

Koesler recalled his recent visit to Charlie Nash's condo apartment, whence could be seen this very same river. There the river was at such a distance that it was challenging to comprehend that the chunks of ice were actually moving. He'd had to focus on a fixed object, such as a building, on the Windsor shore, to detect movement. Now, close up, he could see the ice moving along at a rapid clip. The current was swift and could be dangerous.

As he continued to tune out Oona and her multiple maladies and lamentations, the word "dangerous" struck a chord.

Koesler hadn't adverted to it during his conversation with Charlie Nash, but there *was* an aura of danger to the man, even in his decrepit condition.

The priest had assumed that his first and perhaps only encounter with the famous Charles Nash would involve sacraments. That Charlie was both Catholic and nonpracticing was common knowledge.

So there was Charlie, up there in his aerie, in his midseventies and reportedly so debilitated and ill that it had been many years since he'd been photographed, let alone attended any social function.

In Koesler's experience, that spelled sacraments. He'd had the foresight to have his sick-call kit packed in the pocket of his topcoat. So he had been prepared to offer absolution, Communion, and the Sacrament of the Sick. Then he would have left, gratified to have been of service, while Mr. Nash would have been at peace with God.

To Koesler's surprise, Nash had wanted nothing to do with any sacraments. In fact, the old man was dead right in contending that one must be sorrowful about sin and repentant before sin could be forgiven. Any priest could recite the words of absolution to his heart's content, but God, who alone could actually forgive, would not be fooled.

Koesler had to give the old man credit on that.

It had been Koesler's observation that people—a significant percentage of those who had come to him for reconciliation—tended to kid themselves on that score. Additionally, there was a tendency on the part of the confessing sinner, a tendency that all priests constantly fought against, to invest confessions with a measure of superstition and magic. Sort of like putting sins into an Automat slot and receiving forgiveness in return. A phenomenon that the late theologian Dietrich Bonhoeffer had termed "cheap grace."

Genuine forgiveness was expensive. It might require the forgiveness of an enemy, reparation for harm done, the restoring of stolen property. God *did* forgive. And Catholics believed that a priest could be an instrument of that forgiveness. But nothing happened unless the sinner was repentant.

Very, very sadly, Nash was correct in refusing the sacraments. Instead of desiring reconciliation, he wanted Koesler to use family ties to get the priest's cousin to break off her affair with his son. Which relationship was no more than hearsay.

Koesler had heard the rumors. As far as he was concerned, they were based on nothing more substantial than the two having engaged in some innocent flirtation at a Marygrove function honoring Ted Nash. Added to that, they had been seen together at a few public events—concerts, exhibitions at the Detroit Institute of Arts, a football or a baseball game. All quite harmless.

In the face of nothing more substantial than this, Koesler would keep his own counsel. He preferred not to intervene uninvited in others' lives.

But something was nagging at him. It was Charlie Nash's conviction that Ted and Brenda were having an illicit relationship. Under different circumstances, Koesler was convinced, Nash would not have given a damn. Had Ted been considerably more a chip off the old block, Charlie probably would have cheered him on in the sowing of wild oats.

But Ted tended to be more Catholic than the Catholic Church and had created the reputation of a lavish philanthropist in Catholic causes. The destruction of that image likely would destroy Teddy and, as a corollary, everything that Charlie had created in Nash Enterprises. And Charlie would not stand for that.

And here was where Koesler sensed danger.

Nash, though physically weak, was yet a powerful man of considerable influence. Whether or not his perception of an affair between Ted and Brenda was accurate, Nash was capable of harming either or both. In all probability, if he were to strike out at anyone, it would be the outsider, Brenda.

That is what troubled Koesler. And it troubled him deeply.

"Well, here she is now." It was the change in Oona's tone that brought Koesler back from his musings. Sure enough, Brenda was standing in the living room with Eileen at her side.

Koesler smiled at Brenda, but in some confusion. "How did you get in? I mean . . . I didn't hear the dog . . ."

"You mean Rusty?" Eileen said. "Oh dear!"

"Rusty and I are friends," Brenda said in an amused tone.

"But when I got here . . ."

"You see, dear," Eileen said, "You're the only one. Rusty hardly ever barks at anyone else. He's the least effective watchdog I've ever had. Couldn't really call him a watchdog at all. But he's very lovable."

"Face it, Uncle Bob," Brenda said, "you and dogs just don't hit it off."

"But that's not true. I usually get along fine with dogs. It's just Eileen's dogs . . ."

"It's the odor," Oona said definitively. "Read about it just the other day. They can smell fear. Carries over in the perspiration."

"That's probably it." Maureen entered the room, wiping her hands on her apron. "You've been spooked by so many of Eileen's dogs that you just take it for granted that they're all killers. You start out scared of them and they know it. That's why you never got along with any of Eileen's dogs. Oh, I've got to admit, some of the earlier ones were pretty vicious. But this one, Rusty, he's a pussycat. He didn't bark at any of us."

"Well, maybe . . . maybe," Koesler admitted. "Before I come next time, I'll bathe in antiperspirant *and* deodorant. And I'll try my very best not to sweat when I get here."

"Animals sweat. Men perspire. Women glow." It might have been a humorous remark, but not coming from Oona.

"Anyway," Maureen said, "dinner's about ready. Want to eat first or give the presents?"

"Let's do the presents," Brenda said enthusiastically. "I want to see what Aunt Oona got."

"Some of us are hungry," Mary Lou said. "We've been working on the dinner most of the afternoon and we want to eat it." She made it obvious whom she was singling out.

"Lou, gimmee a break," Brenda said. "I've been working too. A little overtime as a matter of fact. For Pete's sake, it's no big deal. You want to eat first, that's fine."

"Well, then, come on everyone," Eileen invited cheerily.

As they all moved to their places in the kitchen, Koesler stopped at the half bath to wash up. He could not disregard the two girls. Many's the occasion that had been ruined by their bickering. It was as if the world might be big enough for the both of them, but not anything as confining as a house or, *a fortiori,* a room, no matter how spacious.

For a pair who had spent so much time growing up together, the two certainly differed sharply from one another and were usually at odds.

They were in sharp contrast in appearance. Brenda was tall, with straight dark hair, attractive bangs, and a willowy but sensuous figure. Mary Lou, a strawberry blonde with thick curly hair, tended to hold on to baby fat. Not large but a bit lumpy. Mary Lou seemed to spend a lot of time on the verge of pouting, if not actually in tears. Brenda tended to look on the bright side as often as possible.

Neither woman had had an easy time of it growing up. Their most formative years had been spent in the uncertainty of a series of foster homes. Neither had been abused in any of these homes. But they had lacked any sense of security or stability. The experience had to have traumatized them to some degree.

Then there was St. Vincent's Orphanage. The Sisters of Charity did their best to instill a strong sense of religion in their girls. They also tried to provide an atmosphere of caring and love. If there was failure in this, the fault frequently lay with the institution that sought to limit religious women's genuine expression of warm emotion.

In any case, Mary Lou gave indication that she might make Oona's birthday party somewhat unpleasant. It would not be the first time. The food would be good. It always was. The tension might make it difficult to digest.

Koesler joined the others. They were standing at their places waiting for him to lead a prayer before dinner.

"Bless us, O Lord, and these thy gifts which we are about to receive from thy bounty, through Christ, our Lord."

"Amen," they answered.

It was an ancient and traditional Catholic grace before meals. But the three sisters at least were slightly ancient and quite traditional ladies.

There was so much food on the table that some time was spent simply passing dishes around until everyone had an opportunity to partake of everything. After everyone had finally settled into eating, Koesler asked, "So, Brenda, what's new in the Archdiocese of Detroit?"

"You don't know?" Maureen twitted good-naturedly. "You're a priest. You're on the inside. You ought to know everything that's going on in the Church."

"It doesn't work that way, Maureen. I'm pretty far down the information line. Brenda's at the top."

Brenda swallowed some mashed potato, then said, "Hard to say. Almost nothing happened today. There are days like that, when it's just business as usual. But not many. One thing I can say about the chancery: More often than not, it is not a dull place to work."

"You ought to be grateful you work there," Mary Lou said. "If it hadn't been for Father Bob . . ."

"I didn't have that much to do with it, Mary Lou." Koesler sought to defuse the engendering of bitter words. "Brenda just happened to apply at the right time. They were adding staff at the chancery. All I did was to give her a letter of recommendation. Believe me, my letter could have been as much a hindrance as a help. It all depended on who in the chancery happened to read it."

"Just the same—"

"Wait a minute . . ." Brenda was as anxious as the others to head off Mary Lou and her chip-on-the-shoulder attitude. "We did have a celebration of sorts today. But it was a celebration of a nonevent. I guess that shows how hard up we are for excitement."

"A nonevent?" Maureen said. "I don't—"

"We didn't get a shipment of bones." Brenda was smiling.

"I still don't—"

"As far as anyone can remember," Brenda said, "today is the tenth anniversary of not getting bones from Rome."

"Bones from Rome. It's got a nice ring," Koesler said. "Let me guess: relics?"

"Right on, Father Bob."

"It wasn't that hard. Bones from Rome would almost have to be relics of the saints. But after that, I haven't got a clue."

"You don't?" Brenda chuckled. "Who do you think used to put all those relics in the altar stones so you could say Mass on them?"

"Who put them in the stones? Well, if they didn't come all put together, I haven't the slightest idea."

"Excuse me," Eileen interrupted, "but what is this all about?"

"It seems to me," Maureen said, "that we learned something about this in school. Doesn't the altar where you say Mass have to have a relic—a bone or some such—of a saint? A martyr? Doesn't it have something to do with the catacombs?"

"That'd get you a hundred percent, Maureen," Koesler said. "Or at least ninety-eight. Christianity in ancient Rome became an outlawed religion. So the early Christians there had to be very secretive about where they met. Many of them gathered in the catacombs, which were underground cemeteries. Many of them were eventually buried in those catacombs. The majority of them were martyrs. Eventually the Eucharist was celebrated over the tombs of the martyrs."

"And that's where this custom came from—having a relic in the altar?" Eileen asked.

"Uh-huh. Not so long ago the Church made a distinction between 'permanent' and 'portable' altars, which had nothing to do with how heavy or how light they were, but how they were constructed. If the altar was 'permanent,' the relic—just a sliver of a bone from one of the saints—would be placed in the altar. If it was 'portable,' the relic was placed in a rectangular stone and the stone was placed in the altar.

"There also was a cloth into which a relic was sewn. That made it convenient for, say, chaplains, who were obliged to use whatever surface was at hand for an altar—an ordinary table or a rock . . . or maybe the hood of a Jeep. But you can see how much importance the Church placed on continuing that tradition."

"Which gets us back to your celebration today," Maureen said to Brenda. "What is this about not getting a shipment of bones?"

"Yes," Koesler asked, "why would they send just bones? I thought the relics were sent from Rome already in their reliquaries—their containers?"

"Apparently not," Brenda said. "They used to send a bone—a tibia or something—along with authenticating papers. Then one of the chancery priests would get the job of shattering the bone into tiny fragments for the altars."

Koesler laughed. "Knowing the gang at the chancery, they probably called him 'the bone guy' or just 'Bones.' Who was it . . . anybody down there remember?"

"They were talking about that today. They weren't sure who it was. Somebody said it was a priest who later became bishop of Saginaw."

"It may well have been. His name slips my mind. It is . . . uh . . ."

"But how come they stopped doing that?" Maureen asked. "Didn't you say you were celebrating a nonevent?"

"Apparently it's not as firm an obligation anymore. Plus somebody said that the rule now is that the relic is placed *under* the altar—and it's not supposed to be a sliver anymore," Brenda said.

"A recognizable piece of human anatomy?" Koesler immediately regretted he'd said that. In another group such an observation might have encouraged a ribald stream of humor. But not in this setting. He had little to fear.

"Well, that seems to make sense," Eileen remarked.

"They even got rid of the closet where the bones were mashed," Brenda said.

"How do you get rid of a closet?" Maureen wanted to know.

"When they renovated the chancery a while back," Brenda explained, "they just extended the hallway."

"The closet became part of the hallway?" Maureen asked.

"Uh-huh. The closet used to be right across from the archives. Now that area is wide open."

"So then," Mary Lou said, "the saints who contribute their bones to altars don't have to be martyrs?"

"Most of them are," Koesler said. "But I guess they don't have to be."

Koesler and the others had almost forgotten Mary Lou. After her unsuccessful attempts to foul the mood of this party, she had been quiet. And, thanks mostly to Brenda, the ensuing conversation had been light and jovial. Just as it should be.

Now Mary Lou had reentered the flow. Her tone had not improved. Koesler feared the dinner was about to be torpedoed.

"Then just about any saint could qualify to be an altar relic . . . right?" Mary Lou pressed.

"I suppose—"

"How about Mary Magdalene?"

"Hmmm . . ." Koesler thought for a moment. "I suppose . . . I guess so . . . if you could find her. Far as I know, no one's ever found her, or identified her grave. Which brings up—"

"I was just thinking," Mary Lou said, "Mary Magdalene was a whore . . . a slut, an adulteress."

"Well, yes . . ." Koesler feared he knew where this was leading. ". . . but that was before she became a disciple of Christ and changed her life."

"But before she did that," Mary Lou persisted, "before she changed her life, she slept with lots of men. She wouldn't have given a damn whether her partners were married or not . . . would she?"

"Mary Lou!" Maureen spoke loudly, in a shocked tone.

"See, Brenda, there's hope for you after all. If Mary Magdalene could change her life, so can you. Adulteresses can get into heaven, can't they, Uncle Bob?"

"Mary Lou!" Eileen was on the verge of tears.

Koesler, in extreme discomfort, looked around the table. Everyone seemed as uncomfortable as he—with the possible exception of Oona, who, oddly, seemed to be enjoying the contentious atmosphere Mary Lou was creating. Brenda seemed on the verge of being ill. Her face was ashen.

"Dear Brenda, sweet Brenda!" Mary Lou continued, undaunted by the reaction she was getting. "There seem to be so few ways you could become a saint. You'd have to give up Teddy, your sugar daddy. Or . . . or . . . maybe somebody would do you the favor of making you a martyr!"

"Mary Lou!" Maureen leaped to her feet and pounded on the table. "That's enough!"

CHAPTER

6

FATHER KOESLER was slow to claim that anything was the worst, the best, the first, the last, the earliest, the most, etc. Long experience had taught that no sooner did someone proclaim anything the ultimate than someone else was sure to top it.

However, if this evening's birthday party for Oona was not the worst celebration he had ever suffered through, it certainly ranked.

He parked his car in the garage adjoining St. Joseph's and entered the rectory. He checked the messages on the answering machine. No emergencies. Nothing that could not wait till tomorrow.

He dropped some ice into a tall glass and concocted a gin and tonic. As he did so, he found himself casually whistling a tune, the words to which wore a witless path in his mind. "The sun'll come up tomorrow, put your bottom dollar on tomorrow, come what may." A nice melody. The dumbest lyric he'd ever heard.

He had a little time on his hands. He hadn't planned on the evening's ending as early as it did. Parties with his cousins seldom lasted long, but this evening's had set a new record both for brevity and discomfort.

After Mary Lou had drawn the odious comparison between Mary Magdalene in her most disreputable days and Brenda, things pretty well fell apart. Mary Lou kept up a steady offensive, and Brenda, without offering a word in her own defense or any denial of the charges, burst into tears, fled the house, and sped away. Very heated words were exchanged between Mary Lou and Maureen. Eileen pursued peace, but it eluded her. Oona, almost unnoticed, slipped away from the table, retreated to the living room, and opened her presents. No one would ever know whether she *oohed* or *aahed*. No one paid any attention to her. She seemed content.

Koesler had breathed deeply, made a fervent if futile effort to shut down his sweat glands, and somehow made it to the gate, hounded by Rusty. While the endeavor was extremely brave on Koesler's part, it should be noted that the dog was thrown off balance and befuddled by all the clamor and commotion.

51

Brenda was gone, with every indication she would not return this night, perhaps ever. Mary Lou had withdrawn to the guest room, slamming the door behind her. Eileen was attempting to console Maureen, who was teetering between anger and misery. Oona was trying on a new bathrobe. It seemed to fit.

What a family!

Koesler eased himself into a comfortable chair to think it through.

Whatever else was awry between Brenda and Mary Lou—and he thought there must be more to it—Brenda's alleged affair with Ted Nash clearly was the present problem.

Coincidence, that old Charlie Nash should have called him in just a few days ago—the purpose being to get Koesler to intervene in what Charlie was convinced was an adulterous affair between his son and Koesler's "cousin"?

Rumors of such a relationship were so flimsily founded that Koesler rarely if ever adverted to the possibility there might be anything to them. Then, suddenly, Charlie Nash revives such rumors—forcefully; and with no evident connection between them, Mary Lou voices her own suspicion—no, accusation—that the rumors are true.

Koesler was puzzled. He had seen for himself that Brenda had offered no defense, no denial, this evening. It couldn't be because she was slow; on the contrary, Koesler was well aware that, if anything, she was extremely bright, imaginative, and witty. He'd had occasion in the past to trade barbs with her, and she always gave as well as she received. Nothing in his experience with Brenda would have foretokened this evening's defensive behavior.

She had not denied or disputed Mary Lou's insults, but had absorbed them without challenge.

So, what if the rumors *were* true? What if she and Ted Nash actually *were* having an affair?

Koesler's brow furrowed. There'd been plenty of opportunity for Brenda to consult with him. She worked downtown; so, in effect, did he. She was mobile. Such mass transit as existed in the metro area was, at best, undependable and inconvenient, so Brenda drove to work Monday through Friday. It would have been simple for her to hop in her car and visit him here at St. Joe's. She could have done it during her lunchtime or after work. She knew he would be especially available to her. And she knew him well enough to know that he would be open and not judgmental.

She had made no attempt whatsoever to consult him.

Koesler had his own way of dealing with that sort of attitude. Hands off. Fools rush in where angels fear to tread, and all that sort of thing.

But this was different. The way this family relationship had developed, Brenda might just as well have been a blood relative. He cared for her—and for Mary Lou too, for that matter—the way he would for a real cousin.

Particularly now, as he reflected on his closeness to Brenda, he began to worry about her.

Charlie Nash made it clear that Nash Enterprises, this impressive company he had built from the bottom up, was precious to him. Perhaps more precious than anything else on earth. On earth or in heaven.

Now that he was reconsidering it, he thought that Nash's appeal that Koesler convince his cousin to break off the affair was by far the most considerate, humane solution Nash was going to offer.

After that might come who knew what.

On the strength of his one meeting with Nash, Koesler had come to believe the man would stop at nothing to preserve his baby. If that meant that Brenda would have to be physically removed, so be it.

Brenda murdered? It was a possibility. Did Brenda understand that? How would she react if she did know her life might be in danger?

It was next to impossible to know. But Koesler's best guess was that Brenda would rise to the challenge. She was not the type who would be intimidated.

Koesler began to put the whole thing together. He would have to get involved. He would not be able to live with himself otherwise. If something were to happen to Brenda, it would at least partially be his fault. He was convinced of that.

But what to do?

Getting through to Brenda would be like walking through a brick wall. And how much time did he have? No one could tell. Yet the very fact he had been summoned to Nash's apartment, as well as the urgency in the older man's voice, indicated time was definitely a factor.

It would be difficult, then, to try to convince Brenda of the seriousness of this threat. It was unlikely that she would respond to his argument unless he had the luxury of time to explain perhaps repeatedly and in great detail with ever more convincing logic.

If he could not move Brenda in what might be the allotted time, what else might he do?

How about Ted Nash?

Koesler had to assume that Nash had tried to get through to his son, probably very forcefully. If that were indeed the case, the confrontation between father and son would already have occurred, probably shortly before Nash had contacted Koesler.

Why hadn't Nash proposed that Koesler try to convince Teddy rather than Brenda? Because Charlie figured that Koesler would have better luck with his "cousin"? Not a bad supposition; Brenda had grown up respecting Koesler and his priesthood. Except that Charlie Nash obviously didn't know Brenda.

Koesler closed his eyes and leaned back in the chair.

If not Brenda, then Teddy.

The end result, the bottom line, was agreed upon. If there was an illicit affair going on between Brenda and Ted—and from all appearances, and especially from what had happened this evening, there probably was—it would have to end. Their spiritual welfare, and possibly Brenda's very life, might depend on it.

From Koesler's point of view, it didn't much matter which of them, Ted or Brenda, was instrumental in calling it off. If Brenda's cooperation seemed uncertain, Koesler could try his powers of persuasion on Teddy Nash.

It couldn't be *that* difficult. From all Koesler had heard, Ted Nash considered himself a super-Catholic. Even if that reputation was bolstered with a measure of hype, still and all there must be a germ of truth to it. Adultery was adultery, and a Catholic of any stripe would know that.

Yet Koesler could anticipate considerable resistance. There had to be a strong attraction between them, else there would have been no affair. But Ted should be educable.

Whatever else, Koesler was sure Ted would be by far the more malleable of the two.

The next problem: How did one get an appointment to see Ted Nash?

CHAPTER

7

PROTOCOL FOR MAKING an appointment with Theodore Nash, Esquire, Father Koesler learned, depended on who wanted the appointment, and its purpose.

The answers to those questions dictated which if any department head one might see. One was scarcely if ever ushered directly into Mr. Nash's office. Not on the first try, at any rate.

Koesler had to admit he was taken aback.

Priests usually receive some form of preferential treatment. And considering the aura of piety surrounding Ted Nash, Koesler, frankly, expected better. In short, he expected to be granted an immediate interview with the proprietor.

Instead—and, to Koesler, this was a large instead—he was referred to the secretary to Father Arthur Deutsch. Not even the Father himself. His secretary.

It wasn't that Koesler so much minded being shunted off to secondary layers of management. But he'd assumed that a priest asking to see a prominent Catholic layman about a "personal matter" would be ushered into the inner sanctum forthwith—or, that if he were going to be shunted off to an assistant who happened to be another priest, he would at least be able to speak to that priest. If there was no professional courtesy among priests, what then could be said for lawyers and doctors?

At length Koesler did get an appointment to see Father Arthur Deutsch—two days hence. And even then, Koesler was informed, Father Deutsch would have to shuffle his schedule to accommodate this request. Right about then Koesler came close to telling them what they could do with their precious protocol. But he reminded himself he was doing this for Brenda. It helped to have a quest, like the knights of old. Koesler felt like Don Quixote.

Now, ten minutes early, he arrived for his 10:00 A.M. appointment with Father Deutsch.

Father Koesler was impressed. Whatever Deutsch's parochial assignments had been, Koesler was sure none had provided a more opulent setting. The office was located in one of those buildings that springs up seemingly overnight on Telegraph or Northwestern in Southfield or West Bloomfield or Farmington Hills. The salient difference was that this building was a model of tasteful as well as utilitarian design, with a sensible amount of glass, overhang, and passive-energy implementation.

The waiting room was striking, with soft indirect lighting, genuine wood paneling, and superplush off-white carpeting. The secretary was courteous and efficient, but unsmiling. At precisely 10:00 A.M. Koesler was ushered into Deutsch's sanctum.

It was a spacious extension of the outer office, except that where the art displayed in the waiting area was mainly contemporary, here it was almost exclusively religious and traditional. The most prominent portraits were of Pope John Paul II and his alter ego, Cardinal Ratzinger. Together, Koesler thought, these two men did their best to make the Church uninteresting.

Noteworthy by its absence was any depiction of the present archbishop of Detroit, Mark Cardinal Boyle.

A smiling Father Deutsch rose from behind his king-size desk to greet Koesler. The chair behind that desk was also oversize. It resembled one a bishop might use in his cathedral—if, that is, the bishop wanted to be ostentatious.

"You must be Father Koesler. I recognize you from your photos."

"Yes." Koesler could have returned Deutsch's exact words; he had seen Deutsch's picture in newspapers and in his graduation portrait on the cloister wall in Sacred Heart Seminary. But the two men, prior to now, had not met.

Deutsch indicated a straight-back chair near his desk, and Koesler took it.

"Would you like something?" Deutsch asked. "Coffee? A little sherry?"

"Some coffee would be good."

Deutsch pressed a button and a coffeemaker purred into operation. The two men studied each other. Each knew there was about a fifteen-year difference in their ages.

Other than that, Deutsch knew relatively little about Koesler. As was common in the diocesan clergy, older priests were relatively unfamiliar with their younger counterparts. During the early years of the two men's priesthood, chronology had guided priests' ascendancy from associate status to a pastorate. But the drastic priest shortage of recent years had made the position of associate pastor almost extinct.

At the time of Koesler's ordination in the mid-fifties, it had been statistically feasible that few of his classmates would live long enough to become pastors. Now, priests became pastors before the oils of ordination dried. Thus it was understandable that Deutsch would know little about Koesler. What Deutsch did know arose out of the events that had given emphasis to Koesler's career. Deutsch was aware, for instance, that Koesler had been editor of the archdiocesan weekly newspaper, and that the younger man had been involved in some police investigations over the past several years.

It was unclear to Deutsch exactly what the association was between Koesler and the police; but, because priests were among the most faithful readers of the *Detroit Catholic,* he was aware that Koesler was considered to be of the so-called liberal school of theology. An excellent reason to be wary of him.

Never having met Deutsch, all Koesler knew of the man was what others said of him.

Deutsch was reputed to have been a brilliant student. By virtue of that, he had, during the early years of his priesthood, taught in the seminary.

From there, he had been sent forth to found a suburban parish. In which niche he had stayed until retirement. Had it not been for the Vatican Council, his would have been a totally uneventful history.

The council had caught Deutsch, and many other priests, napping. Of course he knew the council was taking place in Rome during the early sixties. But he had no inkling that it would have so radical an effect.

Thus it had come as a massive cultural shock that he found himself facing the people and celebrating Mass in English. After that, one change closely followed another with mind-boggling rapidity. Without having read a single council document through, Deutsch decided that the council was an abomination, and that Pope John, who had convened the council, might well be the antichrist.

Deutsch soon found other priests, mostly his age and older, who were of a similar mind. Leading this fraternity, quite naturally, was Father Charles E. Coughlin.

Father Coughlin arguably was the most widely famous priest in the history of the Detroit diocese. He was not cofounder of the University of Michigan, nor had he been elected to Congress, like Father Gabriel Richard. He was not a profoundly holy man or even a wonder worker, as was Father Solanus Casey.

But Father Coughlin was mentioned in just about every book that chronicled United States history of this century. One scarcely ever read of Father Coughlin without the descriptive suffixal phrase, "controversial radio priest of the thirties."

In the backwash of the council, Coughlin formed the ground zero of its opposition. Many priests gathered round him. Chief among these was Father Arthur Deutsch.

All this—the sketchy reputation of Father Deutsch—was common knowledge, especially among the priests of Detroit. Although little of his earlier history was popularly known, Deutsch had attained a measure of fame when he was selected as, and accepted the role of, chaplain to Theodore Nash, Esquire. That was when he achieved far more than the promised fifteen minutes of fame Andy Warhol ascribed to each human.

The principal item that Father Koesler did not know was what he himself was doing here.

His purpose was to meet with Ted Nash. Once he had stated his name and the nature of his desired meeting with Nash—a personal matter—he had been summarily shunted to Father Deutsch. Since there seemed no way around this rigmarole, Koesler had accepted this route. But he was confused and not at all happy.

Deutsch poured from what looked to be a very expensive coffee service. Koesler thanked him and tasted the brew.

"Like it?" Deutsch obviously did. "It's my own private blend."

Koesler nodded. To him, coffee was a dark, hot drink. He couldn't tell one brand from another. If Deutsch wanted to enter into an informed disquisition on the merit of his creation, it would be a startlingly brief conversation.

There was a lengthy pause while Deutsch savored the satisfaction of his brew. "How are things at Old St. Joe's, Father?"

The question cleared a couple of items for Koesler. First, Deutsch had done some homework; at least he knew where Koesler was stationed. And second, Deutsch wanted to stay formal: It would not be Art and Bob, it would be "Father."

Fine.

"All things considered," Koesler said cautiously, "not bad. The congregation continues to grow . . . although I wish we could attract more black Catholics. Some of the other inner-city parishes are doing very well on that score. But then they offer a liturgy more in tune with the African-American experience."

Deutsch frowned. "I know what you mean. Those other parishes . . . they're more Baptist than Catholic. At least St. Joe's still offers Mass in union with Holy Church. You even have a Sunday Mass in Latin. We were very pleased with that."

We? Who was "we"? Did the Nash-Deutsch connection have spies? And he knew about the Latin Mass. He *had* done his homework.

"Well," Koesler said, "the Latin Mass sort of grew like Topsy. I lucked into a great organist and choir director. It was actually his idea to try the Latin. He and I agreed that one unfortunate consequence of the council was the loss of all that great music—plain chant, Palestrina, Perosi. I don't think the council intended that to happen. But it did: A whole bunch of not very talented musicians wrote a lot of rotten music for the new vernacular liturgy. And all that inspired music that took centuries to build just got lost."

Deutsch nodded. "There are those among us who think the entire Council was 'unfortunate' . . . more coffee?"

"Thanks, no. This is plenty. Look, I don't want to take too much of your time—"

"Don't think of it, Father. This time has been set aside for you." Deutsch pushed the intercom button. His secretary entered and wordlessly removed the coffee service. "Back to St. Joseph's. Got many weddings?"

"Not many. Most of the parishioners live in the high rises and condos. Most of them are pretty well set before they move in."

Deutsch pursed his lips. "Such problems now! Couples these days have no sense of sacrifice, no sense of commitment. Divorce! Why, it's as common now among Catholics as it is among everybody else. And birth control! They think nothing of it at all. I can remember a day when if Catholics got divorced and remarried they had the good grace to stop coming to Mass. And when Catholics would confess birth control and at least tried to avoid it."

"So can I," Koesler said flatly.

More and more, he wondered what this was all about. The state of St. Joseph's parish, the subjects of divorce and birth control . . . what did those have to do with his desire to see Ted Nash about a personal matter?

A less patient person might have walked out, or at least demanded that they get on with the matter Koesler had in mind. But Koesler, when subjected to gamesmanship, usually wanted to find out the name of the game before clearing the board.

"The Holy Father, you know," Deutsch said, "has made it crystal-clear that any use of artificial birth control remains gravely sinful." He paused, but there was no response from Koesler.

"And yet," Deutsch continued, "Catholics—some so-called Catholics, I should say—oppose this teaching openly." Another pause. Again no response.

"What do you think of this, Father?"

Koesler shook his head. "I think the Pope, most of the bishops, some priests, and a few Catholics have problems with methods of family planning. Most priests and all but a few laypeople have solved the problem—and not with the solution the Pope recommends. That this interpretation is not made clear to all the laity, especially in Third World countries like those of Latin America, I think is a tragedy." The statement was made calmly but firmly.

Deutsch was livid. "But . . . but . . . that's heresy!"

"No it's not."

"You're denying the explicit teaching of not one but two Popes!"

"When Paul VI discarded the conclusions of his own blue-ribbon committee and wrote the encyclical 'Humanae Vitae,' he went out of his way to make clear that he wasn't teaching infallibly. And John Paul just restated the earlier encyclical. So any denial doesn't come under the heading of heresy."

Flustered, Deutsch stammered slightly. "M-maybe not. Maybe not technically. But it *is* disobedience to the ordinary magisterium—the ordinary teaching authority of the Church."

"You don't have to translate for me; I know what the ordinary magisterium is. There's more than one way to respond to it."

"I suppose you feel the same way about abortion!"

Koesler sighed deeply. "Look, Father Deutsch, we didn't have to meet each other to know that we differ in certain theological matters. Our archbishop, Cardinal Boyle, has claimed more than once that no one is *entirely* anything; conservative or liberal. But, let's face it, you are generally of a conservative bent, and I am usually in the liberal camp. As far as I can see, our differences are irrelevant to the reason why I want to see Mr. Nash."

"No, they're not!" Deutsch shed his defensive demeanor instantly. "Part of my responsibility here at Nash Enterprises is to interview all clergy and religious of whatever denomination prior to the granting of any donation or funding. And I must say, with your attitude, you don't stand a snowball's chance in hell of getting a penny." He concluded with a triumphant gesture.

Koesler sat with his mouth hanging open in utter disbelief for several moments. Then he began to chuckle. Gradually he began to break up, and burst out laughing. Finally, he said, "Is that what you think? Is that what you've thought all along? That I want some of your money?"

Deutsch, unnerved by Koesler's reaction, became unsure of himself. "St. Joseph's is . . . is an old . . . is an old parish. Why, good God, it's registered as a historical landmark! It's of an age where everything falls apart: furnace, floor, ceiling, roof, tiles, organ, pulpit, you name it. What else would you want but money? And to get that, you go through me. The only way to get it is to go through me. And I can save you time and suspense by telling you there's no possibility whatsoever of your ever getting anything—*anything*—from us! Now I think this interview is terminated! Good day, Father." He did not offer his hand.

Koesler stood. He was grinning from ear to ear. "Yes, we can terminate this meeting. But it was very informative. I'll keep it in mind particularly when I finally have my meeting with Ted Nash. And next time, when I set up that meeting, I'll be a lot more specific about the reason for it."

As he left the plush office, Koesler reviewed his meeting with Father Deutsch. It had not been a waste of time. Koesler had gained some valuable insights into one facet of Nash Enterprises.

What had most intrigued him about Ted Nash was how the man could square his religiosity with some pretty questionable business practices.

Now Koesler began to understand. A meeting with Ted Nash in the flesh might just fill in the gaps.

Koesler's interest in Nash and his empire was expanding far beyond his attempt to help Brenda.

CHAPTER

8

THE GREATER DOWNTOWN AREA of Detroit had become a series of pockets. There were pockets of life and pockets of decay. The hub of the city was now what it had been at its founding. The nucleus was Woodward at the river. Thence it spread north, east, and west like a spiderweb. Tucked into that web were those pockets.

Areas that might be termed "thriving" were the financial district, the riverfront area featuring the Renaissance Center, Hart Plaza, Cobo Arena, Joe Louis Arena, the City-County Building, and scattered hotels and businesses; Greektown and Bricktown; a renovated Fox Theater anchored a budding entertainment center. Most of the rest of downtown once was vibrant, now it rotted.

Running through the outskirts of this area in an endless circle was the People Mover, a series of automated cars that, filled or empty, rattled regularly on their elevated tracks.

Ordinarily, Brenda Monahan brown-bagged it for lunch at the chancery. At one time, downtown workers had had an abundance of fine restaurants available for lunch or dinner. Famed and prized eateries such as the Money Tree, the Pontchartrain Wine Cellars, and the renowned London Chop House now were but a memory.

Today, however, Brenda was going to lunch with her "sister," Mary Lou.

The last time they'd been in each other's presence was at Oona's dreadful, aborted birthday party, a party shattered by Mary Lou's pointed denunciation of Brenda's affair with Ted Nash. A casual observer might reasonably have assumed that the two young women would never converse again.

But this was not their first—nor would it be their last—falling-out. Over the years, the relationship had gone repeatedly from wrangling to reconciliation, marked by a long trail of apologies on the part of Mary Lou—followed by a reciprocal trail of forgivenesses on Brenda's part.

For now, a state of peace and sisterly concern existed between the two.

The occasion for this luncheon was a celebration of Mary Lou's new job. She was about to become secretary and general business manager at St. Raphael parish in Garden City. It was a desirable position with a good salary, and she would be working for a good priest who was the closest thing Detroit had to Mother Teresa.

Rather than meeting in Brenda's office, the two women met in the lobby of the chancery. It was easier than subjecting Mary Lou to the building's obstructive security system.

As soon as Brenda exited the elevator, the two began chatting. They kept up their animated conversation throughout the trip to Greektown on the People Mover. They were a bit early for the noon crowd. And even at lunch hour, few restaurants had much if any overflow patronage; they were seated immediately.

Each ordered coffee and Greek salad, appropriate, they thought for a Greek restaurant. They were correct on both counts.

"Well," Brenda said, "are you happy with your new job, Lou?"

"I'm pretty sure I will be. That's one of the things I wanted to talk to you about." Brenda was the only person who called her "Lou." Mary Lou enjoyed the informality. If the name had displeased her, all could be sure she would let that be known.

"You wanted to talk to me about St. Raphael's?"

"I want to know what I'm getting into."

Considering Mary Lou's track record, Brenda considered it a smart move for Lou to get a second—or even third, or fourth—opinion. With her patchwork employment history, it behooved both Mary Lou and any prospective employer to check things pretty thoroughly.

"I don't know all that much about Raphael's," Brenda said. "Mainly the finances, I suppose."

"I'm supposed to be business manager of the place. It wouldn't hurt if I knew how sound it is."

Brenda nodded. "Okay. When you got the job, I looked into St. Raphael's. I guess I was as concerned as you are. It's not swimming in dough, but it's solvent. Didn't you get any of this information from Father Pool?"

Mary Lou sighed. "I couldn't find out too much about the place. He was too busy finding out about me."

"Huh?"

"He wanted to know if I was satisfied with everything. My office, the furniture, the machines. Was there anything I needed or wanted?"

Brenda giggled.

"Honestly," Mary Lou said, "it was like I was interviewing him rather than vice versa. He couldn't have been more solicitous. But, the bottom line is, I didn't find out much about the parish."

"Well," Brenda said, "right there you've got the good news and the bad. He couldn't be a better guy to work for. But he's the opposite of an efficient money man."

Mary Lou seemed suddenly worried. "Have I done it again? Am I in over my head? Is this another six-month job?"

Brenda waited while the waitress served their salads. Then she spoke. "No, I didn't mean it like that. Father Pool may be a living saint. He just doesn't pay much attention to a Dun & Bradstreet rating. This is his third parish as pastor. While he didn't leave the others bankrupt, they did end up hanging on the fiscal ropes. He just doesn't pay that much attention to finances. For instance, he doesn't accept stipends for just about anything—baptisms, weddings, funerals, luncheons after funerals. About the only thing he accepts is a fee for rental of the parish hall for wedding receptions . . . and then only because he wants to discourage couples from using the hall for that.

"See, he thinks receptions like that ought to be held in commercial halls. But rather than forbid the use of the parish—because he doesn't want to hurt the couple's feelings—he charges for the hall's use. And, of course, the people couldn't care less about the money; they expect to pay for a hall, whichever one they use."

"Well, for heaven's sake—"

"That's not all," Brenda continued. "He never, ever, talks about money from the pulpit. He just obviously is more concerned about people than finances. And that seems to be the way his flock prefers it."

"Oh, my God!" Mary Lou, feeling she might have lost her appetite, laid her fork down. "I'm business manager for a place that has no business."

"It's not as bad as all that." Brenda smiled. "Actually, you're in better shape than it seems."

"Oh?"

"As much as Father Pool doesn't want to hurt his parishioners' feelings, much more he doesn't want to offend you. When it comes to parish finances, you can write the ticket. I've got it pretty well figured out based on his personality and history. You're never going to get him to talk about or ask for money. But that's okay. You'll be the one who schedules weddings, funerals, baptisms. Get the money up front.

There's nothing wrong with that. The stipends for these services are set by the archdiocese. Just don't require any more than the law does."

"What if people complain to him?"

Brenda shook her head. "No problem. He knows the people should make their offerings. He just can't bring himself to ask for them—or even accept them. *You* get them. He won't object. In fact, he'll be grateful you're taking care of what he knows he should be doing.

"Then, he's got the pulpit, but you've got the parish bulletin. Keep an open, running account in the bulletin of the parish budget as compared with the weekly offerings. Keep after the parishioners through the bulletin.

"They know the place can't run on good will alone. Oh, they like to think it can, especially since they're never reminded that they need to support the place. But at Raphael's, the people have the money; it's just that they would rather keep the money than give it away . . . a natural enough sentiment.

"The thing is, Lou, you can do it. It's right down your alley. It's practically made to order for you."

Mary Lou tentatively picked up her fork and resumed eating. At length, she said, "You know an awful lot about this thing, don't you?"

"What thing?"

"This Archdiocese of Detroit."

Brenda smiled. "I work for it."

"You're a secretary! I've been a secretary more times than I like to remember. Depending on the boss, secretaries know as much as they want. As much as they want to get involved, that is. But you know an awful lot about the Detroit Church."

"I guess so," Brenda admitted. "But see: It worked out pretty well for you, didn't it?"

"I have to admit."

As they ate in silence for a few moments, Brenda studied Mary Lou. She was dressed up, rather more than usual. And she looked good.

Ordinarily, Mary Lou's hair looked the same whether she had just gotten out of bed or had just washed and combed it. All those tight little curls. But today it looked different. She must have had it cut and shaped. It could still be improved. But better.

She'd paid more attention to her clothes too, and it showed. By and large, with a good bit of attention, she might just be stunning.

And if she were, then what?

Then a man. A serious man. Not somebody who would chase her till he caught her and then discard her. No, for this, she would need help and support. That Brenda could and would supply.

If Mary Lou were to find Mr. Right, most of her problems would be solved. No more drifting from one job to another. No more insecurity and loneliness. Fulfillment.

It would be almost as big a consolation and joy for Maureen as it would be for Mary Lou. Maureen worried a lot over the ultimate insecurity of her "daughter." Seeing her settled down and reliably cared for would put Maureen's concern to rest.

While Brenda's evaluation of Mary Lou's upcoming job situation was accurate in every detail, Brenda knew that she had oversimplified Mary Lou's ability to handle the problems she was about to encounter.

Could Mary Lou actually accomplish all this fiscal stability in the face of almost no encouragement or support from the pastor? The feat would require a strong personality. Did Mary Lou fit the bill? Maybe.

But in her heart, Brenda doubted it.

And then what? Lou would be out of another job and at loose ends. Maureen would be distraught. Back to square one for the umpteenth time.

No, marriage was the answer. Or somehow, a sudden influx of a great deal of money. But where in the world would that come from?

When Mary Lou spoke again, Brenda was so lost in thought she was startled.

"Did you get me this job?"

"Me! What gave you that idea?"

"The way you explained everything so well. It's as if you planned the whole thing." She fluttered a hand at Brenda. "Don't get me wrong; I'm grateful. If I'm supposed to be grateful to you, I am. I just wanted to know."

Brenda smiled and shook her head. "If you want to blame somebody—or thank somebody—the somebody would be Uncle Bob. He and Father Pool are about the same age. Pool hasn't been a priest as long as Uncle Bob. He did some time in the army before he went to the seminary. Otherwise they would almost have been classmates. But they're friends. Uncle Bob knew Father Pool was looking for a secretary and manager, so he told him about you. But not I . . ." She laughed. "I don't have that kind of clout."

The waitress refilled their cups.

"If you don't mind my asking," Mary Lou said as she stirred her steaming coffee, "what are you doing there anyway?"

"Where?"

"The chancery. Don't get upset, but I've wondered about that for a long time. I mean, you could get a job anywhere practically. You've got the talent. Why would you work for the Church?"

"Because it's interesting."

"How interesting could any job be?"

"It's different. It's more different than any other place I can think of. It's so interesting that I haven't got time to tell you how interesting it is . . . how interesting it can get."

"Okay. So it's interesting and it's different. So will my job be at St. Raphael's."

"No, no. Lou, no parish job can compare with working in the central Church structure."

"Well, there's one thing that's comparable."

"What's that?"

"The salary."

"Lou, you don't know what I make."

"More than I will at Raphael's, but still not much. The Church just doesn't pay. It certainly doesn't pay as much as you could get almost anywhere outside. And you've got the talent, Brenda: With your brains and experience, you could work almost anywhere you wanted. Even without knowing exactly what you make, I'll bet you could triple it tomorrow."

"Lou . . . Lou . . ." Brenda seemed to debate within herself about what to say next. "Lou, money is not that important a factor right now."

It was as if a light bulb lit over Mary Lou's head. "You mean . . . because of . . . Ted Nash?"

Brenda gripped her cup so tightly her knuckles whitened. "Lou . . ."

"I know. I know. You don't want to discuss it. But you can talk about it with me. I'm not going to get all moral on you again like I did at the party. I've thought it over. And I decided I was wrong. I'm not your conscience or your guardian angel. But . . . we might just as well be sisters, you know. And the whole thing doesn't make sense."

"What . . . doesn't?" It was obvious that this topic was painful for Brenda.

Dead Wrong

"You! Working for peanuts when you could have almost any job you wanted and you could almost name your salary. On top of that, you're involved with a married man who is probably going to stay married. So that relationship is going nowhere. Whereas . . . you could have just about any man you wanted. That's what doesn't make sense!"

Brenda drained her cup and paused a few moments. "I really don't want to talk about this, Lou. And if we're going to remain 'sisters,' let's not ever mention this again. But . . . look at it this way: My relationship with Ted—whatever it is—makes it possible for me to not be concerned about money. So, I can work for 'peanuts' without having to worry about a salary . . . see? That makes some sense. And, Lou, if it doesn't make a lot of sense to you, take it on faith."

"Faith?"

"Faith in me. Take it on faith in me . . . okay?"

A pause. Then, "Okay."

"Now, I don't want to rush you, Lou, but it's about time for me to get back to work."

"Oh . . . oh, sure." Mary Lou had only a small portion left of her salad. She proceeded to finish it.

While Mary Lou ate, Brenda had nothing better to do than study her once more. There was something about Mary Lou that engendered in some others an urge to watch over her. Brenda was one of those who felt called to protect Mary Lou. The question was, from what? Brenda's intuition suggested she would soon know.

CHAPTER

9

As HIS ENCOUNTER with Father Deutsch had demonstrated, it was not easy for Father Koesler to get an appointment with Ted Nash.

Nash's secretary had been very firm about the channels that *must* be taken before a meeting could be arranged with Mr. Nash. Mr. Nash was, after all, a most busy executive. At this point she began to list the many and varied ventures that fell under the umbrella of Nash Enterprises.

Koesler had not realized that the Nashes, father and son, had so many irons getting hot in far-flung fires.

However, for the sake of Brenda—and to beat Deutsch at his own game—the normally mild-mannered Koesler was unaccustomedly determined. He made it clear to the secretary that he, a holy, Roman Catholic priest, would take no for an answer only from the Catholic lips of Mr. Nash himself. Most reluctantly—and only because she had doubts that Deutsch had handled this matter correctly—did she permit Koesler to talk to Nash.

Nash quickly concluded it would be easier to grant Koesler a few minutes than to be bugged by so dogged a priest.

And so, Koesler now sat in the waiting area of Nash's private office complex in downtown Detroit's Penobscot Building, where Nash Enterprises occupied three full floors. He had arrived ten minutes early for his 11:30 A.M. appointment. It was now 11:35 and he was getting edgy. Since the appointment had been scheduled for a mere half hour before noon, it seemed obvious that Nash had allotted just thirty minutes, which Koesler did not think was at all adequate. Now, if he was correct about the luncheon break, he had only twenty-five minutes—and counting.

After her initial glare, Nash's secretary had paid Koesler no attention whatsoever—her way of evening the score for his insistence on this interview. Koesler was beginning to feel the martyr. If the silent secretary had been a feral carnivore, it was likely his life would have been demanded.

Just as he was imagining his bones being pounded into slivers for placement in a reliquary for some seldom-used altar stone, the buzzer on the secretary's desk sounded.

She nodded at Koesler and said, in an icy tone, "You may go in now."

Ted Nash obviously subscribed to the dictum: No one's office shall be more plush than the boss's.

The operative word was "too." Everything was too large, too showy, too tasteless, and too pretentious. Koesler couldn't swear to it, but the flowers and plants that decorated the office space appeared artificial. The office definitely made a statement. That Ted Nash was somewhat insecure? If so, the insecurity was probably buried deep.

Nash rose from his extralarge executive chair and circled the king-size desk with hand outstretched to greet the priest. If one were given to hyperbole, it seemed almost possible to play hockey on the desk's surface.

"So good to finally meet you, Father Koesler," Nash said with some enthusiasm. "Up until now, I've just read about you from time to time. The police and those investigations. The homicides and such."

It was a more effusive greeting than Koesler had expected. He was, after all, not the most welcome guest Nash would receive. Particularly since Deutsch, the in-house priest, should have handled and disposed of whatever was on Koesler's mind.

Koesler shook the outstretched hand. "Good of you to see me, Mr. Nash. But please, forget about those investigations. They were mostly the media's invention. At most, I was just on the periphery. It's just that the media like the idea of a simple parish priest and murder. It's like those pictures of nuns playing baseball or on a roller coaster in the good old days: They were almost as compelling as a boy and his dog."

Nash chuckled. "Now, now, Father; remember: He who doth not toot his own horn, the same shall not get tooted."

"Sounds like a good slogan for Nash Enterprises, but not for a parish priest."

"*And* a pastor. We must be nearly neighbors. Father Deutsch tells me you're at St. Joseph's. Now there's a parish with a history. If it weren't for the skyline we could see your church from one of these windows."

Not much homework done here, thought Koesler, who knew precisely which window faced the church. Nash should also have known.

Koesler would wager that Nash knew little or nothing of the parish history as well.

"Your parish," Nash continued, "includes some of those high rises downtown, doesn't it?"

"Recently, yes. Before that, it was a German national church."

"Oh?"

He didn't know much about it at all. "That means," Koesler said, "that anyone of German heritage could belong to St. Joe's no matter where they lived. But recently, the archdiocese gave us territorial boundaries."

"So. But you do include those high rises and condos."

"Yes."

"They must contribute pretty well."

"Our income is improving." Koesler was puzzled; he was also acutely aware that the sand in his twenty-five minutes was running low.

"I must tell you, Father, that I have never gone against the advice of Father Art. Of course, I have come to realize over the years that one should never say never. But I should stress before you plead your case that after your interview with Father Deutsch, the cards are stacked against you." Nash glanced at his Rolex.

Koesler was dumbfounded. "You mean you think . . . that I . . . that I want money . . . a grant from you . . . from Nash Enterprises?"

Nash spread his hands as if the matter were self-evident. "You're a priest from the inner city. But, really Father, there are so many other parishes in the city in far worse shape than yours. Of course—" Nash frowned. "—they have . . . well, many of them have become quite Protestant in an effort to be relevant—I think that's the term they like to use—to their community."

Koesler started to reply, but Nash went on. "What with one thing and another, Father, there is very little that Nash Enterprises—not to mention myself—can do for just about any of our city parishes. Either they're in a financially regenerating area like yours is, or they have almost abandoned the One True Church.

"But I don't want to seem unfeeling. That's why I made time for you this morning. Despite Father Art's decision to refuse your request, I could not turn down your plea for an appointment. However, I must warn you that I take very seriously the opinion of Father Art. Nonetheless, what exactly is it you want?" Another glance at the watch. "We haven't much time."

Koesler almost laughed aloud. But he restrained himself; there wasn't time to relish the misconception.

"Perhaps," Koesler said, "I was not sufficiently clear with Father Deutsch. He thought what with the age of the church and church buildings, that this might be the magic moment when everything falls apart. And, while he was not far wrong, as you said, we do have a financially improving situation."

"You mean . . . you don't . . . you actually don't want money?" It was as if Nash had been told he would never again meet a panhandler on the streets of Detroit.

Koesler smiled. "Well, if you were to throw a million or so at my parish, I wouldn't throw it back. But no, I'm not after a grant from Nash Enterprises or even some spare change from you."

"But then . . ." Nash was almost tongue-tied. ". . . what . . . what could you want? Does it have something to do with the Ford Park Mall development?"

"The what?"

"I know your kind, Father Koesler. Father Art warned me that you are one of those liberals who have abandoned the absolutes of our faith. You probably think the animals that are going to be displaced by our developments are as important as humans."

It was coming back to him. Koesler recalled reading about the development coup effected by Nash Enterprises. He had regarded it as just one more rape of the earth—to go along with the destruction of rain forests, pollution of water and air, erosion of the ozone layer, and so forth. Compared with those disasters, the leveling of Ford Park was a minor atrocity—one more brick in the wall being built against nature.

Koesler would not even have been mindful of the newspaper account had his eye not been caught by the corporation responsible: Nash Enterprises. Even then he would not have paid much attention had he not, at the time, been trying to get this very appointment with Ted Nash.

"You think I've come here to talk to you about a decision you've already made and are not about to reconsider?" Koesler's startled disbelief was evident.

"Before you get started, Father, you should know that we've got the Bible on our side!"

"The Bible?"

"Yes. In Genesis, where God tells Adam, and through him all of us, to 'fill the earth and *subdue* it'! Father Art said so!"

"Oh, that. I think Biblical scholars agree now that a more correct translation of that passage has God telling Adam, *and through him all of us,* to 'fill the earth and *conserve* it.'"

"Don't you wish! Don't you just wish that was true!"

Koesler shook his head. "Mr. Nash, that's not what I came to see you about."

Nash, taken aback, hesitated. "It's not?"

"No. I don't want any of your money, and I wasn't even thinking about Ford Park. But, on top of that, we've used up my half hour—well, really my twenty-five minutes—and I still haven't been able to address the real reason I'm here. What I want to talk to you about is a visit I had with your father a little while ago—a visit at his request."

"Dad? My father asked to see a priest!" Nash's countenance glowed as if he were accompanying Moses and the tablets of the law down from the mountaintop. "I can't believe it! That's marvelous news."

"So, can we talk about it?" Koesler was aware that Nash had—once again—drawn the wrong conclusion. Nash obviously assumed that his father had made his peace with God and the Church. His erroneous conclusion might just buy Koesler a little extra time.

"Yes," Nash said, "of course we can talk about it. But first . . ." Another glance at his watch. ". . . first, there's Mass."

"There's what?"

Nash led Father Koesler to a far corner of the room.

Koesler had not taken note of this area of the office clearly. That was due in part to the "busy" character of the place plus the dimness of this corner. Now Nash touched a switch and soft, indirect lighting immediately brightened the area.

The main feature here was a giant television screen, before which were two neat rows of chairs with kick-down kneelers. The first thought entering Koesler's mind was that someone—Nash?—had finally established a chapel wherein was worshipped the great god TV.

Nash gestured Koesler to sit alongside him in the second row.

Sound—not video—began at the stroke of noon. It was the Angelus, being recited by a man whose deep voice made Koesler think of terminal sanctity. In the background a male choir tendered the "Ave Maria" in Latin plainchant. Both Nash and Koesler replied to the "Aves" during the Angelus.

After that there was silence. What next, Koesler wondered? Then Nash spoke.

"Think of it," he said with unmistakable pride. "Right now, in every office of Nash Enterprises, this is going on via closed-circuit TV."

Koesler thought of it. He didn't much like it. He opposed coercion on principle. He could visualize right now throughout Nash's far-flung empire, glued to the TV screen, masses of Protestants, Jews, and maybe here and there a Muslim. He figured that most of those attending were, whatever their religious persuasion, being politically correct with an eye toward promotion—or even merely just to save their jobs?

In this continuing moment of silence, Koesler took another look around the office. Perhaps there were other surprises tucked away in corners.

If so, he couldn't find them. But the dimensions of the room, sizable enough to allow a minichapel to be comfortably parked in one corner, reminded him of something . . .

Of course: the senior Nash's apartment. That enormous space with, in effect, a medical center in one corner. Charlie has what may be the world's largest private hospital room, while Ted has the least-likely chapel in the business world. Like father, like son?

The screen began to light up, but very gradually, like a slowly lifting mist. Whatever was to come was enhanced by this staging.

The picture was now clear. The setting was a studio. There was what appeared to be a table. Given that Nash had interrupted their meeting by announcing "a Mass," the table was probably an altar.

Now the figure between the camera and the altar was coming through better. Some priest, with his back to the camera, was wearing an old Roman fiddleback chasuble. Koesler guessed it was good old Father Deutsch.

Koesler began to wonder about Deutsch. What was his job description? Screening religious requests for funding, offering a televised Mass—those were things one might expect from a personal chaplain. But Nash had quoted Deutsch to the effect that the Bible tells us to subdue creation. Handy to have a verse like that when one is about to devastate nature. It was truly odd to find a priest playing such an active role in the everyday affairs of secular business.

Koesler began to ponder how much power Deutsch might wield in Nash Enterprises. And, he wondered, did Charlie Nash know a priest was fooling around in Nash Enterprises? Could Deutsch have anything to do with the affair between Ted and Brenda? That seemed to be stretching things beyond possibility. But this whole situation was so bizarre, it could conceivably go off in any direction.

"In nomine Patris et Filii et Spiritus Sancti. Introibo ad altare Dei," Deutsch intoned.

So, Koesler thought, the old Tridentine Latin Mass. He shouldn't have been surprised, but he was.

For some four hundred years, Mass was offered using the exact same words and gestures by every Latin Rite priest everywhere on earth. It was only natural that pre-conciliar Catholics considered the old Latin Mass to be carved in stone. And it was only natural that many of them were bewildered when multiple formats became available in the *vernacular.*

For a while, the old and new formulas coexisted. Then, for some reason known better to himself, Pope Paul VI decided not only to ban the Tridentine Mass but to go to the mat over it.

Traditional Catholics were understandably confused when so ancient a form of worship was forbidden as if it were evil. So symbolic did this controversy grow to be that the Tridentine Mass became a major battleground between the Pope and dissident leader Archbishop LeFebvre.

More recently, after it was far too late to affect LeFebvre, the Tridentine form was again allowed—but only occasionally, and only with specific permission.

Koesler was willing to bet that Father Deutsch used the old rite regularly if not exclusively and *without* permission.

For a moment, the thought of blowing the ecclesial whistle on Nash's chaplain occurred to Koesler. But only for a moment. It was highly improbable that the old Latin Mass ever hurt anybody. And without exceptional cause, Koesler was not a whistle-blower. Interesting, thought Koesler, how those who want everybody else to keep strict rules find excuses when they themselves want to break those very same rules. But, although Deutsch likely was breaking a rule, turning him in would be childishly vindictive.

So, instead of rising in pharisaical indignation, Koesler sat back to evaluate Deutsch's celebration of the Eucharist, or, in terms more familiar to Deutsch, saying Mass.

He was good. The spirit he communicated suggested that he understood the Latin he was using. Not every champion of the ancient language could claim that. And he was reverent. His careful gestures showed an active faith. He believed in what he was doing.

Once again, Koesler was forced to reflect on the grays of life. So few people or things were unremittingly black or white.

From his brief encounter with Father Deutsch as well as from what Koesler knew of Deutsch's reputation, Koesler did not particularly like him. That was the dark side of gray. But Father Deutsch offered a pious and thoughtful Mass. That was the bright side of gray.

Speaking of grays, Deutsch now turned to the camera and launched into a sermon. Within just a few words, Koesler knew this was going to be another dark interlude.

Deutsch opened with a commentary on law. A very familiar point from which to start, thought Koesler.

"You know," Deutsch said, "that there is a Church law commanding all Catholics to attend Mass every Sunday and holy day of obligation—of which there are six. What you probably don't know is that the Church did not just haphazardly make up such a law. The Church never casually makes up any laws."

That, Koesler agreed, was so: The Church is very serious about making laws—and they're usually laws that preserve the institution. This sermon, he realized, was going to engender a host of distractions.

"It is," Deutsch continued, "like Sir Isaac Newton. Newton did not make up, invent, the law of gravity. The law was there all the time. Sir Isaac merely discovered it.

"And so it is with the one, holy, Catholic and apostolic Church. The Church did not invent the law governing Mass attendance on Sunday. What the Church did is discover our need to gather once a week to worship God at Mass. So, you see, just as with gravity, God's law, ordering us to follow what must be done, obliges us to attend Mass on Sunday."

And if you believe that, Koesler thought . . .

Deutsch went on. "But those whom God has selected must obey an even higher law. Just as God calls all Catholics—good and bad, fervent and tepid, strong and weak—to worship him on Sunday, one day of each week, so God has called us to something higher: that is, attendance twice a week. That is why we, members of the Nash family, are expected to attend the holy sacrifice of the Mass not only each and every Sunday but also each and every Friday. Thus we, virtually alone in our special calling, have the opportunity of commemorating Our Lord's resurrection on Sunday *and* commemorating His death on the cross each and every Friday.

"In this, our patron and employer, Theodore Nash, has not made any sort of special law affecting us and our relation with our risen Lord. He, with inspired insight, has discovered our innate need to gather not only once but twice each week."

Koesler half expected Deutsch to add, ". . . Blessed be Ted Nash forever." While Deutsch did not add that doxology, he certainly was acquainted with which side of his bread had butter.

But the manner in which Deutsch got to the butter amazed Koesler.

There had been two published collections of Catholic Church law in the twentieth century. In 1917, in addition to diocesan statutes, the provincial laws of the Council of Baltimore, and, of course, the Ten Commandments, Catholics had 2,414 laws affecting them. Some were more relevant than others. In 1982 the 2,414 laws were reduced to 1,752. To Koesler and others, the reduction was not an unalloyed improvement; in some cases, institutional control tightened.

But in none of the laws—not the 2,414 nor the 1,752—could Koesler find any connection whatsoever with a natural force such as gravity. That was imaginatively creative of Deutsch.

The chaplain was not finished.

Somehow, Deutsch had arrived at moral choices that must be made during "these evil times" and how, in these days of sharply divided liberal and conservative leaders, are we to know which course to follow?

"The problem," Deutsch said, "is not with conservatives versus liberals. We need both conservatives and liberals to balance the Church. The problem is with extremists on either side—while virtue always stands in the middle."

That sounded reasonable. What could have gone wrong?

"Moderates are the answer, but only those who are *loyal* to the Holy Father."

Ah . . .

"There are some who call themselves moderates but they are not loyal to the Holy Father." Deutsch leaned closer to the camera. "And that includes some bishops!" he confided.

I wonder, Koesler mused, if one of those disloyal bishops—in Deutsch's view—might be Detroit's archbishop, Cardinal Boyle, whose picture was noticeably absent from Deutsch's office.

Father Art was summing up with reassuring warmth. "So, my children, when there is doubt, look to the Holy Father for guidance. It is the Holy Father who teaches in the name and with the authority of Our Blessed Lord. Once we align ourselves with the Holy Father, we understand the teaching of the Church. And once we are straightened around, we will encounter those who stray from true doctrine. When that happens, when someone denies the teaching of the Church, we must fearlessly—*fearlessly*—correct him. But with restrained love, as the Holy Father does."

Father Koesler spent a good part of the remainder of the Mass reflecting on that sermon. He choked on most of it.

The third of the Ten Commandments—in the Catholic version— orders that the Sabbath day be kept holy. It does not specify just how the day is to be kept holy. Later Jewish traditions grew like weeds around the Sabbath. Still later, Christian law changed the observance of the Sabbath from Saturday to Sunday. Still later, Catholic law demanded attendance at Mass as one of the ways the Sabbath—Sunday, not Saturday—was to be observed.

In none of this had anyone but Father Deutsch, to Koesler's knowledge, ever found a kinship between this Church law and the natural law.

Then came the familiar conservative emphasis on the Pope as, in effect, a surrogate conscience for all Catholics. The emphasis dulled all distinction between infallible pronouncements and the ordinary teaching authority of the Church.

But, if one were to accept Deutsch's description of the Pope as the sole possessor of dogmatic and moral truth, then of course anyone who differed with a papal opinion would be in error.

Thus, those Catholics—not necessarily all bishops—who possessed *truth* through submission to and agreement with the Pope must *fearlessly* (Deutsch's emphasis) correct the erring brother or sister.

And correction must be made "with restrained love, as the Holy Father does."

Koesler had some difficulty equating defrocking priests, stripping theologians of their teaching tenure, silencing dissidents, removing select powers from bishops, and the like with "restrained love."

But he was most troubled by the tortuous logic and twisted rationalizing so evident in Father Deutsch's presentation. Given this self-serving thinking, what could be condemned? What could be justified? How much influence did Deutsch have over Nash? How much Nash over Deutsch?

Koesler had a feeling he would soon know the answers to these questions.

CHAPTER

10

"*ITE, MISSA EST,*" Father Deutsch intoned.

"*Deo gratias,*" the voice-over responded.

After the final blessing and the reading from the opening of St. John's Gospel, the Mass was completed. Slowly, the image faded and the screen became gray in death for the nonce.

Nash rose. Koesler followed.

"Wasn't that grand?" Nash enthused. "The only thing, maybe it's a little late in the day. Maybe we should schedule the Friday Mass at the start of the workday . . . say, eight o'clock. What do you think, Padre?"

The only time Koesler felt comfortable being addressed as "Padre" was when he happened to be in a Spanish-speaking country or group. Now, he swallowed his irritation. "I don't know. You've probably had the Mass at noon for a long time. It may be a habit by now. But it does make more sense to me to start the day with prayer."

Koesler had unspoken doubts about celebrating Mass throughout this corporate setting. Attendance likely was obligatory. And, of course, there was no way the audience could receive Communion. Sort of like being invited to a banquet and then not being offered anything to eat.

"Good idea, Father," Nash said. "I think we'll try it at eight for a few weeks. See how it works out. But first . . ." He again motioned Koesler to a chair near the superdesk. ". . . let's hear the good news about Dad. Wait: It's after noon. You want some lunch? I can send out. Or, if you want to go to my club . . . ?"

"A sandwich might be nice."

Nash nodded and addressed the intercom. "Loretta, have them send up a few sandwiches: combination cheese . . ." He looked across at Koesler. "That okay? It's Friday, you know."

Koesler nodded and wondered about this man. It had been many years since Catholics had been required to eschew meat on Fridays. There were a few who still abstained. But they were a distinct minority and, in almost all cases, extremely pious. How did any of this—putting a priest on the payroll, having Mass for employees, championing Catholic causes, still abstaining on Fridays—square with being an adulterer and a destroyer of the environment?

"Now . . ." Nash sat back in his chair and rubbed his hands together. ". . . tell me all about Dad. He asked to see you, you said? I can't get over that."

"Uh . . . he did call. And he did ask me to visit him. It sounded like a routine sick call. But when I got there, that didn't seem to be the case."

Nash's expression froze. "I beg your pardon?"

"Your father had no intention of making a confession, receiving Communion or the Sacrament of the Sick."

"But I thought . . ."

"So did I."

"Then what . . . ?"

Koesler took a deep breath, then exhaled. "Your father wanted me to somehow break up the affair between you and Brenda Monahan."

"*What*!?"

"Specifically, he wanted me to talk my cousin into ending the affair." Koesler almost felt like ducking.

"What affair? Who says I'm involved in an affair?"

"Well . . . your father, for starters."

"He's an old fool! I swear he's getting senile."

"I think he gives you credit for covering your tracks skillfully."

"This is ridiculous. Just ridiculous." Nash started to rise from his chair. "I'm afraid I'm going to have to ask you to leave."

"Wait a minute!" At the tone of Koesler's voice, Nash hesitated, then sat back tensely.

Koesler was firm. "I've gone to considerable trouble to arrange this meeting. And I am not one to meddle in people's private lives. I wouldn't even be here today if it weren't for Brenda."

"Now see here." Nash's defense was beginning to break down. "What gives you the right to come in here and accuse me—"

"I'm not accusing you of anything. I want to talk to you about a fact. The fact of your relationship with my cousin."

"You have no proof! I'm a married man. I have a wife and a family. I know who Brenda Monahan is. We've met at a few social functions. I know she lives alone in an apartment. We could scarcely meet in my home—my family, the servants, everyone would know. I know I'm followed from time to time by slime columnists. If ever I met Ms.

William X. Kienzle

Monahan at her apartment, we would have been found out and you'd see it on the evening news or in the next day's paper. So—" a note of triumph—"what do you think? Are we part of NASA? Do we meet in outer space?"

"Mr. Nash, I've already noted that your father said you have been successful so far in covering your tracks. I haven't the slightest idea how you do it. With mirrors? I suppose you have someplace where you can meet in secret. All I know is that your father's allegation is true."

"Now, really, Father, this is too much! One old man accuses me of something he thinks is wrong, and that's it? All I need to do is simply deny it—which I do. It's his word against mine. Now, if you don't mind leaving. I hate to be abrupt but I have a busy—"

"I'm not taking your father's word over yours. In fact, after speaking with your father, I had no intention of bringing up this matter with you. Something else happened that changed my mind."

"Oh?"

"I assume you know the structure of Brenda's pseudo-family." Koesler didn't wait for a reply. "She and Mary Lou were taken in and raised by my cousin Maureen, who has two sisters."

There was no reaction from Nash. He was obviously not about to acknowledge or deny anything with regard to a woman he admitted knowing only casually.

"Well," Koesler continued, "a little while back we celebrated a birthday for Oona, one of the sisters. It was a brief party. It broke up when Mary Lou became abrasive—to put it extremely mildly. In no uncertain terms, she accused Brenda of adultery with you.

"Even then, it was not just the innuendo or gossip or the fact that both your father and her 'sister' raised the issue of adultery. It was Brenda's reaction. I think under ordinary circumstances she could have braved her way through it. Maybe it was that she was under a lot of stress—but she broke down . . . caved in. I've never seen her that way before. And believe me, I know her very well. Her reaction to Mary Lou's accusation betrayed in no uncertain terms that it was true."

He was trapped. It didn't matter how often or how fiercely he denied his relationship with Brenda, this priest was not about to believe him. Obviously Koesler knew Brenda extremely well, just as he claimed. Yet why hadn't Brenda told him of the aborted birthday problem? He'd ask her later. For now, he had to deal with this priest. It was time for a little truth—though not the completely unvarnished variety.

"Suppose," Nash began, ". . . just suppose—nothing more than that—suppose Brenda Monahan and I are more than casual friends. Now, I'm not admitting anything. But if we were, what business would it be of anyone's—starting with my father?"

"You mean, is he concerned about the state of your soul? I wouldn't think so. He doesn't seem much concerned about his own soul. No, he's worried about the business."

"That does sound like Dad. But what do apples have to do with oranges?"

"He's afraid that no matter how careful you are, you'll be found out, and your reputation as a stellar Catholic will be destroyed. He doesn't think you could survive that kind of publicity. And he's ultimately afraid that if your reputation crumbles, so will Nash Enterprises. Now, some could laugh off a disclosure like this. But your father doesn't think you could. And, frankly"—Koesler looked fixedly at Nash—"neither do I."

There was no response. Nash seemed to be pondering his father's projected scenario, perhaps for the first time.

"To be frank, still," Koesler went on, "I don't have any vital interest in Nash Enterprises. My prime concern is with Brenda. Of course, I'm also concerned with your spiritual welfare. But I realize I'm not 'your priest.'"

Nash's expression told Koesler he'd scored again.

"As far as I can tell," Koesler resumed, "Brenda stands to gain almost nothing and to lose everything. She's condemned to be the woman on the side. I can't see any indication that you might get divorced. And even if you did, before you married Brenda—or anyone else for that matter—you'd have to get a declaration of nullity from the Church. There's no guarantee that you'd be successful in that. In fact, even with all your money the odds are heavily against it. I want Brenda to have a life. The longer she stays in this arrangement with you, the more certain it is that she's never going to have a decent life for herself."

There was a knock at the door, and Nash's secretary entered. She placed several tastefully wrapped packages on the desk and left the room, closing the door behind her.

The sandwiches. Koesler was hungry, but this was not the moment for munching. Besides, Nash had made no move toward the food. It would not have been polite to anticipate one's host.

Nash sat looking at the table for what seemed a very long time.

At length, he spoke. "If anything . . . *anything* . . . that is said between us escapes this office, I would, of course, deny it and take appropriate action against you. You understand that, don't you?"

"Mr. Nash, I'm very good at keeping secrets."

"First, I want to know why you didn't follow my father's direction and take this matter up with Brenda. You said that's what he told you: to take Brenda out of this relationship. Why didn't you try this with her?"

"I'm too close to her. I know there is no actual blood relationship, but there might just as well be. I've watched her grow up. She was always my 'cousin' in practice if not in actual fact. Just as doctors are loath to operate on their own relatives, so it would be awkward for me to bring this up with Brenda. Besides, I think the prime responsibility is yours.

"On top of that," Koesler continued, "—and I think I'm entitled to be somewhat personal here—how do you do it? How are you able to do it?"

"What?"

"Your religious activities and projects. You give a sizeable percent of your income to Catholic causes . . . far more, I would guess, than can be written off for tax deductions. You are perhaps the most identifiable lay Catholic, in this country at least. You have a priest on your payroll and a weekday Mass for your employees.

"That's the question: How can you do all this and, at the same time, carry on an adulterous affair? As far as I know, adultery may be the principal fly in your pie. But it is a major league fly."

Nash paused, then spread his hands, palms up. "You don't understand. If you understood, it would look different."

"Understand what?"

"Father Art understands."

"He approves of this?!"

"He knows what's going on."

"If you tell me, maybe I'll understand . . . though what's to understand beats me."

"It's my wife. We no longer live together as husband and wife. It's a sort of brother-sister relationship."

"I'm sorry to hear that, Mr. Nash."

"Ted."

"Okay, 'Ted.' Is this a Church-related ruling?" It was common knowledge among Catholics that the Church regularly demands that couples not canonically married live as brother and sister during the processing of their case or, if that fails, for life.

"No, no. It's children. In the first four years we were married, we had three children. That was just fine for me, but not for her. We couldn't agree on a form of family planning. Either I had a moral objection or the method was not sufficiently reliable for her. So we decided we would stay together for the children's sake—and, of course, propriety."

Koesler knew exactly to what Nash was alluding. Officially, there were only two methods approved by the Church for family planning: the rhythm method and continence. Rhythm would be far too chancy for Mrs. Nash. And abstinence would hold no attraction for her husband. As for the rest of the methods of contraception: one or another might have been appealing to the wife, but all of them were condemned by the official Church. And Nash stood with the Church. No doubt, it was a problem. But . . .

"So," Koesler said, "you and your wife voluntarily agreed to this brother-sister arrangement."

"That's right."

"That's a pity. A real pity. But how does Brenda fit into this picture?"

"You don't see?" Nash's tone connoted genuine amazement at Koesler's ignorance of the next logical step.

Koesler shook his head.

"God didn't intend that I should live as a celibate!" Nash exclaimed.

"He didn't?"

"Of course not! I have no calling for that life whatsoever. If I had, I might have given serious thought to becoming a priest. But the idea never crossed my mind. For the simple reason that I am a sexually active man. Always have been, always will be."

"So?"

"So, that's where Brenda comes in."

"Where Brenda comes in?"

"I don't think it's the gentlemanly thing to do, so I won't go into any detail. But trust me, Brenda and I have really great sex together."

He looked expectantly at Koesler as if hoping the priest would be able to put together the pieces of the jigsaw puzzle.

Koesler returned the gaze, wondering what came next. Gradually, he realized there was nothing more. It occurred to him that it was a case now of seeing the forest for the trees.

Finally, although no further word was spoken, the two men understood each other.

"You mean . . . ?" Koesler ventured.

"Yes."

"Brenda supplies the sex that is no longer a part of your marriage?"

Smiling broadly, Nash nodded.

"You mean Brenda is in effect half a wife?"

"What you've got to keep in mind, Padre, is that God did not will me to be a monk."

"So you've mentioned."

"But my wife refuses to have sex with me . . . at least in any way approved by the Church. So, you see, it's an impossible situation. If I keep God's law I can't have sex with my wife. I might just as well be a celibate. But God doesn't want that. A vicious circle. However—" Nash grew quite intense, "as one of the characters in *The Sound of Music* says, God never closes a door without opening a window."

"You're getting your theology from *The Sound of Music*?"

"No, no. Of course not. Serious and complicated questions like these I check out with Father Art."

"Father Deutsch came up with this solution?"

"No, no. We sort of arrived at it simultaneously, by working it out."

"Would you mind explaining the theology of this thing to me?"

Nash checked his watch and frowned. "I am running late. But, okay, since Brenda is—or might just as well be—your cousin . . . But I must be brief. Basically, I've already explained it to you. It has to do with God's will . . ." He looked sharply at Koesler. "I assume you have no objection to obeying God's will."

"None. I think we often have problems determining what God's will *is*."

"Exactly." Nash nodded. "But it's so clear here. I got married in the eyes of God and His Church for many reasons, not the least being the procreation and education of children."

It had been many years since Koesler had heard the phrase "the procreation and education of children." At least before the Second Vatican Council, Catholic children in parochial schools or catechism classes were routinely taught that the primary purpose of marriage was the procreation and education of children. Catholics approaching marriage were specifically asked if they understood that the primary purpose of marriage was the procreation and education of children. If anyone getting married in a Catholic ceremony were not to agree to that statement, marriage would be denied. Indeed, one of the few reasons a spouse could challenge the validity of a Catholic marriage and seek a declaration of nullity was if one's partner were to refuse the opportunity of having children.

Technically it was *"contra bonum prolis"*—deliberately creating a childless marriage. In fact, it was Detroit's Cardinal archbishop, Mark Boyle, who managed to introduce into a conciliar document language stating that among the purposes of marriage there was none that was "primary."

Thus, the phrase from Nash rang a distant but by no means foreign bell with Koesler.

"So," Nash continued, "I was in perfect agreement with God's will as I entered marriage." He looked at Koesler searchingly, imploringly. "For God's sake, man, we had three kids."

"Mmmm."

"Great Scott, man, don't you see yet!? It's God's will that I marry and thus keep within moral bounds my raging testosterone, my concupiscence. So I did. It is God's will that I do nothing within my marriage to artificially prevent conception. So I didn't. It's my wife's refusal to cooperate with me in natural intercourse that is frustrating God's will. It is Brenda who provides my escape from this vicious circle. Clear now?"

"Not quite. For one thing, in the situation you describe—we'll forget for the moment all those 'God's wills'—you probably could get a divorce, possibly even a declaration of nullity."

"Won't do. Would never do. Melissa was a perfect mate: old money, society connections. She's still the perfect mate. Through her and her family I can have doors opened that I couldn't get through in any other way. Divorce her and Nash Enterprises would lose a healthy portion of its power. Lose that power and many of the Catholic projects would lose our funding. That certainly is not God's will." He shook his head. "No, I could not divorce Melissa, let alone have our marriage annulled by the Church. That would not be God's will."

"Hmmm. Well." Koesler had never been through a more bizarre maze of moral rationalization. "What about Brenda? If she provides the physical benefits of marriage for you, how about the 'procreation and education of children'?"

"Brenda has taken care of that."

"She has?"

"Permanently."

"She's had a tubal ligation?"

Nash nodded. "I know, I know: It's a sin. But she was willing. It was her decision and it was a one-time-only occasion."

Deep within himself, Koesler felt terrible that Brenda had allowed herself to be mutilated. And for Teddy Nash! Yet the use of this radical method of birth control didn't much surprise him. It represented some of what he considered to be the worst pre-conciliar moral thinking.

Back in the days when such things were confessed, couples fought their consciences over artificial contraception, and regularly and painfully presented these "sins" to the priest in confession—"mortal sin" after "mortal sin" over and over, by the week or the month, sometimes finding a sympathetic confessor, more often being severely berated.

Whereas a single operation—a tubal ligation for a woman, a vasectomy for a man—one "mortal sin," and a confessional purgatory was over and done with for life.

But such radical surgery on Brenda—for Teddy Nash! For the convenience of Ted Nash, she would never become a mother!

This moment was as close as Robert Koesler had ever come to decking someone.

Controlling himself, Koesler asked, "She did this . . . she had it done . . . voluntarily?"

"Her idea all the way. Hell, as far as I'm concerned, I would have been delighted to start another family."

"Uh . . . if Melissa had volunteered to be sterilized, you would have gone along with that? Just as you did with Brenda?"

"Of course. It would have been her decision, just as it was Brenda's. Melissa's only contribution was a willingness to use an IUD *and* a spermicide jelly or the pill or . . . uh . . . I'd have to wear a condom. You see, no matter which method Melissa permitted, *I* would be drawn into the sin. I couldn't have had sex with her as long as I knew she or I or both of us were using contraception. I would have been cooperating in a sinful act. But it wouldn't have been my fault if she had gotten herself fixed. But no—not Melissa."

"As I said, I would have been happy to have a family with Brenda. But when she didn't want one, well, I was overjoyed when she suggested—*she* suggested that solution."

"Because then it is not your sin."

"Exactly. The most important thing in the world, Padre, is the state of sanctifying grace. *The most important thing in the world!*"

"I couldn't argue with that. But—"

"And I have never been out of it."

"What?"

"I have never in my entire life been out of the state of sanctifying grace. I have never in my life committed a mortal sin."

Koesler could think of no adequate rejoinder. Finally, he murmured, "I can't think of too many canonized saints who could or would make that claim."

Nash checked his watch. "I'm really pressed for time. So, if you'll excuse—"

"One final question: Father Deutsch agrees with all this?"

"With the bottom line, yes. Although he arrives at the same conclusion by using the principle of the double effect.

"And now, I really hate to be abrupt, Father, but that was your last question. It's been answered, and I must leave. But before I leave, you must leave." He stood. "I remind you, Father: All that we have said here, all that I have told you, remains right here. I know I haven't made a confession—"

"How could you? You never commit a sin."

"That's right. But even though what we've talked about is not protected by the seal of confession, it certainly is a professional secret." He stepped around the side of the desk. "Now, Father, that will be all!"

Koesler rose. He turned to leave, then turned back. "Do you mind if I take one of those sandwiches? I am hungry."

"Take them all."

"One will do nicely."

Koesler took one of the elaborately wrapped packets and, without further word, departed.

He had much to think about.

11

As HE AIMED HIS CAR south on I-75, Father Koesler again thought about his conversation with Ted Nash.

The priest had thought of little else since their meeting the previous day. There was so much to digest, so much to unravel, so much speculation to iron out.

It had then been almost a welcome relief to receive a call this morning from Eileen Monahan, asking if he could visit her this afternoon. With only minor schedule juggling, he could. Eileen had declined to enlighten him as to the reason for the request, stating only that she thought it very important.

It was a pleasant day. He was even able to roll the car window partway down. And, since it was early afternoon, there was little traffic on the freeway; he need pay but peripheral attention to the driving. Thus, with his mind in neutral, he once more played back some of Nash's more outrageous statements.

Koesler had considered his own tendency to rationalize to be one of his more outstanding failings. But his level of expertise in this field in no way approached Ted Nash's proficiency.

It was almost as if Nash began with the premise that he not only never *had* but never *would* commit a mortal sin. Thus, whatever went wrong simply had to be someone else's fault.

This concept of morality—that evil was classifiable into serious or mortal sin, less serious or venial sin, or imperfection—was peculiar to Catholicism.

Koesler could remember clearly as a child having been taught, and believing as he grew up, that individual actions could be mortally sinful, deserving punishment in hellfire. Thus, one could go to confession on Saturday and be headed for heaven (with always the possibility of a stopover in purgatory), and then one might miss Mass deliberately the next day and be headed for hell on Sunday.

This yo-yo theory of spirituality inevitably led to the conclusion that salvation depended on God's getting one's soul on the right bounce.

Yet, strangely, the theory had never seemed questionable to Koesler until Vatican II opened doors to questions.

To a Catholic, the "state of sanctifying grace" implied an intense union with God, freedom from any serious sin. Koesler chose to emphasize the "state." It was comparable to living in the State of Michigan or Ohio or California. One shared in the redemptive sacrifice of Jesus Christ and lived in the state of grace. One continued in that state unless one did something drastic, such as move from Michigan to some other location—or unless, in the case of grace, one decided to live a basically selfish life, using and manipulating others along the way. In that case, the transgression of God's laws was a symptom of the state of sin in which the person now lived. Something radical and decisive had to happen before one entered, abandoned, or reentered this state of sanctifying grace.

There was no doubt that in Nash's mind, the earlier interpretation was in force. Which meant that (by Ted Nash's lights) in all his life so far, Ted Nash had never performed a single seriously evil act.

To believe that, Koesler reflected, demanded an almost superhuman mastery of rationalization. And Ted Nash, to his probable eternal confusion, had it.

As far as Nash was concerned, God was willing the nicest things.

God willed a happy marriage and unlimited progeny. Take sex out of that picture, and God willed a surrogate partner. Ted could not lose.

In this he was not unlike many who claim to be the humble repositories of God's will. Such a claim is substantially more credible when God's will demands unpleasant duties. For instance, the prophets of the Old Testament who begged God not to send them in His name with such ill-received messages. Or someone like Joan of Arc, whose fidelity as a messenger of God's will brought her to the fiery stake.

Or the essential bearer of God's will, Jesus Christ, who shrank from the hideous death awaiting him. He could pray, "Not my will, but Thine be done."

Compared with these, Ted Nash had a piece of cake. One tended to suspect the recipient of a constantly convenient revelation who coincidentally claimed his course of action to be God's will.

Then there was Father Arthur Deutsch.

Nash had called time-out before he and Koesler could go into just exactly how Deutsch could justify Brenda's role in this scenario by the principle of the double effect.

That principle had been around for quite a while. It was one of the few moral determinants taught in Koesler's seminary days that was still in popular use.

It was part of a larger concept known as "the indirect voluntary." The idea being there are certain choices and actions in human life that are neither directly chosen nor the product of force alone. The specific use of the "double effect" occurred when someone did something that spawned two results or effects. To be morally acceptable, the initial action itself had to be either good or indifferent. The first immediate result had to be good and of greater weight than the secondary result, which could be evil and was not directly intended.

Thus, for instance, the case of an ectopic pregnancy—one in which the fertilized egg attaches itself outside the uterus. The doctor may operate—a good or indifferent action. The primary result is good, in that it saves the mother from an impossible medical situation. The secondary result, not intended, but only tolerated, is the death of the embryo.

One could argue endlessly about the principle and its relevance for this age. Is there, for example, any action that is indifferent? And what constitutes a "good" action?

But the principle is still being used by Church ethicists to settle, for instance, complex moral questions fostered by advances in medical technology.

Father Koesler's present puzzle was how Father Deutsch could have twisted the double effect principle into a justification of the relationship of Ted Nash and Brenda Monahan.

How could the "action" be anything other than sexual interaction between two persons, one of whom freely admitting that he is married to someone else? How could such an action be judged "good" or "indifferent"?

What would be the first effect—Ted Nash's sexual gratification?

That's good? That outweighs the secondary effect? Which is what? The harm done to Melissa, not to mention Brenda?

Of the two approaches to the ratification of Ted and Brenda's affair, Koesler preferred Nash's. And he didn't much care for that.

Neither Ted nor Father Art seemed to have an acceptable explanation. Both were rationalizing in the worst sense of that term.

The final question, and the one Koesler found most perplexing, was what, if anything, was Brenda getting out of all this?

"Great sex," according to Ted Nash.

Koesler, never having experienced great, adequate, or shabby sex, wisely decided he was not qualified to evaluate the importance of great sex.

But, he wondered, how great can it get? Even if it were an acknowledged sublime event, wasn't it possible that some other partner could prove every bit as good at it as Ted claimed to be?

Finally, was "great sex" sufficient to cause someone like Brenda to throw away her life?

For that, as far as Koesler could see, was exactly what she was doing.

Everyone who knew Brenda was convinced that her horizons were unlimited. Yet she seemed to have painted herself into such a tight corner. When she had asked Koesler for help in getting a job someplace in the chancery operation, he had readily agreed. As it worked out, his intercession proved effective.

Mary Lou's employment history being what it was, Koesler did not much expect her to hold on to her new job. Even working for a near saint. For whatever reason, her prospects seemed definitely limited.

Brenda, on the other hand, must have had some good reason for wanting to work in the chancery. Again, Koesler had figured that she would not long stay with the archdiocese. Not unless the Pope made her the archbishop—a position she could easily have handled, but one not likely to be offered her.

Brenda had unquestionable talent.

So what was she doing in a job that paid a fraction of her worth? Would she be moving on soon? Every week, Koesler half expected to learn that she had advanced to some more rewarding job, perhaps in some other city or state or country.

Even more, what was she doing in a dead-end relationship with a man like Ted Nash who would stay married to another woman until death did them part? Why had she had herself sterilized? To preserve her fragile union? She had all the ingredients to become an outstanding mother. Nash was more than willing to do his part to make her one. His track record with Melissa indicated he was not lacking in procreative powers.

But Brenda, for whatever reason, did not want his children. Nor, in view of her operation, anyone's child.

Maybe it would be worthwhile, after all, to have a heart-to-heart talk with Brenda about all this.

Koesler had hoped that his hard-won meeting with Ted Nash might have settled this matter. But it had accomplished nothing other than throwing a bit more light on Ted, his house priest, and their peculiar if not unique approach to a bizarre theology.

Out of all this, Brenda emerged as a focal point for both Charles and Ted Nash. Father and son seemed preoccupied with her, yet they could not have been more divided in their attitudes toward her.

Charlie viewed Brenda as a threat to the financial empire he had painstakingly formed and built. He wanted her out of the way. For Ted, on the other hand, Brenda literally completed his life, providing the sexual and romantic gratification missing in his now-loveless marriage. He needed her desperately.

Did Brenda realize the spot she was in? If she was not diligently and unremittingly on her guard, she could find herself at the center of a most uncomfortable collision course. And, without exaggeration, the result could be much more than uncomfortable. It could be fatal.

Koesler hated even to consider that possibility. But Charles Nash had not gotten to the pinnacle of the development business by being Mr. Nice Guy. There was no evidence as far as Koesler knew that Nash had been involved in violence, let alone murder, in the past. But the old man had made it clear that he would allow nothing—*nothing*—to pull apart what he had constructed.

Ted Nash, on the other hand, did not seem quite as prone to the use of any means necessary to achieve his goals. It was, however, quite obvious that he coveted and doted on the success of Nash Enterprises every bit as much as did his father.

While Ted's method of achieving or preserving success might not be as elemental as his father's, Ted had access to a theology that could justify just about anything. Whatever Ted wanted, needed, demanded, could be twisted around to be construed as God's will. Where might that stop? Koesler saw no boundary at all.

If Charles Nash were to perceive Brenda to be a threat to Nash Enterprises, and if no other course could eliminate that perceived interference, Charlie just might remove her by force. And if she became a hindrance or in any way a problem for Teddy, he and his priest were perfectly capable of devising a theology that would remove her from being part of God's holy will.

No matter how one looked at it, Brenda was in harm's way.

Fortunately, the automatic pilot that occupied Koesler's head while driving freeways clicked in. He had reached the turnoff for Grosse Ile. In no time, he was at the familiar gate —front or rear, depending on one's point of view—to Eileen Monahan's island property.

Preoccupied as he'd been on his drive down here, Koesler had given little or no thought to the purpose of Eileen's invitation. With Eileen, it could be anything from a trivial concern to a major calamity. Odds favored a light bulb that needed replacing but was beyond her reach.

Whatever it was, it would give his brain a rest from Brenda's very pressing problems.

CHAPTER

12

THERE THEY STOOD on either side of the fence, Koesler on the outside and the dog on the inside.

The dog barked furiously. Koesler observed that each time the dog barked, which was some twenty-eight or twenty-nine times per minute by unscientific tally, the beast left all four paws off the ground. It actually jumped straight up into the air with each bark.

Why would a dog do that? Koesler wondered. Maybe it was beside itself in a frustrated frenzy. So much commotion for such a little dog! Its small stature notwithstanding, Koesler was not tempted into opening the gate and trespassing on what the dog proclaimed as its territory. It wouldn't have been a large bite—but, large or small, Koesler did not want to lose any portion of either leg.

After what seemed too long, Eileen came hurrying out of the house, calling futilely to the dog as she hustled toward the gate.

Reaching the animal, she scooped it up, tucked it under one arm, and headed back toward the basement door. Shaking a finger of her free hand at the miscreant, she scolded it in no uncertain terms. And, all the while, the dog kept on barking, with passion and vigor.

Only when the basement door was fully and firmly shut behind the creature did Koesler enter the yard. "I tried, Eileen," he said. "Honest to glory, I tried. I tried to turn off my sweat glands. I tried to think positive thoughts. I tried to communicate with the dog, tried to use human-to-canine ESP. Nothing worked."

Eileen stood waiting for him near the house, her hands fluttering as she said agitatedly, "You're early! You're early! I would have had the dog in the basement, but you're early. I thought he was barking at a passing car. And then when he kept it up, I thought it might be the postman or a salesman or something. But Oona said she bet it was Father Bob. 'You know how he has that annoying habit of coming early to things,' is what she said."

"Oona's here?"

"Yes, dear. I hope you don't mind."

Dead Wrong

"What's to mind? I'm just surprised is all. You didn't mention she was going to be here. Did she just pop in?"

"No. As a matter of fact, it was her idea to call you."

"Her idea!" Koesler stopped stock still. "What's this all about, Eileen?"

"I'll tell you—or, more probably, Oona will explain it all."

He followed her into the house.

Oona was ensconced in the recliner, the living room's most comfortable chair, which was tipped halfway back. She seemed listless, weak, as if she were in the early stages of convalescence from some serious operation or illness. Except that she was neither ill nor had she had a recent operation. Her eyes were alert, giving the lie to her seeming lassitude.

Whenever Koesler saw his cousin like this, he was reminded of the hypochondriac's epitaph: *I told you I was sick.*

"Oona! Happy Birthday! I don't remember whether I wished you one the other day when we almost had your party."

"You didn't. No one did," Oona added. "That's why we're here."

"Oona, dear," Eileen said, "maybe we ought to go into the background a bit before we tell him."

Oona betrayed a smidgen of disgust, then said softly, "Oh, very well . . . if you think it's important."

That's Oona and that's Eileen, thought Koesler. Oona tended to think explanations were foolish, a waste of time. Eileen was inclined to prepare people for good news as well as bad.

Koesler preferred Eileen's method.

"It's about our family," Eileen began.

"Whose?" Koesler asked. "Yours or mine?"

"Ours, of course," Oona replied. "But you're included."

"Yes," Eileen said, "we've been talking about it almost constantly since that flare-up at Oona's party the other day . . . the girls, you know."

"Mary Lou and Brenda," Oona supplied.

"Of course." Eileen's tone had an edge. Even she had a threshold of interruption tolerance.

"If it's about the girls, how come Maureen isn't here? No one's closer to the kids than Mo."

"That's what this is all about," Oona said.

"It will be clear as we explain it." Eileen was retaining her narrator's role with difficulty.

"You remember how we grew up together," Eileen said.

"Of course," Koesler replied. "Two families, the Koeslers and the Monahans, living in identical flats—above the family grocery store for you and above the Tamiami Bar for us. Sharing a common staircase and, for much of the two apartments, common walls. On the corner of Ferdinand and Vernor. We might just as well have been brother and sisters . . . that about right?"

"Yes." Eileen was smiling, perhaps at the memory of it. "And then you went away to the seminary. We were so proud of you."

"I didn't know you were particularly proud," Koesler said. "If you were, it was probably a bit premature. It was one thing to be accepted by the seminary in those days, and something else to make it all the way through high school, college, and the theologate. You would have done well to put your pride on the back burner till I got ordained."

"We did. But regardless, we were proud of you all the way through. Each of us spent twelve years boasting about 'our cousin the seminarian.' And then finally, 'our cousin the priest' . . . isn't that right, Oona?"

"I suppose so. I don't remember every year of it." Oona was showing signs of impatience.

"And"—Eileen did not seem to notice Oona's testiness— "before you went to the seminary—when we were very young children—you used to play at saying Mass, and we would be your altar servers?"

Koesler smiled. "I'd almost forgotten that. We sort of anticipated the current introduction of girl 'altar boys,' didn't we?"

"We were all you had," Oona pointed out.

"That's true," Koesler agreed. "It was a very private fantasy I was living as a kid. The fantasy wouldn't have survived any teasing or mocking. I guess that's why I included you girls in my dream. I knew I could trust you."

"Why don't you get to the point?" Oona said to Eileen.

"I am, dear. Be patient," Eileen responded. "We were close. As close as brothers and sisters could get. Maybe closer, since there wasn't any sibling rivalry going on. We trusted each other implicitly."

Koesler rubbed his chin reflectively. "That's true, Eileen. It's absolutely true. I just never thought of it in these terms. I must apologize for taking for granted this lovely relationship we had—*have*," he corrected himself.

"Now?" Oona said.

Eileen nodded. "Remember your first solemn high Mass?"

"Sure. I'll never forget it. June 6, 1954, Holy Redeemer church. Just two blocks from where we grew up."

"We'll never forget it either, dear. Remember how, when it came time to receive Holy Communion, the ushers made sure to line the family up so we would all receive Communion from you?"

The memory was as vivid for Koesler as if the ceremony had been yesterday.

"There was your dear mother and father. Then, next came our mother—God rest all of them now—and the three of us."

"Yes," Koesler said, remembering.

"Well, we haven't exactly followed you around from parish to parish," Eileen continued. "But there are times, special occasions, when we do come together and you offer Mass . . . like the anniversaries of our parents' deaths."

Koesler nodded.

"Well . . ." Eileen seemed to be approaching her objective. ". . . there's a difference now. When we go to Communion. You know what I'm talking about, don't you, dear?"

Koesler had followed Eileen's direction every step of the way. "You mean that's always how it is now? Maureen never takes Communion anymore?"

Both Eileen and Oona nodded in sad confirmation.

"I've wondered about that, of course," Koesler said. "But, as you say, we don't get together all that often at Mass. Yes, I've noticed that Maureen doesn't receive Communion. Neither does Brenda, anymore. Of course, with Brenda . . . there's Ted Nash." He hesitated. "I don't think we can overlook him anymore, or pretend that there isn't something going on between them. And the fact that Brenda no longer receives Communion is, I suppose, confirmation that she realizes the sinfulness of the relationship. I guess I came to accept that that was the way it is with Brenda.

"But I really didn't give it that much thought. I just kept making up excuses why Maureen might not be ready or able to receive Communion." He looked at each of them in turn. "And now you're implying there's a deeper reason, aren't you? That's what this is all about, isn't it?"

Oona caught her breath and at one and the same time sighed in that seamless expression so common to Irish speech. "Didn't you ever wonder enough about it to come right out and ask Maureen?"

"That would be impolite," Eileen chided.

William X. Kienzle

"For the love of God, woman," Oona erupted, "you've already said that we were as close as brother and sisters! Why couldn't Father Bob have talked to her about it? Besides, he's a holy priest of God, save the mark! Who better to talk to her about a matter as important as Holy Communion?"

Koesler suppressed a smile. "I'm sorry, Oona; I just don't operate very well on that score. I guess I respect other people's privacy too much."

"Well, I'd say you certainly do!" Oona seemed personally offended.

"Can't help it," Koesler said. "It's just the way I am. Sometime back I stopped making resolutions I knew I'd never keep. Confronting someone about a matter I know they don't want to talk about comes under that heading. I know there are some priests who do this as a matter of course, but I can't. And it's doubly difficult if the person in question is as close as Mo is to me. Now, if she wanted to talk to me about it, that would be something different."

"What if we tell you what the problem is?" Oona said.

"Do you really think we ought to?" Eileen asked.

"Why do you think we called him here?" Oona said.

"But after what Father Bob has just said, we may be placing a terrible burden on his shoulders."

"No, no, that's all right," Koesler said. "Go ahead and tell me if you want to. Don't you see? You want to tell me something that affects all of us. So, I want to hear it. It's not like I'm prying into your privacy. So, go ahead: What's this all about?"

"Well," Eileen began, "you know us well enough to know that Maureen always was the more active of us girls."

"Wild!" Oona contributed.

Eileen glared at her, then turned back to Koesler. "Anyway, what with one thing and another, it just seemed that none of us would marry, but that if any one of us did, it probably would be Maureen."

Koesler suffered an almost total distraction. Eileen had touched on a topic that was plain as day but one on which he had never dwelt at any length.

Here were these four extremely Catholic children—Koesler half Irish on his mother's side and the three girls 100 percent Irish. In keeping with the trend of the thirties and forties when they were growing into adulthood, odds heavily favored that all, or almost all, of them would marry. And yet not one of them did.

Koesler, of course, had the most obvious reason for staying single.

He had chosen a vocation that had been decreed to be incompatible with marriage. And, now that he thought of it, no one in the family had seemed to expect the girls to marry. On the rare occasion that any one of them had a date, a great deal of fun—and by no means playful fun—was made of the occurrence.

Why was that?

Was it the Irish heritage? Traditionally, though not so true of present Irish youth, the Irish showed no impatience to enter the holy state. One of the native Irish jokes had a prospective bridegroom proposing marriage by asking his beloved, "Would you by any means be interested in being buried in our family plot?" And by the time they did get married, burial was not all that far in the future.

However, this was not Ireland. And when nice young Irish-American women waited for just exactly the right man at just the right time, sometimes life passed them by.

This appeared to be what had happened to the Monahan sisters. Always with the exception of Maureen, who braved her mother's sarcasm and often barbed remarks on leaving for and returning from dates.

As a result, what was really quite normal behavior for this country, this society, and this era gained her the reputation of being "loose."

Whenever he thought of it, which was not often, Koesler surmised that Maureen had caved in to the pressure of her home and remained single as had her sisters. He also figured that Maureen's taking in Mary Lou and Brenda was a type of protest against a spinsterhood that was in effect forced upon her.

This distraction was so compact that Koesler was almost immediately able to return his attention to what Eileen was saying.

"Well, anyway," Eileen continued, "after you were ordained in fifty-four, you got all wrapped up in your assignments and we weren't as close as we had been."

"That's true," Koesler said. "But it's also kind of natural. Those assignments, especially in the beginning when I had so much to learn about being a priest—so much they didn't, and couldn't, prepare us for in the seminary—those assignments took up almost my every waking moment."

"Of course, dear," Eileen said. "But while you were starting a brand new life and career, life was going on for us too."

"Don't go including us with Maureen," Oona admonished.

"I know, I know," Eileen said. She turned back to Koesler. "No, shortly after you were ordained, Maureen began to go her own way. At first, it was just casual dating . . . some of the young men she worked with. Then, some of the affairs got sort of serious. She began to confide in the two of us less and less. We really began growing apart. Then it was . . . when was it, Oona: Do you remember?"

"1959!" Oona said with assurance.

"Yes, 1959. Where were you then, Father Bob?"

"Fifty-nine? I think I was just ending a tour of duty at St. Norbert's in Inkster, as I recall."

"Well," Eileen continued, "that was when it happened. Or, rather, when it began. Maureen met somebody special. She was so sure of herself in this relationship that she began to confide in us again—"

"Not that we could do anything about it, mind you," Oona interjected.

"That's right. In the beginning we hoped it would work out and Maureen would be happy. But as time passed, we both—Oona and I— became more and more convinced that Maureen was living on promises. It was all promises. 'Next month we're going to go to Bermuda.' 'In July we'll go to Montreal.' Just promises and no fulfillment. They never went anywhere. Oh, the movies, or out to dinner. But weekends, almost every weekend, spent in one motel or another."

"Her beau was getting everything he wanted," Oona remarked.

"After a while," Eileen continued, "Maureen began to withdraw from us again."

"Because," Oona explained, "we were asking too many questions. Questions she couldn't answer."

"It wasn't so much the questions, I think, as it was that we were trying to convince her that her boyfriend was leading her down the primrose path."

"She wouldn't listen to us."

"The poor girl just wanted to believe, to hope so much, that she closed her eyes to reality," Eileen said. "She should have remembered that in the beginning we were as happy about her good fortune as she was. She talked herself into believing we were jealous of her because we didn't have any gentlemen friends. Either she talked herself into it or he talked her into it."

"Jealous! *Us?*" Oona exclaimed. "How could we be jealous of the runaround she was getting?"

"Yes, well, anyway, then it happened. In March of 1960." Eileen fell silent. For a change, Oona added nothing.

"Uh . . . *what* happened?" Koesler ventured.

"Maureen got pregnant."

"Pregnant!"

"Yes," Eileen said. "Of course, Maureen didn't realize it until she missed several periods. In June, I think it was . . . yes, June, she went to the doctor and he confirmed her worst fears."

"Then she came back to us. Now that she was in all that trouble," Oona said.

"We were all she had. She had no one else to turn to. Poor thing. She was frightened, bewildered."

"What do you mean she had no one to turn to?" Koesler protested. "She could have come to me."

"You were absolutely the very last person in the world she wanted to know about her predicament," Oona declared.

"But . . . but, why not?"

"Dear," Eileen said, "do you remember yourself back in 1959? Before the Vatican Council? Before you became editor of the diocesan newspaper?"

The question pulled Koesler up short. Himself in 1959. The year Pope John XXIII called for the council and also called for the reform of Church law.

That had been the pre-conciliar Church and a pre-conciliar Koesler. He and the hopelessly outdated Church law were of one mind back then.

How open and nonjudgmental would he have been even to his dear cousin Maureen? According to the testimony of these two cousins who knew him so well, it may have indeed been true: He might very well have been the last person Maureen had wanted to know about her condition.

Somewhat humbled, he pulled himself back to the conversation. "All right, so she couldn't come to me. At that time, anyway. I'll go with that. But she did turn to you. Could you help her? Did you help her?"

"We certainly tried," Eileen replied. "We found her a lovely home for unwed mothers in a Chicago suburb."

"We drove her there ourselves," Oona said. "Visited her regularly."

"Chicago!" Koesler exclaimed. "Why Chicago? There were some good places here in the Detroit area."

"Where she easily could have bumped into people she knew. Or people who knew you. Or people who knew your parents or our mother, all of whom were still alive then."

"Your own mother didn't know?" Koesler was amazed.

"That was the hardest part, not telling mother. Keeping it from her. She wasn't well then; that made it a little easier to keep her in the dark."

"I still can't believe," Koesler said, "that Maureen went all the way through a pregnancy and I didn't know anything about it."

"As I recall, dear, you were just transferring to another parish about then."

"June of 1960 . . . yeah, you're right. I was just going into St. Ursula parish. That was a huge change. You're right."

"It was providential. It really was," Eileen said. "Your folks were barely in touch with us. Mother was quite ill. And you were extremely busy. With all that going on, it wasn't that difficult to cover up for Maureen. And, if directly asked, to explain that a new job called her out of town for a while."

"'For a while'? She planned—you planned for her to return?"

"Oh, yes, when it came time."

"And that was . . . ?"

The sisters looked at each other for a few moments. Neither addressed Koesler's question.

"She did deliver the baby, didn't she?"

"Oh, yes," Eileen said.

"Then, when?"

"November . . ." Eileen said so softly Koesler barely heard her.

"November 1960," he reflected. Then something clicked. "November 1960! The girls—Brenda and Mary Lou! They were both born in November 1960! Are they . . . ? Is one of them . . . ?"

"Yes," Eileen said.

"Which one . . . which one is Maureen's real daughter?" He was aware that he feared the answer.

"Mary Lou," Eileen said. "Mary Lou is Maureen's real daughter. We were able to be with her right after the delivery—in Harper Hospital. Then she pulled a curtain down, as it were. We were not able to see her again for almost two weeks. By then, Maureen had decided she couldn't keep Mary Lou. But she kept in touch—that is, she always knew where the baby was. A series of foster homes and, finally, St. Vincent's Orphanage.

"In the end, she rescued Mary Lou from the orphanage and—to keep her company—Brenda, who was not only born in the same hospital in the same month but was also not taken by her natural mother.

"So," Eileen continued, "it worked out as well as could be expected, I guess. But, I can tell you, it was the most traumatic time we ever had. For Maureen more than us, of course. Actually, she never recovered from it . . . she's never really been the same. Haven't you ever sensed that?"

"Sure, of course I have," Koesler said. "But I thought it was because she—I *thought*—had adopted two orphan girls. I had no idea . . . I would never have guessed."

"And now," Oona said, "you know why Maureen doesn't go to Communion any more."

Koesler needed only a few seconds to evaluate that.

"No. No," he repeated. "It doesn't speak to that question at all. Once upon a time, some thirty years ago, Mo was involved with some guy. They may have been engaged for all we know. They may have been living in sin. Maybe not, for all we know."

"Maybe not!" Oona exclaimed. "My God, she had a baby. Haven't you been listening? She had an illegitimate child!"

"Calm down, Oona. The point is we can't judge anybody else. We can say that something is a sinful action. But we can't say that somebody committed a sin. We don't know what sort of pressures others are subjected to.

"But, okay. Okay, Oona, the fact that she stopped going to Communion sort of tells us that she felt she was unworthy. I guess it means that she may have felt guilty of serious sin."

"I don't think anybody needs a theological degree to know that!" Oona said.

"*Okay,* Oona. But I take it her boyfriend departed the scene about the time she discovered she was pregnant. Otherwise he would have helped her, and you wouldn't have had to."

"Oh, yes, that's right," Eileen agreed. "As soon as she told him—and she told him just as soon as she herself knew, in June of 1960—he dropped her quick as a flash. He forgot all his promises pretty quick."

"We told her so," Oona said.

"I'll bet you did," Koesler said. "So, she was free of him at least since June of 1960. She never took up with him again, did she?"

"No. Not to our knowledge," Eileen amended.

"And we would know," Oona added.

"So, all she would have had to do would be to go to confession. By the time she had her baby, she was no longer living in sin. Not by anybody's measuring stick."

He was reminded once more of sterilization as opposed to any method of artificial birth control. One operation solves all those individual "sinful" actions. In some similar way, having Mary Lou solved Maureen's problem of "living in sin."

Had the baby not happened, Maureen might have gone right on with the "sinful" life she acknowledged by abstaining from Holy Communion.

It seemed a strange way of assessing sin and virtue.

"Confession," Koesler continued, "has been easily available to Maureen for a little better than thirty years. Don't you think by this time she would have availed herself of it?"

"We don't know anything about that, dear," Eileen said. "We just thought that she continued to feel unworthy. I mean, I'm sure the poor dear has been more hard on herself than she need be. But, you see, it wasn't just having the affair or even having the illegitimate child. It also was the years she let her own daughter grow up in foster homes and, of course, the orphanage. I think she still feels guilty about that."

"Well, she shouldn't," Koesler said. "The past is over. No matter what we have done, when we're truly sorry for it, the grace of God saves us."

"That's what we hoped you'd say," Eileen said. "This just seemed the perfect time to bring you into our secret. Mary Lou's outburst at Oona's birthday party just sort of brought things to a head. I'm glad you know."

"So," Oona said, "what are you going to do about it?"

Koesler rubbed his chin. "That's a good question. My heart aches for Mo. She's been through so much . . . so much more than I ever guessed. It still boggles my mind that you could keep this so completely a secret for so many years."

"You aren't the only one who can keep a secret, you know," Oona said.

"The girls—Mary Lou and Brenda—do they know?"

"Oh, yes," Eileen said. "Maureen told us she told them both when she took them in."

"What a burden to lay on them," Koesler said. "But . . . the past is done. It's time to try to pick up the pieces. And, speaking of pieces, do either of you happen to know who Maureen's beau was?"

"Oh, yes," Oona said. "Mr. High Muckety-Muck. Mr. God's-Gift-to-Women . . . in his day, that is."

"Well, then," Koesler said, "who was it?"

"Nash," Eileen said. "Charles Nash."

CHAPTER

13

SON OF A GUN! That bastard! Charlie Nash was Mary Lou Monahan's father!

For a split second, Father Koesler felt as if he were the only person in the world who hadn't known that. If Eileen or Oona said anything in the following few moments, Koesler didn't hear it. He was completely lost in his turbulent thoughts.

Charlie Nash, seemingly nearing the end of his life, calls Father Koesler to a dramatic meeting. Nash knows full well the significant relationships in this affair—Koesler is blood relative to Maureen, Eileen, and Oona Monahan. He and the sisters are first cousins. And, although these four are not popularly believed to be related to the two girls, either in consanguinity or affinity, they might just as well be. Mary Lou and Brenda were taken in by Maureen. From that moment on, they were treated as Maureen's children and thus as cousins by Koesler, Eileen, and Oona.

Did Nash know? Did he know that he was Mary Lou's father?

Koesler broke through his turmoil of thoughts. "Did Nash know that he was Mary Lou's father?"

"Oh, yes, indeed," Oona assured. "Maureen told him what had happened as soon as she had her pregnancy confirmed by the doctor —in June of 1960."

"And?"

"And," Oona continued, "what would you expect? First he insults Maureen by claiming that somebody else must be the child's father. Then, after he humiliates her, he leaves her—deserts her. For a time, she kept trying to call him. But he was never 'in.' Nor would he return her calls. The bastard!"

"Oona!" Eileen put a hand to her mouth.

"Well, that's what he did. And that's what he is. That's how he treated the mother of his child."

"He never owned up to it? No child support? No aid of any kind to Mo?"

"None." Oona shook her head. "After a while all of us just gave up and tried to do as well as we could together."

"It wasn't easy," Eileen added by way of understatement.

Koesler again retreated into his private thoughts.

All these years. Thirty-three years! And no one had done anything about it.

What a coincidence that Eileen and Oona should choose to let him in on the secret just after Nash had exhorted him to talk to Brenda. Pressure situations like this had a habit of coming to a boil willy-nilly. As had this purulent mess.

Nash had told Koesler that the affair between his son and Brenda was a threat to Nash Enterprises. The scenario Nash painted had the relationship of Ted and Brenda revealed. The fear was that if it became public knowledge that Teddy was an adulterer, his facade as a Catholic above reproach would collapse. And when Teddy disintegrated, Nash Enterprises would not be far behind.

So much for the charge made to Koesler by Charlie Nash. But was Nash Enterprises Charlie's real concern? Maybe. However, in the face of the secret just revealed, Koesler doubted it. Undoubtedly there was fear that Ted could not bear up under the infamy that would come in the wake of exposure. But there had to be more to it than that.

Ted was playing with dynamite.

In the wings, just offstage, was Maureen—once Charlie's paramour—and Mary Lou, the young woman who was their daughter. What, if anything, might prompt them to come onstage?

Ted was playing with dynamite, all right. But the detonator was Charlie's creation.

Koesler was amazed when he considered the length of time Charlie Nash had been living with this bomb ticking away. *Thirty-three years.* And at any given moment during all these years Maureen and Mary Lou could have come out of the closet and revealed the truth.

Now that, indeed, might have crippled Nash Enterprises.

Koesler's guess, right off the top, was that neither Maureen nor Mary Lou had any intention of going public with what would be one of the juicier scandals to titillate high society. How those talk shows would slaver over the story! Geraldo might be willing to give his mustache for a first-time telecast, if not an exclusive.

Upon a little deeper reflection, Koesler plumbed his reasons for supposing Mo and Mary Lou would keep their secret. For one, Maureen had an intimate role in this melodrama. Should it become public,

Maureen would perforce share the spotlight with Charlie. And so, of course, would Mary Lou. Koesler could easily understand why they would be most reluctant to expose their private lives to general scrutiny, to the morbid curiosity of the masses. The axiom that no one ever went broke underestimating the taste of the American public was well taken.

Also, he could find no reason why they might choose a revelation now—with an emphasis on the *now*.

No, the time when Mo had really needed Charlie Nash's help was when Mary Lou was growing up. Maureen, with what little financial help she could get from her sisters, had borne the total burden of raising her child—two children actually—from at least the preteen years into adulthood.

In fact, the strapped financial condition in which this family consistently found itself was probably the reason Mo had been unable to support her daughter right from the first—from birth on. Now that he thought of it, it must have been an anguish akin to despair for Maureen to be forced to watch her child drift from one foster home to another and wind up in an orphanage.

Koesler remembered wondering how Maureen could afford to take both Mary Lou and Brenda from St. Vincent's. It had required great sacrifice on her part. What it had actually been was a mother's refusal to be permanently parted from her daughter.

But the statute of limitations on child support must have elapsed many long years ago. If Maureen and Mary Lou had not risked revealing their secret when a favorable judgment could have been a financial godsend, why would they rattle that skeleton now?

Another question bothered Koesler. "A little while ago, you said both Mary Lou and Brenda knew that Maureen was Mary Lou's real mother. Do *they* know who the father is?"

The sisters looked at each other, communicating wordlessly.

"We don't really know that," Eileen said finally. "There are things Maureen won't talk about—even with us. She can be pretty close-mouthed when she wants to be."

"When *she* wants to be!" Koesler exclaimed. "This whole crazy family is a collection of champion secret keepers!

"And," he added, "I suppose we don't know whether Ted Nash knows—what he knows—how much or how little he knows?"

The sisters looked at each other again.

"We have no idea," Eileen said. "I guess that would depend on what, if anything, his father may have told him."

Apparently there was no way, at least at that moment, of ascertaining how much or how little or even *if* Teddy Nash knew. Based on his meeting with Ted and with his priest, Koesler's opinion was that neither Ted nor Father Deutsch knew anything.

Imagine, Koesler mused, having an affair with the—what?—pseudo-sister of one's half sister. And not knowing what was going on!

It put him in mind of the Watergate hearings leading toward a possible impeachment of Richard Nixon. He heard in his memory the soft, gravelly, southern voice of Howard Baker asking over and over, "What did the president know and when did he know it?"

Who knew what, when, and from whom about this mess that had been dumped on him this afternoon suddenly and with no warning?

The only one who could be expected to know the entire story was Maureen. And even she might not know how comprehensive Ted's information might be. Was Charlie aware that Brenda and Mary Lou knew? Did the girls know who Mary Lou's real father was? Even the sisters didn't know the answer to that!

The burning question was: What was going to happen next?

"Well," Koesler said, "let's get back to the beginning. If I remember correctly," he turned to Oona, "you were the one responsible for this meeting."

"It was simple enough," Oona said, "I wanted you to talk to Maureen about confession and Communion. Far as I'm concerned, it's long past time. I wanted you to do it ages ago. But . . ." The explanation trailed off, and Oona looked pointedly at Eileen.

"All right," Eileen said, "I agreed with Oona in everything except that I didn't want to get you involved. Any number of priests could've done the job. But when it came to picking one, we never could agree on which one to ask. And we were afraid that the wrong one might only drive Maureen further away from the Church."

"Okay . . ." Koesler thought for a moment. "We'd better start putting this thing together piece by piece. It's a pretty tangled mess trying to figure out who knows what, who has to be kept in the dark, and who ought to know more. And I agree the place to start is with Maureen. But that's easier said than done."

"What's hard!" Oona exclaimed. "You said it yourself: All she has to do is to go to confession. She committed her sin so long ago. God knows she's suffered enough for it. God knows, all of us have! Far as I know, she hasn't been excommunicated for having an illegitimate child. What does she need besides confession?"

Koesler smiled. "No, there isn't any extra penalty like excommunication for that. There never has been. But there's more to this than we can know, I think."

"What!" Oona sounded exasperated.

"In thirty years?" Koesler said. "In thirty years! Count the weeks that have passed in that time. Think of the opportunities she's had to go to confession. She still goes to Mass, doesn't she? She goes regularly, doesn't she? In that, she's given as good an example as she could to the girls . . . right?"

Both sisters nodded.

"Well, then," he continued, "look at all the chances she's had to confess. Look at all the opportunities she's had. Most Catholic churches offer confession before specific Sunday Masses. Since the Vatican Council, most parishes offer communal penance services. With the communal service, Mo could've just melted into the crowd.

"All in all, she's had more opportunity than many might have. Still, there's no indication she's been to confession. If she had, she certainly would be going to Communion."

"So?" Oona wanted to know.

"So," Koesler rejoined, "it's like taking the proverbial horse to water but not being able to make him drink. Just because we think this would be a real easy step for Mo to take doesn't mean that Mo sees it that way."

"So," Oona said again, "you're the priest. What are we going to do?"

Koesler thought for a minute. "I think," he said finally, "what was said before still holds true. That being so, if I were to bring the matter up, I would alarm her. I can't think of any way I could approach her and not drive her off. Over the years she must have built up defenses. And if I were to contact her, all those defenses would be activated on the spot."

"So,"—Oona wanted action—"what are we going to do?"

"I think Eileen should get in touch with Mo," Koesler said. "Tell her, in the most tactful way possible, that we've had this talk. That I know everything you know, and that I want to help. Tell her all she has to do is get in touch with me and we'll talk it over.

"It doesn't necessarily mean she's supposed to make her confession to me. If that prospect bothers her at all, I can and will set something up with another priest. And I can guarantee that this priest will be kind, patient, and nonjudgmental. All she has to do to get this healing started is to call me. It's as simple as that. Try to make sure you get across how simple the procedure will be.

"And, oh . . ." Koesler added, "maybe it would be good to tell her that I've seen Charles Nash. He's a party to all this too, and I'd be surprised if he has much longer to live."

"You saw Charlie Nash!" Oona said. "You didn't say anything about that! When did you see that bastard?"

"Oona!" Eileen remained shocked at that perfectly legitimate An-glo-Saxon word.

In Koesler's judgment, there was no problem in sharing with his cousins the gist of his conversation with Charles Nash. Not only were the contents of that conversation clearly germane to what Koesler and the sisters were discussing, but there had been no evident intent on Nash's part to protect what was said as falling under the category of either sacramental or professional secrecy.

Koesler filled Eileen and Oona in on his meeting with Nash.

When he finished, Oona said, "I don't believe a word of it! He's not worried about the affair between Brenda and his son becoming public. He's scared over Maureen and Mary Lou. The rotter was the seducer of one and the father of the other. My guess is that the longer he waits for the second shoe to drop the more scared he gets."

"I agree just about completely," Koesler said. "Although at the time he told me all this, I believed him—even if I couldn't quite com-prehend why he had to worry that much about Brenda and Ted's relationship being pulled out of the closet. But after what you've just told me, I tend to agree with you, Oona. Thirty years is an awful long time to live under the sword of a most unpleasant revelation that you think is inevitable.

"But for now, there's no use getting into that with Mo. What we want to do is convince her that confession is just what the doctor ordered. In this case, Doctor Jesus. So, you make the call, Eileen, and I'll take it from there. And, for now, I have just one favor to ask, Eileen."

"Surely. What can I do for you?"

"Don't let the dog out of the basement until I'm well out of here."

FATHER KOESLER recognized the voice immediately. He was surprised only that Eileen had already acted.

It was just this afternoon that he'd had the conversation with her and Oona. Ordinarily, Eileen did not move this expeditiously. He hadn't expected to hear from her for three or four days, maybe even a week or ten days.

Eileen liked to be very circumspect. Faced with a task like confronting Maureen and convincing her to at least talk to her cousin about confession, it would not have been unexpected for Eileen to write and rewrite a script for her part of the dialogue.

Koesler could tell, also immediately, that Eileen was distressed.

"Oh, Father Bob," she said tremulously, "I'm afraid I've spoiled everything."

Koesler thought he detected the choking back of tears.

"Take it easy, Eileen . . . What's the matter?" he asked, even though he was quite sure what the matter was.

"It's Maureen. Oh, I should have written it out—the script—like I usually do when I'm making a difficult telephone call. I don't know where my brains are."

"Well, what happened, Eileen?"

But Eileen was not yet ready to forgive herself. "It sounded so simple when you were talking this afternoon. I thought all I'd have to do would be to let her know that you know all about it and that you want to help her. I thought that would be all it would take. But . . . but . . . I didn't . . ." She was crying.

Koesler felt so sorry for her. "It's all right, Eileen. It's not your fault, whatever happened. Just take it easy and when you're able then tell me what happened."

Several moments elapsed, during which Koesler continued to speak soothingly and Eileen gradually became more composed.

"She . . . she was very angry," Eileen said at length. "More angry than I've ever heard her. She wanted to know by what authority we presumed to tell such an intimate secret to you. She said it was *her* secret, not ours. And that we had no right—*none*—to violate the trust she had placed in us. Oh, she was so angry! As soon as she started to speak, I knew I was going to fail. But I had no way of preparing myself for all the anger and abuse that she heaped on me. It was awful." She sounded as if she was going to break down and cry again.

"Was that all you were able to get through to her, Eileen—just that you and Oona had told me about her situation?"

"No, not quite. When she got over her first wave of anger, I tried to tell her what you were prepared to do . . . that you said she wouldn't have to go to you for confession . . . that you could arrange for her to see another priest . . . one who would be kind and welcoming."

"And?"

"And she got even more upset. She just said the obvious—you pointed it out this afternoon—that if she wanted another priest she could find one just as well as you could.

"And that's true, you know, especially since Brenda works in the chancery and Mary Lou got that job in a parish. It seems that the girls are in pretty good positions to ask around for just the right priest to hear Maureen's confession."

Koesler didn't want his disappointment to show through in his tone of voice. Eileen was dejected enough as it was. "You did your best, Eileen. Don't go blaming yourself. All we're doing is trying to help. The final move, if there's going to be one, has got to come from Mo.

"So . . . that was it? Anything else? Did you mention that I'd been to see Charlie Nash?"

"Yes. Yes, I did." Eileen's voice sounded slightly more upbeat.

"And?"

"And Maureen's attitude seemed to change. She seemed to almost forget her anger and get interested in what I was saying."

"Hmmm."

"It was odd; at first she seemed just as angry that you would see her former lover as she was that we had confided in you. But then, she started to get more . . . uh . . . detached when I told her Mr. Nash had asked to see you rather than vice-versa. She wanted to know what had happened between you two.

"So I told her, as accurately as I could remember your telling us. And when I got to the part where you said that Mr. Nash looked very bad and that you didn't think he had very much longer to live, it was as if all her anger sort of dissolved, and she got kind of lost in thought."

"Did she say anything then . . . that you can remember?"

"Uh . . . umm . . . yes. It was just before we hung up. She didn't say anything to soften or apologize for her earlier anger. But she did say . . . wait a minute—she did say that maybe it was time."

" 'Time'? Time for what?"

"I don't know. I have no idea. I almost forgot that. It was such a minor part of our conversation. The main part—ninety-nine percent of what she said—was all that anger about the fact that we had told you and now you knew all about her secret.

"Honestly, Father Bob, that was the essence of our conversation. And that's what most disturbs me: that part about maybe it being time for . . . whatever . . . That came just at the very end. And I really don't know what she meant by it."

Neither did Koesler. But, mostly for Eileen's sake, he wanted to draw something positive out of the uncertainty. "Maybe," he said, "maybe the fact that Charlie Nash may be on his last legs is what Maureen has been waiting for. Maybe she'll think that over and change her mind about coming around fully and going to confession again."

"Oh, do you think so?" The relief in Eileen's tone was almost tangible. "Do you really think so?"

"Could be. Let's let this stew a bit and see what happens. Particularly if there should be some crisis in Nash's physical condition, I might just try phoning Mo myself. It might just prove to be the opening we've been looking for."

"Wouldn't that be wonderful?" Eileen enthused.

"Yes, indeed it would," Koesler agreed. "Let us pray."

With that, and with Eileen feeling much better, they ended their conversation.

KOESLER REALIZED that he was responsible for Eileen's temporary euphoria. But, he quickly decided, there was no harm in that.

Deep down, he didn't really have much hope that Maureen's reaction to news of Nash's failing health would lead her back to the sacraments.

Whatever that reaction signified, it was an interesting development. For a very long time that evening, even after he retired, Father Koesler continued to ponder what it could mean.

"Time." *Time for what?*

CHAPTER

14

OF COURSE the doorman knew Ted Nash on sight. The liveried gentleman also knew that young Mr. Nash was expected by the elder Mr. Nash. However, no one had mentioned a priest.

It was a nasty moment of decision. Should he simply wave young Teddy and his priest companion through? The doorman's predecessor had done that once. The caller in question was a beautiful young lady who had visited Mr. Charles any number of times. It was obviously an oversight; the doorman exercised his practiced judgment and allowed her to accompany the others, each of whom had been specifically listed for admission.

He never had the opportunity to admit another visitor. He was discharged forthwith. He was unable to obtain another position until he finally found work in Canada.

On the other hand, Ted Nash's short fuse was notorious.

It appeared to be a no-win dilemma.

Then, in an inspired moment, the doorman smiled. "Just let me call upstairs and make sure all is ready for your visit."

Even that conciliatory stratagem almost detonated Ted Nash's temper. It did the waiting doorman's sanity no favor when Charlie Nash's houseboy left him hanging while he checked with his master. By the time Charles Nash had second thoughts on the subject, and word came down to admit the priest, the doorman stood in a welter of sweat.

In the elevator on the way up to the penthouse, Father Deutsch ventured, "Are you sure this is okay? I've never met your father, and he wasn't expecting me. Did you see the look on the doorman's face when I showed up with you? And that call to your father's place—he wasn't checking to find out whether your father was ready for us. I just missed by a hair's breadth being left to cool my heels in the lobby while you went up alone."

"Yes, I noticed all that. I also noticed that Dad had to think about it a while before he evidently agreed to see both of us. But," he added,

William X. Kienzle

"I expected this to happen." He grinned. "Otherwise I would have ripped the hide off that doorman for making us wait."

"I'm still not so sure this is a good idea," Deutsch persisted. "Your father didn't invite me. And I've heard that nobody enters his presence without a clear and specific invitation."

"Don't worry about it. I think it's—yes, providential, that Dad wants to see me now. And to make sure divine Providence is operating, I have you along."

"But there's no indication—"

"The indication"—Nash never lost his temper with Deutsch, but he was perilously close to doing so now—"came to us in the form of Father Koesler."

"Koesler? But—"

"My father has even less to do with Koesler's kind than we have. Yet Dad actually invited that aging maverick to see him. I think Dad knows the end is near. And I want you to be available and on the spot the moment he asks for the sacraments.

"If that doesn't happen tonight, well, that'll be God's holy will. But at least Dad'll be familiar with you . . . so that when he needs and wants you, you'll be there, and he'll be comfortable."

Deutsch shook his head. "I don't know . . ."

"I do!" Nash said emphatically.

The question was settled; Deutsch knew it would not be wise to pursue the matter.

The elevator stopped, the doors slid open, and they stepped out into the tiny vestibule.

Father Deutsch eyed the closed door, the obvious entrance to the apartment. "Do we just go in?"

A sardonic smile briefly crinkled Teddy's mouth. "No one, nobody, 'just goes in' Dad's place."

The door opened, revealing an Oriental houseman in what appeared to be "hospital whites," which were immaculate.

The two men stepped into the room.

It was, of course, Deutsch's first visit. But unless his eyes were able to adjust to the dim interior, he wasn't going to see enough to write home about.

It was a huge room, that much Deutsch could tell. In the early evening, the lighting was remote and indirect. The picture windows, which stretched the length of one wall, and partway along another, revealed the river, Belle Isle and Windsor, twinkling lights, and the rush-hour traffic plowing homeward.

After taking in what little he could distinguish, Deutsch noted the servant leaving by a door in the far side of the room. After a few moments he returned, guiding a wheelchair noiselessly across the room straight up to the waiting men. Then he took the visitors' coats and hats and departed.

Deutsch had spent all but a few years in the Detroit area; like almost everyone else, he was acutely aware of Charlie Nash. Now he was astonished at the man's appearance.

Until about fifteen years before, when he retired in favor of his son, Charlie Nash had been very much in the news. His photo ran in newspapers, magazines, and on television. He was involved in everything from celebrity functions, to ground-breakings, to court appearances when he was being sued—and regularly winning the judgment—or defending the destruction of wetlands.

Deutsch remembered him as a dashing figure equally at home in a dinner jacket or a hard hat.

But all that had little to do with this pathetic, wrinkled creature apparently confined to a wheelchair. Deutsch had deliberately to remind himself that he and Charlie Nash were about the same age— in their middle seventies. The priest recalled shaving this morning. No, the image in his mirror had not looked at all as decrepit as the senior Nash.

Now Deutsch understood why Ted had wanted him to come to-night. Over many long years, Deutsch had ministered to a long, long list of dying people. Charlie Nash qualified. Ted had been wise in bringing them together.

"How are you feeling, Dad?"

"Well as can be expected," Nash replied, borrowing the routine hospital response.

"This is Father Deutsch, Dad."

Nash looked the priest up and down. Deutsch was unsure whether to extend his hand. The question was resolved; Nash made no move whatsoever to shake hands.

"So," Nash said, "this is the deacon."

"Oh, no, Mr. Nash, I'm—"

"It's Dad's way of embarrassing me. He calls all priests deacon. But only when I'm around."

"Well, Deac . . ." Nash began.

"He also abbreviates," Ted interjected, "but generally only when he's feeling good about something, or when, for whatever reason, he likes the priest."

"Well, Deac," Nash began again, as if his son had said nothing, "I've caught your show."

"My . . . ?"

"The service—Friday mornings!" Nash's tone took on a decidedly pedantic quality. Deutsch could see where Teddy got his quick temper. But the priest suspected the son was no match for the father.

"Oh," Deutsch said, "the Mass. But I thought that was on closed circuit, just to Nash Enterprises offices."

"Father Art," Ted said, "there is not very much going on at Nash Enterprises that escapes my father."

"Not anything," Nash corrected.

"I certainly didn't mean to imply that you should be excluded from anything," Deutsch said. "In fact, if there is anything I can do for you . . . if there's any help I can extend, uh, spiritual, of course . . ."

"Don't push it, Father Art," Ted cautioned.

Charlie Nash was making some indefinable sound deep in his throat. It could have been laughter as well as choking.

"Mr. Nash," Deutsch said, "is there something . . . ?"

Still croaking, Nash waved his hand to indicate all was in control, though it certainly didn't seem so.

"Deac," Nash said when he could finally articulate, "you think I let you come up here because I was worried about my 'immortal soul'?" The noise began again. This time a tear or two wended its way through the wrinkles in the old man's face.

"Dad," Ted said, "he's only being solicitous, for Pete's sake."

"Solicitous!" Nash hacked. He tried to force himself to breathe normally. After much effort, he was able to manage a wheeze that, for him, was close to normal.

"No, no, Deac," Nash said, "don't count on hanging my spiritual scalp from your belt." He turned to his son. "You know you shouldn't have brought him, don't you?"

Ted shrugged. "It was worth a chance. Let's be open: You're not all that well, and one of these days you're going to have to get serious about what comes next."

"What comes next," Nash almost roared, "is death! What comes next is death! What is it about the word that frightens you, Teddy? Can't you say the 'D' word?"

"Very well"—Ted's tone took on nearly the same vehemence as his father's—"death! It can't be around too many more corners for you. It's long past time that you should've started preparing for death."

"I am." Nash may have been smiling. It was difficult to tell. He fished around in a pocket of his wheelchair, came up with a cigarette, and lit it. Immediately, he began to cough as if he would bring up his insides.

Deutsch was horrified.

Ted, who had been through similar exhibitions many times before, looked on stoically.

When the coughing abated, Nash held the cigarette up as if it were show-and-tell. "This," he said, "is how I'm preparing for death. Nothing else has been able to kill me. Let's see what the weed can do."

"Come off it, Dad," Ted said. "You're a Catholic. You raised me Catholic. You know what I mean. You should be preparing for what comes after death."

Nash's eyes narrowed. "Your mother raised you Catholic—super-Catholic, come to think of it." He cackled briefly. "I didn't raise you Catholic. I was stuck with it, being Irish and all. I raised you to be a businessman. And I didn't do such a goddam bad job, if I say so myself. Your mother almost ruined my creation. If she hadn't been so off-the-wall holier-than-thou, she might have succeeded."

It took a moment for Ted to swallow what he considered a gratuitous insult to his mother. "If you didn't want a priest," he said, "why did you let Father Art in? Granted, you didn't invite him and I was taking my chances by bringing him along. But you could and—by damn—you would have ordered him to stay downstairs, or to go home, for that matter. But you didn't. You let him come up with me. Why? Why!" Ted finished on a victorious note. "Why, if you are so unconcerned about your soul, about death, about the hereafter?"

Nash licked his lips but didn't seem to moisten them. "Would you gentlemen care to be seated?" As he spoke, he pushed a button on the chair's arm.

The white-garbed young man entered the room. Wordlessly, he moved two spartan-looking chairs from the shadows of the wall to a spot nearby and facing Nash. Then, as silently as he had entered, he departed.

Ted and Deutsch seated themselves. The priest immediately began shifting about, seeking an endurable position.

"No reason you should be more comfortable than I am," Nash commented. He would make no effort to make them feel at ease.

"So," Nash said to either his son or the priest, "you thought I let a priest in here to prepare me for eternity. Now, why would I do a thing like that?"

"To ask God's forgiveness for your sins before it's too late," Deutsch said righteously.

"Sins?" Nash raised an eyebrow.

"Just a few minutes ago, you used God's name in vain," Deutsch pointed out.

Once again there was that guttural cackle deep in Nash's throat. "God's name in vain! If I was worried about my sins, that one would be the least of my worries, as you two soon may discover for yourselves. No, I've got other plans for the deac here."

"Other plans!" Ted sounded genuinely surprised. "Other plans for Father Art? You don't mean that you're going to let Father Koesler take care of your—"

"Koesler!" Nash almost spat the word. "Let's get something clear. I called on Koesler. I called on him to talk to his 'cousin,' your lover. He was supposed to talk turkey to her and get her to leave you alone. Instead, the jackass talked to you!"

"How did you know that?"

Nash shook his head angrily. "I know what goes on at Nash Enterprises. I know what goes on in your life."

Ted wondered whether his father knew about Nebo, the secret hideaway. He doubted it. Just once, Ted wanted to think that he had outfoxed the old fox. "It wouldn't have mattered," he said. "It wouldn't have mattered which one of us Koesler talked to. There isn't anything that could separate Brenda and me."

"That so?" Nash looked piercingly from under his once thick black eyebrows. "Think again, sonny."

"Never!"

"I'll give it to you straight," Nash said. "For one, you're asking for it. Two, you deserve it. And three, I haven't got time to pussyfoot around. "Thirty-three years ago, I had an affair with Maureen Monahan."

"Brenda's—?"

"For want of precise terms—her mother. She got pregnant and we broke it off."

The fact that his father had had affairs did not surprise Ted. He wouldn't have guessed that one of those was with Maureen Monahan. Nor was he at all troubled by his father's choice of words. Of course *she* got pregnant. No *Nash* had anything to do with it. And *we* broke it off. Charlie Nash didn't discard her.

But there was more.

"She had the baby," Charles said. "God knows whose kid it was. Could have been mine. But I've never admitted it. The thing is, the kid became a public ward, until Maureen took it in and raised it."

"If you think," Ted said, "that I'm going to believe that Brenda is that kid, you're sicker than I thought."

"No, Brenda's not the kid. Mary Lou is. Mary Lou Monahan is the kid."

"Brenda's sister? You can't believe that I'm going to accept all this! Out of the blue—all of a sudden? Why should you dump this garbage on me now?"

"Because Maureen dumped it on me earlier today."

"What?!"

"I've been waiting all these years for her to bring it up. Why she didn't try to blackmail me earlier—years ago—I don't know. But, for her own reasons, she picked today."

"But . . . if this is true, why haven't you ever told me? Why did you wait until now to clue me in?"

"You didn't have to deal with it. You don't even have to take care of it now. Maureen's not the only one who's been making plans."

"You . . . ?"

"Of course. I'm not about to be blindsided by some conniving slut. Okay, so she's going for the jugular now. She'll find that we're ready.

"But first, I gotta tell you what we're going to do. I gotta show you how to handle this thing. After I tell you all this, you decide for yourself how important Brenda is to you. If you don't break it up, you're a greater fool than I thought.

"This is where you come in, Deacon. Now, pay close attention, both of you. I'm gonna tell you just what happened thirty-three years ago. And, after that, I'll tell you all that has to be done now.

"And this, Deacon, is how I'm preparing for my death. Now, listen."

1960

CHAPTER

15

HE DIDN'T NEED HELP. He was very good at just about everything he did.

Maureen Monahan indulged in comfortable thoughts about her man as she slowly came more fully awake. It was such a gorgeous beginning to a sunny June Saturday. All seemed right with the world.

She rolled over and looked at her partner in bed.

Charlie Nash slept like a baby, on his back, lips slightly parted, breathing regular.

She smiled. She remembered last night. She remembered all the "last nights." And she wondered again why they didn't just get an apartment, a flat, a house. Or why they didn't simply move into his place or her place. This flitting from motel to hotel was wearing.

Charlie had explained it all, of course. He was a rising young executive in the Lowell Development Corporation. He was moving up the corporate ladder and he had to be focused in his ambition. Competition at his level was intense. Any flaw, no matter how insignificant, or even if not actual but merely perceived as such, could tip the scales the wrong way. The slightest distraction might spell disaster.

It was, he had explained, something like a protagonist in a mystery novel—Sherlock Holmes, for instance. The sleuth could not be involved with anything except the solution of the plot. The hero had to sift through the clues, casting aside the red herrings and eventually coming up with whodunit. Having Holmes emotionally involved in a love affair was out of the question.

"Well, my dear," he had concluded, "that's about the way it is with me . . . with us. Everything is on track. I'm on top of everything at the company. I am the embodiment of a superbly functioning mechanism. I have the solution to anyone and everyone's possible problems. Everyone thinks of me as a machine. No one would think of asking how's my love life. I've got to maintain that image till I really make it. Meanwhile, my dear, we could scarcely want for anything, now, could we?"

She had to agree with at least the final statement. They wanted for almost nothing. Of course, there was this nagging sense of instability. But, outside of that, yes, their life together *was* good.

This was not the first time for him.

He had admitted as much. He'd had to; there could be no other explanation for his skill at lovemaking. But having owned up to a past, he was disinclined to amplify. And she did not press.

On her part, she was much more open. She had told him of her rigid and restricted upbringing and of her two sisters, the once and future virgins.

He was her third . . . well, actually her first. The prior two could only generously be described as love affairs; they were more extended trysts . . . and she never had gone all the way herself. Nonetheless, they had given her some experience in physical relationships.

She'd had no way of knowing at the time, but her first two men were the training wheels of sex. Charlie Nash was postgrad all the way. It was as if Charlie had taken a vow never to leave his partner unsatisfied or unfulfilled.

That was a happy thought. She stretched blissfully, as she recalled all the times—all those times. She flutter-billowed the sheet and watched as it floated down unevenly, outlining the nude contours of her generous curves. Charlie was by no means alone in bringing something to this relationship!

She felt playful. She tried a few maneuvers designed to wake him. Rocking the bed slightly, a foot pressing against his knee, humming softly. Charlie's mouth closed. He licked his lips. He stretched like a large cat getting comfortable. His eyes opened. He looked at her and smiled. "What day is this?"

"Saturday. All day. Even if it rains."

"Do we have anything on today?"

"We have nothing on today." She ruffled the sheet, momentarily exposing their naked bodies. "And we have nothing on right now."

"Then, by all means, let's get something 'on,'" he said, as his head disappeared beneath the sheet. Slowly he lowered the cover, his head preceding its edge as he kissed his way to her toes.

They enjoyed each other leisurely in familiar ways. His satisfaction came first, but he made sure hers followed and was complete.

Now she lay against his side, one leg thrown across his body, her head on his shoulder as he held her and they relaxed together wordlessly.

It was his turn to be lost in thought and memory.

There was no doubt that he had been less than ingenuous with her. Putting aside, for the moment, all the lies, evasions, and inventions, he tried to think of those truths he had allowed to enter their relationship.

He *was* forty-two years old, a little more than ten years her senior. He *did* work for Lowell Development Corporation. He *had* had previous romantic liaisons. Charles Nash *was* his real name. In his own way, he *did* love her. By which he meant that he enjoyed her and, clearly, he gave her pleasure on a regular basis. And revealing their relationship in any way *would* have been disastrous—but hardly for the reasons he had expressed.

That was about it.

All the rest was deception. And he didn't really care. Charlie was familiar with the ethical maxim that the end did not justify the means; he considered whoever had concocted that observation to be an idiot.

The musical comedy *How to Succeed in Business without Really Trying* had not yet been born, but it could have been based on Charlie's life. The title was misleading. The principal character did, indeed, succeed. But he tried. He deliberately, painstakingly, pulled the rug from beneath the feet of each of his superiors, one by one, as he took over their respective positions.

And this was the basic formula Charlie Nash had followed in his ascension at Lowell. But Charlie's willingness to do whatever it took to win, to climb, to succeed was by no means confined to his business life. For Charlie, that method of operation was all-encompassing. It applied to Maureen Monahan as handily as it did to Lowell Development—and everyone and everything else that entered his life.

He would have been dumbfounded had he been asked if he felt sorrow for anything he'd done that had advanced his career or served his pleasure. Remorse was an emotion reserved for advantages not seized or people not manipulated.

Charlie could feel the swell and fall of Maureen's breathing. She wasn't sleeping, just relaxed.

He'd never met or even seen Maureen's sisters. But from her description, he felt he could pick them out of a lineup.

The priest cousin was another matter. From the first moment Maureen had mentioned Koesler—"Father Bob"—Nash had expected him to cause problems. After all, theirs was an illicit relationship. Nash had anticipated some determined interference from the priest. He was surprised when none came.

Eventually, in general and self-confident terms, he commented on the absence of any judgment from her priest cousin. Maureen assured him that not only had she little contact with Father Bob lately, but that further, her cousin was preoccupied with parochial responsibilities and demands. Indeed, she would have been surprised to hear anything at all from him.

In time, Nash learned to live with this shadowy priest so unconcernedly that he, like Maureen, would have been astounded had Koesler appeared on their scene.

All in all, life was very good at this moment. And self-satisfaction was about all for which Nash lived.

Maureen stirred. "Have you given any thought to dinner?"

"Dinner! We haven't had breakfast yet."

Maureen propped herself on one elbow and squinted at the travel clock on the bedside table. "It's too late for breakfast. How 'bout we have a light brunch and then a big dinner later."

"Okay. You got any more ideas?"

"Uh-huh. I'd like to go to the Chop House."

"Carl's?"

"London."

"What? The London Chop House! Did you win big at the track or something?"

"No."

"The telephone company come up with that promotion you've been expecting?"

"Ma Bell may do that one of these days. But not yet."

"Then what?"

"It's a surprise. I want to save it for dinner."

"Gimmee a hint. Is it a good or a bad surprise?"

"It's a glorious surprise. But I want to save it for just the right time."

"You know I can't wait that long for news!" Nash pressed her down by lying atop her. Then he began to tickle her. "What is it? You know I'll never be able to wait till dinner. If you weren't going to tell me till then, you shouldn't have said anything now."

"All right! All right!" she gasped between pleas for him to stop. "All right! I'll tell! Just let me up!"

He pulled back and sat against the headboard. He waited. Without specific reason he was suddenly apprehensive.

She pulled the sheet up, covering herself. "We're going to be parents."

His eyes narrowed. "What?"

"I'm pregnant."

"You can't be."

"I am. I missed three periods. I went to the doctor this week. He confirmed it."

"You can't be pregnant. You're on the pill!"

He was losing control; that frightened her. Charlie Nash, who had written the book on controlled emotions, was losing it.

"I was." She was getting defensive. "Then I started having these side effects—nausea, splitting headaches, bleeding. It was scary. So I started skipping days."

"But you know you can't do that. You know you have to take them every day or it doesn't work."

"I thought I could get away with it . . ." She shrugged. "I guess you're right. But I was still getting the side effects, so last month I went off the pill completely. But it was earlier—in March—when I started skipping. And that's when I got pregnant. So," she concluded, looking at him imploringly, yet trying to sound confident, "we're going to have our baby in November."

There was no immediate response. He just sat there. She had expected something. Initially she'd talked herself into believing that he'd be happy. As she had explained her condition, hope for an encouraging reaction dimmed. Now, nothing. He just sat there.

AT FIRST it was as if there were a tiny crack in the brick wall that represented his future. As Maureen talked, the crack widened, then split and fanned out in myriad directions.

His plans, all those carefully constructed plans! In his imagination, they seemed to crumble.

His deep, sustained depression lasted actually only briefly. Then he began to function in his customary way. It was a battle between fate and his will, a fate that would shape his destiny, or his invincible will that would conquer, overcoming every obstacle and controlling his future.

In the end, it was no contest: Charlie Nash would be the master of his fate no matter the cost to others.

HE GOT OUT OF BED and reached for his clothes. "How do I know it's mine?"

"How do—? Are you saying—?"

"You're saying it's impossible for it to be anyone else's?"

"You're goddam right that's what I'm saying!" She never blasphemed. "How can you even suggest you're not the father!?"

"You were willing to sleep with *me* without any guarantees, without being married to me. Why couldn't you do the same with somebody—anybody—else? Besides, you told me that I wasn't your first. How about one of the other guys? I mean, if you can go to bed with other men, why can't one of them be the father?"

"You bastard! I told you about them just to be honest with you. They were long gone before I even met you. I can't believe you'd accuse me of being unfaithful. I can't believe it!"

"I don't give a damn whether you can or can't believe it. Our agreement was that we weren't going to have a kid."

"There was no agreement!"

"Not on paper. But then we didn't have any papers saying we were married or could live as if we were. What do you think all that talk was about that you would go on the pill? Once you started fooling around with the pill, you weren't protected any more. I, or any of your lovers, could have fathered a child with you."

"I can't believe you're saying these things!" If she hadn't been so angry she would have wept.

"You knew! You knew I didn't want a child. You knew that was the last thing in the world I wanted. I don't give a fat damn *who* the father is. I'm not going to be it. Not by a long shot!

"Besides, if you were having all those problems with the pill, you, I, we, your other studs, could have taken some other precautions."

Maureen began to feel guilty again. "It was no use," she almost whispered, "nothing else we could have used would have been as reliable as the pill. And the pill was driving me nuts."

"It wasn't up to you to make that decision by yourself. You led me to believe that you were safe. And you weren't using anything. You trapped me!"

"We never gave ourselves a chance," she said quietly. "Neither one of us ever had a child. One or both of us could have been sterile. We had no way of knowing. It could have been."

"Now there's a great gamble: Two healthy, normal people and you presume that one or both of them is sterile!"

"Wait a minute"—her tone became more aggressive—"what is it with you, anyway? What's so horrible about our having a baby? We love each other . . . or, I thought we did. There's no reason we can't get married: People do it every day. You've got a great job, and you've got nowhere to go but up. Where's the catastrophe?"

"And then, what would your next little surprise be: Your family coming to live with us?" He was now fully dressed. "Your virginal sisters would be pregnant with a double virginal birth? Your boy-friends add babies to our little family? It could become a guessing game: I could try to guess which of the kids were mine." He slipped his watch onto his wrist. "Well, no, thanks. No, thank you, dear. This stud is getting out. Now!"

He scooped up his overnight bag and left, slamming the door without a backward look.

NEVER IN HER LIFE had her emotions been so stretched.

When it had happened the first month, she hadn't been unduly concerned. After all, it wasn't the first time she'd missed her period—although that, for her, was extremely rare. But heightening her uneasiness was the fact that she and Charlie were freely, sexually active, paying no attention whatsoever to her rhythm of fertility. And she had been skipping days she was scheduled to take the pill.

It was with some anxiety that she had gone to the doctor for tests. When the results were affirmative, she was thoroughly ambivalent.

Gradually, she had talked herself into believing that it would work out.

She was not eager to have a child just now. She could welcome a baby, but, deep down, she knew that Charlie was adamant on the subject. Using the pill was entirely his idea. She was well aware of his reasons for this: the status quo, the unencumbered advance, the slow but steady growth of their life together, and so on.

But she'd been sure—actually, she had convinced herself—that he would change his mind: Once aware that it was a *fait accompli,* he would come around.

In her worst possible scenario, she'd never imagined the response she'd just witnessed. It was unbelievably horrible, the complete antithesis of what she had planned, what she had hoped for.

A candlelight dinner, gracious ambiance, a satisfying meal, perhaps some dancing. Then, when the mood was totally romantic, she would tell him, tenderly, lovingly.

And he would be receptive. Not the best timing, at least as far as he was concerned, but, all in all, good news. Oh, initially, he would be startled, shocked even; then he would recognize that sometimes fate steps in and changes human plans.

In her worst nightmares she could never have envisioned what had just happened.

He was gone. And forget the daydreams, the rose-colored glasses, the happy endings: He was gone for good.

And she was alone. More alone than she'd ever felt.

But not totally alone. There was someone growing inside her.

She would live for her child, completely for her child.

And someday, somehow, she would make Charlie pay for what he'd done.

Someday. Somehow.

She refused to let herself cry.

16

THEY MET AT A small restaurant on State Street in downtown Chicago. It was a pleasantly warm day in late August. Street traffic was heavy, with cars searching for a place to park or an avenue of escape, and pedestrians intent on business or pleasure. Few people in the Windy City were concerned with the condition of Maureen Monahan. Just the family with whom she was staying, and her two sisters.

Maureen, Eileen, and Oona were in no hurry. This restaurant served as kitchen, dining room, and visiting parlor for them. Their leisurely approach to lunch did not endear them to their waitress, who would have preferred that they eat and move along. As it was, she tried to be gracious in hopes of a generous tip.

Maureen had been living in Chicago a little more than two months. Fortunately, she had not begun to show her pregnancy until July. At that point it was necessary to get out of Detroit if she was going to keep her condition concealed from general knowledge.

After her bitter breakup with Charlie Nash, Maureen had confided only in her sisters. They had discussed the situation for hours—for days—before all the questions were answered, all the emotions were aired, all the plans made.

In the end, it was agreed that it was the three of them against the world. They also agreed that "the world" held most of the cards. But they would hang in there and press on regardless.

Maureen might have received a maternity leave from the telephone company, but that would have entailed informing the company of her condition. And that was absolutely unacceptable. So she applied for as much combination vacation and sick leave as she had accumulated. That would not begin to cover all the time she needed, but it was the best she could do. And it was not at all certain she would have a job waiting on her return.

Next, they made arrangements through the Legion of Mary in Chicago for a private home that would take Maureen in for the final few months of her pregnancy. The legion was an international association of Catholic laymen dedicated to helping out in the day-to-day charitable needs of the Church.

The Chicago couple who took Maureen in were kind and helpful, particularly the wife. But there was no avoiding the bottom line: During this most momentous event of her life, Maureen was a stranger among strangers.

Almost constantly her thoughts were on Charlie Nash. All that she was undergoing had been made necessary by his rejection of her at the most vulnerable moment of her life.

The distance between Chicago and Detroit, approximately three hundred miles, was sufficient to discourage frequent visits. Faced with that distance, neither Oona nor Eileen was a confident driver. And, in her condition, Maureen found driving increasingly challenging.

Trains came to the rescue. The rails enabled Oona and Eileen to visit occasionally, and Maureen to steal into Detroit periodically for checkups by her gynecologist. Through him, Maureen was scheduled to deliver at Harper Hospital in Detroit's center city.

The women had just ordered their third refill of iced tea. Under her breath the waitress groused that they had just better leave a considerable tip.

"Would you like to leave here and walk around a bit?" Eileen asked. "You don't look very comfortable."

Maureen smiled ruefully. "It doesn't matter all that much. It isn't standing, sitting, or moving that's the problem; pregnancy is uncomfortable."

Her sisters knew that Maureen's statement was, in plain evidence, incontrovertible. The condition of their flesh-and-blood sister was as close as either Eileen or Oona had ever come to being pregnant. They were used to the sleek, coordinated sister they'd always known and secretly admired. This gross, pear-shaped edition of Maureen seemed to need strings attached to keep her from becoming a float in the Thanksgiving parade.

"Are things working out with the people you're staying with?" Oona asked.

"It's all right. They're nice enough people—and their kids are young enough not to question a brand-new 'Aunt' Maureen living with them for a little while." She smiled again, weakly. "And they're too blessedly young to know that there has to be a father that goes with my condition. So there aren't many embarrassing questions . . . at least none I can't field."

"How about the couple?" Oona pressed.

"They're okay. Mr. Peterson is preoccupied. He's got his job and family to worry about. I get the impression that taking in people who need a temporary home was Ethel's idea, not his."

"And her? What's she like?"

"A real help. She's gone through three pregnancies herself, so she can tell me what to expect, and really sympathize. It's not home . . . it's not even close. But for what it wants to accomplish, it's not bad."

Eileen touched Maureen. "Dear, won't you come back with us? You've only got a couple of months to go. We'd love to have you. You know that, don't you?"

Maureen nodded. "Of course I know that. You've really been such a big help, both of you. I don't know what I'd have done without you. But, no . . ." She shook her head. "I couldn't go back with you. I've put enough into this Chicago stay that I don't want to blow it all now.

"Besides, it would just be trading one problem for another. Here, even in the best circumstances, I'm a stranger in exile—but at least nobody knows me and I can get out and around without any questions.

"If I went home with you, it would be marvelous. But I'd be so afraid of meeting someone I know, I'd be a virtual prisoner and I'd go stir crazy or get cabin fever or some such.

"No, I think our original plan was well made. I'll stick with it. And, while we're at it, I think it would be best for this to be the last visit till I come home for the delivery. There's only a couple of months left."

"Whatever you say," Oona said.

They sipped their tea in silence for a few minutes.

"Oh!" Maureen exclaimed.

"What? What's wrong?" Eileen, startled, drew the attention of the few customers still in the restaurant.

Maureen smiled. "Nothing. This iced tea must be getting to the baby. It decided to take a walk and it hasn't got an awful lot of room in there."

"Really? Is it moving?" Oona asked. "Can I feel it?"

"Oona!" Eileen said. "We're out in public. Control yourself."

"It's all right." Maureen glanced around. "Nobody's looking now. Go ahead." She took Oona's hand and directed it to the spot where tiny feet were romping.

Eileen looked around the restaurant and saw that indeed no one was any longer paying any attention to them. "Do you think . . ."

"Of course." Maureen took Eileen's hand and placed it near Oona's. Fortunately, the baby was active enough at this moment to entertain both sisters.

Eileen's eyes were glowing. "Isn't it marvelous!" she enthused. "That's our nephew," she said to Oona.

"Or niece," Oona countered.

Maureen just smiled at both of her impressed sisters. She released their hands and rubbed her own expanded self. "It's the one beautiful thing in this whole sorry mess. Whenever things get particularly bleak, I focus on this baby growing and getting stronger inside me. It's a miracle."

"It *is* a miracle." Eileen grinned.

"I hesitate to mention his name," Oona said, "but have you ever wondered why Nash didn't suggest an abortion? As far as he was concerned, that would pretty well have taken care of things."

Maureen looked into the distance where there was nothing to see. "Yes . . . yes, I've wondered. But he never mentioned it. I thought that when I told him about the baby, he might have been too shocked to be thinking clearly. But if that had been the case, he would've called me later. He could've done that. But he didn't. The only thing I can think is that he knew I would never have agreed to it. I guess it wouldn't have been a big thing for him, but . . ." She shook her head vigorously. "I could never have agreed to that."

"I'm not saying that all you just said isn't true," Eileen said tentatively, "but there may be another reason."

Maureen and Oona looked at Eileen inquiringly.

"There was a piece in this morning's paper . . ." Eileen said hesitantly, "in the business section . . ."

"Well, what was it?" Oona asked. "I don't remember anything special."

"I cut it out before you got to the paper."

"You what? I didn't notice anything missing. But then," she added, on reflection, "I didn't look at the business section this morning. But why on earth would you do a thing like that?"

"It would just have upset you," Eileen explained. "I didn't want to have you upset when we had our trip to make. I would have shown it to you eventually."

"Well, what was it?" Maureen asked. "Was it about Charlie?"

Eileen nodded.

"Well, what?" Maureen was becoming exasperated.

William X. Kienzle

"He's been promoted. He's now senior vice president of Lowell Development. He's one step from the presidency of the company."

Maureen reflected on that for a moment. "It doesn't surprise me. I knew all along he would succeed. That's one of the reasons I thought he'd be happy about the baby. There was never any doubt that he'd be able to afford a family.

"So . . ." She sighed. "He made it. Correction: He's making it. He'll go a lot farther than that.

"But . . ." She looked intently at Eileen. ". . . what's that got to do with me?"

"The article in the paper," Eileen said, "also mentioned his age and a few other things . . . along with the fact that he's married."

"Married!" Oona exclaimed.

"And," Eileen continued, "he has a son named Theodore."

Maureen looked as if someone had struck her. "How . . ." She spoke haltingly. ". . . how old is the boy?"

"Seven." Eileen spoke so softly it was difficult to hear her, even though there was little noise in the restaurant. "I hated to tell you this, dear. But you were bound to hear it. And there was no *good* time. I'm so sorry."

"I don't believe it . . ." Maureen spoke as if in a stupor.

"I'm so very sorry, dear. It was in this morning's paper. I'm sure it's true."

"It couldn't be. It's impossible. He was with me so much of the time. Not all the time, but . . . how could he love me so much and then . . . a wife . . . and a child . . . a family?"

"Perhaps it's a mistake," Oona said. For Maureen's sake, she was shocked. And Oona did not shock easily. "God knows the papers make mistakes."

"I don't think so," Eileen said. "Sometimes they get the wrong name under the wrong picture. But not something like this."

"There was a picture?" Oona said.

"How did Charlie look?" Maureen wore a bemused smile.

"Quite well," Eileen said. "Handsome, I'd say."

"Oh, yes, handsome. That was Charlie all right," Maureen said. "Not pretty, but handsome, in a rugged sort of way. I'll give him that. Good looking. I'll give him that and more."

"He's a bastard!" Oona said definitively.

"No . . ." Maureen was in an almost dreamlike state. "That's what my child will be."

^ə "Maureen!" Eileen exclaimed.

"It's all so clear now," Maureen said. "It wasn't that Charlie was really all that upset about having our child. That was all for show. And that's why he never even mentioned an abortion.

"He could easily have afforded two families, with one child from each woman. He certainly was satisfying me and spending as much time with me as I could expect from a man in his position. He wasn't with me all the time. He said the job required a lot of travel. That made sense. All the while, he was traveling to his wife. He could have kept that up even if we'd had a child. I suppose he was telling the other woman—his wife—that he had to spend a lot of time out of town. I guess she believed him—just like I did.

"No, there was nothing wrong with that situation as far as he was concerned, even with another family. And he didn't mention an abortion for the simple reason that he didn't want me to have one. And why not? I can't believe he has any religious scruples or any kind of qualm about abortion. But, if he'd demanded or even suggested it, and if I'd agreed, he'd have had no reason to break up with me . . . That's it, don't you see?

"It was made to order," Maureen continued. "It must have seemed to Charlie like a gift from out of the blue. It was time. It was time to get rid of me. Oh, maybe there was no particular hurry. Maybe he saw this big promotion coming. He'd be moving into a different stratum. He'd have his picture in the paper. They always do that with a big promotion in a major corporation. They'd publish his vital statistics, including the fact that he had a family. The item would a pleasant little surprise to his family, of course. But it would be more than a little surprise to me.

"No, it was time to get rid of me. And I handed him the reason for it on a silver platter: I got pregnant."

Maureen was smiling ironically: She had unwittingly collaborated in the destruction of her own love affair.

"I got pregnant," Maureen repeated. "It was my fault. *It was my fault!* Can you imagine? *I* stopped taking the pill. The fact that I was pregnant was *my* fault. It was *my* fault that he had to break up with me. It wasn't *his* fault at all. He must have thought he had written the script. How could I have been such an idiot? How could I have been such a fool!"

There followed a long silence.

The waitress approached tentatively. She could sense that the mood of these three women had changed, and that something terribly serious—even tragic—was being discussed.

Did they want anything more? Oona declined, and paid the bill, leaving a generous tip.

Still, none of the three could speak.

"I hope to God you get him," Oona spat. "I hope you nail him!"

"Oona, dear, that doesn't sound very Christian," Eileen responded. But inwardly she agreed with Oona.

"The very least you can do," Oona said, "is to get him for child support. And, with this promotion, he'll be able to contribute quite a nice sum, I do believe. That, and it's about time his wife knew of your existence. Yessirree, it's about time Charlie Nash began to pay the piper."

"No!" Maureen startled her sisters with the vehement tone of finality. "No. Don't either of you do anything. I've got to think this through. Until now, I've been seeing all that's happened to me in one way. Now everything is topsy-turvy. I'm not much older, but a whole lot wiser. I have a premonition that what I do next is going to change my life forever. What I do next is liable to change a lot of lives."

She looked at them and smiled—a strong, warm, genuine smile. "God love you, dears. I know you are not only my sisters, but you're the dearest friends I have in the world. Now, I may have to ask you to trust me without knowing everything I'm doing.

"For some strange reason, I feel as if I've switched places. From being a helpless passenger, I may be in the driver's seat now. Just, please, believe in me!"

"We will," Oona said.

"We do," Eileen said.

17

EVERYTHING SEEMED SO WHITE: the walls, the cabinets, the towels, the fixtures, and, most of all, the ceiling. She had nothing to do but look at the ceiling while hurting all the time and tensing for the next incredibly painful contraction.

Every so often the nurse would come in to take her blood pressure and check for dilation. The nurse was pleasant enough, but she gave the impression of having done this too many times. She seemed untouched by Maureen's wondrous and frightening new experience.

Back in Chicago, just a couple of days ago, Ethel had tried to prepare Maureen for the delivery that was imminent. The information and advice was helpful and appreciated but nothing could convey this reality.

For one, Ethel had not adequately described the pain. Maybe birthing had been relatively easy for her. Maybe she'd forgotten the special pain of a firstborn. Maybe there just weren't words to do the job.

For quite some time now, Maureen had been second-guessing the decisions she'd made.

One of those decisions was to enter the hospital on her own. Both Oona and Eileen had argued long and hard against that. They wanted to be with her. But Maureen refused. Her only explanation was that having her sisters—or anyone, for that matter—with her did not fit into her plans.

So, against her sisters' strong opposition, Maureen had come to the hospital directly from the train that had brought her from Chicago.

She had been alone.

Alone when she rode in the cab to the hospital. For once, she'd wished for a talkative driver. It might have proven a distraction from the inevitability of her destination. But, just her luck, the driver kept his eyes on the road and his own counsel as the meter ticked away.

Alone when she checked into the hospital. She hadn't been a hospital patient since a childhood appendectomy. This process was new to her but routine to the clerk, who, like Joe Friday of "Dragnet," got just the facts, in just about the same disinterested, mechanical manner as the fictional police officer had used.

From the registration desk, Maureen was taken to her room, which she would share for the moment with another maternity patient. This woman had just lost her baby through complications during delivery. All this, Maureen learned by just one question. After that, it was clear the woman did not want to discuss her private tragedy further. She was merely waiting for the process of discharge. So, once again, at a time when Maureen wanted to talk to someone, especially one who had been through the actual event, she was, instead, very much alone.

This business of loneliness had dogged her footsteps for the past six months. And that time had taken its toll.

In the beginning it had been self-inflicted; she had freely removed herself from her relatives and friends to endure exile in a city of strangers. Now it had become a self-fulfilling prophecy. It seemed that everywhere she turned for companionship, she found only walls of isolation and silence. It was more than beginning to reach her.

There was another decision she'd made that was making her think again. That was the determination to use no anesthetics or painkillers. She wasn't trying to be either heroic or idiotic. She feared that if this process were in any way numbed or deadened by painkillers, she would too easily forgive what Charles Nash had done to her.

She reasoned that if she tasted to the dregs whatever measure of discomfort and pain that pregnancy and delivery might entail, and if she endured without the solace loved ones would normally contribute, she would never, ever, forget or forgive Charles Nash.

ACCORDING TO the wall clock, she had been in labor now for almost thirteen hours.

That was longer much longer—than she had expected, even though her doctor had cautioned that labor with a first child could be prolonged—and perhaps problematic. The doctor had been right on the money: This child was a problem.

For a considerable time, contractions had been coming every five to seven minutes. At first, she tried to swallow the pain. She did not want to appear a weakling, particularly since it had been her own idea to forgo any painkilling drugs.

After a while, it just wasn't worth the effort to appear brave. She started to whimper. But once the barrier had been lowered, she cried out unreservedly. All that accomplished was a slight venting of emotion; it did nothing to alleviate the pain.

The contractions intensified in their now all-too-predictable regularity. The baby stayed floating comfortably in its warm amniotic fluid. The womb retained its occupant. The nurse continued her periodic visits, measuring the cervical dilation, taking Maureen's blood pressure, checking the baby's heartbeat.

The nurse seemed genuinely solicitous. But as much as she might wish to stay with Maureen, it was impossible; there were other laboring mothers to tend. So, once again, Maureen was alone and in incredible agony.

In her misery, she resolved not to make any more resolutions. Then she sank once more into the dreadful depths.

THERE WERE SCREAMS that didn't seem to stop. Why wouldn't they stop? Through the haze of grinding pain, she felt a hand on her arm. It was her doctor, and, as the screams abated, she realized they were her own screams. The doctor was talking to her, she knew that; she could see his lips moving. She tried to focus on what he was saying.

The doctor, who was well aware of her decision to forgo drugs, was offering her a heavy dose of Demerol.

Maureen wavered not an instant. She declined the doctor's humane offer.

After that, there was nothing for him to do but wait for her to deliver. And there was nothing for her to do but wait for whatever it was that persuaded an unborn baby to be born.

The doctor did not want to see her suffer. But it did make things easier for the child. Because any analgesic she received would pass on to her baby. And, so far as anyone knew, the baby did not need a painkiller.

It was also better for the postpartum mother in that without drugs her recovery would be far more speedy.

And so, everyone waited. There was nothing else to be done. For Maureen's part, she would never, ever, forget this ordeal.

Then, it happened.

Or so it seemed.

Her water broke. Her cervix dilated measurably. "It's time, honey," the nurse said.

Like a well-oiled machine, a tried and true routine slipped into high gear. Maureen was wheeled into the delivery room. All that white was replaced by green. Her doctor arrived almost simultaneously, along with another nurse, who, in time, seemed redundant. Maureen's feet were once again placed in stirrups. The position was so familiar by now, she felt like a pony express rider hopping from horse to horse.

The doctor's head disappeared behind the sheet stretched across her knees. "It'll be just a little while now, Maureen."

She groaned.

"Lucy," the doctor addressed the nurse positioned next to Maureen's head, "did I tell you about the guy who was touring in Ireland and was having trouble finding a place to stay the night in one of those little villages?"

"No . . . not that I remember," she said tentatively.

Maureen almost bit through her lip.

"He finally got to the last possible bed-and-breakfast place in the village, but the owner told him they had no rooms. So the tourist was reduced to begging for any place to sleep. Finally, the owner said he did have one empty bed, but it was in a room where another man was staying. And this guy snored so loud he kept the cows awake; the tourist would never get any rest in that room."

Maureen could not find any humor anywhere in the world.

"But the tourist assured the owner that arrangement would be fine. So, against his better judgment, the owner let the tourist have the extra bed. Next morning the tourist was up bright and early for breakfast, well rested and everything. The owner couldn't believe his eyes. 'You slept?' he asked.

" 'Like a baby,' the tourist answered.

" 'How'd you do that? . . . with that snorer in the room and all that?'

" 'Simple,' the tourist said. 'Just before I went to bed, I kissed him.' "

Maureen screamed.

Light-humor time was over. "Okay," the doctor said, "when I tell you, push."

The nurse, so close that her head was almost touching Maureen's, began coaching her to breathe in rhythm with the contractions.

"Now!" the doctor commanded.

With a half scream, half grunt, Maureen complied.

Several "Nows" later, the doctor said, "Okay, here we go! Now!"

The nurse repeated the "Now." Maureen, covered with perspiration, pushed with what was left of her might. Would this go on forever? Logic told her it would end. But logic had little impact in the face of this protracted pain.

"Uh-oh," the doctor said. "We've got a stargazer . . ." The rest of his words were lost to Maureen.

"What? *What?*" Maureen tried to see what was going on, but, on the one hand, she couldn't raise her head enough, and, on the other, the draped sheet blocked her vision.

"The baby was coming out face up," the nurse explained. "The doctor has to turn it."

"Oh, my God!" Maureen shrieked.

"Oh, Lord!" the doctor exclaimed, "Now it's turned sideways! I'm gonna have to use forceps. Okay, Maureen, hold on. Don't push for a minute."

She fainted.

She came to as the nurse was, as gently as possible, shaking her and slapping her face.

"What? What? Stop!" Maureen shrieked.

"Okay, Maureen," the doctor said. "I've got the baby turned and it's ready to come out. We need your help. Now, again, when I tell you, *push*!"

She did, again and again, grunting with the effort and screaming with the pain. But her screams grew increasingly guttural and her grunts weaker. Maureen was at the end of her rope.

Then, through the wracking waves of agony, something seemed to break, then something was sliding out of her. Her tears came at the same time as the smile that widened into a grin.

"Okay," the doctor said, "come on. We're ready for you."

There were a few brief moments of silence as the final stages of this miracle of birth were played out.

"This," the doctor said, "is where your decision not to have any drugs is going to pay off. Although I don't know whether, after all you've gone through, it will be worth it. But you're alert, and your baby is not at all groggy. You'll see in a little while when you start to nurse a very frisky baby."

"Doctor," Maureen said weakly, "doctor, what is it?"

"Oh, yeah. Plumb forgot to mention that. Maureen, you've got a fine, healthy girl."

Maureen closed her eyes. Her smile was almost beatific.

"Perfect," she said, and relaxed.

CHAPTER

18

HE STUDIED the birth certificate for a full minute. Then he looked across the coffee table at Charles Nash. There was no expression on his face whatsoever. His eyes held some sentiment, but it was impossible to tell what it might be.

His name was Rick Chardon. He was of average height, with thick, dark hair, brushed back and clinging tightly to his patrician head. His eyes, as already described, were very much alive, but with an intent frequently veiled.

Wordlessly, he handed the certificate back to Nash.

"What," Nash asked, "is wrong with that certificate?"

"Your name is on it."

"Exactly."

Nash had used Chardon's services several times in the past, mostly to get information on Nash's immediate superiors or fellow workers at Lowell Development Corporation. Information that could compromise their professional and/or private lives. Information that could undercut their standing at Lowell. It was one of the telling ways Nash had climbed the corporate ladder to his present position—one rung from the top.

Chardon simply did whatever he was paid to do. His services did not come cheap, but they were virtually guaranteed.

One never needed to tread lightly or be at all squeamish with Chardon. Everything was conducted in a business milieu wherein that which some might consider morality had no bearing.

Chardon in no way worked for Nash. Chardon free-lanced. He could not, of course, advertise. His reputation grew by word of mouth from a series of satisfied customers.

"I need to have my name taken off that record," Nash said. "My name, and all other statistical information about me."

Chardon nodded. "I'm not familiar with the Wayne County Clerk's Office. Is there any problem getting a copy of a record?"

"None. I got this copy without showing any identification at all.

You ask for a record—anyone's—birth, marriage, death, you pay the fee, you get the record. Simple as that. No questions asked."

Again Chardon nodded.

Nash knew that already Chardon was hatching a plan. There was no substitute for dealing with a professional. "So, do you have any ideas?"

Chardon nodded.

"I suppose it would be good to talk money," Nash said.

Chardon shrugged. "A little early. I don't know yet what it will take."

Nash looked concerned. "Time is a factor. At the end of each month, they send all these records to Lansing. They're kept in the state capital, as well as in the county. That means you're going to have to take care of this by the end of the month. That leaves a little more than three weeks. Not too bad, except it has to be done within that time frame. Otherwise we'll have to have someone doctor the records in the county *and* in the State."

Slight frown lines surfaced on Chardon's forehead. "Three plus weeks."

"That's all we've got." Nash felt a tightening in his chest. He was so confident in Chardon's efficiency that he hadn't even considered the outside chance that this undertaking might be impossible, even for Chardon. "We can't squeeze out anything more. Those are the rules. The records are kept by the state as well as by the various counties. We've got just to the end of November, and then the job gets twice as hard."

Chardon shook his head. "Not twice as hard, damn near impossible."

"Well, can you do it? Can you get the record changed before December?"

Chardon said nothing for several moments. Then he looked squarely at Nash. "The price just went up."

"You haven't quoted me a price."

"I know. But it just went up."

"My resources aren't bottomless."

"They will be." Chardon almost smiled.

Nash read Chardon's words as well as his demeanor and concluded that Chardon's price would not only be fair, but that Chardon's appraisal of Nash's financial future was that it would be endlessly prom-

William X. Kienzle

ising—and that he was counting on many future commissions from Nash.

It was Nash's turn to nod. "Do you need any more information?"

Chardon took the birth certificate from the end table where Nash had laid it. "Not any more than this. You want your name and identification off this record. You don't want it ever to get back on it. And you want it done before the end of this month."

"That's it."

Chardon tipped his head sharply. "Done."

HE CASED THE OFFICE of the county clerk several times. He always kept moving, under the theory that you're less likely to be noticed if you seem to know what you're doing. People tend to take you for granted.

He was canvassing the women clerks. He knew what he was looking for, but he was having trouble finding the perfect foil. Yet he was confident he would. No racist, he weighed black women as well as white. But after several near misses, he was almost ready to compromise.

Then he saw her.

She was perfect. Mousy, her hair pulled back and pinned in a bun so tightly it almost made her eyes appear oriental. Her dress was carefully modest, with lace at the high neck and long sleeves. She had a habit of compressing and rolling her lips inward, making a tight line of her mouth. She glanced fully at applicants just long enough to check their physical appearance against the record's description—if the customer was asking for his or her own record. The rest of the time, she kept her eyes modestly cast down. Her ring finger was bare.

She was it.

Now, he needed a new identity. He had already done his research. He had all the information he needed.

The next day, Chardon returned to the clerk's office. This time he stood for an extended time, seemingly trying to make up his mind which line to enter. He waited until he knew she'd noticed him. Then he took his place at the end of her line.

As the line moved forward, he knew she was glancing at him, taking him in surreptitiously.

In time, he was at her station. "I need a copy of my birth certificate. My name's Peter Arnold."

"And your date of birth?" She almost stammered. She noticed his smile. And of course she couldn't bank on it, but she sensed that he was taking some interest in her. She was reluctant to believe her own intuition.

He smiled again. "Sorry. November 7, 1939."

"Just a moment, please." Her heart was beating more rapidly, and she felt her cheeks flush. She tried to control her emotions. This was silly. She was just doing her job. Then she did some quick mental arithmetic. She was good at her job.

She made the copy, returned to her station. She handed him the copy, holding her end of it a trifle too long and too firmly, so that he was momentarily slightly surprised. "Happy birthday."

"Thanks." He started to leave, then turned back. "Today I am a man, as they say. Uh . . . I don't mean to be too forward, but . . . would you be willing to help me celebrate? Dinner, maybe?"

There was only the briefest hesitation. "Well . . . yes . . . I guess that would be all right."

"Great. What time do you get off work?"

"Five-thirty."

"I'll pick you up then."

From their first date through all the subsequent dates, which occurred almost daily, he knew that if it weren't for the money, he wouldn't be caught dead with her on a date.

She slowly opened up to him, confiding her background, her academic experiences, her political preferences, her secret ambitions. He created a portfolio for himself that closely resembled all she told him about herself.

It was a cautious and painstaking beginning. He forced himself to appear not only interested, but obsessed with every detail of her life.

After the ice was broken, Agnes Ventimiglia poured out her soul to this marvelous man. After a lifetime of hoarding her feelings, secrets, aspirations, she finally had an outlet, another human being in whom she could confide. It was wonderful. She couldn't bring herself, she couldn't dare hope, to believe that this was the man of her dreams. Could this be the one she was destined to marry and, with him, spend the rest of her life? She could only pray.

Chardon was measuring time carefully.

His objective was to gain her absolute trust. In this there were no shortcuts. There needn't be. It would take only a few minutes at most to alter that birth record. It would not pay to scrimp on any single bit of preparation. Because if this didn't work, he'd have to fall back on something a lot more fraught—something that would involve break-ins or bribery.

He would know he'd gained her complete confidence when she had little new to tell him about herself.

The next step was to turn a corner and make himself indispensable to her and thus make her dependent on him. He must create the impression that not only was he in love with her, he was contemplating marriage.

All this was accomplished with relative ease. Except that time was definitely a factor—and he didn't have much left.

He didn't really want to have sex with her, but he would have had it furthered his purpose. Fortunately, she was shy, and, reading her correctly, he perceived that she wished to save herself, if not for their wedding night, at least until a firm proposal of marriage.

November was coming to a close before all was ready for the moment of truth.

They spent a weekend together in Cadillac, Michigan. They stayed at a multipurpose resort in separate but adjoining rooms.

Most of the leaves had fallen from the trees. Fall was sliding toward winter. They hiked through the skeletal forest. They swam in the heated indoor pool. They ate in the nearly deserted dining room. They laughed and shared intimate glances and chaste kisses by the huge log fire.

Almost as an aside, he mentioned one evening that a friend of his was going to have a problem with a paternity suit. The friend, of course, was not the real father. But the mother was intent on blackmailing him. So she had given the friend's name for the birth record. It would be a crying shame for this friend to have to go to court and spend possibly thousands of dollars fighting this malicious suit that would ruin his life if he lost. Chardon would consider it a favor of love if Agnes would correct the record by removing his friend's name from it.

Though such an action would of course be illegal, the request was straightforward enough. It was his understated tone of voice that gave her the clear impression that this was of great and significant importance to her Peter Arnold.

The thought crossed her mind that this might be the entire purpose of his relationship with her. He certainly knew that she worked in the clerk's office; that's where they'd met. And he had gone where no man had entered before—into a love affair with her.

Could it be? Could he have trifled with her affections for the sole and simple purpose of getting her to change an official record?

No! Thoughts like that were an insult to their relationship. They had shared too much. She had confided in him too deeply. They had had too much fun together. He respected her too much.

No man—no man!—would have done all he'd done for her for so trivial a reason.

"Yes, darling. Yes, of course I'll do it for you. I'll do it for your friend, for your sake."

NOVEMBER 30, 1960. Agnes had drawn a heart around the date on her calendar.

Unless she missed her guess, either at the conclusion of dinner or in the privacy of his apartment, Peter would propose. She would accept. For the first time in their relationship—for the first time in her life—tonight they would consummate their love and commitment to each other.

Dinner was lovely, as usual. The Pontchartrain Wine Cellars lived up to its reputation. Agnes reflected that they had never dined at the same place twice. She attached no particular significance to that.

There was no post-dinner proposal. But the evening was by no means over.

At his apartment, once they were settled in, he offered her a glass of sherry. A large sip of the amber liquid warmed her. But she didn't need the drink; she was ready for him.

He had noted the changes in her appearance tonight. Her hair style, the makeup, her perfume—all were new and attractive. Having assisted her in being seated at the restaurant and just now as he bent over her from behind and offered her the glass of wine, he was aware that she was wearing a lacy black slip. The fact that her dress was cut low enough for him to see that was also significant.

Adding it all up, he concluded that she had plans for tonight. After all this time and all these dates, this freshly suggestive transformation had to have some special meaning.

Perhaps she expected him to propose this evening. Perhaps with or without a proposal, she was ready to go to bed with him. Whatever, she was ready for romance, and all the barriers would be down.

He had to admit she looked good. And her perfume was seductive. The way she was tonight, he would not at all mind going to bed with her. It might be a lot of fun. Loosing all those years of her repression could be a fantastic aphrodisiac. But . . . this was business, not pleasure.

For just a moment, he was tempted to compromise. He could let things follow their natural course and conduct his business after the lovemaking. No, that was sloppy thinking. Let emotions run away, even momentarily, and pretty soon his reputation could be in jeopardy. He could not afford compromise in any form. He would have to do it now.

But first, one final check.

He had already run one test. Knowing her lunch-break time, he'd gone to the clerk's office in her absence and obtained a copy of the Monahan birth certificate. It had, indeed, been altered. The father of "Baby Girl Monahan"—evidently Maureen had not yet selected a name for her child—was "unknown."

Now, the only item left to be verified was that Agnes was the one responsible for the change . . . that she hadn't collaborated with anyone else . . . that she was the only one besides himself and Nash who knew.

From behind her, near the wet bar, he said, "By the way, Aggie, did you do that favor for me? In the records?"

The fact that he had never again mentioned it after his initial request was further indication, if any were needed, that the record had nothing whatever to do with their love affair.

She smiled. "Yes, I took care of it . . . there was no problem; nobody will ever know."

He was standing behind her, the blackjack ready. There was no purpose in further delay. He delivered an expert blow to the right temple.

For his line of business, he had not killed all that often. By actual count, this was his sixth victim. The only time he'd had any doubts was prior to the first murder. He had wondered how he would react to killing another human being. He had been slightly surprised that he had felt . . . well, nothing: not shock, not horror, not pleasure, certainly not remorse. If anything, there was satisfaction in a job well done.

Now, having bludgeoned Agnes, he again felt nothing. It was part of his job.

He inventoried the apartment. Earlier this day, he'd gone through the place, removing every trace of his stay there. This was merely a fail-safe check.

In a little while, he would leave with Agnes's body. He would never return. The bill for this month had been paid in advance. He would leave the security deposit behind. No evidence, no questions; it would be as if he had never been there.

All was ready. He checked the body. Agnes was dead. Only he and Charles Nash would know what had happened to the birth record.

This was the hard part—physically. He hoisted the canvas sack containing her body onto his shoulder, carried it down the stairs into the parking lot and slid it into the trunk of his car. He then drove out onto the nearly deserted streets of Detroit.

He rarely smoked, but he needed one now. He rolled down the window and lit up. The cool breeze quickly dried his perspiration.

He turned onto East Jefferson and headed for Belle Isle.

He drove slowly across the bridge to the island. There were a few other cars on the bridge. That was not encouraging. He would check the island for oncoming traffic. It didn't matter how long this procedure took, he wanted to be sure there would be no one around when he got rid of his bundle.

He circled the Scott Fountain. There were a few parked cars, no lights, windows raised and fogged. He had one thing in common with the couples in those cars: He and they wanted privacy.

He swung around the fountain and once again approached the bridge, this time heading back toward the mainland.

The traffic was as it had been, sparse . . . but the bridge was not empty. It would be risky to stop here. Everything had gone so well, he wasn't going to take any risks.

He turned onto Jefferson and drove back toward downtown. Then he swung down to Atwater, the street closest to the river. There, in an utterly deserted spot, he disposed of his bundle.

He did not wait to see it hit the water, although he heard the splash. As soon as it was out of his hands, he turned and reentered his car and drove away.

This would cost Charlie a bundle. But the work was of vital importance to Nash.

However, Chardon would not bill exorbitantly. He had done business with Nash before. Nothing approaching murder, but several hatchet jobs. Charlie paid well and promptly. Chardon wanted to continue to free-lance for Nash. The bill would have to be carefully computed.

Chardon, after all, had worked hard on this job and invested a considerable amount of his valuable time. The bill would have to be impressive but not offensive. He had time to figure it out. He had plenty of time now.

He did not give a thought to the dead body he'd thrown in the water, to be swept downriver by a powerful current.

ACTUALLY, the canvas sack had caught on a piling just at the surface of the water, where it would bob up and down for the better part of two weeks.

All in all, not Chardon's idea of a best-case scenario.

19

PATROLMAN Walter Koznicki was a mite old to be a rookie Detroit police officer.

After graduation from the University of Michigan, he served a hitch in the army; after mustering out, he enrolled in the police academy. All this was a preparation for law enforcement, which represented his highest ambition in life.

Almost every course he took at U-M would be relevant to police work and investigative science. His term of army duty as a military policeman constituted direct preparation.

His maturity and single-minded dedication won him the only two trophies awarded by the academy: one for the highest academic score, one for marksmanship on the shooting range.

So it was with genuine promise that Koznicki graduated and was assigned to what was then termed a patrol car, under the guidance of a senior officer. Sergeant Cooper preferred street smarts to what might be achieved in any educational institution. He didn't let Koznicki, his maturity, or all the prizes and book learning in the world impress him. On the contrary, this rookie was under special pressure to prove himself. And just such a test was coming up.

The police had received a call about a suspicious object in the water off Atwater in the vicinity of Woodward. Cooper's unit was dispatched to check it out.

Cooper hoped for the worst. And he got it.

It did not take them long to locate the object. It was a bag or sack of some kind, canvas perhaps. It appeared to be snagged on a fractured piling.

It was Cooper's guess that it had to have been dumped from this very spot where they were standing. If it had been dropped in from any point further upriver, it would probably have been sucked under by the current long before it reached this point.

If it had just been the bag that was visible, no one might have paid much attention to it. But there was an added point of interest. Evidently, the zipper had not been firmly closed or the canvas had ripped; in any case, something was sticking out of the sack. It looked like a human arm. No doubt about it, the bag would have to be retrieved.

Similarly, there was no doubt in Cooper's mind about which of the two of them would be doing the retrieving. "We're gonna have to get that sack." Cooper pushed his cap back and scratched his head.

"Were you going to help?" It was Koznicki's form of jest.

Cooper did not get the joke. Even a lightly made proposal that he drag a possibly rotting corpse out of the river lacked any measure of humor. "No, no. You're a big, strong young buck. I'm just an old copper waiting around for merciful retirement. Why don't you be a good lad and go get the bag?"

Cooper was absolutely correct: Koznicki was a big, strong, relatively youthful buck. Standing a few inches over six feet, big-boned, about 230 pounds and few of those pounds fat, he was at about the peak of his physical prowess.

It being mid-December, Koznicki was more than loath to get wet. But if he was careful, he might be able to keep himself, at least from the knees up, dry.

He studied the piling and its supports for a few moments. He knew that this operation might better be carried off by a team, with perhaps a diver present in case the bag was fumbled and dropped into the water. But if Cooper wanted to make it a test, so be it.

As Koznicki swung a leg over the side and began his descent down the pilings, he noticed Cooper surreptitiously applying Vicks Vapo-Rub under his nostrils. Koznicki knew it was a maneuver intended to mask the putrid odor of a decaying corpse.

He'd been through this as an MP, not in the context of a murder, but with dead bodies nonetheless. Some officers smoked cigars, others used products such as Vicks. No matter how accustomed one became to the singularly distinctive necrotic odor, blocking that odor was the easier way out. That Cooper did not offer the rookie the salve was part of the test. Koznicki was resolved to take whatever the senior officer chose to throw at him, including this difficult and unpleasant task.

If he had not been strong as an ox, he could never have carried it off. Holding on with his left hand, he balanced himself carefully, while with his right arm he reached for, grasped, and lifted the water-soaked sack and its dead-weight contents off the spike of jagged piling. Then, laboriously, he struggled back upward to street level, tugging the sack after him. As he was about to attempt to heave his burden over the ledge, Cooper stepped forward and helped haul the ponderous package up onto the frozen ground.

Koznicki stood by, his breath coming in chunks, as Cooper pulled down the zipper and threw open the sack.

At that point, Koznicki, gulping in air, was most grateful for the cold. At least there had been no heat to intensify the putrefaction. Also, the body could not have been immersed more than a month at most; it was just beginning to show the "washerwoman" syndrome of wrinkles.

"Better call Homicide. And while you're at it," Cooper added, "you better stay in the car. With those wet feet, you'll have icicles in your shoes." He was somewhat in awe of Koznicki's strength. Cooper knew he could never have retrieved that sack unaided, not on the best day of his life.

Koznicki didn't waste a moment. He was in the patrol car as quickly as he could move. While he radioed Homicide, he turned on the car's heater and focused its output on the floor. Fortunately, the engine had not cooled off too much, so there was still some residual heat.

Now enjoying the warmth that enveloped his wet feet and chilled legs, Koznicki studied the site just a few feet away. It was his first homicide scene.

Was it a homicide? Though the answer seemed obvious, he thought it a logical question. It was either homicide or a suicide. But who would zipper herself inside a canvas bag and dive into a river? Or had someone chosen this method to dispose of Aunt Sally rather than pay for a funeral?

Was she a drowning victim? The medical examiner would have an answer to that. But again, even a casual glance at the corpse revealed that mark on her right temple. That probably did it. The murderer had to be pretty strong if he killed her with one blow. *He?* Well, a reasonable supposition since superior strength was required.

And the victim? Young, Koznicki thought. Perhaps late twenties, early thirties. Nicely dressed. In life she might have been attractive. Now, the soul long gone, only the shell of what had been a young woman with most of her life ahead of her.

Something came over Koznicki. It was as if an inner voice was telling him something special. The feeling, he thought, must be similar to that which a bird experiences when it first leaves the nest and finds itself flying. This is what he would do for the rest of his life . . .

William X. Kienzle

the rest of his working life—which he now hoped would encompass his mortal life.

He was utterly captivated. Who had done this? Who had killed this young woman? Of all the questions on his mind, this was paramount.

He looked around. The homicide team was gathering. The immediate area was cordoned off. Each member of the team was doing what he specialized in. One was taking photographs of the area, concentrating on the victim. Two plainclothesmen were taking notes. One of them was questioning Sergeant Cooper.

So completely was Koznicki caught up in what was going on, he became inured to his discomfort. He got out of the car and approached the detective who was not talking to Cooper. The officer seemed to be drinking in the scene, memorizing it perhaps. Koznicki, not wanting to interrupt, said nothing.

In time, the detective became aware of this huge man. He turned and slowly appraised Koznicki from head to toe. He noted the patrolman's damp trousers. "Cooper make you get the body?"

Koznicki nodded. He did not like being reminded of what he'd just been through. He was still soggy enough to have belonged inside the heated car.

The detective looked Cooper up but mostly down. Dry. Completely dry. He turned back to Koznicki. "You bring that body up all by yourself?"

Koznicki hesitated. The truth might have compromised Cooper to some extent. Koznicki was aware that they should have called for help. Cooper had simply imposed a test, and Koznicki had submitted to it. But it was a direct question from a superior. "Yes."

The detective chuckled and extended his hand. "Davis. And you are . . . ?"

"Patrolman Koznicki."

Davis was struck by some memory. "Oh, yeah, I've heard of you. Just out of the academy, aren't you?"

"Yes . . . uh . . ."

"Oh, Lieutenant Davis. I've got Squad Three, Homicide."

After a pause, Koznicki asked. "What happens next?"

"Huh?"

"What do you do next? If you do not mind my asking."

Davis nodded. "Find out who she is . . . was."

"How do you do that? Do you mind my asking?"

Davis smiled and shook his head. Some detectives definitely would mind. He did not. Especially not over questions from so promising a rookie.

In fact, two near clones had found each other.

Most people would find homicide work interesting in the abstract, perhaps in murder mysteries or crime novels. Most would have no taste for the reality. Some few would find a macabre fascination with the sordid details. For some homicide detectives, it was a job. For a precious few, it was the ultimate and consuming passion. For these, nothing surpassed the drive to discover who did it and, perhaps, why. In this latter select category were Davis and Koznicki. Koznicki recognized this, at this time, only in a hazy way. Davis recognized it in himself and in Koznicki as well.

"There's always the possibility we'll never find out who she is. She could be from some other part of the country, even a foreign country. Maybe she was a discard; nobody wanted her and nobody cares what's happened to her. But I don't think that's the case here."

"Why is that?"

Davis shrugged. "A feeling."

Koznicki reacted internally. He had the identical feeling.

Davis noticed Cooper getting ready to get into the patrol car. "Your partner looks like he's ready to leave. And you look like you could dry off some more."

Koznicki started toward the car, then turned back. "Would you mind if I followed this case? Would it be all right if I looked in from time to time?"

Davis, who had turned away, did not look back, but merely nodded.

Actually, he was pleased. Koznicki was precisely the type who ought to get into Homicide. And all the better that he choose it rather than be tapped for it. Davis resolved to take Koznicki through this case step by step.

In the car, Cooper was heading back to the station. His partner needed dry trousers and shoes. Both could use an extended coffee break. But first . . .

"You were talkin' to that lieutenant."

"Lieutenant Davis."

"Uh-huh." Pause. "What was that all about? I mean, you were wet 'n' all. You shouldn'ta been out there. I told you to stay in the car."

"I wondered how the investigation would begin." Koznicki had to smile; it was a little late for Cooper to be worried about Koznicki's health. Sort of like an arsonist-firefighter who works to put out a fire he started and then figures everyone should be grateful he was there when the blaze started. If Cooper hadn't ordered Koznicki into the water instead of calling for help, the patrolman would likely be dry and warm now.

"That's all it was? He didn't ask how come you were wet? Or how we got the body out of the river?" Obviously Cooper was concerned that what he'd done would filter up through the lieutenant to Cooper's superior.

"That was mentioned," Koznicki admitted.

"And you said?"

"Only that I got the body." Koznicki knew what was on Cooper's mind. "I think he did not think it that odd that I should have retrieved the body. He took it in the lighthearted way in which it was intended. We talked mostly about identification of the body."

There was something about the way Koznicki talked that bothered Cooper. It was . . . what? . . . too formal. Cops didn't talk that way. It was like the guy got off the boat from some place in Europe not long ago. It wasn't that his English wasn't good; it was *too* good. "Well, we're goin' back to the station. You got spare stuff there?"

"Yes."

"Okay. We'll get you dried off and warm. It's not gonna sit well if I kill you." Cooper's laugh was forced. "Then, we'll take a break. But, say, how 'bout we just let what went down at the river be between us . . . that okay with you?"

"That will be fine." Inwardly, Koznicki was enjoying the sergeant's discomfort.

There he goes again, thought Cooper. Not "Okeydokey," not "Like hell," not "Don't shit me!" *"That will be fine."* He doesn't talk like a cop. Cooper more than ever couldn't care less about the rookie's academy trophies. So he was big! And so he was stronger than anybody Cooper had ever known. So what!

Why, the galoot hadn't even questioned Cooper's order to go get the corpse—just went over the side. On the one hand, Cooper appreciated the absence of hassle; on the other, he'd like to see more spunk.

Cooper did not subscribe to the theory that in order to give an order you have to be able to take one. Koznicki did. It was Koznicki's experience that those who were the poorest leaders had been the most recalcitrant followers. They could give orders, all right, but mostly in the spirit of an attempt at proving their domination.

Koznicki was, in a word, secure. He had little or no need to prove anything.

And so Koznicki easily agreed not to mention anything to anyone beyond the fact that they had been called to investigate a suspicious object in the river, they had retrieved it, it had turned out to be a dead body, and Homicide was now on the case.

Having extracted this assurance from Koznicki, Cooper freely told the story to his cronies, whom he could depend upon to keep it within the fraternity. They laughed over it, and were in some small agreement that a guy with Koznicki's attitude was not going to go far on the force.

CHAPTER

20

SO IT WAS A bent-nosed bunch of Detroit cops who learned that Patrolman Walter Koznicki had been transferred to Homicide.

Two days and many questions after he had pulled a body from the Detroit River, Koznicki was summoned to a meeting with Lieutenant Davis. Over lunch at a Greek restaurant near headquarters, Davis, in effect, made an offer Koznicki would not have turned down under almost any circumstances.

Membership in the Homicide Division, then, was not attained by any sort of seniority system or chronological order, or even by application. One had to be sponsored by a high-ranking officer, or by someone in Homicide. After which both the inductee and the sponsor were held responsible for the novice's work. Thus, sponsoring a new member of this elite division demanded conviction that the newcomer would not foul up, but rather that he or she would measure up to every demand made.

Davis had that sort of trust in Koznicki. And, as luck would have it, Squad Three was short one member. An officer who had been shot in the line of duty, and as a result paralyzed from the waist down, had just been granted disability retirement.

Everything had been prepared, so that not only was Koznicki's induction immediate, but his first assignment was the case he'd begun by retrieving the body of a murdered young woman.

Even as the two men were finishing lunch, other members of the squad were coming up with a positive identification. Davis and Koznicki returned to headquarters to learn that the decedent's name was Agnes Ventimiglia.

One Rosemarie DeFalco, a fellow employee of the deceased at the County Clerk's Office, had reported Ms. Ventimiglia as a missing person. DeFalco's description had been close enough to Jane Doe #23 to warrant a trip to the morgue, where the hysterical Ms. DeFalco made the ID.

Koznicki was dispatched immediately to question DeFalco, who had been given medication and was now more self-controlled.

His first impression was that DeFalco was a very attractive young woman. He was particularly impressed, since her beauty was evident even though she had just undergone a horrible shock. A puffiness about her red eyes testified to that.

After introducing himself and expressing sympathy, Koznicki asked his first question. "How is it that her family did not file the missing person's report?"

"She . . . she moved out of her parents' home . . . oh . . . a little less than a year ago, maybe nine months. They wouldn't have been aware that she was missing."

"But, you . . . ?"

"I work with her. I'm . . . I was . . . her friend." Her eyes filled with tears. "A very close friend." She shook her head. "When she didn't come in to work the next day, I thought . . . oh, that maybe she was just taking the day off to sort of . . . you know." Koznicki's face was impassive. "Then, after the weekend, I started to wonder. But . . ." She shook her head again. "I thought that maybe they'd gone off together . . . you know, eloped or something. And if they had . . . well, I knew Aggie wouldn't want somebody to barge in on them, and she'd have died of embarrassment—" She stopped, realizing that Agnes had indeed died, and of more than embarrassment. "Well, she would have been so terribly embarrassed if the police or some sort of investigator had tried to come after her, especially if it had gotten into the papers.

"So, I tried to cover for her at work, and make excuses . . . although really nobody else paid much attention . . . they didn't pay any attention to her when she was there, so they didn't even miss her when she wasn't. And it always slows down around the holidays anyway."

The tears overflowed. "I just kept waiting, hoping she'd come back. hoping I'd at least hear from her . . . and . . . I really didn't know what else to do. I didn't want to call her parents and get them all upset and make things worse."

Koznicki nodded sympathetically. "She had no contact with her family?"

"No. Not really. I think they never let her grow up. So when she moved out, there were . . . bad feelings."

"Bad feelings?" Koznicki was taking notes in his own form of shorthand. "How bad? Was there physical violence?"

"Oh, I don't think so. At least she never mentioned any. And I think she would have. It was just a kind of, 'If you leave, don't ever darken our door again' . . . that sort of thing.

"But," DeFalco continued, "if you're looking for whoever killed her, I don't think it was anybody in her family. I think I know who did it."

Koznicki, who had been standing, sat down next to her on the bench. "Oh? Who?"

"His name is Peter Arnold."

"Who is he?"

"He was . . . well, I guess you'd call him a boyfriend." She sounded uncertain.

"Do you know where we can find this Peter Arnold? Do you know where he works?"

She thought a moment. "No, not really. Aggie never mentioned . . . I mean, she was a very private person—even with me."

"Tell me all you can about this Peter Arnold. What does he look like? Can you describe him?"

"Well . . . not really. I've never seen him. But Aggie did tell me about him. She said he was average height, and he had dark hair, and very strong eyes—that's what she said: 'strong eyes' . . . no, wait—" She squinted, in an effort to call up her friend's words. "She said . . . he had dark, brushed-back hair that clung tightly to his head—she said he had a patrician head—and he had heavy eyebrows and . . . and riveting eyes. Yes, that was it: riveting." She thought for a moment. "He was considerate, she said . . . and she said they had a lot in common—"

"A lot in common?"

"Yes . . . things like he was Catholic, he had voted for Kennedy . . . like that. And the big thing was, most of all, he didn't try to take advantage of her."

"Oh? What do you mean, 'take advantage'?"

"Well, I mean . . . Aggie was very innocent. She was a virgin." She reddened. "That's what she said. And I believe . . . believed her. As a matter of fact, the last time I saw Aggie—I remember it was last month, the thirtieth—we thought that was going to be the night when he was going to pop the question. She was ready to spend the night with him—make love for the first time . . . the first time for her, that is.

"That's what I meant that he didn't take advantage of her. He never pressed her. He didn't rush her. They dated almost every chance they got . . . even spent a weekend or two in a resort motel—in separate rooms."

"Separate rooms?"

"That's what she said. And I believe her. I have no reason not to.

"In fact," she added, "that was one of the things that helped me identify—" She bowed her head and held a handkerchief to her nose. After a minute she continued. "That was one of the things that helped me identify Aggie. Even if I hadn't recognized her face, I would've recognized the clothes she was wearing. I helped her pick out most of them, especially the lingerie."

"And that was the last time you saw her alive . . . November 30?"

DeFalco nodded and dabbed her face with her handkerchief.

Undoubtedly, the medical examiner had determined a time of death, but Koznicki was not yet advised on that. He would learn that November 30 was well within the M.E.'s ballpark time frame.

"You said," Koznicki continued, "that they—Agnes and this Peter Arnold—dated frequently. Do you have any idea how long that had been going on?"

Her expression brightened. "I can tell you exactly when it began."

Koznicki was amazed at how quickly this case was coming together. His first homicide interrogation, and his informant—the decedent's closest friend—could testify on virtually every important question, and—most significant surprise of all—believed she knew who the killer was. Beginner's luck? He waited for DeFalco to recall the precise date Ventimiglia and Arnold had begun dating.

"It was his twenty-first birthday. I remember she said he asked her out to dinner to celebrate his becoming a man—an adult. It was . . . November seventh, I forget which year—wait a minute: If that was his twenty-first birthday, his year of birth would have to be . . . 1939, wouldn't it?"

"My arithmetic agrees with yours."

"So that's it, then," DeFalco said. "Peter Arnold was the only man she was ever serious about . . . golly, the only man she ever dated! They saw each other constantly for about a month. As far as I know, he was the last person she saw before she disappeared . . . unless . . . unless she was on her way to her date with Peter and maybe she got mugged. Was she . . . uh . . . attacked?"

"I will know that when I talk with the medical examiner, which will be immediately after I finish talking with you. But, if she did not keep her date with Arnold . . . or if she disappeared after her date, I would think it only natural that he would report that and probably join in the search for her. Unless, of course, you are correct and he killed her.

"One would think," he added, "that if she were missing, he would check with her place of employment. He did not call or get in touch with you, with anyone in this office?"

"Not with me, and I don't think with anyone else. Everyone here knows I am—" She shook her head. "I *was* Aggie's friend; they would've come to me if they'd gotten a phone call or an inquiry like that. What happens now?" she asked, half-hopefully, half-hopelessly.

"We will proceed with the investigation. Meanwhile, if you think of anything else that might be helpful, any bit of information, please get in touch with me." New on the job, he did not have a business card to give her. He wrote his name and the Homicide number on a page of his notebook, tore it out, and handed it to her.

As he was leaving, she called after him. "Officer! Officer Koz . . . Koz . . ." She read his name from the paper he'd just given her. "Koznicki. I just remembered: where they were supposed to go on their last date. She mentioned it just before she left me. It was the Pontchartrain Wine Cellars. She also said that they never went to the same restaurant twice; it was always different ones."

Koznicki entered that in his notebook.

"Thank you, Miss DeFalco. You have been very helpful. Remember, if you think of anything else, please call us."

Teary-eyed again, she nodded, as her shoulders slumped and she gave herself up to grief.

Before leaving the Wayne County Morgue, Koznicki checked with the M.E.'s office. Among the things he learned: The November 30 date was well within the parameters established for the time of death of the deceased. And there was no indication of any sexual assault; indeed, physically the dead woman had been a virgin.

There was no doubt in Koznicki's mind that Rosemarie DeFalco was an accurate witness, both as to the facts in this case and in the conclusions she had drawn.

Lieutenant Davis took charge of what was, with the information DeFalco had supplied, now a fast-paced investigation.

It was not difficult to locate Peter Arnold, *the* Peter Arnold born on November 7, 1939. Father: Samuel Arnold, white, age 22, born in Michigan, owner of a small auto parts factory, living at 30105 West Seven Mile in Redford Township; mother, Laura Jean Trucky, white, age 18, born in Michigan. Peter Arnold's birth had been in Redford Community Hospital.

It scarcely could be any other Peter Arnold.

But it was not Agnes Ventimiglia's Peter Arnold.

Peter Arnold, at six feet four, was hardly of "moderate build or average height." His hair was not dark, but blond. His eyes were undistinguished. But above all, he traveled extensively for his employer-father. He had been out of town, indeed much of the time out of state, during most of November—including November seventh and November thirtieth. And this was corroborated by a variety of business associates and customers.

The explanation was simple enough: Anybody could get anybody's vital record as long as it was filed in the county clerk's cabinets. It would be many years before that system was tightened and regulated.

Somehow, the killer had learned that Peter Arnold was about to have a twenty-first birthday. It could have been anyone. Statistics are easily available. Births are even listed in the daily newspapers, back issues of which are available at any library. The twenty-first birthday would be a logical event to celebrate, giving the killer a pretext to invite someone out to dinner.

But why?

Not why would someone want to date Agnes Ventimiglia; she may have been rather plain, but plain girls dated. Besides, from what Koznicki could tell, she had had the potential of being attractive. With a little work, and help from Rosemarie DeFalco, Agnes had become a desirable package for the occasion of her murder.

But why would a man who wanted to date her pretend to be someone else? And why would that man date her on a practically incessant basis rather than merely periodically, for nearly an entire month, only to kill her at the end of that month? And if he lied about his name in the beginning, was it because he had planned from the beginning to kill her?

Every ounce of logic would demand that there be some purpose, some goal, some reason, something to gain from this.

If it was some pathological, insane killer, why the month? He could have killed her on any one of the early dates.

If he had wanted to string the encounters out to gain her confidence so he could have sex with her, why hadn't he? According to DeFalco, Agnes was indeed ready, primed, for romance on that last date. If he wanted sex he could have had it for the asking.

But no. He didn't. He killed her in as cold-blooded a manner as possible.

The consensus of the members of Squad Three was that the killer had wanted something from Agnes Ventimiglia. There was no way of telling whether he had gotten it.

He killed her either because he got what he wanted and was done with her . . . or because he did not get what he wanted and was frustrated and furious with her.

A check of resorts in the state revealed no reservation in either the name Arnold or Ventimiglia. A further check revealed a few names of people who had checked in together in two separate rooms. But the follow-up led only to a dead end. On investigation, most of the couples registered had legitimate reasons for their stays . . . and in every one of those cases the woman involved was still very much alive. In the remaining few cases, the rooms had been paid for in cash at the time of check-in; the phone numbers and addresses given were spurious, and in any case, none of the employees even recalled any of the couples. Koznicki believed Agnes had told Rosemarie the truth. Probably Arnold had convinced her it would be wiser not to use her real name. By that time, Koznicki concluded, Agnes undoubtedly would have done anything he'd asked.

Which probably applied to whatever it was the killer had really wanted from her. Koznicki believed that the killer had gotten what he was after, then killed her.

They checked for insurance, but the only policy they found was one that had been taken out years before, naming her parents as beneficiary. They checked her bank accounts, but there were no out-of-the ordinary withdrawals. She had had no jewelry outside of the usual—a string of simulated pearls, a few pins and bracelets, a couple of gold-filled necklaces, some earrings—all clip-on, her ears were not pierced—a high school ring, a Mexican silver ring, two watches, one the Timex that she wore daily to work, the other a Longines that was on her wrist when she was pulled from the water.

To the best of Rosemarie's knowledge—and her grieving parents confirmed this—Agnes Ventimiglia had possessed nothing worth killing her for.

They checked with Joe Beyer, proprietor and customary maître d' of the Pontchartrain Wine Cellars. Joe did not keep a record of reservations running weeks back. Nor did he or any of his staff recognize the photo of Agnes Ventimiglia, nor the description of Peter Arnold.

And, according to the declaration of Agnes herself, they never went to the same restaurant twice. So the Wine Cellars was not the only restaurant checked, but the investigators came up empty on all of them.

However, that said something to Koznicki. Of all the restaurateurs in the Detroit area, no one took better care of his patrons, paid more attention to them and remembered them better than Joe Beyer. It was natural for the killer to save the Wine Cellars—one of the best—for last. But he would not chance going there more than once with the likelihood that Joe Beyer would remember him and his date. And for the killer to know that, he had to know Detroit and its restaurant scene intimately. Or so ran Koznicki's line of reasoning; probably the killer was a Detroiter, possibly a native Detroiter.

It wasn't much. But they didn't have much to go on.

This killer was a professional in every sense of the word. He was a man of mystery. He entered from nowhere. He used someone else's identity. He was known to one person and one person alone. And he killed her. Before that, he took her out on dates. But no one could remember seeing them. His victim had one close friend, and only one. Yet, even though Agnes confided in her friend Rosemarie, DeFalco had only the vaguest notion of what this man looked like. Finally, he simply disappeared. No record of any kind. No fingerprints. No footprints, for that matter.

In an investigation such as this, the more time that elapses the less likely the case is to be solved.

The critical time in this case had not yet passed, but leads were growing thin. The police were perilously close to an "open murder" charge, at which point they would move on. Although Davis assured Koznicki that no murder case is ever closed. As long as anyone maintains an interest in it, it lives.

AGNES VENTIMIGLIA was to be buried tomorrow. Koznicki decided he would attend the funeral. One never knew; it was always possible a suspicious person might attend, of average height and weight, with dark, brushed-back hair clinging tightly to a patrician head, with heavy eyebrows shadowing riveting eyes.

One never knew.

CHAPTER

21

ST. URSULA'S PARISH was tucked away in a heavily compact neighborhood on Detroit's near east side. Within its boundaries was a cemetery and Detroit City Airport, and the aroma of the potato chip plant across Gratiot wafted over its streets and sidewalks. Its population was approximately 40 percent Italian, 40 percent Polish, and 20 percent black. Most of the Italians and Polish were Catholic; most of the blacks weren't.

At one time the neighborhood had been nearly 100 percent Italian. It had been known as—and was still called by some—Cacalupo, an ambiguous Italian pun that Father Robert Koesler never bothered resolving.

This was Father Robert Koesler's third parochial assignment in five years—considerable shifting about in a day when assistant pastors usually lasted five years per parish.

This would be his second Christmas at St. Ursula's, an occasion that brought pastor Robert Pompilio's bosom buddy, Father Joe Farmer, to the parish to help out with seasonal confessions and Masses.

The three priests were at dinner. As usual, Koesler felt odd man out. He was quite tall, they were quite short. The two older men had been close friends for many years; Koesler had known Father Pompilio only a little more than a year and had been in Father Farmer's company only occasionally during this time. Koesler, with a still-youthful appetite, ate rapidly; his companions ate at a leisurely pace. Koesler was eating steak; the other two were eating smelt.

Pompilio had caught the smelt in a fast-running Canadian stream. When he caught the fish, he was garbed in a present from Joe Farmer— a sleeping bag that, when properly folded, became a water-resistant ski suit. And, when properly unfolded, turned back into a sleeping bag.

The two buddies were inveterate gadgeteers who were constantly giving each other odd contrivances. Half the fun was trying to figure out what if any purpose such contraptions served.

Father Koesler reflected that the separate but unequal dinner they were eating was not nearly as bad as it might be. Early on, it had been established that he did not care for smelt. He could eat the fish—he could eat most anything—but smelt was far from his favorite dish.

There must have been thousands of the little devils in the rectory's freezer. Pompilio had the housekeeper prepare masses and masses of smelt for him; out of consideration for his young assistant's taste, steak was served for Koesler.

That, in those days when it was a seller's market, was an extremely thoughtful gesture on the part of the pastor—far, far better than the treatment accorded one of Koesler's classmates, whose pastor regularly ate steak while his assistant was served hot dogs.

Despite the preparatory seminary's insistence on submissiveness to one's pastor, mortal flesh can absorb only so much harassment no matter how inadvertent it might be. So, one day, the assistant stated he would no longer tolerate such manifest second class treatment. The pastor, in his own way, agreed: Henceforth, the pastor dined on his steak while the assistant continued to be fed hot dogs—but they ate at different times.

Such was the state of the Church in those days.

Koesler felt fortunate indeed.

Father Pompilio cut a tiny portion off the minuscule fish. He put the knife aside, stabbed the small bite, squeezed a bit of lemon juice on it, dabbed it in the tartar sauce, put it in his mouth, and laid the fork on his plate while he proceeded to chew the morsel. This routine would be observed, in agonizing repetition, for the length of the meal.

Koesler, nearly done with his supper, thought he might go mad.

"Say," Pompilio said, "I heard a good one today. Seasonal too."

Farmer grinned. "Let's have it."

"Seems that"—some people are described as having an ear-to-ear grin; Pompilio had it almost literally—"a Dominican and a Jesuit priest died and went to heaven—"

"This has got to be fiction," Farmer interrupted. "They don't let those guys into heaven now, do they?"

"C'mon, Joe, let me finish." Pompilio cut an infinitesimal piece of smelt. "Anyway, St. Peter asked them what, in all of history, they wanted to see. They talked it over and finally agreed that they wanted to see the original Christmas, the way it really was.

"Well, sir, they got whisked off and there they were, right there at the original, authentic Christmas—Mary and Joseph and the baby and the shepherds and the animals.

William X. Kienzle

"Well, sir, the two priests fell down on their knees in adoration. And that's where they stayed for a good long time." He laid the lemon slice down and dipped the morsel in the tartar sauce.

Koesler, having finished both steak and potatoes, lit a cigarette.

"Finally," Pompilio said, "the Jesuit got up and went over to St. Joseph, and tugged at his sleeve. 'I beg your pardon,' he says, 'but have you given any thought to the child's education?'"

Koesler chuckled. Farmer laughed generously. Pompilio chewed on the current morsel with great and evident satisfaction.

"That's pretty good, Pomps," Farmer said. "It reminds me of another Christmas one."

"Yeah, Joe, yeah." Pompilio, knife and fork both resting on his plate, was not even sawing off another bite of fish.

Koesler decided he would try not to count the mounting number of cigarette butts in the ashtray. It was too discouraging, what with his trying to cut back. Since the housekeeper apparently was not going to empty the ashtray until it overflowed, Koesler decided to take the drastic step of emptying it himself.

"The way I heard it . . ." Farmer began to chuckle.

Koesler decided to concentrate on Farmer's story. Toward the end of every joke he told, he had the tendency to break himself up. In a way, it enhanced the humor. It also made it nearly impossible to make much sense of the punch line.

"The way I heard it," Farmer repeated, "the Holy Family was in the stable with the animals and the shepherds. And Joseph was standing there with his brow all furrowed. Mary asked, 'What's wrong, Joseph?'

"And Joseph said, 'I was just thinking. I was trying to think of a name for the baby.' Just then, the three wise men arrived. Well, the last of the three, Melchior, was very tall, and when he entered the stable, he banged his head on the low door frame. He rubbed his head and mumbled, 'Jesus!' And St. Joseph said . . ." Farmer began to laugh so hard Koesler feared he might be choking on a morsel of food. But he was just convulsed with his own punch line.

"And St. Joseph said, 'That's it!'" he finally concluded, between gasps of laughter.

"What? What did he say, Joe? What did he say?"

"'That's it!' 'That's it!'"

Even Koesler thought it funny . . . sort of blasphemy in reverse.

The laughter subsided. Farmer finished eating. Pompilio cut off another slice of the microscopic fish. Koesler stubbed out his smoldering cigarette and wondered if Pompilio had discovered the secret of multiplying fishes. "By the way," Koesler said, "while we're all over the subject of Christmas, have you seen what the choir is getting up for the carols before Midnight Mass?"

"No, I haven't caught that. What's going on?" Pompilio dipped the fish fragment in the tartar sauce, put it carefully in his mouth, placed the knife and fork on his plate, and recommenced his contented chewing.

Farmer spoke from an abundance of unassimilated experience. "What could be different about that? You heard a few Christmas carols, you heard 'em all."

"It's not the carols," Koesler said, "it's the staging."

"Staging?" Pompilio repeated.

"The way the organist has it set up," Koesler said, "he has spotlights all over the church, and he's getting them programmed to light up what he thinks is an appropriate picture or statue to go along with each carol."

"I'm not sure . . ." Pompilio fumbled. "The 'appropriate statue'?"

"For instance," Koesler explained, "when the choir sings 'Away in a Manger,' the spotlight illuminates the manger scene that's mounted on the Communion railing."

"That sounds pretty good to me." Pompilio sipped from his glass of white wine.

"Yeah, it does," Koesler seemed to agree, "but we don't always have an appropriate painting or statue."

However, the interior of St. Ursula's church came close to having a representation of nearly every saint imaginable. It was an iconoclast's dream come true.

Apparently with this in mind, Pompilio asked, "Who don't we have?"

"Well, for one, the Archangel Gabriel. When the choir sings the 'Ave Maria,' the organist wants to shine the spot on Gabriel—who announced to Mary she's going to be the mother of Jesus. After all, half the words of the 'Ave Maria' are Gabriel's."

"So we don't have Gabriel," Pompilio said. "Who does he shine the light on?"

"Michael," Koesler answered. "He's the only archangel we've got."

Farmer, trading on his former statement, said, "You seen one archangel, you seen 'em all."

"Not quite," Koesler responded. "While the choir sings the words of the gentle angel who humbly asks Mary if she will consent to be the Mother of God, the spotlight reveals an archangel in battle gear, with his foot crushing the serpent-devil and his arm raised to strike the serpent with a huge sword."

Neither Pompilio nor Farmer seemed to find this tableau either humorous or ridiculous. "You seen one archangel, you seen 'em all," Farmer repeated.

"They'll never notice," Pompilio promised.

Koesler did not wish the congregation's Christmas piety to be punctured. But he did hope they *would* notice.

Later, as Christmas Midnight Mass neared, Koesler would, somewhat sadly, come to agree with both Farmer and Pompilio.

The pastor gave every indication that he had finished dinner. There were no more little smelt to be found anywhere. Until he saw it with his own eyes, Koesler had given serious consideration to the possibility that the fish really weren't dead: that they were propagating faster than rabbits and that forever—morning, noon, and night—there would be smelt in the serving dish and Pomps would be eating them into eternity.

Pompilio rang the little silver bell. Sophie entered, cleared away the dishes, returned with coffee and cookies, glanced at the overflowing ashtray, and left the room.

Koesler lit another cigarette. What would coffee be without a cigarette?

"Would you like me to take that funeral tomorrow morning?" Farmer asked.

"No!" Pompilio said emphatically. Then, more softly, "No."

Koesler smiled inwardly. There was some chemistry going on here. His pastor was not the most secure person Koesler had ever known. Pompilio had difficulty believing that everyone, including himself, recognized that he was, indeed, the pastor of this place.

There would be a funeral at St. Ursula's tomorrow morning. This funeral was out of the ordinary in that the deceased was a murder victim. Agnes Ventimiglia was to be buried from St. Ursula's because her parents were parishioners, at least nominally.

Everyone who knew Pompilio—as Farmer certainly did—knew that his self-confidence was flimsy. An occasion such as tomorrow's funeral, which undoubtedly would be turned into a media event, was a rare and signal moment to make one thing perfectly clear: that he, Father Robert Pompilio, was definitely in charge.

Farmer must have been joking, thought Koesler, in offering to take the funeral. The two old buddies did that sort of thing between themselves with some frequency, Farmer more so than Pompilio.

"She was a graduate of our school, wasn't she?" Koesler asked.

"Yes . . ." Pompilio sighed. "She graduated before my time—my time as pastor, that is."

Pompilio had been an assistant at St. Ursula's years earlier under a most severe and uncompromising pastor. That might have been part of his problem—trading the image of subservient assistant for the role of pastor.

"What do you think happened to her?" Pompilio threw out the question for general comment. "Who do you think did this to her?"

Joe Farmer dunked his cookie in his coffee. Koesler concentrated on the smoke curling from his cigarette. He hated to watch dunkers. The process was so messy.

To date, the police had released only the information that the body of a young white woman had been found in the Detroit River; that she hadn't drowned, she'd been bludgeoned to death; that she'd been killed on or about November 30; and that she'd been identified as Agnes Ventimiglia.

In a later item, not related to the investigation, the announcement of her funeral arrangements appeared in the paper.

It was definitely a media event.

Local news media—TV, radio, and the press—had been replete with statements and photos of the deceased's friends, co-workers, neighbors, and, last but by no means least, her pastor.

The police had not mentioned the name Peter Arnold because the real Peter Arnold had amply proved that he'd had no knowledge of Agnes, let alone of the crime.

Farmer leaned forward, elbows on the table, and in a savant-soaked tone, said, "Personally, I think it was a boyfriend. Happens all the time nowadays. It's the result of all this steady dating. Not good old-fashioned courtship like there used to be, with parental supervision and all. You hear confessions from young people that age and what are they doing? Necking, petting, fornication—what do they call it?—*making out*. Sin, mortal sin! And what do they care? One confession and it's all wiped away; they can start all over again. The Ventimiglia girl and her boyfriend were probably making out and he got carried away and—"

"I think," Koesler interrupted, "the paper said there was no evidence of sexual intercourse."

"All the more," Farmer insisted. "They probably went all the way any number of times. This time she said no. Probably got some grace and virtue from a confession and decided to have a chaste courtship or nothing. He got mad and killed her . . . whaddyou think, Pomps?"

Pompilio, sucking bits of fish or bone from between his teeth, did not immediately reply. Then, as if suddenly aware that the ball was in his court, he said, "I couldn't disagree with you, Joe. But I think it goes back further than that. It's the home."

"There you have it," Farmer agreed.

"Particularly the father," Pompilio continued, running with the ball. "The Ventimiglia case is a good example. If it hadn't been for the mother, the girl would never have gotten a parochial education. As it was, she had only half a Catholic upbringing. Her mother did the best she could. And God knows the sisters gave her good Christian teaching in school. That's probably what made her say no to another mortal sin . . . like you said, Joe."

"Damn right!" Farmer agreed with his own statement.

"But what can you do," Pompilio pontificated, "when the father's a pagan? Won't go to church. Won't make his Easter duty. What kind of example is that? And so, consequently, therefore"—a habitual phrase with Pompilio—"there is no unity in the home. The mother going God's way while the father has no virtuous example to give."

"What a hypocrite!" Farmer exclaimed. "Have you seen him on television? He makes out like he's St. Francis of Assisi. And like he's got nothing left to live for now that his darling daughter is gone. Makes out like she's St. Maria Goretti who died rather than let someone have his way with her. Whereas she probably was steady-dating. And she had been taught in school how evil that was. Now she knows what we were trying to warn her about. Too late. Too late," he ended in a melancholy tone.

"What do you think, Bob?" Father Pompilio did not want to suggest that he and his friend considered Koesler too young and inexperienced to contribute to this bull session. Which, in fact, they did.

"I don't have the slightest idea, really," Koesler confessed. "I've just been following the story in the papers. They've been giving it a lot of coverage."

"You can't believe what they print in the papers," Farmer said.

"Especially the Detroit papers. They're anti-Catholic. Always were and always will be."

"Tell you the truth," Koesler replied, "I haven't noticed that."

"Why, my God, man!" Father Farmer quickly became testy. "Just read the letters to the editor they publish! They must run seven or eight to one against the Church."

"I've never counted them." Koesler now thought he might just do that in case Farmer ever made the charge again. "But I think Nelson Kane, Ed Breslin, and Herb Boldt are pretty darn good police reporters. Besides, all three of them are Catholic."

"That doesn't matter as long as they work for the godless *News* or *Free Press,*" Farmer stated.

"Still . . ." Koesler didn't believe a word of it. "I think they do a good job, especially on this story. And if you follow them closely, they seem to agree in thinking this had something to do with the girl's job. And that would have to have something to do with the records kept by the county clerk."

Farmer snorted. "A guy wants a copy of his wedding certificate and the Ventimiglia girl can't find it—so he kills her?"

"No, no, of course not." Why had he bothered getting into this discussion, Koesler wondered. He should have bailed out when Pompilio asked for an opinion. But he was in it now; he'd just have to get out as quickly as possible. "It's just that her friend—who is it?—something DeFalco, I think, said that Agnes and whoever the killer is seem to have met at the clerk's office. If that's true—and each of these three reporters thinks it is—then they only knew each other for about a month."

"I know that," Farmer said. "I read the papers too, you know."

"Good," Koesler said. "I was beginning to wonder."

The remark did not sit well with Farmer. "What are you, a wise-ass?"

"Now, now . . ." Pompilio preferred a smooth digestion to a quarrel after dinner. "We're just airing this out. No need to argue."

"It's not an argument," Farmer insisted. "I just wanted to point out to our young man here that when a couple goes out on dates practically every evening and even on weekends—as it said in your precious papers that Ventimiglia and the killer did—that can constitute steady dating, as all legitimate Catholic theologians teach. So we go back to what I said in the first place: It was a lovers' quarrel, it got out of hand, and he killed her. Any couple who see each other that often should be formally engaged. And they have to take precautions to avoid the near occasion of sin!"

Pompilio pushed his chair back from the table, a clear sign that the meal, as well as the after-dinner conversation—which tonight had gotten somewhat out of hand—was finished.

"I'm sure we all have things we've got to do this evening. And so, consequently, therefore, we'd best get busy. I'm sure we can all agree we must pray for the poor young woman."

"And," Koesler added, "I suppose for her killer, too."

Sensing Farmer was about to object to this turn of another cheek, Pompilio put a cap on all further comment by leading the procession out of the dining room and saying, over his shoulder, "Yes, we should be praying for everyone."

ABOUT AN INCH of snow had fallen overnight. It was the first measurable snow of the season. Coming so near to Christmas, it was welcomed by most Michiganians. Soon the local citizens would tire of it.

The narrow streets of Culver and Georgia and most neighboring streets were clogged with cars. Parking here, at the best of times, usually presented problems. But this would be one of the most well-attended funerals in recent memory.

On top of that, the intrusive TV vans and their crews had movement around the church area pretty well bollixed up.

It was 10:00 A.M.

Father Koesler stood at a school window absently watching the people—some of Agnes's friends, parishioners, and outside curiosity seekers attracted to media events—cautiously making their way over the slippery sidewalks en route to the church.

Koesler was administering a written test to the seniors to whom he taught a class in Church history. He was totally unqualified to teach that or just about any other academic course. A lot of this sort of thing went on, as priests discovered that *ex officio* they were expected to handle many things for which they had not been trained.

He could not help feeling the contrast in this morning's parish events.

All through the school, holiday and holy day decorations were hung from and plastered to walls and ceilings.

Just at this moment the seniors were not bubbling. But they would be as soon as they were finished with their test. Then only a few more days would separate them from vacation and the lovely feast of Christmas.

In the school, as well as around the world, people were celebrating new life, fresh hope, and the love of God.

In the church this morning, people were marking death. The saddest of all deaths: that of a young person who should have looked forward to many, many more years of life.

Another sad feature was the dearth of genuine mourners. A few of Agnes's co-workers were moved, but mostly just pro forma. None of them, with the sole exception of Rosemarie DeFalco, had been a real friend. Their reasons for mourning ranged from a sort of dutiful sadness to the intrusion of death upon their young lives. They realized that Agnes had died long before her time. It reminded them that, youthful though they were, inevitably death waited for them too.

And so, in this complex of buildings at the corner of Georgia and Culver, life and death were being noted.

Inside the church, Father Pompilio officiated at the Ventimiglia funeral, ably assisted by Father Joseph Farmer.

Television cameras had recorded the bearing of the casket to the church, and the priests' welcome of it. The TV crews then retreated to their vans, two of them to return to their stations; the third would wait to film the departure formalities. Radio reporters narrated some of the rite and recorded some of the ceremony's sounds.

Sounds such as the small pipe organ and the voice of the children's choir. Choir members had been excused from classes for this very important ceremony.

Few in the choir or in the church understood the Latin words, but the genius of plainchant conveyed the somber plea for peace and rest. Father Pompilio's strong tenor added conviction to the finality of these services.

Beyond these, the most wrenching sound was the intermittent sobbing of the dead girl's mother.

All this was noted by Patrolman Walter Koznicki, who had surveyed the crowd at the funeral home as Agnes Ventimiglia's casket was closed for the final time.

After that, Koznicki had hurried to the church, where he studied everyone who entered. There was no doubt about it, the man he was looking for, the man Rosemarie DeFalco had described from Agnes's description, that man was not present. He had not come to view the finale of his handiwork.

The leads were running thin. In a few more days, Homicide would shelve the investigation of the death of Agnes Ventimiglia. It would be filed under "open murder."

Koznicki could not remember another incident in his life that had left him more frustrated and disappointed. This, his first homicide investigation, had begun so promisingly. It had taken almost no time to identify the victim's remains. Rosemarie DeFalco had been so cooperative and helpful. They had gotten rid of the red herring of Peter Arnold's name quickly. They had a bit—albeit just a fragment—of a general description of the killer. They had the name of the restaurant where Agnes and her murderer had had her final meal.

The result: nothing. One dead end after another.

The killer was clever, no doubt a professional. And yet, Koznicki sensed that someday, somehow he would catch up with this murderer. Koznicki believed in divine Providence.

Some sort of providence was at work here far beyond his ken. He had come within a hair of meeting Father Robert Koesler. Yet, some years down the line the two would meet when a nun would be murdered in this very parish.

Koznicki and Koesler were destined to become close friends. One of their meetings would relate to the murder of Agnes Ventimiglia. But that would be many years in the future.

1993

CHAPTER

22

THE SILENCE was eerie.

It was as if they were staring at a larger-than-life television screen with the sound turned off.

Lights in office buildings were winking out. Lights in residences were going on. The quaint lights atop the Belle Isle bridge were flickering. Auto traffic was letting up.

It had taken Charles Nash almost an hour to tell his tale. His son and Father Deutsch had forgotten the discomfort of their straight-back chairs; both sat immobile, mouths ajar.

If anyone had made a sound, or uttered a word, it would have cracked like a thunderclap.

Finally, in the face of their silence, Nash said slowly, in a low voice, "Well, that's the way it was." Then he added, more loudly, almost defiantly, "And that's the way it is."

Still no one moved or added any words.

Finally, Father Deutsch, as if half in and out of a nightmare, spoke, barely above a whisper. "You had a young woman killed?"

Nash tipped his head toward the priest. "Of course not! I knew enough not to get involved with that. At least not for such a piddling reason. If there was a mistake made, it was in not spelling out precisely how far Chardon should have gone. Changing the record would have been enough. But . . ." Nash paused a few seconds. "It doesn't matter. Chardon proved himself a very careful professional. His tracks were well covered. The police investigation went nowhere. They threw in the towel. And, as it turned out, it was a good move. It meant there was no one in the clerk's office who knew what happened."

"I can't believe it!" Deutsch said. "You actually approve of what that murderer did?"

Nash appeared to shrug, although his shoulders moved so imperceptibly it was difficult to tell. One thing was clear: He wasn't going to respond to the priest's question.

Ted leaned forward so that his head was only inches from his father's. "Were you . . . were you the father? Mary Lou's father?"

"Who can say?" Nash's response was nonchalant. "Back then they didn't have all these fancy scientific ways of proving paternity. Most of the time it came down to whether the kid looked like you.

"When it happened—when Maureen told me she was pregnant, I denied it flat-out. Maybe I even believed I wasn't the kid's old man. Maybe I talked myself into believing I wasn't. After all, the last thing I needed was a second household. I already had your mother and you. It was one thing getting away from you and your mother to shack up with Maureen in a bunch of hotels, motels, and apartments. It would really have been tough if she'd started carting a baby around."

He gestured violently with both hands. "It was out of the question! Simply out of the question! And it was all her fault. All that time, I thought she was on the pill. She was supposed to be protecting herself. But, no! It 'made her sick'!" He mimicked a cloying tone.

"If she had told me . . . if only she had told me, I would have done something."

" 'Done something'? What? What would you have done?" Part of Ted was inwardly smirking at the thought of his father's being taken in by Mary Lou's mother.

"I dunno," Charles mumbled. "Something. Used a jelly, a condom . . . something. We didn't have much protection that was dependable then like what they've got now." He shrugged, this time perceptibly. "Probably I'd have made my farewell speech right then, as soon as she said she was going to quit the pill. I could've bailed out and there wouldn't have been any kid to deal with. Anyway, the instant Maureen gave me the glad news, I knew . . . I saw my life going down shit's creek without a paddle.

"So I denied it could have been mine. The fact was, Maureen was gonna have a baby and it wasn't gonna be any virgin birth. Somebody had to be the father. Why did it have to be me?"

Nash was becoming overly agitated. He took a pill bottle out of his sweater pocket, extracted a pill, put it in his mouth, and waited while it dissolved.

"But it more than likely was me," Nash said matter-of-factly. "Who'm I trying to kid? What kinda girl was Maureen, anyway? She was a good Catholic girl with a—my God!—a goddam priest for a cousin! She was stretching things as it was by sleeping with me. The only reason she did is because she thought we'd get married. If push came to shove, I couldn't imagine her sleeping with anybody else. So . . ." Charles spread his hands, palms up. "Probably the kid is as much mine as you are, Teddy. The thing is, she would have one hell of a time proving it."

"Proving it?" Ted's voice was sharp. "What do you mean?"

"Chardon!" Nash said. "Chardon! He got the girl to change the birth record. It lists Mary Lou's mother as Maureen Monahan, but the father"—he gestured to himself—"is unknown. And this is supposed to be information the mother supplied. The way it looks on that record is that the mother herself doesn't know who fathered her kid. Or, that she simply won't tell. Gonna be a little tough for her to claim I'm the one after all these years. She sure ain't gonna prove much from that record."

"But Maureen is Catholic," Father Deutsch said. "Wouldn't she have had the child baptized? Did she? Did you have that record tampered with too? I know a baptismal record doesn't carry the same impact as a birth certificate. But it surely has to be considered, especially if Maureen were to claim the discrepancy between the two records was the result of someone's tampering with the clerk's record. If the authorities were inclined to believe her claim, the baptismal record would gain importance. You'd be listed as the father in the baptismal record—just like you were in the original birth record."

Nash almost smiled. "Way ahead of you on that one, Deacon. Yeah, she had the kid baptized. Took me a while to find out where. There's a little church used to be near the hospital, Santa Lucia, Italian parish. See, she might not have got the kid baptized at all. Or, if she did, it could have been anywhere—hell, there's more than three hundred parishes in this diocese alone. Yeah, it took my people years to find the place."

Nash began wheezing faintly. All this talking was draining him. But he was determined to get everything out in the open for these two now. "Maybe you remember—nah, you wouldn't've paid any attention to it, Teddy. Maybe you remember, Deac, along about 1970, there was a fire in the priest's house at Santa Lucia . . . eh?"

"I don't think . . ." Deutsch hesitated. "Wait . . . yes, I think I do. It wasn't much of a fire. Didn't touch the church, just the rectory. Even so, they put it out before it destroyed the building. I think they blamed the blaze on smoking. The old pastor there—Father Gombino—I knew him slightly—he smoked like a chimney. The way I remember it, the fire started in the pastor's study where the . . . the . . . uh . . ."

". . . records were kept," Nash supplied.

"You were able to have the records destroyed without burning down the whole place?" Deutsch seemed almost in awe of the feat.

"Chardon again?" Ted asked.

Nash nodded. "Shows you he could do the job just the way you wanted it. Doesn't it? Later on, they closed the place down. All the Italians moved out and no one moved in to take their place. There's nothin' there anymore. Just flat ground, a few bricks."

"Amazing!" Father Deutsch was deeply impressed.

There was a pause.

"Well, Teddy," Nash said finally, "whaddya think?"

Ted looked up. "You mean about finding out that I have a sister—a half sister?"

Nash nodded.

"Frankly, Dad, I wouldn't have been surprised to learn that I have brothers and sisters all over the world. But *Mary Lou*? I've never met her. Oh, Brenda has told me about her. But not much. I was never particularly interested. But that she's my sister! That's going to take a lot of rethinking."

Nash grew very serious. "The way it worked out, she might just as well be Brenda's sister. That's the way they grew up."

"But they're not sisters! They're not related in any way!"

"History's repeating itself, son."

"What?"

"I had a family when I was having an affair with Maureen Monahan. And now you've got a family while you're having an affair with someone who practically grew up in the same Monahan house. Don't you see that?"

"No! And you're not seeing it straight either. What ended your relationship with Maureen was when she got pregnant. And she got pregnant because she didn't keep your bargain to protect herself from that. With the kind of marriage I've got, it doesn't make a damn difference whether or not I've got a relationship on the side. You had Mother to deal with. She wouldn't have stood for your having a girl on the side—not for a minute.

"So, okay, your life would have been too complicated to handle when Maureen had Mary Lou. But the difference is, just to make sure our life together stays completely uncomplicated, Brenda had herself sterilized."

From Nash's reaction, it was clear that this was one—perhaps the only—facet of Ted's life that had remained hidden from the old man's information network.

"What'd she do?" Nash asked. "A hysterectomy?"

"She had her tubes tied."

"She did that for you?"

"Does it make a difference?"

From his change in attitude, obviously it made a significant difference to Nash. It was completely foreign to his experience that any woman would voluntarily make such a drastic sacrifice for any man. He was profoundly impressed.

"On top of that"—Ted pressed his advantage—"I didn't ask her to do that. Hell, I didn't care if we had a dozen! I can afford as many kids as God sends. And as far as Brenda's concerned, I could hire as many nannies as needed to take care of the brats. She just didn't want to muddle things up. She insisted on it!"

It was rare, very rare, but Nash was taken aback. Ordinarily, he never asked a question whose answer he did not already know. Similarly, it was not his wont to wander into an area where he was not familiar with the topography. Brenda had flabbergasted him. It seemed she might actually love his son.

To Nash, it didn't matter how many wives or mistresses a man had. If a man actually found a woman who would love unconditionally, such a man was fantastically lucky. In all his life, Nash had never encountered such a person.

"Okay, I was wrong. It happens. Maybe you shouldn't get rid of her after all. Maybe she can be a help."

"Help?" Ted asked. "Help in what?"

Nash was growing noticeably weaker. He seemed to be calling on some inner strength to continue. "Help in the matter—the reason I called you. I told you, I got a message from Maureen."

"How?" Ted asked. "How did it come? The phone?"

"Registered mail. It was short and to the point." Nash pulled a paper from a drawer beneath the wheelchair seat and handed it to Ted.

" 'Now is the time for you to pay your dues,' " Ted read.

"And it's signed, 'Maureen Monahan.' " Nash snorted. "As if there were more than one Maureen who would send me a note like that."

Ted returned the note. "What's it mean?"

"It means she's ready to drop the other shoe."

"Huh?"

"When I dumped her," Nash said, "and after she had Mary Lou, I kept waiting for the lawsuit. I thought sure she would demand child support. Hell, I didn't give a damn about the money; my only worry was how to keep it quiet. It wouldn't have been good for business to have to juggle a paternity suit at that time in my life. Your mother wouldn't have gotten a kick out of it either," he added.

"Matter of fact, I wouldn't have minded kicking in child support without any court order. But I didn't want to give Maureen the idea that I was changing my mind about ending our affair. And I wasn't real anxious to make the first move either.

"The way it turned out, she surprised me: She didn't ask for a penny. And she didn't have any money; hell, she was so poor she couldn't even hold on to Mary Lou. She had to farm the kid out to a series of foster homes. That took a lot of guts—"

"Do you mean you actually sat by and did nothing to help that poor woman?" Father Deutsch interrupted. "Even though she didn't have enough to keep her child—*your* child?"

"I'll get to you in a few minutes, Deacon." Nash did not even look at the priest. "As I was saying, I thought that took a lot of guts. But I knew she was mad as hell at me. I had to wonder, though, when there wasn't any paternity suit.

"The first shoe dropped when she had the kid and didn't do a damn thing to get me involved. She had to have something else in mind for me—"

"Didn't you think it possible that she could have forgiven you in the spirit of Christian charity?" Father Deutsch interrupted again.

"You don't know Maureen. And you don't know how goddam mad she was. Besides," Nash almost growled, "I said I'd get to you in a minute.

"The thing is, I've been living with this sword over my neck for the past thirty years, just waiting for it to fall. But that's okay; I can take it. It's just that it looks like it's time . . . at least as far as Maureen's concerned."

Ted shifted forward as if to say something, but his father waved him away.

"I can take it," Nash repeated. "I don't want you to get the wrong idea. I've been waiting for this to happen and I've been planning a bunch of counterattacks. Only thing is . . . I don't have any idea how long I'm gonna last. It's getting harder every day—just to go on living.

William X. Kienzle

"And that's why I called you in as soon as I got her message. Whatever she does, I want you to be ready for it just in case I'm not here."

"Dad . . . I . . ."

Again Charles waved his son off. "No pious shit, Ted. Nobody lives forever. And I'm not even gonna come close. So, pay attention . . ."

CHAPTER

23

WITH ALARMING debility, Nash dropped a trembling finger to the button on the wheelchair's arm. Immediately the young man in white entered the room. He went first to a tank alongside the hospital bed and picked up a coil of plastic tubing that unwound in his wake as he came over to the wheelchair, where he inserted a two-pronged device into Nash's nostrils, bringing the instant relief of oxygen.

It was undoubtedly a routine that had been repeated many times, for it was accomplished smoothly and flawlessly.

After making sure Nash was breathing with some ease, the young man left the room. Not a word had passed between them.

"Look, Dad," Ted said, "this is too much for you. We can come back anytime you want us. Tomorrow—"

"No!" Nash's voice had regained its strength. "No." He relaxed a bit. "It's the old joke about the guy who doesn't buy green bananas. I don't know if I've got a tomorrow. We do it now."

"Whatever you say."

"Now, as I was saying, I expected her to hit me hard with a paternity suit. When she didn't I was sure she had something else in mind. The longer she held off, the more sure I was about what she was after." Nash paused and looked intently at his son.

"Which is . . . ?"

"Can't you guess?"

"You don't mean—"

"I sure as hell do!"

"What?!" asked a frustrated Deutsch.

"Nash Enterprises!" said Ted with fervor.

"At least half the company," Nash confirmed.

"She can't get away with that!" Ted blurted. But no one endorsed that view. "Can she?" Ted added feebly.

"That's it!" Nash said. "We got to be ready to stop her. It's not a bad plan," he affirmed. "If you'd listened to Brenda better, you'd have a better idea of the whole scheme. Because it's got as much to do with Mary Lou as her mother.

"See, Mary Lou has been a loser just about all her life. Okay, so she had a couple of strikes on her right off the bat. But she had damn good genes going for her. The only way I can explain it is that Maureen brought her up to become a lemon. And why, I ask myself? So that Maureen can manipulate the kid to do whatever Momma wants her to.

"You should see Mary Lou's work record! She's worked at more places than I've done business with. She's not gaining experience; she just can't hold a job. *That's* what's waiting in the wings to take over half of Nash Enterprises. Half of what I built and handed over to you, Ted."

"But why?" Ted was nearing anguish. "In God's name, why? Does Maureen want to ruin the company? Just out of spite against you? She's not even hitting at *you* anymore. You're retired. It's me she's going to destroy! Why? *Why?*"

"Think, Ted," Nash admonished. "Maureen didn't wait until I died. Although she easily could have. She's waited this long; what's another few months? A few weeks? A few days? Whatever.

"No, she waits until now. I'm still alive, but not by much. Maybe she thinks the pressure will push me over the edge. Maybe she wants to hit us while I would take up the challenge, but, she figures, I wouldn't be able to stand up to her now when I'm a shadow of my former self.

"But it doesn't matter. We're not gonna waste our time trying to second-guess Maureen. The hell with her! I'm gonna give you our battle plans. We'll be ready for her whether I'm here to lead the fight or not. There isn't any way in hell that Maureen Monahan's gonna take half our company so she can run it through that mannequin daughter of hers."

"So that's it!" Ted exclaimed. "Maureen wants to get fifty percent of our company for her idiot daughter so Momma can run it. Well, fat chance!"

"Damn right!" Nash removed a medium-sized portfolio from the drawer and handed it to Ted, who immediately opened it and started riffling through the papers.

"Those papers are for your eyes only," Nash said. "Not even the deacon here. The first thing we gotta take care of is the damn DNA test. That's one they didn't have when Mary Lou was born. They say it's pretty accurate."

"More than 'pretty accurate,' I'm afraid," Ted said. "If a test of cells or blood from you and Mary Lou proved compatibility, any court would rule in favor of your paternity. It happened to Mayor Cobb a few years back."

"I know; I know all that." Nash gestured toward the papers Ted was holding. "You got a list there of labs and technicians that either we own or are into us plenty deep and owe us some big favors. And just in case there might be a problem there . . . remember, just now, you said 'any court' would rule against us? Well, there's a list in that packet of judges who you can depend on to look the other way.

"If push comes to shove, Teddy, remember what's at stake. Not just the billions our company is worth, but everything we put into it. God, my whole life is in this company! So, for chrissakes, don't pinch pennies. Whatever we got is worth this fight."

Ted nodded firm agreement.

"One final thing, and one final list. There's names and contacts of some people who have proven themselves, people we've used in the past. With each name there's a description of the guy's specialty. They don't come cheap, but they're worth every cent."

Ted studied the list, then, suddenly looked up. "Chardon!"

"Yeah, he's still with us and still good enough to stay on the list. Remember the fire in the priest's house—gutted the place where they kept the records? Just make sure you explain exactly what you want done. He's gotta be the most dependable guy on the list. Which is not to take anything away from any of 'em. They're all good. And you got their specialties right there.

"Now"—Nash adjusted the oxygen tube and inhaled deeply— "you should have everything you need. You know the whole story. You know what the threat is, and you know who the players are. But you're the dealer now, and you can call the game."

It was something like a last will and testament; in spelling out the priorities, the testator reveals much about himself. Charles Nash laid bare his priorities. They came as no great surprise to his son.

In all probability, Nash had never really cared for Maureen. She was just one of many pleasant diversions. Nor did he give a damn for their offspring, Mary Lou. Even without the bombshell of Maureen's pregnancy, Nash would have dumped her eventually, whenever the relationship became inconvenient. But he would have tried to make the split far more amicable. He would have had the luxury of time to engineer an unhurried break.

Nash did not care for his wife. But every respectable tycoon should have one. So he got one.

Nash did not care for his son. The son's purpose in the scheme of life was to preserve, enlarge, and perpetuate Nash Enterprises.

That's what he cared about. The care and feeding—the survival and prospering—of his company; that was his sole and abiding concern.

And, upon reflection, Ted had to admit that he himself was not far removed motivationally from the old man. This reflection became clear as Ted clutched to his bosom the sheaf of papers his father had just committed to his care.

Ted wanted to save and protect the company every bit as much as did Charles. Perhaps more, if not for the same reason. Nash Enterprises was Charlie's baby. No matter how many human children he had sired, the only one that truly counted was the company.

For Ted, the company was a most comfortable vehicle through life. And the span of his life was a prime concern. If the company were to perish after he had entered into his eternal reward, that would be unfortunate. That would also be a major problem for those he left behind, principally his wife and children. Those who survived him could make or break what he bequeathed them. But as long as he lived, by God, Nash Enterprises would remain dominant in the development field.

Another major difference between father and son was the matter of an interest beyond the company. For Charles, there was none. For Ted, there was Brenda.

Nash never understood why his son had become so obsessed with another human being. It was, for Nash, a defect in his son's character. But as long as Teddy could keep the store going, that was enough.

And Nash was positive he had just given his son all the weapons Ted would need for the upcoming battle.

Nash had but one more base to touch. Then he would be able to rest. "Now, Teddy, why don't you go into the next room with Chan for a while? Give you a chance to look through those files. Maybe you'll have a question or two . . . you never know."

"If it's all the same with you, Dad, I think it would be a good idea for Father Art and me to leave . . . that is, if you haven't got anything else to tell me."

"I don't have anything more for you. I got something for the deacon here. I didn't know he was coming, but now that he's here, I want to talk to him a bit."

"But I can stay—"

"No, you can't. I want to talk to him one on one. If you hadn't brought him along, I'd've sent for him soon anyway. Now you go on. I'll let Chan know when we're done. Go on. Git!"

Ted gathered up the papers, packed them back into the portfolio, and left the room.

Nash studied the priest intently. But before he could speak, Father Deutsch said, "You're going to ask me to do something—a favor, aren't you?"

Nash almost smiled. "I didn't think of it like that."

"That's because you don't ask for many favors, if any. You give orders. And I'll bet they're carried out. But what you're about to do is ask a favor . . . right?"

"Well, what makes you so sure?"

"I don't work for you. I don't owe you anything. You're not in a position to order me or even threaten me."

"What if I was to say that you're off the payroll of the company? What if I was to take away your office, the secretary, the whole she-bang—your TV Mass?"

Cool confidence emanated from the priest's face; clearly he did not feel threatened. "I am a retired priest of the archdiocese of Detroit in good standing. I did a good job saving my pennies. I've got a home in Boca Raton. I was very comfortable down there before Ted asked me to be chaplain here. I could return to Florida. I could return there very easily. So we're getting back to what you're about to say to me. It's what people call a favor. It has to be."

Nash's body shook ever so slightly. He might have been chuckling. "Okay, okay, if it'll help us get on with this, I'll admit it's a favor. I'm gonna ask you a favor, okay?"

"Not quite. Before I consider whatever you have in mind, I'll ask a favor of you."

"A bargain! That's nice." He *was* chuckling—mirthlessly. "You're a little different than I expected. Most of you guys—you priests—if I ask a favor, you'd do it. You'd just do it. That . . . what's his name? . . . Kelzer—"

"Koesler?"

"Yeah, Koesler. He'd probably just do whatever favor I'd ask."

"Maybe that's why he's pastor of a broken-down church in the middle of this miserable city and I'm very comfortably retired."

"Well, I like it! You wanna strike a deal. Okay. I can understand that. Whaddya want? You want my immortal soul? You want me to confess? That it?"

"Oh, I'd like you to make your peace with God. I'd even like to be the one who absolves you. But that's not it. I don't believe you can sell your soul either to the devil or to God. That's not the stuff that a bargain can be struck over."

"Then?"

"Quite simple, really. From now on, for as long as we live, as often as we are in contact with one another, you will address me as 'Father.' And you'll do it with respect."

"Hey . . . nobody talks to me—"

"Have it your own way. Maybe I'm demanding something more important than what you have in mind to demand from me. If so, you'd be justified in refusing my request. In that case, I'd say what you want to ask of me can't be of much importance to you.

"Up to you, Mr. Nash."

Nash worked his lips silently. Then he nodded. "Okay, *Father,* you got it. Now hear me. I don't know exactly what Ted's gonna hafta do to protect the company or himself . . . or me, for that matter. Depends on what Maureen does. But I do know that thanks to the brainwashing my dear wife gave him, he's gonna hafta justify whatever he does. Somehow he's gonna need somebody to tell him God's not sore about what he does. That's where you come in—"

"Now, just a minute—"

"No, no, you're good at it. I've watched you. We want to put up a high-rise or a mall and in the process we chase all the damn animals out of the wetlands to hell and gone. In my day, we'd just the hell do it. Nowadays we got the damn environmental freaks climbing all over us.

"On top of that, Teddy's got a *conscience.* You do very well at manipulating that conscience. You do good work. I'm surprised all the time the way you can pull out a Bible verse that justifies the whole thing. A talent. And . . ." Nash spread his hands. ". . . that's all I'm asking. Just keep up the good work. You know." He winked.

"That's impossible!" Deutsch's dismay was clear. "How can I possibly promise that whatever Ted does will be morally correct?"

"You're not listening. I didn't say that what Ted does will always be good. I'm saying, he'll ask you if it's okay. Your only job is to justify whatever will protect or help the company."

"You've got it backwards. You're presuming that everything that aids the company is good while everything that hurts the company is bad. Morality is just the opposite. Morality is an objective norm: It measures what you have the company do and decides whether it's good or bad."

"Let me help you, *Father.* Think of all the good things the company does. Helps missionaries. Helps the poor every once in a while. Helps Ted to contribute to good causes that you pinpoint for him. Gives you a very meaningful TV pulpit.

"And—I was saving this as a surprise—we're gonna set you up for network TV—just like those TV evangelists. Top quality and everything. You'll have influence all over the nation . . . who knows, maybe even the world if it catches on like we figure it will.

"Now, how about that, Father! Did we or did we not sweeten the pot?"

Father Deutsch gnawed at a knuckle. "Well, I must admit," he said finally, "so far it's worked out that way. Everything Ted has done has been justifiable—though sometimes marginally. I suppose . . . given all the good Nash Enterprises can do, does do . . . that with the principle of the double effect—"

"That's the way I like to hear you talk, Father. Now, one thing more: Ted can't know what we've just talked about. He can't know about the bargain we just struck."

"I understand."

"Because he can't, he *mustn't* have any doubts about any advice you give him. If he thought I'd talked to you about this, he could think you maybe were bending the theology a bit. Don't get me wrong; I'm not saying you would do such a thing." The old man's expression was sardonic. "As a matter of fact, I haven't asked you to do anything more than you're already doing. I certainly didn't ask you to do anything wrong. God almighty: You wouldn't agree to do anything wrong! I just don't want Ted to have any doubts. I don't want him to think you've changed your standpoint in the way you advise him. So, not a word about our conversation. You can handle this, can't you?"

"Don't worry. I can handle it."

Nash looked intently into the priest's eyes, then nodded decisively several times.

Nash pressed the button on the chair. In a few moments, Ted and

Chan reentered the room. After a few words of parting, Ted and Deutsch were dismissed.

The two men rode the elevator in silence. They did not speak until they were in Ted's car and headed toward Deutsch's residence.

"So, what was that all about? What did Dad have to say to you?"

"Ted, I can't tell you."

"What? I demand—wait: He didn't go to confession, did he?" There was anticipation in his voice.

"Uh . . . almost. Not quite. What he said clearly falls into the category of a professional secret, which, as you know, is almost as inviolable and sacred as the seal of confession."

"But surely you can tell me."

"I can tell no one. All I can say is that your father put a lot of trust and confidence in my advice. I think he may be leaning in the direction of actually confessing to me. I can't risk ruining that strong possibility. You wouldn't want me to."

"Hmmm." Ted did understand. Unfortunately, he also was not getting his way. If there was anything Ted was very much used to, it was getting his way. The combination of wanting to know what his father had said to the priest in confidence and at the same time understanding that the priest would not—could not—reveal the contents of that conversation set up a mean little dilemma in Ted's psyche. He could think of no better way to give vent to his conflict than to pout. And this he did in expressive silence all the way home.

CHAPTER

24

BRENDA CLOSED THE DOOR QUIETLY. She always did when she was unsure whether Ted had preceded her to Nebo. He might be dozing. This was especially likely when, as tonight, she arrived in the late evening.

She heard music coming from the living room. It was classical, somebody's symphony, so it couldn't be Valeria working late. Valeria's musical preference tended toward country and western or folk rock. It had to be Ted.

She put away her packages, purse, and coat and entered the living room. Something—an atmosphere, an attitude?—was profoundly different. Ted sat in the recliner facing her. There was no sign of a glass, empty or full. Apparently he had not had his relaxing drink, a ritual he called his "attitude adjustment hour." He was brooding about something.

"Hi, honey," she tried tentatively. "Sorry I'm so late. Work piled up."

He gave no response.

"Is there . . . is something wrong?"

"Why didn't you tell me?" He paused. "Why didn't you tell me that Mary Lou was my sister? You must have known."

She stood as if struck. "How did you find out?"

"My father. He told me the whole story this evening." His eyes bored into hers. "I'm living with someone who grew up with her, and I learn about this from my father! I felt like a fool. Why? Why didn't you tell me?"

She sank down onto the couch. "It just happened," she said after a minute. "That night at Marygrove—the night we first met . . . I knew who you were, of course. But something happened between us right from the start. There was no opportunity, no opening for, 'Oh, by the way, I grew up with your sister.' Maybe there was a time later when I should have told you but . . . I let it pass. After that, I just let it stay buried.

"I'm sorry your father chose to tell you," she said softly. "I'm

198

sorry you learned it from him and not me. But . . . it's not the end of the world."

She showed no sign of tears or any emotional stress. That was one of the many characteristics Ted loved about her. But . . .

"Not the end of the world!" He was almost shouting. "Dad just got a threatening note from Maureen. As far as she's concerned, it could very well be the end of the world for Nash Enterprises. Dad wants me to dump you! He figures you have to be on their side."

"And you?" She remained calm. "How do you feel about me, after all we've been through together? After all we've meant to each other? How do you feel about it? Want me to leave?"

He came over and sat next to her on the couch. "God, no! I told you before, I'll say it again: I can't live without you. But I just couldn't understand." He shook his head. "Why? Why didn't you tell me?"

"Why didn't your father tell you until now?" She let the question dangle for a few moments. "Obviously, as far as he was concerned, there was no need for you to know until now. With me . . . it was a stupid blunder. I suppose I should have told you. But . . . honestly . . . as I look back over our time together, I don't see a single instance where it really would have been in any way appropriate. And the more time passed, the more pointless it seemed to bring it up. Until . . . until now, when you need to know. So, how about it?" She looked at him steadily. "Are we still a team, or what?"

His look of relief spoke for him. "We're a team." He shook his head again. "I guess I really knew all you just told me." As he looked at her, his face seemed to soften and relax. "I just wanted to hear it from you. It's all settled. We're a team."

"Okay, then." She relaxed back into the sofa. "Now . . . I've only heard this remarkable tale from Maureen's side. Tell me everything your father said. Maybe I can help."

And so he did. Meticulously, Ted recounted everything his father had earlier revealed. Brenda listened most attentively.

After he'd finished, she said, "That part about the baptismal record—I don't understand that. Why was it so important to find it and destroy it? I don't think it carries much if any weight in civil law."

"A couple of things: It does have my dad listed as Mary Lou's father. But, more important, it shows the discrepancy between the birth and baptism record. It might . . . it *might* trigger an investigation.

"And then there was that murder of the woman who changed the birth record. Of course, Dad had nothing to do with the murder," he added.

"But he didn't seem to let it bother him a whole lot."

Ted shrugged. "That's Dad."

"Well," she said thoughtfully, "if it's that important, I think we've got a problem."

"A problem? What problem?" In spite of foreboding brought on by the suggestion of trouble ahead, Ted felt comforted by her use of the first person plural. They were in this together.

"The problem is that the fire in that rectory didn't destroy the baptismal record."

"What? Sure it did. Dad was certain. Whatever else, Chardon is dependable."

"No. I'm not referring to the records at the church. Up till some-time in the mid-eighties—I think it was 1983—all parochial records were microfilmed. The copies are kept in the archdiocesan archives, the originals were returned to the parishes." She paused. "I think that record is in the archives."

"So if Maureen . . ."

"Exactly."

"Oh, my God! Dad didn't know. What're we going to do?!"

"If it's that important, we'd damn well better get in there and get it."

"Do you know where the archives are?"

She smiled. "On the same floor where my office is in the chancery."

"No! Then you can do the job."

"It's not that simple. It's kept locked all the time. Even if someone was working in there, I couldn't just go in and rummage around. No way."

"How about at night?"

She nodded. "I could get into the building, even though the security is quite good. But I could never get into the archives room. See, the door to the archives—well, picture the door to a bank vault."

"Heavy metal with a combination lock?"

"Uh-huh. And there's a separate alarm just for that door. There's no way I could get that combination. And even if I did, I couldn't stop the alarm before it went off."

They sat thinking.

"We need a professional," Ted said finally. He picked up the port-folio from the coffee table and began paging through the papers.

"Dad gave me this list. It's a list of people who . . . well, people we can call on if we need help." He studied several papers carefully. "It's almost poetic justice or some such thing," he said, half to himself.

"What?"

"The perfect person for this job." He turned the paper toward Brenda and pointed to a listed name.

"Rick Chardon," she read, "The guy who . . ."

". . . arranged for the doctoring of the birth certificate."

"And," she concluded, "the one who killed . . . uh . . ."

"Ventimiglia, Agnes Ventimiglia," he supplied. "Look at these qualifications. Among other talents . . . proficient at breaking and entering—and an expert safecracker." He looked up at her. "He's our man," he said decisively.

He leaned back, elated. "Good Lord, this feels comfortable!" He turned to face her again. "I didn't realize it until just now, but all the plans Dad has are contingent on whatever course Maureen takes. This—what we're doing now—puts us on the offensive. Just where I want to be. Now . . ." He was almost businesslike. ". . . how do we do it?"

"I've got a key to the front door on Washington Boulevard."

"It's that easy? No security?"

"Wait. The key just gets me into the building. Next, I've got to punch in a code, or the minute I step in the elevator all hell breaks loose. Fortunately, my code does get me passage to the third floor where my office and the archives are both located. But then, there's still the archives door, the combination lock and the separate alarm. I can only get Chardon onto the third floor. After that, he's on his own with the door and its alarm. But I can give you the exact location of the parish records so he won't have any trouble finding them once he gets in."

"How about guards? Any security personnel in the building?"

"Yes. But they get off about six in the evening. After that the cleaning crew comes in. But Chardon should be able to handle them. He can wear almost any kind of uniform—Consumer's Power or something like that . . . just say he's been called in to repair something. Most of the crew speak very little English. His only problem is going to be that door and the alarm. But if he's an expert at B&E and a safecracker to boot . . ."

"It should be a cinch." He looked thoughtful. "Think I ought to tell Dad?"

"You know him better than I."

"I think I'd better. Besides, I want to give him more proof that he was wrong and that you're on our side. Let's see . . . this is Wednesday. Let's set it up for Friday night."

"Only two days?"

"Why not? Thursday we brief Chardon and Friday he gets the uniform. What's he going to do—practice opening safes? Fooling with combination locks?" For the first time this evening, Ted smiled broadly. He felt much more at ease when he was in control of a situation.

He phoned his father. Brenda could hear only half of the conversation. It seemed that Charlie Nash needed a measure of assurance that Brenda could be trusted, but, in the end, he was convinced. Finally, he gave his approval to the plan.

After Friday, it wouldn't matter whether or not Maureen was aware that a copy of Mary Lou's baptismal record was kept in the chancery. After Friday, it wouldn't be anywhere.

RICK CHARDON walked down Washington Boulevard. Once it had corresponded to New York's Fifth Avenue, Chicago's Miracle Mile, Los Angeles's Rodeo Drive. Now it could not be described even as a shadow of its former self.

As far as he could see, and his vision was excellent, there was no one else in sight. Here and there among the shadows there might lurk a prospective mugger or two, but that thought did not occur to Chardon. Even if it had, he would merely have been amused. The idea of some misfit attacking Rick Chardon was ludicrous; such aggression might well have proven fatal to the mugger.

Chardon was wearing the working uniform of a Michigan Bell Telephone Company repairman. It was determined that there was precedent for Ma Bell repairmen coming in for night work. The chancery phone system was accorded high priority. Partly because it was a busy and important system and also due to some influential Catholics in influential positions at Ma Bell, this telephone company deferred to the needs of the Catholic bureaucracy as often as possible.

The uniform's pockets contained a variety of items, only a small percentage of which were of the telephone repair category. In addition, Chardon carried a metal box with everything a professional safecracker needed to feel at home.

He paused only a moment before the plate glass window of the

Catholic Bookstore, and glanced in both directions. Nobody. He stepped to the chancery door and slipped the key in the lock. It turned smoothly. Chardon had good vibes about this job. The preparations had been hurried, but then there hadn't been much to prepare.

On the left side of the foyer, near the now-empty guard's stand, was the code box. He punched in the number he'd memorized, pressed the "stay" button, and punched the code number once again. The information he'd been given was so simple and logical, he anticipated no bombshells. However, shrewd professional that he was, he came ready for the unexpected.

The elevator stopped at the third floor. The doors slid open. No alarm. He exhaled in relief. However, not all was quiet. From the distance, around the turn of the corridor, came the sound of a vacuum cleaner. It was unusually loud. He surmised it must be a powerful, industrial-strength machine.

All the lights in the corridor were lit. That didn't matter. He was not relying on darkness as a protection against detection; his uniform would explain his presence.

As he came to the first turn in the corridor, he flattened himself against the wall and peered cautiously around the corner.

His first surprise of the night. A uniformed guard stood with her back to him.

He remained calm. He had a series of decisions to make.

He could not continue his mission while she was around. If he tried to pass himself off as a repairman, she could and would check to see if such a person was expected. Besides, no way could he crack a safe while a security guard looked on.

He could turn on his heel and retrace his steps and perhaps come again to fight another day. Or, he could eliminate the guard.

For him, the professional, the perfectionist, there really was no choice.

He took his blackjack from his pocket. The grip felt natural—an extension of his hand. Noiselessly he stepped up behind her. He swung with all his might. The blackjack struck her squarely on the right temple. She crumpled to the floor.

As with every other time he had used this weapon, there was no outcry, no external blood, no lingering consciousness. Death would follow in a matter of minutes.

He opened a nearby door and turned on the light. It was an office that evidently had already been cleaned. The crew would have no reason to return here. He dragged the inert form into the office, turned out the light, and stepped back out into the corridor, closing the door behind him.

Should any of the cleaning crew ask about the missing guard, he was prepared to say that she had to check another floor and would be back soon—and meanwhile, he had to repair the phone in the archives room. He anticipated no further trouble. But he was confident he could handle whatever came up.

As he continued down the hall toward the archives room, he froze for a moment as an elderly woman came toward him. She wore an old, threadbare dress, an apron in similar condition, and stockings that sagged around her ankles. She paid him little notice, glancing only at his clothing as she went past. Evidently the uniform was sufficient explanation for his presence. Everyone had a job to do. She cleaned offices, he repaired phones. She wouldn't get in his way if he didn't get in hers.

She continued down the corridor, pushing her silent vacuum ahead of her. In a few moments, he heard the roaring sound as she began another room.

The combination lock did not appear to be much of a challenge. And, with a setup like this, he was certain he could neutralize the alarm wires. A piece of cake.

He had been at work on the combination for no more than ten minutes. Everything was falling into place; a few more turns and he would be ready for the large metal door handle, which he knew would yield.

He didn't hear them approach, probably due to the infernal noise of the vacuum. But he heard the voice clearly. "Okay, turkey, hold it right there!" It was a woman's voice, but harsh. "Just lean forward and put both hands on the door where we can see 'em!"

Chardon did as he was told. He also glanced back briefly. Two Detroit uniforms, one male, one female, both with guns drawn and aimed. No question of going for his own gun; he'd be dead before he could make his move.

These things happen. But not to him. At least not often. Nothing to do now but play the hand he would be dealt.

The male officer nudged Chardon to his feet, patted him down, and cuffed him. "Robbin' the Church. My, my. Ain't nothin' sacred anymore."

The female officer, checking out Chardon's tool collection, realized this was no penny-ante thief. Somehow they had nabbed a considerable fish. She pulled a card from her pocket and began to read. "You have the right to remain silent . . ."

He was going to hold on to that right like a life preserver.

CHAPTER

25

IT WAS EARLY Saturday morning. Things were off to a slow start at 1300 Beaubien, police headquarters for the city of Detroit.

As usual, among the earliest arrivals were Lieutenant Alonzo Tully and Inspector Walter Koznicki. Each was in his respective office in the Homicide Division.

Tully—most of his confreres and closer acquaintances called him "Zoo"—was studying last night's cases. The load was surprisingly light for a Friday night. Tonight would probably make up for that shortfall.

One episode particularly caught his attention. And this he studied for some time with utmost care, stopping only to make an occasional phone call.

Half an hour later, after a cursory knock, Tully entered the tight office of the head of Homicide.

Koznicki smiled at his most prized detective. "Something, Alonzo?" Koznicki was almost the only officer who did not use the nickname.

Tully, rubbing his chin, did not look up from the report as he stood across the desk from the Inspector. "You're familiar with the Chancery Building on Washington Boulevard." It was a statement. A Catholic as faithful as Koznicki could safely be presumed to be quite familiar with his Church's structures.

Koznicki leaned back in his chair and, as Tully looked up, nodded.

"Did you," Tully asked, "ever know of anyone who was murdered there?"

Koznicki's eyes widened. He thought for a moment. "No. No. There have been some strange occurrences, particularly when one includes St. Aloysius parish with the chancery. They occupy the same building," he explained, almost as an aside. "But no, neither the parish nor the chancery. Although there was a time," he added, thoughtfully, "when the head of a murder victim was found in the church itself.

"But," he continued, "since you ask about it, it must have happened. I did not hear of it on the news this morning."

"That's because we get up early. The media is on the story now." Tully passed the report to Koznicki, who immediately began reading.

"Happened about 1:00 A.M.," Tully commented. "Mangiapane and Moore responded. This is their report." Tully paused, waiting for Koznicki to digest the report. When the inspector seemed to be reaching the final notations, Tully spoke again. "The first surprise is how the guy got through security. It's a pretty good system."

"I did not know that. And it surprises me somewhat."

It was Tully's turn to be surprised. "Walt, they're in the middle of downtown, right off the street. Lots of other buildings in that neighborhood have bars on the windows and alarms all over the place."

Koznicki shook his head. "It is probably part of my upbringing. Churches were open all day, sometimes into the night hours. And yet, I would assume this security system is relatively recent."

"Maybe. But it's there. And this guy just sailed straight through it."

"Someone from the inside?"

"Maybe an inside job. There are lots of possibilities."

Koznicki glanced back to the report. "There is no name?"

"The perp hasn't said more than 'yes' or 'no' since we took him in. And that's mostly 'Do you want to use the john?' questions. We sent his prints out with an urgent. I got a hunch when we get his ID, it's gonna ring bells in some other states. This guy's a high roller. You should see the tools he had.

"As far as we can tell, the killing was casual. He had lots of options. Apparently he killed her because it was simpler for him." Tully looked thoughtful. They both knew it was unusual for a B&E to kill. It wasn't the usual M.O. But nowadays there were fewer and fewer absolutes.

Koznicki shook his head sadly. There had been a more gentle time even for criminals, a time when murder was a rare occurrence. Now it seemed to replace an angry letter.

"Hot from the soup," Tully said of the photos that had just been developed and that he was laying out on Koznicki's desk.

Some of the shots showed the corridor as viewed by the perpetrator as he approached the guard. Other shots were of the door to the archives vault, as well as the tools the killer carried. Finally, an exhaustive series showed the victim from all possible angles.

Koznicki seemed to be engaged in some peculiar game as he slid the pictures around his desk. Soon he had them in an order he found satisfactory. "This . . ." He pointed to an object in one of the photos. ". . . this is a standard blackjack?"

Tully moved behind the desk to look over Koznicki's shoulder.

"Uh-huh," Tully affirmed. Then, "Well, yes and no. It certainly does the job like any other blackjack. But there's something different about it. I talked to Mangiapane on the phone. He said it was . . . like . . . custom-made. Something like a specially made cue that a professional billiard player uses. You know, he carries it around with him from parlor to parlor, takes it out of its case, screws it together. Like Paul Newman," he added, "or Jackie Gleason in *The Hustler.*"

Koznicki's eyebrows lifted slightly. "This was the only weapon the killer had?"

Tully shook his head. "He had a gun, but he never got a chance to use it. The uniforms got the drop on him. If he'd gone for the gun, he'd be the M.E.'s patient now."

Koznicki, preoccupied with the photos, did not look up. "Who called our people?"

"One of the cleaning ladies," Tully said. "She was coming down the hallway when she spotted the guy. She took him to be a repairman, so she didn't give him much thought—until she realized that the security guard wasn't at her post. That's when she decided she'd better call for help. Lucky she did," he added.

Koznicki absently drummed his index finger on one photo. It was a head shot of the victim; the finger was touching the spot that had been crushed. "Strange," he mused, "a blackjack made to order and apparently the weapon of choice. And he needed only one blow to kill . . ."

"Yeah, that is weird. Guns do the job. For something like this, probably a silencer. And if not a gun, a knife. I'd almost think something manual like strangulation before a blackjack. That's like one of those vintage movies."

"There is something . . ." Koznicki's finger continued its unmindful dance on the glossy. "There is something, but it will not come . . . Oh, well . . ."—the finger stopped—"it will come in due time."

Tully returned to the other side of the desk, took a chair, and leaned in so the two detectives were close. "This looks like a platter case, Walt. I can't think of anything that could screw it up. Getting through that security system constitutes B&E. The prints on the 'jack are all his, and the M.E. is checking the death wound to confirm that it was caused by this 'jack. Only a couple of questions don't have any answers yet. But they bug me."

"Oh?"

"One," Tully said, "why was there a security guard there?"

"You yourself said they had adopted a security system in keeping with their changing neighborhood. Would it not be expected that they would employ guards?"

"Yeah, that's what I thought. But Mangiapane asked them how many guards were assigned every night. Just a routine question. But it comes out that the guards go off duty around six in the evening. *Every* evening. So, he asks, how come there are guards last night? And the answer is the cleaning people say they were afraid, so they asked for the added protection."

"Afraid? Afraid of what?"

Tully shrugged. "I don't know. Mangiapane doesn't know. As far as I can tell, the cleaning people don't even know. 'There was talk,' is all Mangiapane and Moore were able to get out of them.

"So, that's one. And two: What was in the archives room that a pro would be after? Did somebody hire him? And what was so damn important about it all that he would kill somebody in the process of getting it?"

"I take it there is no answer as yet?"

"Uh-uh. Nobody—at least none of the cleaning people—had even the slightest idea what was in there. Seems the guy in charge of that department does his own cleaning."

"It would be helpful if we had some answers to those questions, would it not?"

"It certainly would. The questions probably will come up in the trial. Even without the answers I don't see our perp walking—not ever. But it would be nice if the prosecutor could fill in the blanks." Tully paused. "We could use some help."

"Help? What do you have in mind?"

"Most of the time it doesn't make any difference to me that I never got religion. Nine times out of ten religion doesn't play too husky a part in a criminal investigation. But every once in a while . . ." Tully's thought trailed off.

"Such as now?"

"'Specially when we're smack dab in the middle of the Catholic Church with all its rituals and its bureaucracy, and its rules and regulations, and its jargon. I mean, Walt, you are the most Catholic person I know—with one exception . . ." A hint of a smile played at Tully's lips.

Koznicki's expression mirrored Tully's. "Father Koesler?"

"You read my mind."

"Would you like me to call him?"

"I already did."

"You set me up."

"He'll be here at nine. Wanta join us?"

"I would not miss it," Koznicki said with finality.

Tully gathered up the photos on Koznicki's desk, with the exception of one. The shot showing most explicitly the effects of the fatal blow Koznicki extracted from the pile. Tully did not question his boss, but departed, leaving Koznicki to study the photo as he pondered. *Something . . . there is something here . . . something I cannot quite put my finger on.*

He continued his study, but the specific memory continued to elude him.

CHAPTER

26

THEY HAD NOT slept a wink all night.

Ted and Brenda had alternated between sitting, pacing, and lying down, futilely hoping for revitalizing sleep. They had expected Chardon to call in the early hours after midnight, 2:00 or 3:00 A.M. They could not relax before that time, so anxious were they that everything would go off perfectly. They could not relax after that time in anxiety over what might have happened.

There was no point in trying to call anyone. The chancery switchboard was shut down at night. If Chardon had completed his task, he would contact them.

All they could do now was listen to local radio news. This they did through the early morning hours, with no result.

Then 8:00 A.M. arrived, and the first reports of the attempted break-in at Detroit's Catholic chancery, headquarters for the local Catholic Church. In the break-in attempt, a security guard had been killed. The name of the guard was being withheld pending notification of the family. A suspect was in custody. Police spokespersons declined to divulge the suspect's name. Nor was any motive for the break-in advanced. More details would be reported as this story developed.

Ted and Brenda were stunned. Chardon had been caught. Their scheme was in shambles. The only possible silver lining was the possibility that he had somehow taken care of Mary Lou's baptismal record before he'd been apprehended. And even that would not be an unadulterated blessing.

In any case, the story had broken; it was now feasible for Brenda to make some calls. After all, she did work at the chancery; it was only natural she would be concerned.

One of her greater challenges was to put off explaining to Ted each and every call she made. One call quite naturally led to another, and she didn't want to interrupt the flow by going over each in detail. She kept promising Ted he'd get every bit of information she could pry out of a series of people, each of whom had only a fragment of the story. To that end, she was scribbling copious notes.

After a while, Ted gave up trying to read them. He wondered whether she would be able to decipher her own scrawl.

Brenda was grateful when Ted gave up his vigil over her shoulder. It was much easier to function without him draped over her.

Finally, the last call, at least in this series, was completed. Brenda motioned Ted to sit across from her, and there would be a self-administered debriefing. She spread her notes in front of her on the coffee table.

"Well . . ." Her hands were trembling almost imperceptibly. ". . . realistically, there is practically no good news. So I'll give you what little there is right off the top. Chardon appears to have said nothing. They don't even have his name yet."

"They'll get it." Ted ran his fingers through his hair repeatedly.

"The important thing, I think, is that he's not running off at the mouth. If he had, there'd be some cops looking for us—or, rather, for you, since you're the one who hired him."

Ted stared at her in disbelief. *Doesn't she know the rules of this game?* Then, on second thought, *Why should she?* This was her first time through this netherworld. "He won't be talking, honey."

She looked bewildered. "He won't?"

"The worst that can happen to him—at least in Michigan, because we don't have the death penalty—is that he'll get life without parole for killing that guard. Now, we'll make sure he gets a top lawyer. But, if he loses his trial . . . he loses. Nothing can change that. The time he does either will be very hard or it will be the best money can buy. If he drops the Nash name, he knows we'll get him—even in prison. If he keeps his mouth shut, he knows we'll grease the way and won't stop trying to get him out. Rest easy: He won't talk."

She was not playing poker; she really seemed relieved—greatly relieved. But, she reminded herself, that did not mean they were out of the woods. Their plan had disintegrated; now to pick up the pieces. "Okay. The good news is better than I figured. Now for the bad: Chardon didn't get into the archives room. He was working on the combination when he was arrested."

"Damn! It could have gone either way, couldn't it? You read about it all the time in the papers. They're always complaining about the slow response to emergency calls. Dial 911 and take your chances. Sometimes the cops get there in seconds; other times an hour or more goes by. Just a different response from the cops and Chardon could have taken care of the record. Hell! He might even have gotten away—"

He stopped, his brow knit, then said thoughtfully, "What was a security guard doing there in the first place?" He looked at her searchingly. "I thought you said the guards leave about six in the evening. What happened?"

An ironic smile appeared. "You wouldn't believe it," she said. "We're responsible for that—in a roundabout way."

"Huh?"

"Remember Ford Park?"

"How could I forget it?"

"Remember when you told me about how you were going to rebuild and renew the area? You said it would be a great deal for the archdiocese to buy up some of that adjoining property for new parishes?"

"Yes, yes . . . I remember."

"Do you remember what came next?"

"Sure. I suggested that you present the proposition to your boss, McGraw. And you said you did."

"And I did. And he bought the whole concept. He was as enthusiastic about the prospect as I've ever seen him about anything.

"What I didn't know was that he was going to become a Nervous Nellie. The closer the time came for the archdiocese to buy the properties, the more McGraw got frantic that somebody else would hear about it . . . that there'd be a leak somehow, and that the archdiocese would get into a bidding war for the land. He warned everyone to be extra careful to prevent any word escaping.

"I knew about that. Most of the people in Finance and Administration reacted kind of lightheartedly . . . like McGraw was getting paranoid. Nobody was going to steal our plans any more than anyone was going to leak any information. Only a few of us know what was in the works anyway.

"What we—what *I*—didn't know, is that McGraw had stashed all the paperwork for this project in the archives for super safekeeping. And then he spooked the cleaning crew. He told them they'd have to be on their guard for about a week. He didn't bother telling them what they had to be so cautious about . . . only that their very lives were at stake."

"My God! 'Paranoid' doesn't begin to describe McGraw. It's too weak a word."

"That's the way he is," Brenda said. "Anyway, that's how it happened. I didn't know—hardly anyone did—but the cleaning people demanded protection for the duration of whatever it was that so scared Mr. McGraw. They weren't going to be in that building alone during nighttime hours, especially when somebody might invade the place. They knew about the security system, but that wasn't enough: They wanted people—real live guards. They wanted the same company that provided daytime monitoring to send someone while they were there at night."

"Who okayed it?"

"McGraw."

"And he didn't tell anybody outside of the cleaning people?"

"That's the way he is. Never let your right hand know what your left is doing. Even though extending the guards' hours wasn't his original idea, he wholeheartedly endorsed it."

"And that's why our well-laid plan failed."

"And that's why we'll never be able to try that again," she responded, "at least not in the foreseeable future. Now they know someone wants to get into the archives—although they don't know why . . . Say, there's a thought—"

"What?" Ted was eager to grasp at straws.

"If McGraw buys this—if he believes that Chardon was hired to break into the archives to get the papers McGraw squirreled in there, then as soon as this land deal is completed there won't be any need for the increased security. We might be able to try it again." She looked at him encouragingly. "Certainly there must be another safecracker in that list your father gave you."

Ted stopped running his hands through his hair. He folded them in his lap. "Maybe. Maybe a second try would work." His brow knit again. "But something else has been bouncing around in my head while we were waiting this morning. And the idea is stronger now that we know what happened and why."

"What?"

Ted looked at her steadily. "I think what we did to try to get hold of that baptism record was the right thing to do. I didn't realize how much I disliked Dad's defensive strategy until I got this aggressive plan going. And I was right: Going after that document was right on. It was just a freak accident that fouled up a damn good plan.

"Dad's going to be sore as hell about this. He'll want to go back to counterpunching whatever moves Maureen makes. But I can handle that.

"What occurs to me now is that with all the things we've planned

William X. Kienzle

to outwit Maureen, there's something we haven't considered that's fundamental to this whole thing." He paused.

"What's that?"

"We haven't established whether or not Mary Lou is actually Dad's daughter."

"What!?"

"Oh, sure, Dad seems to have accepted his paternity. But that's based on his presumption that Maureen was such a 'nice girl' and that she was so exclusively in love with him that she wouldn't have had anything to do with anyone else. But that's an unconfirmed presumption. Just an unconfirmed presumption.

"And it's so like Dad. *'What else could it be? No one could be unfaithful to me. Impossible!'* But it's not impossible. Unlikely, maybe; impossible, no!"

"What are you getting at?"

"What I'm getting at is that very likely someplace down the road, somebody may demand a DNA test to prove whether or not Dad *is* Mary's Lou's father. Now that could just be a bluff to get Dad to accept the claim. All we've got for that eventuality is a whole bunch of stalling tactics. But what if . . ." He looked firmly at her. ". . . what if, in the end, Dad is *not* Mary Lou's father? And what," in rising excitement, "what if we had proof of that? The ball game would be over." He smacked his knee in elation. "Don't you see?"

"I see, all right. But how could you prove such a thing? If you had a DNA test made, everyone would know the result. And, if what we believe is true—that Mary Lou *is* your father's daughter—then the game's over. And we lose. Isn't that an enormous chance to take?"

"That's the whole idea!" Ted was enthusiastic. "We're not going public. This is—what shall we call it?—a trial run."

"A trial run?"

"Uh-huh. All I need is a little information from you, and we're in business. And this time my plan is not going to fail."

CHAPTER

27

FATHER KOESLER had suggested meeting Inspector Koznicki and Lieutenant Tully at the chancery. But, to simplify matters, Koesler accepted their offer to pick him up at St. Joseph's rectory.

No introductions were needed. All three knew each other from previous episodes when the priest had made available to the police his expertise in matters Catholic. So, Koesler fitted himself without additional comment into the rear seat of Koznicki's car for the very brief trip to the Chancery Building, whose memorable address was 1234 Washington Boulevard.

During the drive, Koesler reflected on the familiarity of a setting: 1300 Beaubien, or any precinct station for that matter, was a home away from home for the police. No matter how many times a civilian might enter such a place, he or she would never be as "at home" as an officer. Sharing a specialized way of life, with its distinct dangers, duties, and rewards, created a bonding that no outsider could penetrate.

However, these two policemen were about to enter Koesler's peculiar venue, headquarters for the Roman Catholic Church of Detroit. While he did not actually work there, the "business" of the chancery was his business. And while he did not know the identities of all the employees there, Koesler was on a first-name basis with all the chancery priests and auxiliary bishops. And he needed no introduction to the Cardinal archbishop. Priests and bishops were the heart and soul of what the chancery was all about.

Just as the police were at home in their stations, so Koesler was at home in virtually any rectory or church or, *a fortiori*, the chancery. He could well understand and empathize with the police desire to have him along.

Under ordinary conditions, the chancery, as well as Washington Boulevard, would have been virtually deserted on a Saturday; one could fire a cannon down the boulevard without harming a soul. Conditions today were not ordinary; such a shot might wipe out many of the local television and radio crews, print reporters and photographers, as well as quite a few uniformed police.

This weekend had begun slowly as far as crime was concerned: some bar brawls, domestic disturbances, a few muggings, armed robberies, and the popular drive-by shootings. Most Detroiters owned guns, and Detroit's mayoral administration never saw a gun it did not want to protect.

In the context of these mundane and repetitive crimes, a B&E topped off by a murder in the Catholic chancery was deemed major news.

As it turned out, the police were fortunate to have a priest expert walk them through this investigation. On their own, the news media were almost foreordained to blunder on any number of Church technicalities. Today or tomorrow, or in the weeks to come, priests watching or reading reports on Catholic events would grimace at such errors as: Vatican for Viaticum; missile for missal; Georgian for Gregorian; beautitudes for beatitudes; beautification for beatification; cannonize for canonize; immaculate conception for virgin birth; celibate for chaste; leaving the Church for leaving the priesthood; sea for see; blessed bread for consecrated bread; and the ever-popular Villa della Rosa for the Via Dolorosa.

Such blunders are the result, most charitably, of finding oneself in a foreign culture. A complication that would not be a problem for Koznicki and Tully thanks to their resource person, Father Koesler.

Koznicki parked as near the building as possible. Few cars were legally parked today. News people tried for a comment but none was given. A no-nonsense attitude and IDs gained the trio entry to the elevator through a harried security guard who, but for last night's shocking events, would have been home in bed.

The third floor was swarming: Chancery personnel were looking officious, distressed, or confused, depending on their respective involvement in the problem area. Uniformed police were busy securing what was deemed necessary. Police technicians, armed with the tools of investigation, were examining, collecting, and recording anything and everything that could be construed as evidence. Rounding out the assemblage were several officers from Tully's Homicide squad, including Sergeants Phil Mangiapane and Angie Moore, who, sighting the new arrivals, made their way along the corridor to report.

After greeting Koesler, familiar to them from previous investigations, the pair informed the newcomers about what was now common knowledge, at least on the third floor. Which was that the likely objective of the intruder most probably was the land purchase plans and proposals that had been placed in the archives room.

Mangiapane in particular seemed pleased that everything was falling into place. The suspect was in custody. And, although he as yet had said nothing and was stoically awaiting his attorney, the perpetrator had been taken *in flagrante delicto*. And now, to cap the climax, they had a credible motive: the theft of documents that could mean millions of dollars to the right people.

Tully looked at Koznicki. "Too pat?"

"I think that a distinct possibility," Koznicki responded.

Mangiapane appeared wounded at their doubt. "Zoo, whaddya mean? It's on the platter. This is a gift horse . . ."

"And one," Koznicki completed, "that you do not want to look in the mouth. Is that it, Sergeant?"

"Well . . . yes," Mangiapane admitted. "We got the perp. We got the corpse. We got the weapon. And now, we got the motive. Believe me, before we found out about what was locked away in that room, we were up . . ." He paused, considering the attentive presence of Father Koesler, and decided on a substitute phrase. "We were up a tree for a motive. I mean, what in chancery archives could be worth all this?"

"It's okay, Manj," Tully said. "We're with you. It's just that this thing maybe is a little too pat. Now, we hope it comes down just like you've got it. We just want to take another look. We don't want to take a chance of this thing blowing up on us when it comes to trial."

"Is the person in charge of the archives here?" Koznicki asked.

"He got . . . sick when he heard what happened," Mangiapane said. "Ulcer acting up—uh, just a minute . . ." The sergeant stepped around some nearby technicians and returned immediately with a young man who seemed to be enjoying all the excitement. "Inspector, this is Mr. Maher. He's one of the few people who knows the combination that opens the vault door."

Koznicki and Tully identified themselves to the new arrival. Koesler and Maher already knew each other; Koesler addressed him as Harry.

"Has the door been opened yet?" Koznicki asked.

"No," Maher replied. "Nobody's touched it since the burglar. Some of your people were looking for fingerprints, I think."

"Then, would you open it, please?" Koznicki requested.

The group walked to the door, sidestepping people occupying the crowded corridor.

Maher noted the lock's indicator was pointing at the number twenty. He leaned forward so that his finger movements were hidden from view, and, in a few seconds, the door was open.

"That was fast," Tully commented.

"I noticed the lock was aimed at the number twenty," Maher replied. "That's one of the numbers of the combination. I took a chance and simply went on from there. The guy who was working on this door was almost done. And he was right on with the combination as far as he got. That's really something," he marveled. "This is a tough lock."

"Interesting," Koznicki commented.

The group entered the room and fanned out, examining the various cabinets and shelves, taking care to touch nothing.

"Can you tell us what is in here?" Koznicki asked.

"Not as well as the archivist. But, in general, anything regarding Church teachings; building records; appointment letters of priests; anything having to do with parishes; files on bishops; parish records—baptismal records; confidential letters to the apostolic delegate that might have to do with disruptions in the diocese or problems with priests; appointments of bishops to Detroit; documents from the Pope; correspondence between the diocese and the Vatican; and, of course, those plans for land purchase that were placed in here very recently, and which seem to be the focus of everyone's attention."

"You do yourself poor service, Mr. Maher," Koznicki said. "You seem to know quite a bit about this room."

"Really only a general knowledge of what's kept in here. I would have a devil of a time trying to put my finger on any of these things specifically," Maher said.

Tully turned to Koesler. "So, what do you think? Outside of the land purchase plans, what's exciting enough in here to provoke a robbery and a murder?"

Just then, a uniformed policewoman entered the room and handed a packet to Koznicki, identifying the contents as mug shots of the suspect. Koznicki opened the envelope and studied the photos as Koesler addressed Tully's question. "Beats me," the priest admitted. "It could be almost anything—or nothing. Judging by the contents that Harry just enumerated, I'd guess those land acquisition papers might be the most financially valuable item here.

"There are other possibilities worth speculating on. But I'm afraid they're pretty thin. There's lots of information about priests who've gotten into trouble of one sort or another. Maybe even a bishop or two—"

"The possibility of blackmail or extortion," Tully interposed.

Koesler nodded. "I would guess so . . . at least the possibility. Then there's the Vatican correspondence and confidential letters to the apostolic delegate." Koesler noted a fresh furrow in Tully's forehead. "The apostolic delegate," he clarified, "is something like an ambassador, but not quite. He's a representative of the Vatican sent by the Pope to provide the Vatican connection between the Catholics of this country—really the bishops of this country—and the authorities in Rome. He lets the bishops in on what's on the Pope's mind. And, probably more important, informs the Pope about the state of the Church in whatever country we're talking about. Here we're considering the United States," he explained. It was Tully's turn to nod.

"But, outside of some delicious gossip, I can't think of anybody's being so interested in who's had trouble or what relations are between U.S. bishops and the Vatican as to risk breaking in here. And in any case, it boggles the mind to think anyone would kill for that kind of information." He shrugged. "I suppose if you went through this stuff pretty much page by page, you might find something that rang a bell. But that could take almost forever."

Tully shook his head. "Yeah, without a confession by the perp, it might just take forever. And he hasn't said word one about what he was doin' in here."

Koesler and Tully simultaneously realized that Koznicki hadn't been at all involved in this speculation.

The inspector, having most carefully studied the mug shots, was gazing into space.

"Something, Walt?" Tully asked.

"Father," Koznicki said, "do you recall our conversation about how we had just missed each other when you were a young assistant pastor at St. Ursula's and I was in the midst of my first homicide investigation?"

Koesler grinned. "I sure do. There I was in the parochial school, giving the kiddies a test, as I recall. And there you were in the church looking for the killer who was responsible for that funeral. Like ships passing in the night. And it wasn't till years later—when I found the body of that murdered nun—that we actually met." He thought for a minute. "That first murder—where we just missed each other—that was never solved, was it?"

"No, it was filed as an open murder. But," Koznicki continued, "something has been troubling me this morning. And whatever it is, I think it has something to do with that murder. The name of the victim . . . Agnes . . ."

"Ventimiglia," Koesler supplied. "I think the reason I remember it is that we priests talked about her death at some length. And, of course, the news media made it notorious."

Koznicki seemed to be barely listening. "Earlier this morning I was almost mesmerized by a photo of the guard who was killed here. Something about the fatal blow jarred a memory. I couldn't quite figure out what it was. But now . . ." He tapped the two photos that bore no name, only a number. He then held up the pictures—full face and profile—of the man, so that Koesler and Tully could view them.

"You can see," Koznicki said, "that the suspect appears to be of an indeterminate age. He might be in his forties or fifties. There are few lines in his face. You will note his height: five feet eight inches. Not tall, not short. He has a full head of hair. It might have been dark brown or black at one time. Now, of course, it is salt and pepper. Even though he has just been through a harrowing experience, being arrested and processed, there is hardly a hair out of place. It clings so tightly to his head—a head that one might describe as 'patrician.' Now, I call your attention to his eyes. Those thick eyebrows, and the eyes themselves—riveting, extremely expressive, dominating, almost cruel."

He looked first at Koesler then at Tully. "Would you agree with this description?"

Tully and Koesler glanced at each other. It was Tully who spoke. "Yeah, Walt. It describes him. But what's the point?"

"I have just given you an almost word-for-word description of the man we suspected of having killed Agnes Ventimiglia."

Tully looked startled, Koesler astonished. "How," Koesler asked, "could you have remembered all those details after all this time? That must be thirty years ago!"

"Thirty-three," Koznicki corrected. "It was my very first homicide case. I thought we were so close to solving it. I knew I would never forget it.

"Earlier, when I saw a picture of the wound that killed the guard, I wondered where I had seen such a wound before. It was Agnes Ventimiglia. A single, powerful blow to the temple. I think the two blows are identical."

Koznicki seemed to shift into a higher gear. "There are several things I must check out. Alonzo, you will remain in charge here?"

"Sure."

"Father—we are not taking you from your duties . . .?" As Koesler shook his head, Koznicki continued, "I wonder then, would you be willing to accompany me?"

"Of course. I'd like very much to see this thing through."

CHAPTER

28

IT WASN'T that she had to work Saturdays. Mary Lou Monahan insisted on working not only every Saturday but on Sunday too, at least until the collection was counted and placed in the night depository.

Mary Lou was an answer to Father Pool's unspoken prayer that God would send somebody to take finances and the budget off his back. It was ideal. Mary Lou's duties at St. Raphael parish were well within her talent and training. She loved it.

This Saturday, Mary Lou had just finished sharing a light lunch—which she had made—with her pastor. She had taught him to eat regularly. He had taught her to eat sparingly. Both were the better for it. He was no longer distressed with hunger pangs. She had lost weight. Which, in addition to a newly acquired sunny disposition, made her more vivacious and attractive.

Father Pool had gone to make sick calls. Mary Lou was typing announcements to be made at Masses later this afternoon and tomorrow.

Normally when the front doorbell rang, she knew who would be answering it. Pool always insisted on going to the door. She was far too busy, he had explained, to attend to such mundane duties. Besides, he said, rectory callers usually wanted to speak with him anyway.

From time to time Mary Lou reflected on what a waste it was that a man like Pool couldn't marry. He would have made an outstanding husband.

While she had no plans to force the issue, such as seduction, she vaguely decided she would hold on to this job just in case this or some future Pope decided to rescue the cultic priesthood by reevaluating this business of mandatory celibacy.

She had nearly finished the announcements when the doorbell sounded. It startled her; for one reason or another, few people called at the rectory on a Saturday.

Her first view of him almost took her breath away.

He looked down at her from a couple of inches more than six feet.

Whatever he wanted, he was serious about it. His rectangular, strongly featured face she found most attractive. He wore a light London Fog topcoat and a dark gray homburg. He was among the very few men who could carry that off.

He smiled. It may have been because her mouth was hanging open. "I hope I'm not disturbing you coming here on a Saturday."

Odd; he had a common midwestern twang. She had half expected a British accent. "No, not at all. Come in—please."

She led the way to her office. He waited till she sat down behind her desk, then he took the chair opposite. He removed his hat. The shade of his wavy graying hair matched that of his pencil-thin mustache. He might be in his mid-forties, perhaps some ten years her senior. "My uncle," he began, "was buried from this parish this past week. Mr. Ned Speakman?"

"Oh . . . yes . . . I'm sorry."

"Perfectly all right. One of those deaths to which people add the words, 'It was a mercy.' He'd suffered a long while. I wonder, could you possibly arrange to schedule a Mass for the repose of his soul? If it wouldn't be too much trouble, I'd like to have the Mass offered on April twenty-fifth? That way it will be a month's mind."

Mary Lou consulted her parish calendar. "Yes, we can do that."

"Fine. Very good. Now, if you don't mind, it's been quite a long time since I've had this done. Could you tell me, what is the offering for such a Mass?"

Mary Lou could not suppress a chuckle. She immediately apologized.

"Quite all right. Did I say something peculiar?"

"No, no, just the opposite. You got everything perfectly correct. I haven't heard anyone do that in the time I've been here. I just can't think of too many people who could or would do it."

"Really . . ." He seemed interested. "What did I get right?"

"Everything, amazingly. Most people ask for a Mass for a dead person rather than for their soul. Almost no one anymore knows there are special Masses for thirty, sixty, and ninety days after death that are called month's mind. And, most of all, everybody asks, 'How much is the Mass?' But you've avoided every single one of those clichés. Do you mind telling me, just how did you do that?"

He smiled. "No tricks involved. It probably comes from my days in the seminary. And I've kept up pretty well with all the changes. As a matter of fact . . ." He paused. "I'm not taking up too much of your time, am I?"

Mary Lou smiled delightedly as she shook her head. She quickly had become enchanted with this stranger.

"You're too young to remember a column that used to run weekly in the *National Catholic Reporter* called 'Cry Pax.'"

Although she had heard others refer to the column, she was indeed too young to have read it. Obviously he was not. She would have to reassess her estimate of his age. Not mid-forties, more like mid-fifties. The reevaluation did nothing to dim the fact that she found him extremely charming.

"It was a column," he explained, "that poked fun at some of the more flagrant blunders we Catholics make. The particular item that comes to mind was an excerpt from a column published in a parish bulletin. I haven't the slightest idea now whose bulletin it was, but it had to do with deadbeat parishioners who requested Masses be scheduled but never made an offering. The pastor was incensed because other parishioners, who were willing and able to pay, couldn't get their Masses in the overcrowded schedule. Following the item was an editor's note wondering why we Catholics could never convince people you cannot 'buy' a Mass."

They laughed. Over the next forty-five minutes they continued to laugh as they enjoyed each other's company. They learned each other's name. He was Ned McDonald, once of Detroit, now of Chicago. He was a corporate attorney—very successful if she was any judge, though he himself made no such claim. She soft-pedaled her employment vicissitudes, giving the impression that she quickly became disinterested in a job once she had mastered it.

"But, say . . ." McDonald looked at his watch. "I must be keeping you from something. And I've got some business I have to take care of." He rose to leave, then hesitated. "I wonder . . . this is terribly forward of me . . . but would you consider dining with me tonight? It would just be an early dinner; I have to get back to Chicago tomorrow. But it's been such fun talking with you."

Mary Lou needed no time to consider. "That would be nice. I'll be done here by six."

"I'll call for you then."

They shook hands warmly and he left. Immediately she began anticipating a delightful evening. And with a man like him, it didn't much matter where it all would lead. She smiled wickedly. She didn't even know whether he was married! Worse, she didn't care.

One could get very old and dried up waiting for the Pope to change his mind about celibacy.

INSPECTOR KOZNICKI drove Father Koesler on a series of converging trips around the city on this bright, sunny Saturday afternoon in March.

They dipped into nostalgia, again reminiscing first about their near miss of each other at the Ventimiglia funeral at St. Ursula's. If Father Pompilio had not decided to officiate, if Koesler had not been scheduled to administer a test to the school kids, if Koznicki had called at the rectory—at least they would have seen each other.

But none of these missed coincidences would have prepared them for what happened years later when Koesler had stumbled upon the dead body of a nun in the otherwise vacant convent at St. Ursula's.

That had led to a series of opposite coincidences that brought the two men together. If Koesler had not happened to be the one who found the body, and if he had not noticed the peculiar presence of a rosary—so incongruous in the hand of a nun who had been taking a bath—still they might not have met.

But they did meet, and had, over the years, become good friends, easily sharing confidences.

On the drive this afternoon, they first had returned to police head-quarters to pick up additional copies of the suspect's mug shots.

Next, they visited Dr. Wilhelm Moellmann, medical examiner for Wayne County. It was he who had performed the autopsy on the murdered security guard. And he wasn't at all happy about it. The police had requested priority for this postmortem. Such a request almost always set off Moellmann's short fuse.

Fortunately, most of the doctor's explosive force had been spent before Koznicki and Koesler arrived. That, plus the fact that he had a special if well concealed respect for Koznicki, plus the presence of a priest, rendered Moellmann fairly cooperative. But for the person making the request, Koznicki's query about an autopsy performed here thirty-three years before could well have set the doctor's aggression on full throttle.

"Well, you know," Moellmann said, "I wasn't here then." He had a clear and quite appropriate German accent. A hortatory tone that was put to use as he asked—commanded—some browbeaten assistant at the other end of his phone line to locate the ancient file and bring it to him "*now.*"

They did not have long to wait before a clerk appeared with a grungy folder, which Moellmann grabbed without comment. He mumbled beneath his breath as he rummaged through the file. "There are notes and pictures. Ja . . . ja. Hmm. Hmm. Hmm. Interesting." It became obvious that he was comparing the old case with this morning's autopsy. "Well, I can't say. But it is very interesting. The right temple. The internal damage. The force of the blow. Well, you see, I cannot say for sure that the same weapon was used in both deaths. And I cannot say the same person was the killer in both cases. But the similarities are striking. Oh! Ho! That was a pun. I didn't intend it, but that was a pun."

He recovered quickly. "I would say that this is well worth the investigation. If you get somebody who is a suspect in both murders, I could testify as to the similarities. The evidence would be circumstantial, but, put it together with other indications, it could be quite strong."

So far, thought Koznicki, so good. Or, as good as he had any right to expect.

"Where to now?" Koesler asked as they headed back to Koznicki's car.

"The Beyers . . . Joe and Mollie."

"The couple who owned the Wine Cellars?"

"Yes. You know them?"

"Sure. I think everybody who ever ate downtown must have dined at the Pontchartrain Wine Cellars. And if they did, they probably knew Joe and Mollie. What a rotten shame that great restaurant had to close. I've missed it for—what is it?—two or three years now. But"—he turned to look at Koznicki—"what in the world could Joe and Mollie have to do with this case . . . these cases?"

"According to the Ventimiglia girl's best friend, Agnes and her mystery man probably were to dine at the Wine Cellars the night she was murdered."

Koesler paused to think that over. "Then," he said slowly, "that's why you picked up copies of that photo of the suspect. But even assuming they did eat there that night, do you actually think the Beyers might remember the man? It's been more than thirty years!"

"There's always a chance. And in this work, one depends on whatever attention to detail may bring." The car headed east, with the priest and the Inspector now each deep in his own thoughts.

BOTH KOZNICKI AND Koesler were gratified when Joe Beyer answered the door. They had not determined beforehand that he would be home.

Beyer recognized Koznicki immediately, but had to be introduced to Koesler—a fact that discouraged the priest from thinking the former restaurateur might possibly recall the suspect. Koesler had dined at the Wine Cellars with some regularity. The suspect might have visited there but once.

After they were seated in the living room, Koznicki explained that he wanted Beyer to see if he could remember or identify any of the men in some police photos.

Beyer took the photos, turned each so it would not reflect the glare of sunlight, then studied it carefully. Finally he looked up at Koznicki. "This is important, isn't it?"

Koznicki nodded soberly.

Beyer returned to his perusal. He looked up again. "Can you give me a hint? Is it someone who's been in the news lately?"

"Sorry," Koznicki said. "It would do the case no good for me to prompt you. All I will say is that you may have seen one of these men some thirty years ago. Do you recall ever having seen any of them?"

Beyer returned to the study, but he was slowly and steadily shaking his head. "No, no, Walt . . . sorry. But I can't. Sorry."

At that moment, Mollie, his wife, entered the room like a fresh and welcome breeze. "Walt, Father, don't stand."

But they did, and shook hands with her. "Do you remember me?" Koesler asked, although he had assumed that if the husband did not remember him, neither would the wife.

"Yes, of course," Mollie said. "You used to come in with some other priests."

That, thought Koesler, was a safe enough bet. As usual, he was wearing a clerical collar with his black suit. Surely it was a safe guess that he was a priest. And priests had a habit of dining together with considerable frequency.

"You're . . ." She rubbed her forehead. "You are . . . uh . . . Father Kelzer. No . . . wait! Father *Koes*ler." Sure of herself, she brightened.

"Amazing!" Koesler acknowledged. "I haven't seen you in years."

Joe handed his wife the mug shots. "They want to know if we recognize any of these guys, Mollie. I struck out. Wanta give it a try?"

"Sure." She sat on the couch alongside him. She examined each picture with evident care. There was utter silence while she shifted back and forth among the photos, trying to stir up a forgotten incident in the past. "Look at those eyes!" She held up one photo. It was the shot of Chardon. Koznicki's face was impassive. "They're scary," she said. "Looks like they could penetrate right through you. Otherwise, a kind of good-looking guy. Seems as if I ought to remember him. And . . . I kind of do . . . sort of."

"I can tell you this much," Koznicki said. "You would have seen the man we're looking for about thirty years ago, and probably not thereafter. So you could assume that his hair would have been dark instead of gray. Obviously, since each of the men in these pictures still has a full head of hair, we can assume the hairline would have been the same as it is today."

She returned to the photos. "I'm drawing a blank, Walt. But . . . there's something nagging at me. Can you leave the pictures?"

"Of course. If you have any recollection at all of any of these men, you know where to reach me."

Koznicki and Koesler left. As the inspector drove away, Koesler looked back. Joe Beyer was waving good-bye. His wife was studying the photos.

CHAPTER

29

THEY DINED AT Meriwether's on Telegraph Road near Ten Mile. It was Mary Lou's choice. Ned McDonald protested that she should have picked a posher place, but she assured him that all things considered—food quality, service, management—this was her favorite.

They had been seated in a walled booth that afforded them a modicum of privacy and created for her a sense of romance.

During their chatty dinner, she learned that he was a widower of ten years whose children were grown, on their own, and scattered around the country. She was thrilled to be with this handsome mature man whom she found engrossing, humorous, attentive, and, all in all, delightful company.

He had ordered wine with their meal. Twice. Because he anticipated her desire—another prized trait—and kept her wineglass full, she was only peripherally aware that she had consumed well more than half of the two bottles they emptied during the meal. Neither did she notice the alcoholic content of the wine. It was high. And so, as the evening wore on, was she.

She didn't become aware until they were leaving the restaurant and the chill spring wind hit her that she was somewhat more than tipsy. But she felt so secure, so cared for, that she simply relaxed and let McDonald take over.

She was able, barely, to direct him to her apartment. When they arrived, her only desire was to prolong this enchanted evening. "Won't you come in for some . . . coffee . . . or something?"

He smiled as he helped her from the car. "Maybe for just a little while. You look as if you could use a little help."

"Oh, I'm so sorry! Am I embarrassing you?"

"Of course not. We've just had a lovely evening."

Leaning on him as little as possible, she let him guide her up the steps and into the building and her apartment. Once inside, she excused herself and went immediately into the bedroom.

He located the kitchen and began making coffee. He was still at it

William X. Kienzle

when she noiselessly came up behind him and encircled him with her arms. He jerked erect from surprise.

He turned within her arms, which continued to encompass him. She was wearing a nightgown and robe, both flimsy, both diaphanous.

He pushed her away easily and held her at arm's length. He could see through her garments quite clearly. A little too round here and there, but all woman. He smiled.

As she drew herself close to him again, she swayed. He quickly grabbed and supported her, leading her to the living room, where he helped her lower herself to the couch.

"Just sit there a few minutes, Mary Lou, and I'll get us some coffee. You'll feel better with some coffee in you. And then we can go on from there."

"As long as we go together, Ned." She wasn't slurring her words quite as much as when they'd left the restaurant. Remarkable recuperative powers, he thought.

By the time he returned to the kitchen, the coffee was ready. He glanced back at the figure on the couch. Mary Lou had shifted to a recumbent position and was stretching luxuriantly.

His heart beat a bit more rapidly, and he started to perspire. She was a lot of woman. And she was his without even having to ask. Quite beyond his power of control, he was ready for her.

He shook his head and smiled to himself. Going with emotion was amateurish. He was a pro. "Milk? Sugar?" he called out.

"Black."

Better. The coffee would be at its peak heat. He looked at her again. He frowned and calculated. He took from his pocket a vial of small white pills. He dropped two in a cup, then filled it with coffee. He waited a few moments for the pills to dissolve.

"Oh, forget the coffee and come on back," she called.

"Coming right up."

He entered the room, bearing a tray with two cups. He handed one to her. "Here, just try this. It'll make you feel better." He took the other cup.

"I don't think I've ever felt better." She was smiling, leaning toward him, figuratively giving herself to him.

"Come on, drink up. Then we'll go from there." He sipped his coffee.

"Oh, all right." She sipped. It was hot. She blew across its surface, then sipped again. Ned apparently wanted her to have the coffee. It wasn't a bad idea at that. It might enable her to be a bit more bright-eyed and bushy-tailed. But she would not take her eyes from him.

She had nearly drained the cup. "Oh, Ned, I'm getting so tired." Strange, she thought; the coffee should keep me from feeling sleepy. "Help me stay awake."

He moved to support her as her head dropped to his shoulder. "It's been a long day. Maybe you just need a little nap. Don't be afraid of it. You'll feel fresher after a little nap."

"Well . . ." Her voice was trailing off. ". . . maybe . . ." She slumped limp. Carefully, he removed himself from her and the couch.

He checked her breathing and pulse. Normal and steady. He had been twice concerned. His first challenge had been in balancing the drug with all that wine. Too strong a dose could've been risky—even fatal. His second worry occurred when she seemed to bounce back from the alcohol. He hadn't counted on such a tolerance. Until now he had feared the dose in her cup might not be sufficient to affect a relatively sober person her size.

But it had all worked well.

He took a compact leather case from his topcoat, opened it, and spread the contents on a pillow that had fallen from the couch. He moistened some cotton with alcohol and vigorously swabbed the crook of her arm. He fingered her arm and applied pressure until a bluish vein stood out. He delicately but firmly inserted a hypodermic needle into the vein and filled the syringe with Mary Lou's blood.

He packed his instruments back into the case. He did not anticipate any search for prints, but one could not be too careful: With a handkerchief he wiped clean everything he'd touched in the apartment.

He scribbled a note: "Mary Lou, I had a wonderful day. I guess it got to be too demanding for both of us. I have your number. I'll call soon. Ned." He left the note on the kitchen cabinet near the coffee, which he unplugged.

He surveyed the apartment. Everything seemed to check out. As he was closing the door behind him, he took one last look at the sleeping Mary Lou. *Well, so long, doll. I wish I could've taken what you offered. It'll be interesting finding out the alcohol level of this blood. It'll be even more interesting establishing the DNA structure.*

FATHER KOESLER was unwinding.

Inspector Koznicki had returned the priest to his church barely in time for the late Saturday afternoon Mass, which, by ecclesial fiat, satisfied Catholics' obligation to attend Mass on Sunday.

Fortunately, he had a long-standing habit of preparing over an entire week—as time allowed—for his weekend homilies. Saturdays, however, were usually reserved for tying up loose ends. There hadn't been time for that today. The homily was a bit frayed. So, after Mass, and after the dependably few confessions, and after a warmed-over dinner, he had reworked the sermon until he felt more confident about tomorrow.

After the natural excitement of a police investigation—for him at any rate—and the repairs made on the homily, he was understandably exhausted. He knew that today's activity would not have so wiped out a younger priest, a younger Koesler. But he also knew he was not what he once was.

He sat in his room in the spacious but otherwise vacant rectory. A glass of wine perched on the nightstand next to the chair. Gershwin's Piano Concerto in F was on the record player. An open book lay on his lap. He was having no success reading. He found himself going over the same paragraphs again and again without comprehending the printed page. It was not the book's fault. His mind was restless.

It was easier listening to the music than trying to comprehend the book.

The events of the recent past were distracting by nearly anyone's measure. All that hubbub with his cousins. Then the cataclysmic revelation that Maureen wasn't just playing mommy, she actually was a mother to Mary Lou.

And the father of it all was tycoon Charlie Nash!

That, by itself, was food for thought enough. But somehow, all those things seemed jumbled together in today's events. And he had no idea why. Something today . . . What would it have been? Everything seemed to revolve around the secret archives of the archdiocese of Detroit. But how? What?

On a whim, he thumbed through the phone book. There it was: Maher, Harry, on Archdale. He dialed the number. He recognized the voice that answered. "Harry? Father Koesler here. Sorry to bother you so late."

"Perfectly okay. It isn't every day I get sucked into a homicide scene. Matter of fact, I was just telling Peg all about it for maybe the fourth or fifth time. She's grateful for the break."

Koesler chuckled. "I'd probably be doing the same. Except Mother

Church protected some lady from becoming Mrs. Koesler. Good grief! It even sounds strange. The only Mrs. Koesler I've ever known was my mother. But . . . what I'm calling about: Remember this morning when someone—I forget who—asked you what was kept in the archives?"

"Yeah. I remember thinking he was asking the wrong guy. But I listed all the things I could remember being in there."

"That's it. Can you give that list to me now? And go slow; I'll be writing them down."

Maher did precisely that, and after exchanging a couple more pleasantries, they hung up.

Koesler sat looking at the list of disparate items and listening to the music. He drifted off in the direction of the music.

He was thinking about *The Joy of Music,* a book written many years before by the now-deceased Leonard Bernstein. In the book was a chapter entitled, "Why Don't You Run Upstairs and Write a Nice Gershwin Tune?" It was an all-but-rhetorical chapter. The foreordained conclusion had to be: All well and good if your name is George Gershwin; otherwise you're doomed if you want to write one of his unique tunes.

Koesler's mind turned back to the concerto, now in its third and final movement.

Gershwin moved from those marvelous songs to serious music. Purists might quibble about the classic structure—or lack of structure—of a composition such as the concerto. It seemed evident that the composer had grasped a basic concerto form, the established divers distinct themes in the first two movements, then tied them together in altered configurations in the third.

And that was just about what Father Koesler was trying to do. There were any number of seemingly unrelated events here. Something—an instinct?—told him there were not only obvious relationships between certain facts but there also were as yet undetected couplings.

His head felt like the wire used for recordings before tapes came along. Back then when things went wrong, the result was literally haywire. The strands would tangle in a hopeless mess. That pretty much described the condition of his mind.

He finished the wine and determined to try to empty his brain and get some sleep. All the while he knew he wasn't going to be successful. Not thinking was a feat he had never come close to mastering.

And these thoughts were going to distract him with no resolution in sight all through the day tomorrow.

CHAPTER

30

FROM WHERE he was seated, in a corner of the ample kitchen of St. Joseph's rectory, Father Koesler could see little of the traffic. But he could hear the whooshing of the procession of vehicles on their way down Gratiot to the call of Monday-morning business.

He felt somewhat out of the mainstream of American life. Here half or more of humanity was picking up the thread of commerce left behind when they'd murmured, "Thank God it's Friday." And here was he, immobile and beginning a day not unlike any other.

He hadn't yet begun to page through the *Free Press.* He was working through a bowl of cold cereal and banana in milk. Experience had taught that it was counterproductive trying to read and spoon dripping cereal simultaneously.

As was his morning habit, he had turned on the kitchen radio eternally dialed to 760—WJR-AM and Detroit's perennial radio king, J.P. McCarthy. So far, Koesler had learned that the Pistons had won, the Red Wings had lost, and so had the Tigers. That took care of basketball, hockey, and the grapefruit league. There had been twelve shootings over the weekend, eight of them fatal. Given a gun, Detroiters did not fool around. Traffic was backed up on the Lodge, Ford, and Chrysler freeways and on I-696—the Reuther—as well. Given little or no mass transit, Detroit drivers managed to torture each other through rush hour.

He finished the cereal and poured a cup of last night's coffee that he had just now reheated. There were those who would have found it bitter. To Koesler, it was dark and hot. And that, to him, was coffee.

J.P. (Joseph Priestly) McCarthy was about to do one of his patented phone interviews.

"On the other end of *my* line is Theodore 'Ted' Nash," the familiar, confident voice said. "Good morning, Ted. According to an item in Bob Talbert's column in this morning's *Free Press,* your father is willing to submit to a DNA test to settle a paternity matter. News to you?"

"Not at all," the voice of Ted Nash replied. "J.P., I've been in touch with my dad over the past couple of days. This thing goes back some thirty years, if you can believe that!" His tone made it clear no one could believe that.

"That's a piece of time, all right. Any idea why *now*?"

"Well"—a playful tone—"it's probably not child support."

"The lady mentioned in Bob's column"—all business, but still a light touch—"a Maureen Monahan. Know the lady?"

"Never met her." Jaunty tone.

"More important, obviously: Does your dad know her?"

"In the Biblical sense, J.P. no. But"—more seriously—"he did know her years ago. He hasn't seen her since then. He does remember her. They dated a few times, then they broke up. Like what happens to lots of relationships. They were both very young at the time."

"But, we keep coming back to the question, why now? After all these years?"

"Well, J.P., the best we can come up with is that when they went together briefly back in the sixties, Dad was just a struggling young executive. Now, of course, he has built Nash Enterprises. What shall I say? The pot is richer? The stakes are higher? If her daughter were—and she's certainly not—my father's child, she would make some ridiculous claim *now*. Now that we're talking empire!"

"I'll say. Just the two of you? How about half the whole enchilada?"

"It'll never happen, J.P."

"We tried to reach your dad, but no luck."

"He isn't in the best of health, J.P. That's the only reason he's not talking to you this morning."

"But you can speak for him?"

"I sure can, J.P."

"Then one last question: How come Charlie Nash doesn't wait until a suit is filed against him? Why does a man like him—prominent in the community as a philanthropist of the first order—why would a man like that volunteer to take a DNA test before a complaint has been filed against him? Doesn't he sort of lend some sort of credence to, let's face it, an allegation that no one even knew was going to be made, by volunteering for the test?"

"It might seem that way, J.P. But anybody who knows Dad real well knows that that's just the way he is. He didn't get to where he is by sitting back waiting for people to do things to him. He's an aggressive kind of guy. When he got word this allegation was going to be made, he decided to settle the matter once and for all. The ordinary guy would do everything in his power to stall and pull legal maneuvers to sidestep a test as credible as a DNA. But Dad knows there's nothing to this claim. So, to nip this thing in the bud, he's offering to take the test and get the thing over with."

"Well, okay. You can be sure that everybody's going to be following this story. Thanks for talking to us.

"Ted Nash, commenting on a decision made by his dad, Charlie Nash, a name familiar to every Detroit-area adult. Aware, *he* says, of a pending legal action against him, a paternity suit, Mr. Nash has decided to throw down the gauntlet, as it were, and challenge the claim by agreeing to take a test that will settle the matter one way or the other. Good story. And, as it develops, you'll hear about it here on WJR, radio 760, in the Golden Tower of the Fisher Building."

Father Koesler, who had gone rigid at J.P.'s first words, turned off the radio and flipped through the morning paper to the feature page. There, in its usual place across the top six columns, was Bob Talbert's "Out of My Mind on Monday Moanin'." And there was the item, with an added disclaimer that Talbert had been unable to reach Maureen Monahan but had corroborated the story as it had been released by the Nash people.

Had Koesler left his radio on, he would have heard a similar disclaimer by J.P. McCarthy, including the statement that WJR had been unable to get through to Ms. Monahan.

Koesler was stupefied, his brain numb. All his previous reasoning was in shambles. Everything about this matter was topsy-turvy. Nothing made sense.

But it *had* to make sense. He just wasn't seeing it clearly.

In the light of all that had happened, including this morning's bombshell, how could this event square with a reasonable conclusion?

Koesler's brain was a near maelstrom. But gradually, as he began to fit things—people, events—into place, one possibility loomed ever larger. Now, he needed just one more bit of information to have everything come out right. There was one person he simply had to talk to.

He dialed her number ten separate times, by actual count, before he gave up. He would have to make an unannounced and uninvited visit. Something he scarcely ever did.

But first, he left a desperation-filled note for Mary O'Connor, parish secretary, general factotum, and his right arm. He apologized profusely and stressed what an emergency he faced today. He had no idea where he would be nor how long he would be gone. He asked her to try to find a spare Jesuit to offer the noon Mass. Short of that, she might contact one of the parish's extraordinary ministers of the Eucharist to conduct a prayer service with the distribution of Communion.

All of this Mary would have thought of on her own, once she knew he'd been called away. He was going into detail only to indicate how sorry he was to dump these emergency burdens on her.

Next, he asked her to reschedule today's appointments for later in the week.

For all of this, all he could promise her was that he would not make coffee for her tomorrow. For some reason, she never cared for any of his brew.

He had only to remove his cassock and don the black jacket and clerical collar. And he was gone.

As HE NEARED Maureen's modest home in the suburb of Warren, Father Koesler was met by an array of departing vehicles. Several vans with prominent TV logos were headed out of the neighborhood. The rest of the motorcade he took to be radio and print people.

His initial surprise gave way to an acknowledgment that it was only natural that Maureen and the girls would be among the hottest news items in town following Nash's announcement.

As he parked in front of Maureen's house, he thanked God he had not arrived earlier when the reporters must have been swarming all over the place. There was only one man left, who was about to enter his car as Koesler pulled up. A radio personality, he would have gone unrecognized except that Koesler had been interviewed by him in the past. WJR reporter Rod Hansen smiled as the priest approached. "If they didn't call for you, I don't think you're going to get in here, Father."

Koesler nodded toward the house. "Anybody home?"

"Oh, somebody's home all right. They just don't want to talk to anybody. Not anybody from the media anyway." His innate curiosity and reportorial skills were piqued by this priest who had arrived conveniently after the mass of newspeople had departed. "It's Father . . . Koesler, isn't it?"

"Yes."

"So what brings you here, Father?" Hansen switched on his tape recorder as he moved closer to the priest.

Koesler's reaction was one of gratitude. Rod Hansen's traplike memory had pulled up his name from previous episodes with the local media. But obviously Hansen was unaware that Koesler and Maureen were related. Otherwise, the priest's telephone would have been ringing this morning. As long as he could keep the relationship quiet, there was a good chance he would move through this storm unscathed.

"Well," Koesler said, "in a sense you're right, Rod. The Monahans and I go back a long way. I think they kind of expect me to come. At any rate, I'll soon find out."

Leaving the reporter standing at the curb aiming his recorder at a departing back, Koesler climbed the steps and rang the doorbell. He prayed Maureen would let him in. Otherwise he would be forced to deal with Rod Hansen once more. Faced with such an astute reporter, Koesler knew he would soon run out of evasive statements. He had no intention of lying to the reporter. But neither did he want to be hounded.

He breathed a sigh of relief as the door was opened. "You're lucky," Maureen said. "I didn't intend to answer the phone or the door all day. But I hadn't counted on a priest and a cousin as well. Come on in."

As Koesler stepped inside, he glanced back in time to see Hansen shrug. As Maureen closed the door, the reporter entered his car and drove off.

INSIDE THE HOUSE it was more like the dead of night than morning. All the blinds were closed and the draperies drawn. Lights were turned on. The only sound came from the whir of the refrigerator in the kitchen.

He entered the living room, to find Brenda seated on the couch. Maureen joined her. Koesler sat opposite them in an upholstered chair. "Everybody's here but Mary Lou," he said.

"She was here," Maureen said, "earlier. She left quite a while ago."

"In a huff?"

Both Maureen and Brenda looked at him with interest. "What makes you say that?" Maureen asked.

"Earlier this morning," he said, "after I heard the news, a whole bunch of scattered thoughts, suppositions, theories, what-ifs, began to fall into place. Now I can think of more than one reason why Mary Lou left in a huff. Maybe why she may not be back.

"I haven't filled in every single space," he explained, "but I think I'm close." He looked at each of them in turn. "Suppose I tell you the story the way I have it figured out. And you tell me if I'm wrong. You might even fill in those blanks that are left."

Maureen and Brenda looked at each other, then returned their gaze to Koesler. "Okay," Maureen said. "Go ahead."

Koesler settled back in the chair that was much more comfortable than it appeared. "Let me begin at the end—the break-in and murder in the chancery building the night before last."

Brenda shot an "I-told-you-so" look at Maureen.

"A number of things about that whole mess sort of begged for somebody to make sense of," Koesler said. "It occurred to me as the investigation proceeded that it was the head of your department, Brenda, who put these documents in the archives. I found that interesting. Also interesting was that the archives are on the same floor as your office. So, if you wanted to, you could have provided a key to the chancery's door as well as the combination that would get somebody through security to the third floor, where your office and the archives are located."

"Lots of people could have provided as much. Or the intruder could have obtained the information from any number of sources," Maureen objected.

"Uh-huh," Koesler admitted. "But there's more. The presence of the security guard. Under ordinary circumstances, no guard would have been there. But the cleaning people demanded added protection as long as those valuable papers were in the building. How did they hear about the danger? All they've said is, 'There was talk.' I wondered, was it your boss, Mr. McGraw, who put out that word, Brenda . . . perhaps prompted by you?"

"It—"

"Then there was the killer," Koesler said, cutting off Brenda's attempted reply. "The police have since identified him as Rick Chardon. The possibility that Chardon is the same person who killed a young woman thirty-three years ago—coincidence? Inspector Koznicki is trying to establish the connection.

"Now I was trying to figure out some connection between the two crimes besides the apparent motive that Chardon was trying to steal the land purchase documents. After Mr. Maher provided me with at least a partial list of items stored in the archives, I started wondering: What if both crimes were related to some sort of records?

"In the case of the girl who was killed thirty-three years ago—Agnes Ventimiglia—she worked in a county office that dealt almost exclusively in records—birth, death, marriage. Among the things contained in the archives are microfilms of parish records—including baptismal records. What if that's the relationship?

"So far, Brenda, we have the possible use of your key, your ease of entry, your floor, documents that belong to your department—all this leading up to the possible theft or destruction of what—a baptismal record? By a person who is also the probable killer of a young woman in charge of birth records that go back to the time and place of *your* birth. What a coincidence!"

The two women were gazing at Koesler, Maureen with a frown, Brenda with what Koesler took to be a slight smile.

"The question I asked myself then," Koesler continued, "is 'Why?' What is there about these records? Why would they involve murder—the first very premeditated, the second a matter of necessity?

"That led me to consider what happened to you, Maureen. At the time you were dating Charles Nash, I was pretty completely preoccupied with my pastoral duties. But Oona and Eileen have recently filled me in. So I'm aware of how deeply involved you were with Charlie. You expected—understandably, I might add— him to marry you. Then you became pregnant. And he was the father of your unborn child.

"But, he dumped you—brutally. You were filled with shame and anger and," his voice softened, "I suppose a measure of despair. But," he added, "it looks as if in your emotional reaction, that anger won out."

He looked at her questioningly. But Maureen, her face a mask, merely gazed at him wordlessly.

Koesler pushed on. "You went away to Chicago during your pregnancy. You returned to Detroit for the birth of your baby. Undoubtedly, you loved your baby as much as any other mother. Other than that, you were one deeply angry young woman— especially when you discovered that Charlie had had a family even before he began seeing you. And that he'd kept hidden from you the existence of a wife and a son.

"You would be the only source of information for the recording of your child's birth. I can't think of a single reason why you would not have listed Charles Nash as the father of your baby." He paused, but with no response from Maureen, picked up the thread of his speech.

"Now, I must admit I've never seen a copy of that birth record, but I would be powerfully surprised at this point, with everything that's happened since, if that record doesn't show 'Father unknown.'"

No reaction from either woman. In the absence of any response, Koesler assumed he was on the right track. "If you supplied the father's name, Maureen, and later the record was changed, who but the father—Charlie Nash—would have been responsible for the alteration? What if he hired Chardon, and Chardon provided the 'romance' that filled that unfortunate young woman's last days? What if in return for that 'gift' of 'love,' Chardon required—that Agnes remove Charles's name from the birth record . . . ?

"Since Agnes was killed at the end of November, the month of your child's birth, the record would have been altered around about that time. I know that at the end of each month, copies of that month's records are forwarded to Lansing to be kept at the State Capital. That's why they had to get Agnes to alter the record before December. It also explains why they would kill her then. They had no further use for her.

"But you wouldn't have known all this. And good Catholic that you are, you would have had your daughter baptized. Now here's a record that would present a considerable challenge to tamper with. For one thing, no priest would allow it. But beyond that, you could select any parish you wished and Nash would have the devil's own time tracking down the parish of baptism. And his name definitely would be on *that* record.

"Now, why would Chardon be trying to get to this record in the archives? I'll bet if we looked up that record in the archives and found the church of baptism—and that would be easy enough—I'll bet we'd find that something had happened to change or destroy the original baptism record in the actual parish.

"Not that many people knew about that microfilming program. So I'm assuming—and I'm sure I'm correct—Nash had something done to the parish record, thought he could rest easy, then found that the record still existed in the archives. Thus, Chardon again.

"But there's one more twist to this story, I do believe, Maureen." Again he paused, this time seeming to look off into the distance. The two women didn't know whether he was thinking or, possibly, praying.

"I don't think I've ever come close to gauging just how deeply and totally you hated Charlie Nash, Maureen . . ." He turned back to her.

"... nor how deeply determined you were to have revenge—the most complete revenge I have ever encountered." He shook his head.

"At one point, you may have contemplated seeking a mind-boggling child support from Nash. But after you discovered that Charlie had gone so far as to have your daughter's birth record altered . . ." He paused. "When did you discover that, anyway?" Maureen's only response was a shrug. After a moment, Koesler went on. "At any rate, whenever you discovered it—and possibly even the concomitant murder of an innocent young woman further motivated you—you started on your careful, painstaking long-range plan of revenge.

"When it finally dawned on me what you've done, I couldn't believe it." He looked at her, then shook his head with a pained expression. "That's when I decided I could scarcely recognize you as the kid I grew up with.

"Here's what I think happened. In a huge county like Wayne, there must be many more than one child per month whose birth record lists 'father unknown.'

"You didn't assume custody of your child immediately. That may very well have been a necessary financial decision. But I think it was much more than that.

"Somehow, you kept track of two children—one a foundling, the other your daughter. Eventually, you brought one, then the other, to your home. As far as most of us—myself included—knew, they were both more or less adopted by you to take the place of the daughters you would never have.

"Then your sisters were let in on that secret—and much later, they informed me, as one born out of due time: Mary Lou was your real daughter. She was my real cousin.

"But now, Maureen"—he looked at her fixedly—"I think not."

Both women remained impassive; it was as if they knew his conclusion was inevitable.

After a moment, Koesler went on.

"As a good Catholic girl, you very probably considered your love affair with Charlie Nash as one prolonged mortal sin. For one raised as you and I were, there was no possible way you could have escaped that self-condemnation. But you could see light at the end of the tunnel: He would marry you and make your love legitimate.

"Then he discarded you because you were pregnant—with his child.

"At this point, as sorry as your situation was, you could have returned to confession and Communion.

"And, at this point, I asked myself, why not?

"Okay, your hatred of him is so great that you can't see yourself reconciled with God. But years pass—thirty-three of them—and you're still that angry? We Catholics have remedies for lingering anger. Given time, we can take measures—praying for those who have wronged us, at least trying to forgive. But none of these measures can coexist with deliberate, premeditated, and unresolved revenge.

"That, Maureen, was why you couldn't bring yourself to confession. The revenge you planned was as fresh and rampant as when you first laid your careful plans.

"But I wasn't certain how such a complicated scheme of revenge could involve Mary Lou. Granted, if she was Charlie's daughter, she could make a lot of trouble for him. And then it hit me: but not nearly the misery that would befall him if it turned out that *Brenda* was his daughter."

He looked at Maureen, who returned his gaze unflinchingly. "That's it, isn't it?" he said. "Brenda is Charlie's daughter. Brenda is my cousin, not my 'niece.'"

They sat looking at each other. It seemed that each was trying to think of something to say.

"Uncle Bob . . ." Brenda said finally. But she immediately corrected herself. "Actually it's *Cousin* Bob." She smiled, a real smile this time. "At least now I can address you as a relative and mean it."

"Brenda!" There was warning in Maureen's tone.

"It's all right, Mother. It's over now. At least as far as Father Bob is concerned." Brenda turned her full gaze on Koesler. "The break-in was Ted's idea," she said resolutely. "He told me about the Ford Park land development. I told McGraw. I also told Ted about the microfilm copies of parish records. When Ted decided to go for those records, the development plans became the perfect smoke screen. Any vandalism in the archives would seem to be aimed at those plans. Ted chose Chardon with the understanding that he would do only what was ordered, as long as one was specific."

"Then," Koesler said, "it was Chardon who killed Agnes Ventimiglia?"

"Yes. Charlie—" She stopped. "I can't think of him as 'Father.'" After a moment, she continued. "Charlie told him only that he wanted his name off my birth record and that no one should know that it had been altered. By Chardon's lights, he was simply doing his job efficiently. Ted didn't know any of this until a few days ago when Mother issued her threat—a veiled threat, but enough to start the ball rolling."

"And the security guard on the third floor?"

"I told the cleaning people about the important papers being kept in the archives. I suggested it would be a dangerous situation until the matter was resolved. Which is probably true for that matter. But actually, I knew of no plan—besides Ted's—to do anything about the vault.

"When it comes to that," she added reflectively, "I really doubt that anyone would actually try to break into the vault—not just for those plans."

"And the killing?"

Brenda's lip trembled. "That was tragic. Chardon was explicitly told, *no* violence. For all I cared, he could get caught or, when he spotted the guard, he could have aborted the job.

"But even if the cleaning crew hadn't forced the issue, none of it would have mattered. You see," she explained, "I had already made a copy of the microfilm that contained my baptismal record." She shook her head. "It wouldn't have mattered . . ." Her voice trailed off. After a moment, she continued. "But once I learned that they had arranged to put guards on that night, I knew it wasn't necessary for me to do anything.

"Either way it would have forced the Nashes into something more desperate." She shook her head again. "He wasn't supposed to get violent. He wasn't supposed to kill. That was tragic," she repeated. "But it was entirely his own decision."

With Brenda near tears, Koesler turned to Maureen. "How did you ever do it, Mo? Juggling two infants in foster homes and, when you were ready, taking them home with you?"

Maureen didn't reply. She seemed to be weighing whether or not to open up, even now. Finally she sighed. "It's been a long, hard time. What would you both say to some coffee and cake?"

Koesler wasn't sure whether "long, hard time" referred to the past thirty-some years or the past few hours. But he suddenly realized that the thought of coffee and cake was indeed appealing. He nodded to Maureen, who rose and went toward the kitchen, followed immediately by Brenda.

As the age-old homey sounds and aromas of coffee-making emanated from the kitchen, Koesler leaned back in the chair and, arms above his head, stretched his muscles. *I wonder,* he thought, what the inspector is doing?

IT HAD BEEN a long and exhausting Saturday, but a satisfying and rewarding one.

Inspector Koznicki walked slowly along a series of Spartan holding cells on the ninth floor of police headquarters. When he reached the last cell, he stopped and stood looking in. The occupant was aware immediately of the officer's presence. Both men evaluated each other silently. The occupant rose from his cot and walked to the bars where he stood only inches from the inspector. Still neither man spoke.

Koznicki rubbed his cheek and chin, scratching a now more than five o'clock shadow. "Rick Chardon," he said.

There was no change in Chardon's expression; only his eyes seemed to react.

"You have been busy," Koznicki said. "Wanted in five states to face murder charges. And detained here on a charge of murder in the first degree."

There was no response from Chardon.

"I have ascertained that none of these states including our own has the death penalty. I wonder if you considered that when you accepted the contracts."

A slight smile appeared on Chardon's face. It remained there, a sort of mocking expression.

"But," Koznicki said, "my greatest pleasure in this day harkens back to 1960. I had not been long out of the academy. We got a call about a suspicious article in the river. I pulled the bag from the river. The bag you threw in the river."

Chardon's eyes registered surprise, but only for an instant. Then the slightly mocking expression returned. But now it seemed forced.

Koznicki took some pleasure from that. "I do not have to tell you what was in the sack. You know all too well. There are, perhaps, only a few details you did not know.

"If Agnes Ventimiglia did not tell you, it will be interesting for you to know that she had a 'best friend' at work. She confided in this friend especially regarding the romance of her life. Although you were careful to keep your identity hidden from those who worked with Agnes, she gave a fairly detailed description of you to her friend— who in turn gave it to me. I have kept it fresh in my mind ever since. I have a rather good memory. And within that memory I have kept a special place for my first homicide investigation.

"So, when I saw your picture, a part of the jigsaw puzzle came together.

"Oh, it was not just the photo. Any number of men could fit the description that we had of you. Important is the fact that your fitting that description keeps you in the picture for the rest of the puzzle.

"What moved me to look more closely into the connection between you and the Ventimiglia murder was the weapon you used this morning." Koznicki paused in thought. "It seems as if that happened days ago.

"In any case, when I saw the photo of the fatal blow you gave the security guard, the first piece of the puzzle fell into place. As I looked at that photo, I saw in my mind's eye the head wound of the Ventimiglia girl. To my eye they were identical. Our M.E. said that the similarities were so close it could hardly be a coincidence. As I say, seeing your mug shots made part of the puzzle come together.

"There is a third piece that just fell. You may or may not remember which restaurant you took Agnes to for her last supper. It was the Pontchartrain Wine Cellars. Agnes told her friend that she had asked you to take her there. And you didn't want to upset her for her last supper, did you?"

The mocking look remained in Chardon's eyes, but they flickered.

"This afternoon I took some mug shots to the home of Joseph and Mollie Beyer, the owners of the late restaurant. Joe could not identify you. Neither could his wife—until just a few minutes ago. She just called me and without any coaching whatsoever, she picked you out. She remembered you. It was the eyes. She was frightened by your eyes. Once she remembered you, she recalled your companion for that evening: a very happy young lady. She remembers seeing Agnes's picture in the papers after her body was discovered and identified. She did not recognize the girl in the picture as the happy young woman who had been in their restaurant a few weeks before. Agnes, plain innocent young lady that she was, was not particularly memorable. You were. Mollie put the two of you together at that dinner.

"So you see, Mr. Chardon, the pieces of the puzzle are beginning to fit rather snugly. We are in touch with those states that have warrants out for you. I suspect you understand why we are following all these leads when we have you dead to rights in this morning's murder. There is always the possibility some present or future governor will be moved to pardon you. He or she might be able to do that without an enormous backlash of public opinion if you have been convicted of only one murder. That is not likely to occur if your record shows a history of multiple murders.

"And of course there is a very special reason. I have a personal need to close the case of the murder of Agnes Ventimiglia. I feel I owe it to her, to her memory. And now, you see, I am very close to doing so.

"Now, Mr. Chardon, you may think you were very clever in never committing a capital offense in a state that had the death penalty. But of course"—Koznicki spread his arms wide—"if you were clever you would not spend the rest of your life in a cage."

Koznicki walked away. He was, of course, aware that Chardon had said nothing. It didn't matter. The inspector had enjoyed his monologue.

HE WAS SURPRISED that he'd had that much of an appetite. As he finished brushing off his black clericals the crumbs that were the remnants of several slices of coffee cake, he looked up to see Maureen and Brenda watching him with some amusement. "I didn't get a chance to finish my breakfast," he explained in a non sequitur. Then, realizing that his breakfast was not the only thing left unfinished, he said to Maureen, "Do you think you could fill me in on the rest now?"

Maureen pressed her lips together. Then she took a deep breath and let it out with a sigh. "Making the decision was the hard part. Once that was done, the mechanics of the thing weren't all that difficult. I don't mean the first decision. As you said, that was a financial necessity. I couldn't be a working mother, I couldn't afford to pay somebody to take care of Brenda, and I couldn't keep her with me and depend on the dole or charity. I just couldn't do that.

"It was deciding to involve two children in my plans: That was brutally tough."

"But Mo, what if you'd had a boy instead of a girl?"

"Things would've changed. I would've planned differently."

"I don't understand."

"That, Bob, is because you're a man. Men make plans and if something goes wrong, they have to start all over again, usually from the beginning. Women don't usually make such elaborate plans, so they can bounce off unexpected obstacles, change course and keep going.

"The only thing in my mind was to make him pay for what he'd done to me . . . and to our child. And, in the process, make an example of him that other people could learn from.

"That driving urge is what got me through those months of exile—and a delivery you wouldn't believe. The compulsive desire for revenge just intensified with each rotten trick he'd play on me.

"Leaving me twisting in the wind was bad enough. Then I found out about his wife and son. But when he had his name removed from his own daughter's birth record, that was the last straw! No ordinary revenge would be sufficient.

"That's when I decided to bring two girls home and confuse the matter."

"You certainly succeeded in that!"

"After I had Brenda baptized, I let her become a ward of the court. Then I found another baby, also a ward of the court. I tracked down their foster homes, visited them, contributed all I could afford regularly to support them.

"Back then, foster care was intended to be temporary. So it wasn't difficult to get them into St. Vincent's Orphanage. And later, it was simple, after my record of interest in their young lives, to take them home with me permanently. From that time on, it was a tricky business to train them for vastly different destinies."

Brenda stood and began pacing behind the couch. "When I was old enough, Mother confided in me, and me alone. Together we planned everything. We were of one mind. My goal was to insinuate myself into Ted's life. He was super-Catholic, so I got a job at the chancery—the local hub of Catholicism.

"That was it in a nutshell, Uncle Bob. Our plan was to bring down both father and son—and their baby, Nash Enterprises. And . . ."—her face telegraphed satisfaction—"that's what we're about to do."

"But you've been . . . uh, living with Ted Nash!"

Brenda, without emotion, nodded. "We were pretty sure that with a father like Charlie Nash, the son would develop into a male chauvinist pig and worse."

"And Ted did not disappoint us," Maureen said.

"I went to lots of places where I knew Ted would be. I always dressed modestly in black and white. We knew that's what Ted wanted in a woman. Then one night at a gathering honoring Ted, it clicked."

"But Ted claims you had your tubes tied. Is that—?"

"That part's true."

"But—"

"Father Bob"—Brenda looked at him unflinchingly—"this was an incestuous relationship. I wasn't going to have a child we produced, even by accident."

It was Koesler who flinched. "Oh, my God! I was so busy trying to figure all this out that I lost track . . . Ted is your half brother," he said in a strangled voice. "And he doesn't know it! Brenda, how could you . . . ?"

Revenge. It was the motive for all they had done. No price for this vengeance was too high. The look on their faces told him that.

"And Mary Lou? The reason she left in a huff was because you finally told her everything?"

"We will," Maureen said sadly. "There's a limit to what she can handle at one time."

"You mean she doesn't yet know she isn't your real daughter!?"

"She will . . . soon. Right now she's angry because she was used as a guinea pig."

"Another one of Ted's ideas," Brenda explained. "The one we were provoking him to come up with." She was standing behind the couch now. "From his father's rogues' gallery, Ted came up with a smooth operator, a doctor whose license had been lifted. He was to take Lou to dinner, get her drunk, and get a sample of blood to check against Charlie's for a DNA test.

"She woke up with a hangover and a bruise on her arm. When the story hit the papers and the airwaves, she came over to see what was going on. We explained what that much was about. It was a real shock for her. That's why she's so angry." Brenda shook her head. "After she calms down a bit, we'll explain the rest—everything—to her.

"She'll be furious, of course," Brenda added. "But we're counting on the money she'll be getting to help heal a bunch of wounds."

Koesler's brow knitted. "Money . . . what money? What money will she be getting?"

Brenda and Maureen exchanged glances.

"Wait a minute . . ." The light was dawning for Koesler. "That's what this business is all about this morning," he said slowly. "The DNA test has indicated that Charlie is definitely not Mary Lou's father."

Maureen nodded. "But all of them 'know' that Mary Lou is my 'daughter.'"

"So," Koesler said, more sure of himself now, "they're convinced that they're home free. And they've issued the public announcement that they're going to have the test made because they think they already know what the test will prove."

"That's it," Brenda said. "What they don't know but will soon find out is that Charles and Maureen did have a daughter, but her name is not Mary Lou."

"And then?"

"And then," Brenda responded, "we will demand half of Nash Enterprises. And then," she concluded, "Ted will lose a love partner and gain a sister—and a business partner."

"Wow!" The fervent exclamation was all Koesler could muster.

"But," he said finally, "isn't there a different way to go about this?"

"What?" Maureen asked bluntly.

"A less conspicuous way," Koesler said. "What I mean is . . . if the Nashes were convinced of the validity of your claim, maybe this could be settled—what's the term?—out of court?"

"No," Maureen said.

"Wait, Mother," Brenda interrupted. "I can see some big advantages if we do it—or at least try to do it—Uncle Bob's way. All the negative publicity would do the company no good. And I have some definite plans for a new environmentally conscious Nash Enterprises."

"He'd never believe either of us," Maureen said.

"What if I try?" Koesler asked.

"You'd do that?" Brenda said wonderingly.

"I've talked to Charlie Nash before. No reason I couldn't do it again."

After some brief thought, Maureen spoke. "All right. It couldn't hurt. And I have to agree, your way is better. But the agreement will have to be . . ." She chuckled. "I almost said, 'in blood.' It'll have to be in writing, witnessed by an infinite number of lawyers."

"You don't trust *Dad*?" Brenda smiled.

"Don't use that word again," Maureen said.

Koesler stood. "Before I go . . ." He looked intently at one, then the other. "It's over. 'The comedy is over.' The opera is ended. Do you think now you can finally bury the hatchet? Your plan seems to have worked perfectly. And some good may come of this. Will you return to the Sacraments now?"

Neither woman spoke for several moments.

Then, after a deep sigh, Maureen spoke. "It's too early. It's way too early. There's lots left to heal. I don't know. I just don't know." Another pause. "That's all I can say."

Koesler's gaze moved again to Brenda. Again she met his eyes unflinchingly. She said nothing, merely shrugged.

"I'll pray for you," Koesler said. "I really will."

31

FATHER KOESLER was more than mildly surprised at how easily he was granted an audience with Charles Nash. And yes, midmorning, this very time, would be fine.

Of course Koesler did not need to be a psychic to know why the tycoon was feeling magnanimous. He had played a hand that didn't stand a chance of winning, and he had won. What could Koesler do to him? What could any of his enemies do? He was on a roll. He sensed it.

However, Nash had not advanced to an "open door" policy. The security was as uncompromising as ever. The doorman checked for Koesler's name among the admittables, then the priest was announced. Once out of the elevator, he was immediately admitted to the huge white room.

This time, Charlie Nash was not hidden in some other room; he was right out in the open. His wheelchair was positioned opposite a straight-back chair. Nash motioned Koesler to the vacant chair. He seated himself as the white-clad young manservant, taking Koesler's topcoat and hat, disappeared into the adjoining room.

Koesler studied Nash for a few moments. The old man's mouth resembled a slit in a craggy rock, but, yes, Charlie was smiling. "Heard the news, have you?"

"Yes"—Koesler nodded—"from several sources."

"You probably think I've lost my marbles. Come to see if I should be committed?"

Koesler smiled tightly. "No, I don't think you've lost your marbles. I think they're scrambled around more than you think, though."

Nash inclined his head and looked more intently at Koesler. He was unsure what to make of the priest's reply. He decided to put it on the back burner and forge on. "Stole a little thunder from the Monahan woman, didn't I? Sort of nipped her move in the bud. Imagine . . ." There was that look again; it must have been a smile. ". . . spending most of your adult life planning a coup—almost living and breathing for revenge, and then having it all fall apart on you. All these years she's been expecting to dump Mary Lou on me as my daughter! Hell, I can be frank with you. You're not going to tell anyone and it doesn't matter anymore anyway. But I gotta tell you: I believed it. What a load off my mind. But"—he looked at Koesler intently—"you don't know what I'm talking about, do you?"

"Oh, but I do. I've just come from Maureen's home."

"They know?"

"Mary Lou told Maureen about her very brief 'romance.' And about the bruise around the puncture mark on her arm. That, along with your announcement that you were prepared to be tested for a DNA match, pretty much brings them up to date."

Nash's laugh was a cackle. "Generous of me, eh? Like betting on a one-horse race. Between you and me, I gotta give a lot of the credit to Teddy. He's the one who thought of rigging the game. Him and that Brenda of his." He shook his head. "And to think I was after you to break them up. Imagine that! Brenda's maybe the best thing that ever happened to the kid."

"Well, as William S. Gilbert once wrote, 'Things are seldom what they seem.'"

"What's that mean?"

Koesler hesitated. Charlie Nash was in such high spirits, it seemed a shame to bring him down. But, sooner or later, it had to be done. And with the news media snapping at their heels due to Nash's announcement, the time to do it was now. Definitely now.

Painstakingly, Koesler recounted the story of Maureen Monahan, the Monahan sisters, Mary Lou and Brenda.

It was interesting watching the emotions just below the surface of Nash's facade. First there was mild amusement, then doubt, then denial, then anger. Then rage exploded. "You expect me to believe this cockamamy pile of bullshit!"

"You? You above all others! I expect you to believe every word."

"Never! It's impossible! Why, for God's sake, man, you want me to believe that Brenda was in on this from the beginning? That she conspired against my son? Hell, before she proved herself, I would've agreed. But not now! My God! She even had herself fixed for Teddy!"

"It wasn't for Teddy. It wasn't only adultery. It was incest! Teddy is her half brother. Brenda wasn't going to have any children born of an incestuous relationship."

Nash began to gabble; a light froth appeared at the corners of his mouth. Koesler was concerned anew for him.

"Well . . . well . . ." Nash sputtered, "what about the fact that I challenged Maureen publicly and agreed to a DNA test? You're trying to tell me that I've made this disaster for myself. Do you expect me to believe that she was clever enough to foresee that I'd have the wrong girl tested and then put my head on the block with the media?"

"The reason we have a problem with this is that we're men."

"What?!"

"If you or I had been planning this, we would've had to back up and start over any number of times."

"What?"

"But women are able to bounce off obstacles and go right on."

"What?" The old man's face was screwed up, his eyes squinted, in an attempt to comprehend.

"Maureen assured me—and I believe her completely—that she had only one plan regarding you: the ultimate possible revenge. If the child had been a boy, the plan would have been different, but it would have gone forward. Now, she was determined to keep after you until you made an error. Then she would pounce.

"So you secretly test Mary Lou's DNA against yours—and then you announce that you're willing to take a DNA test with Maureen's child and make the results public. Now you've done it: You've made—what she considers—your inevitable blunder. And she's ready to pounce."

Nash's lips worked soundlessly. Then the words burst forth as the spittle flew. "I can't believe it! I don't believe it! I won't believe it!"

"You don't want to believe it. But you do believe it," Koesler said calmly. "Let me give you the final argument. You know Maureen about as well as anyone. Now, just a few minutes ago, you said you had believed that you were the father of Maureen's child. And you believed—I believed—everybody believed—Mary Lou was that child.

"You knew Maureen well enough to know she loved you and there was no way in the world that she would have been unfaithful to you. You granted that her child was yours. There really wasn't any doubt at all: Her child is your child. In your heart you know that to be true. All you've discovered through that test is that Mary Lou is not your child. And you know what that means. If you now submit to the test you've told everyone you're willing to take, you will not test with Mary Lou. You'll test with Brenda. And you know . . . in your inner heart you *know* what that result will be."

Koesler had never seen anything to equal the sudden transformation that came over the old man.

Nash fairly sprang from his chair. It was as if he were a young man. Even the creases in his face seemed to smooth away for an instant. He raised both arms to heaven, his hands clenched. As Koesler, in dismay, started to rise, Nash cried out in an unexpected loud and firm voice, "I am consumed! Good God, it's the end!"

He pitched forward, almost knocking Koesler to the floor as he fell.

The priest was completely unnerved. He had witnessed heart attacks, he had seen death. But never anything like this.

He grabbed the empty wheelchair and pressed every button he could find. Lots of things happened. The room experienced a drastic change in configuration—walls ground slowly to new positions, forming where none had been before; a gigantic TV screen swung slowly down from the ceiling; and, most distressing of all, the empty wheelchair started to roll on its own. Koesler, in near terror, looked about. The door at the end of the room burst open and the manservant dashed in, expertly dodging the moving obstacles. He hurried to the wheelchair, first pressing the button that halted the chair's motion, then pressing the others so that the walls and TV returned to their former positions.

"Call 911, quick! *Quick!*" Koesler said.

"No, no! Mister Nash has own crew. I call!" He hurried to a phone on the stand near the hospital bed.

Koesler could not hear what was being said, but, satisfied that aid was being summoned, he immediately became engrossed in trying to help in the only way a priest could in this situation.

He knelt next to Nash, who lay face down in a crumpled heap. Koesler turned him over as gently as he could. Nash's eyes were open wide but seemed to see nothing. His mouth was grotesquely contorted as if struggling for every precious breath.

Koesler grasped the dying man's hand and bent his head close to Nash's ear. "Charles," Koesler shouted, "you're dying. In a few moments you'll be judged by a loving God! Give Him your love now. If you're sorry for all the sins of your life, squeeze my hand!"

In response there was something . . . a pressure. A conscious act . . . ? A dying twitch? There was no way to tell.

As far as Koesler was concerned, it was enough. He shouted in Nash's ear, "The Lord, Jesus, absolves you. And I, by His authority, absolve you from every bond of excommunication or interdict inasmuch as I am able and you need such forgiveness. Therefore, I absolve you from your sins in the name of the Father, and the Son, and the Holy Spirit. May the suffering of our Lord Jesus Christ, the merits of the Blessed Virgin Mary and all the saints, whatever good you have done or evil you have suffered, be, for you, a remission of sins, an increase of grace, and the reward of eternal life. Amen."

Charles Nash was gone. Koesler was sure of it.

NO SOONER HAD Koesler finished the words of absolution than the emergency medical crew—Nash's private crew—dashed into the apartment. Koesler was impressed. They went to work immediately and expertly. Koesler was convinced they were beating a dead horse; but they had been retained to keep Nash alive and they were going to strive for that even if he was beyond resuscitation.

With two of them working on Nash, the others lifted his inert body onto a gurney and wheeled it toward the elevator. Koesler asked if he might accompany them. One of them nodded, and, but for the house servant, away they all went.

He rode in front with the ambulance driver. From time to time, Koesler glanced back; the crew was still working feverishly. Whatever Nash paid them, they were earning it. He ruminated that once Nash was no more, that excellent income would go down the drain along with him.

Koesler was surprised that they were not heading for Harper, Receiving, or any of the nearby trauma centers. They were speeding, siren blaring, eastward toward St. John's Hospital. It had to be a prior arrangement.

After they arrived, and Nash was whisked into emergency, Koesler found a seat in the waiting room. There he looked from person to person, composing a scenario for each. This woman was waiting for a husband who had cut himself trying to fix something around the house. That couple was worrying about their child's unexplained fever.

And those three who had just walked in were anxious about Charles Nash.

Koesler of course recognized Ted Nash and Father Deutsch, but the third man was a stranger. No, he wasn't; at second glance, Koesler recognized him from photos in the news and society pages. Avery Cone, a highly prominent and extremely wealthy attorney.

Ted led the way to the receptionist desk. He didn't need to identify himself; the attendant knew who he was. She disappeared into one of the emergency cubicles.

A few moments later, a white-clad woman with a stethoscope tucked into a pocket of her smock emerged and walked directly to the trio. "Mr. Nash . . ." She looked grave. "I'm sorry, but your father is gone. There was nothing we could do. He was dead on arrival. So sorry. If you wish, I can get somebody from Pastoral Care to be with you . . ."

Koesler noted that Deutsch bristled at the mention of incidental spiritual aid. What was he—warmed-over stew?

"Did he have a priest with him?" Ted asked. "Was there a priest with him when he died?"

"Not from our hospital," she replied. "Our chaplain isn't here just now. And, of course, your father was gone by the time they brought him in. He probably died almost instantly. But I heard someone say a priest arrived in the ambulance with him." She looked toward Koesler. "Could that be the one?"

Heads turned. "Father Koesler! You!" Nash's exclamation was ambiguous.

Koesler rose and came over to the group. "I'm sorry about your father, Ted."

"You were with him? He sent for you?" There was so much hope in Ted's voice.

"Actually, *I* called him. But he invited me over."

"Did you . . . ? Did he . . . ?"

"It was terribly sudden. He just pitched over. But I'm pretty sure he gave me a sign that he wanted absolution, so I gave it to him."

Ted's smile was sublime. "He did? You did!" He seemed near-ecstatic. "We were just on our way to see him about this morning's announcement when one of my people called on the car phone. We came right away." He turned to the attorney. "Avery, this is Father Koesler . . . the priest I told you about." Then, turning back to Koesler, "Father, I don't think you know our attorney? Avery Cone."

The two men shook hands, but had no opportunity to speak in the face of Ted Nash's exuberance. "But this is really providential. I can't get over it!"

Before anything else could be said, Father Deutsch, who was obviously trying to control some inner ire, jumped in. "Just a minute. You said earlier that *you* called *him*. Why?"

"It was about . . . uh . . . this morning's announcement." It was clear Koesler was uneasy talking about this in public. "Perhaps," he suggested, "we could discuss this somewhere more private?"

"What's wrong with here?" Deutsch was enjoying Koesler's discomfort.

Cone sensed that some seclusion was in order. "There are private rooms here for Pastoral Care," he said. "I suggest we use one."

The foursome repaired to the room Cone indicated. Once there and seated, Koesler reviewed the morning's events, beginning with the J.P. McCarthy program (which of course Nash knew about), Bob Talbert's column (ditto), through the visit and exchange with Maureen and Brenda, to Charles Nash's reaction.

Though Koesler went over the events in detail, it did not take as long as it had with the senior Nash. In capitulation, Koesler was able to streamline the story. Woven into this account, prompted by questions from the lawyer, were all the contributory details. Things such as the roles played by Chardon and the ersatz attorney from Chicago.

As Koesler reported on his conversation with Maureen and Brenda, Ted waxed feisty. But as Koesler related the gist of that conversation, an appalled Ted turned first beet red, then ashen with horror and shock, and finally sank back in a dispirited pallor.

He collected himself somewhat as Koesler recounted the particulars of his visit with Charles Nash, climaxing with the old man's death.

At this point Ted leaped to his feet. "You killed him!" he raged at Koesler.

"Calm down, Ted." Cone waved the distraught Nash back to his seat. "Father Koesler didn't kill your dad. If anything, he seems to have presented the facts as gently as possible. Besides, it was inevitable that Charlie would learn about it all.

"The way I understand it," he said, "Father Koesler, in effect, volunteered this morning to represent his cousins' claims to Charles in the hope of effecting a quiet settlement out of court." He turned to Koesler. "Would that be about it, Father?"

Koesler nodded.

As his father before him, Ted Nash continued to argue against the facts, as he had done throughout Koesler's presentation. Unlike his father, at no time did he give complete credence to any of the story beyond those incidents for which he or his father was responsible. "I still don't believe it!" Nash disclaimed. "Not Brenda. She wouldn't have taken any part in this mad scheme. She can't be my . . ." His voice quavered. ". . . my sister. Why . . . my God . . . that would make her . . . that would make us . . . our relationship incestuous. Incestuous!" He looked at Koesler challengingly.

Koesler nodded firmly. "That's the word she used."

"I can't believe it!" Nash insisted. "Not Brenda!" He looked to Father Deutsch, who slowly shook his head. Ted and he had carefully constructed a patchwork of rationalism to justify more than half an adulterous affair between Ted and Brenda. But Deutsch could not bring himself to trot out the dependable double effect principle in order to whitewash incest.

This left Ted in a series of unbelieving dilemmas. He could not believe that Brenda would plot against him. He could not believe that Brenda was his sister. He could not believe that Brenda, knowing she was his sister, could make love to him—could allow him to make love to her. He couldn't believe that he could live without her.

And deep down, just like his father, he knew that all of it was true.

"Wait . . ." Something occurred to Father Deutsch. "With Charles Nash dead, doesn't that do something to the will? Surely Brenda was not mentioned in Mr. Nash's will! Wouldn't that make it impossible for her to inherit?"

"A good point, Father," Cone said in his most attorney-like tones. "But—" He stopped, and looked at Koesler. "Father . . . would you mind?"

Koesler immediately nodded and stood up. "I'll be in the waiting room." He quietly closed the door behind him.

"Now," Cone proceeded, "to get back to your point, Father Deutsch. We would have to allege that Charles knew that Brenda was his daughter and refused to include her in the inheritance. And I should tell you," he explained parenthetically, "in such cases, it is usual to specifically mention this in the will.

"However," he continued, "if he didn't know she was his daughter, her claim would be much more sound. If he did know that she was his daughter, the fact that his name had been expunged from the birth record but not from the baptismal record would have to be addressed and explained. That would, of course, introduce the participation of Chardon—"

"Wait!" Deutsch could see where this was leading, and he didn't want to follow that path until every escape route was examined. "Everybody thought that Mary Lou was the daughter. Tests prove she is not. Now everybody seems ready to believe Brenda is the daughter. What if she's not?"

"You can't think she'd fall for something like we pulled on Mary Lou!" Nash said.

"No," Deutsch replied. "I mean, challenge her. Go through with the test just as we planned. Let the chips fall where they may." He looked around brightly.

"Father," said Cone, "if such a test proves positive—as it almost undoubtedly would—and if the results were made public, which they must be, Ted would be lucky to come away from this with the clothes on his back.

"Further, even the threat of such a test—the publicity attendant thereto—well . . ." He looked squarely at Ted. "Do you want to take the chance that all this will come out in the media? Your father's affair with Ms. Monahan? Your affair with her daughter? Adultery, incest . . . even the mere alleging of incest? Even if it managed not to affect your business, what will it do to your home life? To your religious position?"

Ted, stricken, sat with his head bowed.

"Gentlemen," Cone said, after a minute, "what we have here is a classic can of worms." He addressed Ted again. "Should you try to pry the lid open, or worse, remove the cap, we will be trying to deal with all these worms for longer than we have any right to believe we'll live.

"Ted, you brought me along for legal advice. I'm giving you the best advice you could possibly get from anyone anytime. Settle!"

The word seemed to infuse some spirit in Ted. "But . . ."

"Settle!"

Ted slowly deflated. Cone said nothing more, seeming to give the floor pro forma to anyone who thought he had a better solution. No one did.

The attorney stepped to the door and opened it. Locating Koesler in the nearby waiting room, he nodded.

With Koesler having rejoined the party, Cone once more took the floor. "Now, Father . . ." He could well afford to be cool; it wasn't his money. " . . . in the matter of the Misses Monahan, what do they want?"

"I cannot speak to that, Mr. Cone," Koesler replied. "I think that must be about the only topic that Maureen, Brenda and I did not cover."

"Well," Cone said, "it shouldn't be too hard to ascertain. Gentlemen—" he included each of them—"why don't we go have a relaxing lunch. On me."

Koesler had to return to his parochial duties. Nash, feeling as if he might not eat again for the rest of his life, begged off. Deutsch went to lunch with Cone.

CHAPTER

32

THE PRINCIPALS in this drama had been involved with each other to varying degrees for thirty-some years. Father Koesler had been drawn into active participation for only a few weeks. But the fallout from his entanglement shook the roots of his extended family and affected the manner in which he would relate to the people closest to him for the rest of his life.

It was now some months after the death and burial of Charles Nash. According to his wishes, Charles had been cremated. A memorial Mass was offered at Blessed Sacrament Cathedral. Given the life he'd lived, there well might have been some question about granting him Christian burial. Koesler had been prepared to testify that he'd been with Nash at the moment of his death and that absolution had been—apparently—requested and given.

But no one asked. They just had the memorial Mass, which was very well attended by not only many high-rolling entrepreneurs but also by lower and higher clergy.

His father's sacramental exit was, at that time, the singular consolation in Teddy Nash's now turbulent life, which was rapidly crumbling around his head.

KOESLER WAS THINKING about Charles Nash and the aftermath of his life while seated in a confessional in an otherwise empty St. Joseph's Church of a Saturday evening waiting for someone, anyone, who sought forgiveness for sin.

Maureen and Brenda had been cold to the notion of arbitration and cool to mediation. They were not in a bargaining mood. They demanded.

In his defense it should be said that Avery Cone had been given little leverage or room to maneuver. To begin, the shoe very definitely was on the other foot. Maureen at first insisted that the DNA test be performed. Convinced of the certain result of such a test and most conscious that the media would take that result and run with it, Cone found himself in a hole before he'd begun to fight. Not only were Maureen and Brenda holding most of the cards, Ted Nash had gone limp, metaphorically. What cursed him most was the impossible dilemma that he could not live without Brenda. And, now that he was convinced theirs was an incestuous relationship, he could not live with her.

In the end, Brenda had demanded and eventually was ceded 41 percent of the stock of Nash Enterprises, making her the largest single shareholder. She also gained the chair of chief operating officer, and made it clear she had her sights on Ted's position of chief executive officer.

The final step was spin control: explaining to the public via the news media the sudden ascendance of Brenda Monahan into the Nash empire. Avery Cone adapted Henry Ford II's M.O. and did not complain, while explaining very little as he put the best face possible on the situation.

Maureen, in calling Nash to account, had not specified which of the girls was his alleged daughter. Thus, Mary Lou, hitherto heiress presumptive, could now be excluded, letting Brenda take center stage.

Cone opened his statement with a brief eulogy of Charles Nash—paying tribute to the departed's munificence as he fashioned a panorama of all that worthy man had done for the local community, not to mention the world at large. In keeping with this blessed memory, the fallen hero's remains would not be subjected to desecration in the slightest degree.

Whereas in life, Charles Nash had challenged the validity of Ms. Monahan's claim, in death, no matter what the result of a DNA test might indicate, the late Mr. Nash would have no further redress. And, no matter how reliable such a test was reputed to be, it was not infallible.

However, in the face of the Monahans' adamant, inexorable, and implacable claim of consanguinity, together with the Nash family's resolve to subject themselves to no further legal action, and to close the chapter, an agreement had been reached between the parties.

Under this accord—without admitting any part of the Monahan claim—Ms. Brenda Monahan would be granted a seat on the Board of Nash Enterprises, as well as an unspecified financial settlement.

Note was made of the fact that Ms. Monahan's background in the planning and administration offices of the archdiocese of Detroit brought to the Nash Enterprises board room yet another level of expertise as well as a special insight into the "pro bono" work that had always marked the endeavors of this company.

No additional comment would be forthcoming from either party.

And so it was reported by those in the hard news category. Columnists, opinion vendors, and pundits, on the other hand, had a field day speculating. Environmentalists were near ecstatic in the expectation that Nash Enterprises, once one of their most hard-nosed adversaries, might now become an ally in the cause.

Meanwhile, before Ted's coffers were completely depleted, Melissa began divorce proceedings. Financially, Ted was bleeding from every pore. Emotionally, he was near dead.

Whether Brenda would ever return to the Church of her youth was completely open to conjecture. At the moment, she showed no desire for such a reconciliation. At the moment, she was expertly steering Nash Enterprises along unfamiliar paths. Ford Park plans had been discarded, and all the small animals indigenous to that sanctuary were frolicking freely.

Mary Lou had been furious. Realistically, almost everyone had taken advantage of her. From her reputed mother, to a best friend who had been as a sister to her, to Charlie and Ted Nash and their fake lawyer from Chicago.

As some people need time to mourn, Mary Lou needed time to pout. When that time expired, she was won over by explanations and assurances from Maureen and Brenda that no other way could their plan have worked.

And there was the money. Brenda cut her in for a not-insignificant percentage. Mary Lou had tried it poor and tried it rich. Rich was better.

Yet, despite her newfound funds, she held on to her job at St. Raphael's. One could never tell when the Pope was going to get real about this celibacy thing.

Then, there was the side issue of Inspector Koznicki finally getting his man. Koznicki and Zoo Tully had painstakingly tracked down and followed up every thread of evidence. They were, of course, convinced Chardon had murdered Agnes Ventimiglia. It was a matter of gathering enough proof to make an extremely strong case with circumstantial evidence.

In the end, they convinced the prosecutor's office. Chardon was convicted of first-degree murder of the Ventimiglia woman.

In a separate trial, he was convicted of the murder of the security guard. He was sentenced to two concomitant life terms without parole. Now the other states who wanted him could have their days in court with Rick Chardon.

As yet, Chardon had said no word implicating anyone else. And, while it was unlikely that he would, there was always the possibility. In any case, Inspector Koznicki had never felt more satisfied about an investigation. And probably never would.

Father Arthur Deutsch was now rather redundant. And so he had retired once more to his Boca Raton manse, there to regale his fellow "senior priests" in retirement with tales of power and excitement and that crazy, meddling pastor of Old St. Joe's. In Boca Raton, with the return of the patron of most of the senior priests, the sun never climbed above the yardarm.

Last, but definitely not least, in Father Koesler's thoughts, was his dear cousin Maureen. He was aware of the Native American aphorism, "Never judge a man until you have walked a mile in his moccasins." No one, Koesler felt, deserved such consideration more than Maureen.

Certainly hers was an abiding hatred, a deeper, stronger, and more bitter hatred than he had previously encountered. But she had been pushed over and over again by a callous, underhanded, and thoroughly un-Christian Charlie Nash.

Now that it was finally over, and, with the death of the senior Nash it certainly was, what would Maureen do? To this date, nothing had happened. Everyone seemed busy with something or other except Maureen. Once Brenda was ensconced in her expanding empire at Nash Enterprises, Maureen had quietly disappeared from view. Further, neither Oona nor Eileen nor Koesler had been able to contact her. If this continued much longer, he resolved to get serious about locating her.

In the meantime, he hoped she was well. And he prayed that she was at peace with God. For now, he could do no more.

KOESLER GLANCED at his everpresent watch. Time's up. For all you people out there who haven't come to confession, time is up. Time to lock the church, retreat to the rectory for a little TV, some reading, and a good night's sleep before tomorrow's Sunday schedule.

33

FATHER POOL, pastor of St. Raphael's, sat lost in prayerful thought. There were so many for whom to pray. The ailing parishioners he'd visited this week in hospitals and at their homes. The men and women out of work with no good prospects. Children with that age-old antagonism to their parents. The elderly with only loneliness to keep their infirmities company. There surely was no dearth of favors needed from God.

Father Pool was about to commence his litany of favors received from the all-good Lord when there was a knock on his confessional door. The janitor was reminding him that it was time to close up and lock the church. Without that prompting, Pool probably would have drifted on in prayer for God only knew how long.

Indeed, it was due to Pool's praying in the church till all hours that the janitor had assumed the responsibility of at least getting the priest off to his rectory at a reasonable hour.

Pool smiled at the janitor's intervention, and began gathering up his belongings, mainly books. He was about to leave the confessional when he heard the outside door open, then shut. He waited. It might be a penitent.

Shortly, someone entered the penitent's compartment. As with most church confessionals of the current era, one side was set up to allow priest and penitent to sit informally facing each other with no screen or wall separating them. The other side was an older-style confessional where priest and penitent were separated by a screen that preserved the penitent's anonymity.

It was into the latter style confessional that this penitent had entered.

Father Pool shifted his chair so he could hold a whispered confession in the darkened recesses of this boxlike compartment.

"Bless me, Father, for I have sinned," came the muted but distinctly feminine voice. "It's been a bit more than thirty-three years since I've been to confession." There was a pause. "Father, I'm Maureen Monahan. You know . . ."

"Bob's cousin!" The smile of recognition colored his voice. "Maureen, what are you doing over there in the dark? If you come in this other door, we can sit and visit."

"I . . . can't."

"But you've already identified yourself. There's no need . . ."

"I know. But this is the only way I've ever gone to confession. I guess it's silly . . . but I've got to do it this way."

"That's okay. It's not silly. I forgot this open confession was introduced a long time after your last confession. You just relax. There's nothing wrong with doing it this way."

"Well, I don't know whether I should make one of those 'general confessions' that go back to when I was a kid."

"Does anything back there trouble you? Is there anything back there that bothers you?"

"Mmm . . . not really."

"Listen Maureen, God loves you no matter what you've done. Just relax, and whatever's troubling you, let's get rid of it."

"Okay." She sounded grateful. "Well, thirty-some years. A long time. I've missed Mass, oh, I don't know how many times. Not every week . . . but often. Then, there were those petty things. You know, gossip and anger, occasional bad language, and—oh, who'm I kidding? What's really bothering me is the relationship I had with Charles Nash. You probably heard about it."

"If I've got eyes and I can read, yeah, I did. But that was a while back."

"Well, that's it. The worst thing about it is all the time I spent hating him. I despised him. I wasted thirty-three years plotting against him. Now that it's over, I just feel drained.

"Looking back, I can't believe that I could be that mean-spirited. But I was. I was obsessed. I lived and ate and breathed my anger, my hatred of him. And, God forgive me, I won. I beat him. And you know what? It wasn't worth it. Now that I look back, I wish I hadn't done it.

"But I'm still sort of confused. I don't know whether I'm sorry enough for God to forgive me."

"Maureen, believe me, your contrition sounds solid to me. If nothing else, you sure are headed in the right direction. If you aren't yet as sorry as you'd like to be, remember, God knows you've had a tough time, trying to take care of those girls all by yourself. You'd have had to be superhuman not to have been affected. But you're moving in the right direction now. You're okay. Believe me!"

"That's good to hear."

He could hear the relief in her voice. "Anything else?"

"Just what started this whole thing: my affair with Charlie." She paused, obviously recollecting. "In my favor, I certainly didn't know he was married. And the only reason I went ahead and slept with him is because I was sure . . . I was so sure . . . he was going to marry me.

"But . . . that doesn't excuse it. We had relations probably two or three or more times a week for a couple of years. And, for a while, I was taking the pill. Does that figure in the sin?"

"Not really. Is that about all?"

"I guess so. No, wait. There's one more thing. It's kind of odd. But, once . . ." She stopped. From the silence, he gathered that she was pulling herself or her memories together. Finally, it seemed that she had come to a decision. "Well, you see, I had dated—plenty more than my sisters ever did. And on those dates, I may have necked and petted and gone pretty far. But I never went all the way. The only person I ever had sex with, really, was Charlie Nash. Toward the end of our affair . . . this is embarrassing . . . but I began to wonder if . . . well . . . if it was the same with everybody . . . or whether sex felt different . . ." She fell silent again.

"And . . . ?" Father Pool prompted.

"Well, there was this one night about three months before Charlie and I broke up. Charlie was supposed to pick me up after work. He called and said he couldn't make it; something had come up. I asked one of the guys at work to drive me home. On the way, I got to wondering . . . about other men.

"Well, the thing is, I invited this guy in, and we had sex. That was the only time, and . . ." She took a deep breath. "I guess that's it."

Three months before the break-up. Father Pool hesitated only a few moments. "That's it?"

"I think so."

"Then, you make a sincere act of contrition while I give you absolution. And know, Maureen, that God loves you. 'The Lord Jesus Christ absolves you. And, I, by His authority, absolve you . . .'"